"Reliable entertainment for fans who enjoy nooks, crannies, subplots, and carpentry tips." —*Kirkus Reviews*

"Home repair is Graves's gimmick, and she uses it very successfully. But it is her light, humorous tone and well-chosen cast of characters that grow and evolve from novel to novel; her obvious love for coastal Maine and its inhabitants; and her ability to marry all of those ingredients to serviceable plots that make this a series whose popularity will continue to grow." —*Alfred Hitchcock Mystery Magazine*

"Entertaining . . . a nicely drawn cast of characters, both human and animal, plus humor built around domestic bliss and angst, personal foibles and outrageous situations, all make for plenty of cozy fun." —*Publishers Weekly*

"Hours of cozy entertainment." —*Kirkus Reviews*

"Anyone who can mix slaughter and screwdrivers is a genius. Plus, anyone who has bought a home that needs even a new toilet seat is probably consumed with murderous thoughts (against the previous owner, the mortgage company, the lousy inspector, the spouse)." —*Boston Herald*

"Graves provides an entertaining read sprinkled with practical tips. A recipe for success—even if it makes you want to start one of your long-overdue home-repair projects!" —*Wichita Falls Times-Record News*

"Another well-plotted whodunit . . . I love this series." —*Kingston Observer*

"Sarah Graves is in top form. . . . As always, Graves's trademark home repair tips add utility to fun."
—*Mystery Lovers Bookshop News*

"Like the old Victorian homes she describes . . . Graves's stories seem to grow better with the passing of time. . . . Readers who enjoy solving mysteries and fixing up older homes will appreciate Jake's do-it-yourself expertise in both areas." —*Booklist*

"[An] innovative cozy series . . . Readers will relish the author's evocative descriptions of small-town Maine, strong characters whose relationships evolve, sense of humor, and, of course, helpful home-repair hints."
—*Publishers Weekly*

"Offers all the pleasures of the 'cozy' subgenre . . . [with] its feisty amateur sleuth . . . [and] quirky assortment of friends and family . . . The plot is leavened with home repair passages full of detail and a nice dose of attitude." —*New England Today*

"An enjoyable read for those who like their mysteries well-built." —*Bangor Daily News*

"Graves makes rehabbing shutters and other chores suspenseful. The novels are as well crafted as the household projects are carried out."
—*The Boston Sunday Globe*

"Charming." —New Orleans *Times-Picayune*

"With an intricate plot, amusing characters and a wry sense of humor, Sarah Graves spins a fun, charming mystery that is sure to make you smile and keep you guessing right up until the end."
—*Booknews* from The Poisoned Pen

Praise for the Home Repair Is Homicide Mysteries of Sarah Graves

"Graves transcends the boundaries of the conventional mystery by allowing her protagonists to indulge in heroics that land them in the shark-infested waters of the thriller." —*Library Journal* (starred review)

"Reigning master of the [cozy] genre." —*Romantic Times*

"Relentless pacing, an appealing heroine and perfectly loathsome antagonists will more than satisfy series fans." —*Publishers Weekly*

"Laugh-out-loud funny and laid with enough false trails to delude a troop of Boy Scouts. But they shake it out to a terrifying finale." —*Romantic Times*

"This Home Repair Is Homicide series is more fun than a soap." —*Booknews* from The Poisoned Pen

"There's plenty of slapstick, farce, and home-repair tips amid the mayhem." —*The Boston Globe*

"Graves once again delivers an atmospheric setting in small-town picturesque Maine. . . . A fun read . . . There's plenty of ambience and colorful characters in this cozy of a mystery." —*The Santa Fe New Mexican*

"As usual, Jake, an engaging first-person narrator, keeps the story rolling along smoothly. A little cozier than John Dunning's series of antiquarian bookman Cliff Janeway, but fans of both series won't mind crossing over." —*Booklist*

BY SARAH GRAVES

Books published by The Random House Publishing Group are available at quantity discounts on bulk purchases for premium, educational, fund-raising, and special sales use. For details, please call 1-800-733-3000.

CRAWLSPACE

A

Home Repair Is Homicide
Mystery

SARAH GRAVES

BANTAM BOOKS • NEW YORK

Crawlspace is a work of fiction. Names, characters, places, and incidents either are the product of the author's imagination or are used fictitiously. Any resemblance to actual persons, living or dead, events, or locales is entirely coincidental.

2011 Bantam Books Mass Market Edition

Copyright © 2010 by Sarah Graves
Excerpt from *Knockdown* © 2011 by Sarah Graves

Published in the United States by Bantam Books, an imprint of The Random House Publishing Group, a division of Random House, Inc., New York.

BANTAM BOOKS and the rooster colophon are registered trademarks of Random House, Inc.

Originally published in hardcover in the United States by Bantam Books, an imprint of The Random House Publishing Group, a division of Random House, Inc., in 2010.

This book contains an excerpt from the forthcoming book *Knockdown* by Sarah Graves. This excerpt has been set for this edition only and may not reflect the final content of the forthcoming edition.

ISBN 978-0-553-59113-2
eBook ISBN 978-0-553-90727-8

Cover design: Jamie S. Warren and Stephen Youll
Cover images © Peter Doomen/Shutterstock (staircase); © Kulish Viktoriia/Shutterstock (shoe); © Carol Russo (house graphic)

Printed in the United States of America

www.bantamdell.com

9 8 7 6 5 4 3 2 1

Bantam mass market edition: April 2011

CRAWLSPACE

Now that it was too late, she knew how wrong she had been. Watching her own hand slide wetly across the kitchen countertop, her fingers clutching uselessly at its edge before slipping off in a slick of her own blood, she understood at last.

"Roger," she whispered. Her husband's name. But it came out a wordless sigh.

They'd been fighting again. In the past few months, ever since she'd begun fearing that his brother, Randy, might still be alive, Roger had changed from loving husband to punishing enemy.

The idea that Randy might have faked his own death was irrational, even paranoid. But it kept coming back, and this morning's argument over it had been the worst yet.

The memory unfurled dreamily now as she lay on the kitchen floor. "Stop!" Roger had shouted, shaking her by the shoulders. "Do you understand me? I'm *sick* of it!"

Of her fear, he meant, not only that Randy still lived but that he had killed her sister, Cordelia.

Poor murdered Cordelia, who'd believed until she died that the extravagant double wedding they'd had—the Dodd brothers, Roger and Randy, marrying the Lang girls, herself and Cordelia—was a dream come true. . . .

She studied her hand, the fingers curling weakly, as it went limp on the tile. She didn't want to think about why the usually spotless surface felt wet and sticky.

Or about whose shoes those were, inches from her head. She whispered again. But this time no sound came out at all. Instead, this morning's battle went on replaying in her mind, the past more real to her now than anything in the present. More alive . . .

"This crazy obsession of yours," he'd bellowed at her, his eyes wild and frightened. She'd tried to get away, to wriggle out of his grip, but he wouldn't let go.

"I'm sorry," she'd babbled. Could it have been only an hour ago? "I'll never talk about it again, Roger. Truly I won't."

About how she'd awakened one morning to the realization that her brother-in-law, Randy, had not fallen off his fishing boat and drowned two years ago, as everyone believed. That the reason his body never turned up had nothing to do with tides or currents.

That he was alive, that he'd killed Cordelia . . . and that now he was coming back to kill her, too.

Roger's hands had released her shoulders, only to close on her throat. Terrified, she'd torn at his grip, but he was bigger and stronger than she was, and so angry.

So . . . frightened. *Why?* she'd wondered as, with a breathless shriek, she shrank from him.

"Please," she'd begged him. As if even then it could all be undone and things could be all right again.

But they couldn't. As if realizing this, Roger had let his hands drop and slammed out of the house.

Now her cheek pressed the floor where a pool spread away from her. At eye level, it reminded her of the wine-dark sea she'd studied about in school so long ago.

Too late now for fear, for apologies or regrets. Too late . . .

Now she knew.

Chapter 1

Y ou're awfully quiet," **Carolyn Rathbone** complained as Chip Hahn pulled the Volvo sedan into
the empty parking lot and turned the ignition off at
last.

He looked down at his hands. He'd had a bad feeling about this trip all along. Still did.

She tried again: "Don't you like these people you're going to see tomorrow, or what?"

It was just past eight in the evening. He'd been driving all day to reach Eastport, Maine, before nightfall and had missed by about four hours. God, it got dark early here in November.

"I like them. It's been ten years since I've seen them, is all." More than ten, actually, so long ago that he hadn't even called to let any of them know he was coming.

He just meant to stop in and say hello if they were at home. And anyway, his silence had nothing to do with his old friends, but Carolyn had stopped listening and got out of the car before he could finish saying so.

Sighing, he hauled the heavy satchel containing her laptop, BlackBerry, iPod, and vodka bottle plus six hardcover copies of her latest book, *Young Savages: Bad Drugs, Sick Sex, and Bloody Murder in the Richest Town in America,* out of the Volvo's backseat. The parking lot overlooked a wooden pier sticking out into Passamaquoddy Bay, he knew from his map. The long, narrow body of salt water divided Moose Island, which the little bayside town of Eastport perched on, from the Canadian island of Campobello.

Tonight the bay was inky black, with thin, silvery crescents shining atop the waves, reflections of dock lights illuminating a long concrete breakwater about a hundred yards distant. The salt air smelled of seaweed, creosote, and wood smoke.

"Come on, Chip," Carolyn called petulantly from across the street. "Hurry up."

The cold wind off the water cut through his jacket, adding another complaint to his already full list of them. He was tired, hungry, and unaccountably nervous, and the sharp tang of sea salt in the night air somehow made him feel worse.

As he shouldered Carolyn's satchel another unpleasant shiver went through him, as if he not only wanted to be home in his own small, familiar Manhattan apartment, but that he should be. That something bad might happen because he wasn't.

And so far, nothing about Eastport was doing much to change that. Old two-story brick commercial buildings lined the main street. All were dark now except the one open restaurant on the corner, a half-dozen cars clustered in front of it.

Other than that, this end of the street was dead. A few of the storefronts had plywood sheets nailed over their windows. Kids hung out near the benches at the far end of the parking lot, laughing and cursing, showing off for one another.

A police car cruised past, slowing to give the kids a long looking over. Other than that, hardly anyone was around.

Well, but it was nearly winter, Chip reminded himself. Any tourists this remote, thinly settled coastal area got in summer had gone home weeks ago. He felt another pang of homesickness for the city, where sirens and garbage trucks and the low, constant thrum of human activity at least reassured him that someone was alive 24/7.

"Come on, Chipper," Carolyn whined from in front of the restaurant. With the satchel digging what felt like a trench into his neck, he hurried to catch up with her, looking both ways unnecessarily before he crossed the street.

"So, does this place meet with Madame's approval?" he asked her when he reached the other side.

He'd have been happy to get a sandwich and fries at a burger joint on the mainland. But Carolyn had vetoed those, supposedly on the grounds that she wanted to eat authentic Maine seafood.

Why that could be gotten only on an island she didn't bother explaining, and anyway he wouldn't have believed it. He knew the real reason was that none of the places they had passed served drinks, and because they were way out here in the boonies, she was saving the rest of the vodka in the satchel for later.

"Listen, about tomorrow . . ." he began hesitantly. He'd been thinking all day about how to tell her. Might as well get it over with. But she brushed him away with an impatient flutter of red-tipped fingers, while diners inside the restaurant's large plate-glass windows observed her with interest.

No surprise there; in her late twenties, Carolyn was still girlishly striking, with long, glossy black hair, enormous blue eyes, and expert makeup he knew she'd paid a mint to learn to apply. Tonight she wore skinny black jeans with a white silk shirt, heeled leather boots, and a black leather jacket that made her tiny frame look even slimmer than it was.

But then, Carolyn's outfits always looked good, too, even after a long drive or a hellish transcontinental flight or a mob-scene book signing, because no matter the difficulty of the task, she always made sure someone else did the heavy lifting.

A beat-up old Ford pickup went by with a low rumble of bad muffler, one fender hanging on by a glob of Bondo and the other heavily patched with duct tape. All Chip could hear of the music coming from the truck was the bass line: *boomp, boomp, boomp.* When the kid behind the wheel spotted Carolyn, his jaw dropped and the truck slowed suddenly, as if the mere sight of her had taken the strength from the driver's body.

Chip rolled his eyes. Makeup lessons or not, he personally thought that her eyeliner was way too heavy, and that the blood-colored lipstick Carolyn wore made her mouth resemble a wound.

"Oh, tomorrow," she mimicked him, ignoring the kid who now revved his truck's engine show-offily and had to rescue it from a stall before roaring away.

"We've been through that already, Chip, okay?" Carolyn said. "Spend all day with these friends of yours if you want to, but I have other plans. I mean, I didn't come this far just to chicken out at the last minute."

"Fine. Whatever you say." It wasn't what he'd wanted to talk about. But when she got like this, there was no point arguing with her. He held the restaurant door for her, then abruptly forgot his troubles at the aromas greeting him inside.

Grilled vegetables, garlicky shrimp in some kind of wine sauce, and a heap of rice pilaf went by on a platter. He felt as if all the delicious smells were seizing him by the nose, floating him through the air like a cartoon character.

A hostess swiftly seated them at a table near the window, brought glasses of wine, and recommended a combination plate containing samples of the day's specials. A short time later—Carolyn hadn't even finished her wine before the food began arriving, a first for her, in Chip's experience—ecstasy ensued.

Smoked-salmon pizza slid down like ambrosia, the lobster in spinach sauce tasted like heaven, and the duck with a conserve of ginger and passion fruit . . . absolute bliss. After half an hour Chip sighed, relaxing into the pleasure of a decent meal after a long day's drive, then looked up to find Carolyn eyeing him sourly.

The spinach sauce curdled on his tongue. "What?"

She'd ordered a whisky neat and was sipping from it, never a good sign. "I should be asking you."

Her blue eyes regarded him coldly across the table. He wondered if her legions of devoted fans ever noticed that they looked like ice chips, shaped and polished to resemble human eyes.

She sipped more single malt. "Because I got an e-mail today. A very puzzling e-mail. From Siobhan Walters. About you."

Oh, hell. He felt the comfort of the good food slide away. Siobhan—pronounced *Sha-vaun* but spelled the old Irish way—was Carolyn's New York editor.

He'd felt he could trust Siobhan. He'd believed he could confide in her, without everything he said to her getting back immediately to Carolyn.

He'd thought that Siobhan could just possibly manage to keep her mouth shut. *Wrong.*

He swallowed some wine, felt it go down badly and barely saved himself from a coughing fit.

"And Siobhan says"—another harmless-looking sip of the single malt, the way gasoline was harmless when you trickled it onto a fire—"Siobhan says you've got *ambitions*."

She gave the word a knowing twist that told him the jig was up, so under her ice-chip gaze he decided to come clean.

"Look, Carolyn, don't take it the wrong way. You had to know that being your assistant wouldn't be a permanent career for me. I mean, don't get me wrong," he added. "It's been great."

He could practically feel his nose growing. He hadn't told Carolyn about his foray into online music criticism, either. But that was minor compared to this.

"But I do have a book of my own in mind, and I did talk to Siobhan not long ago, just in an exploratory way—"

Carolyn laughed, a cawing sound of derision that drew looks from people at other tables nearby. She drank off the remaining whisky.

"Hey, it's not that I blame you for trying to slide in on my coattails," she said. "And Siobhan doesn't, either."

Outside the big window, the junky pickup truck went by again. The kid behind the wheel looked happy, like he didn't want any more than he already had.

Or if he did, he wasn't worrying about it; Chip wondered enviously what it felt like not to be always desperately trying to achieve something while at the same time being afraid you couldn't.

"So I'm not very pissed off," continued Carolyn. "I mean, I do get it. You want something all for yourself, and it's perfectly understandable that you would try for a shortcut."

He looked down at his plate, where a smear of passion fruit sauce stained the edge of a remaining bit of pizza crust. He had not been trying to take a shortcut.

"You called Siobhan?" he asked. But of course she had. At one of the rest areas on their way here, probably, on her cell phone.

Miserably, he imagined how the talk between her and Siobhan must've proceeded, their pitying laughter. His own call to the eminent editor now appeared to him for what it was: a pathetic try at raising himself above his station.

He put his napkin on the table. "I'm sorry if I embarrassed you." There was wine still in his glass, but he didn't want it.

"You embarrassed yourself, that's all. Think of it as a learning experience."

Right, he thought bitterly—learning his place, which was that of a paid servant. He hadn't always been one, he reminded himself. But he'd bought that trip when he'd started working for Carolyn, and now he was on it. So if he was unhappy, he supposed he had no one to blame but himself.

A naturally gifted researcher, he'd discovered fifteen years earlier how easy it was to go online, learn all about nearly any subject, then sell the info nuggets he had mined to his less adept classmates for their essays and term papers.

Later on, he'd found his talent for writing things himself. He'd learned that he was fast and accurate, with an effortless knack for the phrase that summed up a whole subject in a smooth, easy-to-read way. He'd sold a few of them, too.

But stories and articles in publications that paid

pennies per word didn't put food on the table, even if you liked instant mac-and-cheese alternating with ramen noodles. He'd been teaching part-time at a rural community college in Kansas, still trying to get a freelance career going, when he found Carolyn's card pinned to the student center bulletin board and called the number on it.

She'd been struggling toward writing for a living, just as he was. Six months later, he'd gathered every possible fact about the violent deaths of two pretty young women in Nevada.

After that, together he and Carolyn had come up with the kicker. The killer, a high-school track star and honor student from a wealthy family, had been stalking and murdering other young women for years, unsuspected by his parents and teachers.

Armed with the knowledge, Chip had written part of Carolyn's first draft and, let's face it, most of the book's rewrites. When the sensational trial ended in "guilty" just as their work on it came out, *Young Blood* had started climbing the bestseller lists, and *Young Savages* was doing even better.

Immersed in these thoughts, he didn't notice Carolyn getting the check. But now he got up and made his way between the tables to pry the charge-card receipt from her.

It was part of his job to record every penny Carolyn spent, a routine she liked in theory but got irritated about in practice. But never mind, she would thank him in April, when he also handled the visits to the accountant.

Or rather, she wouldn't. His paycheck, she'd once

informed him when she was feeling prickly enough to be honest, was gratitude enough. And anyway, he'd already decided he wouldn't be working for her anymore by then.

Tomorrow, he promised himself. After they'd met up with the anonymous e-mail informant they'd come here to see—Mr. Mystery, Carolyn had begun calling him—then he would tell her.

Music criticism, fact-checking, even freelance researching again . . . anything was better than this. He followed her outside, where Eastport's main street seemed even more empty than before. No cars moving, no people; at just past nine-thirty it might as well have been midnight.

Across the bay a few lights gleamed, sparsely sprinkled over Campobello. To the north, a lighthouse beam stabbed rhythmically at the sky.

A foghorn hooted, though the night was clear and the stars overhead shone frigidly. Shivering, he headed for the car.

"Come on," he told her over his shoulder. "We'd better go find our rooms before the innkeeper turns out the lights and goes to bed."

He'd wanted a place here in town, but Carolyn had chosen a rental cabin on the shore of a nearby saltwater inlet instead. It would be more authentic, she'd said, more atmospheric.

Yeah, yeah, he thought. "Nearby" meant at least ten miles in this part of the world. Also, the car's on-screen mapping gadget didn't work here, so on top of everything else, he would have to find the place himself.

Digging his car keys from his pocket, he hoped the

cabin at least had hot running water. Then he realized that she wasn't behind him. "Carolyn?"

A self-described free spirit, she was capable of wandering off on her own, especially with a few drinks in her. A spurt of mean glee seized him at the idea that she might get lost, but the self-indulgent emotion was fast followed by a pinprick of real fear.

The guy they were meeting tomorrow was no model citizen, at least if what he'd told them about himself so far was true. But then Chip spotted her slim figure hurrying along, already halfway up the street.

"Carolyn, come on, it's late, and—"

I'm tired. From the way she ignored him, though, he knew it was pointless. She would do what she liked, as usual. With a sigh, he hoisted the satchel again.

Not that she would use it, but if he didn't bring it, she would send him back for it. And as he traipsed after her, he saw what had attracted her: a block away, the red neon window sign of a bar.

By the time he got there, she'd already gone in. He followed, resigning himself to an hour of witless barstool conversation, the smell of stale beer, and maybe football on TV way out here in the middle of nowhere. But inside, he got a surprise.

In a room overlooking the long, L-shaped concrete breakwater he'd seen earlier, a dozen or so young hipster types drank Amstel Lights and played darts to the sound of Coldplay's most recent release, being played on a good if not exactly spectacular sound system. Apparently, driving a truck up and down the main street wasn't all there was to do in this town.

He looked around, his discontent banished for the moment by the varnished plank floor, the mahogany bar with a polished brass rail, and the eight-foot mirror on the wall behind it. There was even a jar of pickled eggs by the cash register.

The glass lamp shades weren't Tiffany, he felt sure, but they weren't junk, either. Chip decided an Amstel of his own wouldn't hurt him.

"On the house," said the bartender to Carolyn, who'd already named her poison. "Welcome to Eastport." She'd asked for another straight scotch—a double, Chip saw with an unsurprised sinking feeling.

The bartender was a fortyish, sandy-haired guy in jeans and a white polo shirt. His smile didn't reach his eyes as he slid a glass of amber liquid across the bar at Carolyn.

But then again, why should it? The guy wasn't here for the laughs. Chip nodded at the draft spigots.

The bartender drew Chip a cold one and returned to the cash register, where he'd been balancing the till, laying fives, tens, and twenties in neat piles. Despite this clear signal that it was nearly closing time, Carolyn knocked her shot back efficiently, then put money on the bar's gleaming surface.

At this rate, he'd be pouring her into the car, Chip thought. On the other hand, it would cut down on conversation, and after what had happened in the restaurant earlier, maybe that was just as well.

Ignoring her, he took his beer and sat alone at a table while she got her fresh drink and started bragging about who she was, what she'd written, how successful she was getting.

Chip glanced around, embarrassed for her. Luckily,

the only other person within earshot was a silent, slump-shouldered guy in a pulled-down Red Sox cap, staring into a beer mug.

Morosely, the guy dug a peanut out of a half-empty packet and ate it, washing it down with the remaining suds in the mug. Chip wondered what a guy like that did the rest of the time, then forgot about him.

Carolyn gabbed on while the twentysomethings in the darts game laughed and chatted among themselves and the Coldplay tune on the sound system changed to something that Chip hadn't heard before.

The Tough Alliance, maybe? Tin Can Logic? Whatever, it was good. Someone in here knew their indie music. Behind the darts area was a small stage, too, with the amplifier, mixer, and speakers plus microphone and video screen of an elaborate karaoke system, for patrons who wanted more than just a passive music experience.

"So, what do you know about the Dodd case?" Carolyn asked the bartender. "Those two sisters who were killed? One of them only about six weeks ago? You must hear plenty in here," she prodded.

The bartender's smile stiffened. Chip waited for his reply, wondering if maybe his partner and pal, Carolyn, had pushed it a little too hard. But just then somebody in the darts game got a bull's-eye and fresh laughter erupted from the group.

"Can't help you there," the bar man was telling Carolyn when Chip could hear again. Another indie fave, BC Camplight, filled the room with their most recent release: synths, brass, and piano melodies, topped by a self-assured vocal.

Chip's estimation of whoever chose the music for this place went up another notch. Neither Camplight nor the previous tune was exactly blaring out of the average commercial radio station; even in the city, if you wanted that stuff you had to go looking for it.

The guy down the bar rose without speaking, left money and his empty peanut bag, and limped out, dragging one foot a little.

The bartender ignored the guy as the front door swung open and fell closed again. "I don't know any more than anyone else around here," he told Carolyn. "Which is basically nothing."

He made a last round of drinks for the darts group, then returned. "You're going to write a book about it, though? Mind if I ask how you're going to do that when nobody knows what happened or who's guilty?"

"Oh, well," Carolyn replied, her voice full of the too-loud confidence of one who could not walk a straight line, much less blow a Breathalyzer test successfully. "I'm not worried. When I'm finished, everyone'll know. Just like last time."

She swiveled on her barstool, reached clumsily for the satchel that Chip had placed near her, and drew out a garishly jacketed copy of *Young Savages*. The cover art featured yellow crime-scene tape, a glistening red blood drop, and cash so real-looking, you could almost try to spend it.

The cash represented the money the teenaged killer's rich parents had spent trying to get him off. The parents' prominent friends and well-respected fellow country-club members had all testified to the youth's stellar character, too, though many had privately already known or suspected otherwise, Chip and Carolyn had discovered.

The result had been a scandal so juicy, *Vanity Fair* ran two long features on it: one an insiderish piece by Dominick Dunne, and the other by Carolyn herself. In place of the usual glowing blurbs from other authors, the book's dust jacket capitalized on this by featuring outraged quotes from residents of the exclusive enclave whose reputation had been shredded within.

The bartender eyed the book warily. "So that's what you want to do?" he asked. "Rip our little town up one side and down the other, like you did in that one there? I can't really say I look forward to that."

Alert as always to the merest hint of someone getting in her way, or threatening to, Carolyn backpedaled expertly.

"Oh, no," she reassured him in a voice like warm oil. "Nothing like that. It was another kind of situation entirely. Those people—"

She waved at the book's garish cover. "They were a bunch of rich snobs, just trying to get some poor innocent guy blamed."

Which wasn't at all what had happened; there'd been no other suspect, only the son of a prominent entertainment attorney who'd been brutalizing his other girlfriends for years.

There had never been any question about what he'd done, in the community where he'd lived. But Carolyn was on a roll now. She might get too loaded to see straight once in a while, but she never lost sight of her own interests.

"That won't be the story this time," she reassured

the bar man. "I can already tell this isn't some snooty place where all anyone cares about is money. I think that here the bad guy'll be somebody from away."

That wasn't true, either. Just the opposite, in fact, if the hints they'd already gotten from tomorrow's mysterious interview subject were any indication. But the bartender relaxed, or seemed to.

Good old Carolyn, Chip thought. Barely an hour on the island and she'd already figured out the question that really mattered: *Born here?*

Or—and this was what put you behind the eight ball most definitively in a place like this—*not?*

"So you're going to find out who." The bartender smiled. All but his eyes, which remained curiously stony. "Bring the bad guy to justice even if the cops couldn't." His tone sounded skeptical.

"That's the plan," she replied brashly, which was when Chip stopped listening. He'd heard it before.

From his table by the front window, he could see all the way down the dark street. The lights in the restaurant where they'd had dinner blinked out, and the last car was pulling away out front.

Behind him the music changed once more: to Amy Winehouse, her voice as heartbreaking for what happened to her later as for its beauty now. Listening, he drank what was left of his beer and signaled for another.

He would get through tonight okay, at least. Carolyn had been furious with him for daring to talk to Siobhan Walters about his book plans, but it seemed she had already forgotten about that.

She'd put her foot down and that was the end of it, or so she probably believed. It was the way things had always gone between them. Tomorrow, though, he would finally summon the nerve to tell her that he was quitting. Then her attitude would be different.

He wanted to write a novel; he'd come up with the perfect plot, and now was the time. Or at least he doubted there would be any better. So he intended to take his swing at it.

Carolyn would pitch a world-class fit when she heard what he had to say, and she would have plenty to say in reply, too, he knew from experience. And all at top volume . . . but as soon as they got back to the city, she was still going to be on her own, he resolved very firmly.

Case closed, as Chip's dad—better known to all and sundry as the Old Bastard—used to say. After he delivered the bad news, Chip could relax, maybe even enjoy dropping in on his old friends here in Eastport.

"Chipper." Carolyn's sharp voice pierced his thoughts. She'd left the bar area without his noticing and was standing over him impatiently.

"What?" he snapped, too tired even to bother moderating his tone.

She didn't mince words. "There's one other thing. I should have told you before. From now on, if anyone needs to call Siobhan Walters, I'll do it."

He nearly spit beer in outraged surprise. "What?"

Who did she think she was, anyway, to be revoking his phone privileges as if he were a naughty child? Putting his mug down carefully, wiping up a spilled drop with his napkin, he tried summoning some composure, but without success.

Carolyn dragged a chair out and sat facing him, her

limpid blue eyes full of what he used to think was sincerity, before he got to know her better.

Now he knew it was just personnel management.

"Division of labor, sweetie. Don't take it personally." She patted his arm. "Siobhan and I talked about it. She's busy, too, you know. She doesn't have time for hand-holding."

He stared at her, speechless with anger.

"Trust me, honey," she said. "I know what I'm talking about. You should stick to what you're good at."

She preened unconsciously, throwing her glossy hair back over her shoulder. It was another gesture he'd gotten used to, a part of her off-the-charts regard for herself.

"It's a jungle out there, and honestly, you know I've got your best interests at heart, don't you? Believe me, Chip, you're better off behind the scenes," she went on persuasively.

Then she dropped the bombshell. "And while we were talking, Siobhan and I also decided that after this—"

Behind them the darts game ended. The music stopped; in the sudden silence, people paid their bar tabs and went out in clusters of two and three.

"—we think, Siobhan and I, that I should write a novel. A thriller about a famous true-crime writer who accidentally finds out about a secret online society of serial killers. And one of them targets *her*."

Stunned, he shoved his chair back and got to his feet. Carolyn was a bitch; he'd never kidded himself otherwise. But this . . .

In the mirror behind the bar, he saw himself with

sudden, unwelcome clarity: a pale, plump man, pushing thirty and already paunchy and balding, whose
limp shirt collar hung open and whose pudgy fingers
kept on making slow, deliberate hand-washing motions.

You wouldn't know how strong they were, those
fingers. But there was all the typing he did, plus the
exercises to ward off repetitive stress syndrome. He
even had spring-loaded grips that he squeezed for a
few minutes every day, because a hand injury could
be career-crippling.

Such as it was: his great career. He stifled a bitter
laugh at the thought.

"But that was my idea," he said, already knowing
it was useless. "That's exactly the idea that I told
Siobhan Walters I wanted to . . ."

Carolyn got up, too, and without any shame at all
met his wounded gaze in the glass.

"You can't just *take* my idea," he told her reflection. But the cool, dismissive pity in her blue eyes
gave him his answer, as if he'd needed one, even before she spoke in tones of strained patience now: she
already had.

"Chipper, don't be a child. You'd never get anywhere with it. You're nobody," she pronounced with
her usual blithe cruelty.

Glancing back at her own beautifully groomed
image in the glass, she went on: "I'm the one who
sells books. My name, my face. That's always been
the deal, and that's the way it'll stay. Especially after
this baby gets written."

She patted the satchel fondly. The laptop inside
held the e-mails they had gotten from the man—Chip

assumed it was a man—whom they were to meet tomorrow.

The messages had begun arriving shortly after Chip started doing online research on the Eastport case, the murders of the two Dodd women. Those anonymous e-mails, more than anything else, were why they were here.

Those, and the research he'd done on account of them. As he thought about all the hours he'd put in, he had to stop himself from snatching the satchel up and cradling it.

What was in there was his work, hardly any of Carolyn's. Not just doing all the research and answering all the fan mail, but also ferreting out that one additional, just-too-weird-to-be-a-coincidence detail. . . .

The detail that had tipped the scales and brought them here tonight. "I don't get it," he said, still not quite able to believe Carolyn's treachery. Or, for that matter, Siobhan's.

"Siobhan's too classy a person," he protested. "She wouldn't go along with this." But then he saw the faintly guilty look on Carolyn's face and realized: she'd probably claimed *he'd* stolen the idea from *her*.

And that was the last straw. "Fine," he said. "I quit. Now. I'll just write my own novel, and then I'll . . ."

"And then you'll what?" she asked acidly. "Sell it? To who, Siobhan Walters? You think she wants you to compete with me? To give me an excuse to go elsewhere for more money, better terms?"

Her laugh was like a slap in the face.

"And the editors at other houses you could try," she went on, "who're all just dying to poach me off

Siobhan's list, you think they'll antagonize me for you?"

She dug in her purse, threw bills onto the table. "Oh, honey," she sneered, "dream on."

He felt it sink in, what this meant and how disastrous it was. He'd been counting on an advance, on selling the book before he finished it, basically, so he'd have money to live on.

It was an uncommon arrangement for a first-time author, but he'd worked with Siobhan Walters often enough so that he'd thought he could swing it. She knew he always showed up on time, in shape, with the stuff. That he was a professional. But if Carolyn stood in his way . . .

"Chip." Her eyes filled with tears. But this was just one more of her manipulative tricks, he felt sure. "I really can't do it anymore, okay?"

Yeah, right. She was just trying to rationalize her crappy behavior. Grimly, he examined his options. Taking money from his estranged father was a complete no-go; cash from the Old Bastard came with too many strings attached.

He couldn't go back to the community college, either, to the tedium of pounding basic grammar into corn-fed young numbskulls for starvation wages. Back there, the library shelved Dr. Phil's hideous volumes in the philosophy section, for God's sake.

And even if he did that, wrote the novel in his spare time and put up with a life that was like thin gruel meanwhile, in the end there would be two competing manuscripts: his and Carolyn's. So guess which one would end up in print? Unless . . .

"I can't stand thinking about them anymore," Carolyn said suddenly. Her face had gone somber, and her voice had the soft tonelessness he recognized, which meant she was telling the truth.

For once. "Dead girls," she said. "Every time a royalty check comes in, or a . . . it's like someone sent me a lock of their hair. Or a piece of bone."

She shivered faintly, as if shaking off memories. She had plenty of them, he'd give her that much. But then, so did he.

"I've got to do something else. And I can't just come up with ideas like you can," she added plaintively. "I'm not . . . I'm just not creative that way. I told Siobhan I'd do the next one as true crime, but no more," she finished.

That doesn't give you the right to take my ideas, he replied silently. Moisture glistened on her cheeks. *Crocodile tears,* he thought, as he produced a tissue and handed it to her.

Well, maybe not all of them, he conceded. But he was still very angry.

Sniffing, she twisted the tissue's corner to a point and blotted expertly with it, not even smearing her mascara. When she passed the tissue back to him, her composure had returned.

"So, anyway, that's it," she said, all traces of emotion gone with her tears. She was efficient about things like that.

Tears. Gratitude. Whatever. "That's the way it's going to be. My way. We can go on together or not, your choice."

She dug in her bag for a compact mirror, checked her face in it. "But if you're really quitting," she added, "I wish you'd let me know right away, tomorrow. I'll need to find someone else."

As she snapped the compact shut, the awful thought he'd had a moment earlier flitted across his mind once more. He lifted the satchel to haul it to the car for the final time that night.

"Let's go," he said tiredly, then stepped out onto the dark sidewalk, where the wind, honed to an icy dagger, made his jacket into a joke.

Like me, he thought bleakly, hunching his shoulders against the inclement weather. If only he wasn't so linked to Carolyn, if only they didn't—he had to admit this much—work so well together.

If only her sudden success hadn't given her such power, and if he wasn't so dependent on it.

Or if she didn't exist at all. If something happened to her, clearing the way for him to start over without her weight on him, crippling him like the satchel's strap.

His name wasn't Chip or, worse, Chipper. It was Charles, but she'd found out somehow what his nickname had been as a kid back in Manhattan, and ever since, she'd used it all the time.

No matter how many times he asked her not to, it was *Chip, do this. Chipper, do that.* He'd have thought she did it to annoy him, but he knew better. She'd simply forgotten what he'd said.

But what if he could change things? What if in one decisive stroke he could end Carolyn's petty tyranny and his own habit of being a victim forever?

Siobhan Walters would almost certainly want him to write the current book if Carolyn couldn't, and that might open a door for his novel, too. So he'd have work, money, and freedom.

A dust devil whirled down the otherwise empty street and collapsed as, stepping between two old buildings to escape the frigid wind, he felt his hands flex with unaccustomed urgency.

The bar's door opened and closed, and her boot heels clicked confidently if a bit unsteadily toward him. Only hers . . .

For a moment he thought he heard something else, quick and stealthy, like a foot being dragged hastily on concrete. But no . . .

He listened again. She was alone. Alone on a dark street, a little tipsy, late at night in a strange town . . .

Anything could happen. And she'd come here to meet someone, hadn't she? Mr. Mystery, their anonymous correspondent.

Chip even had the e-mails to prove it.

But in the next instant he realized how ridiculous he was being; self-dramatizing, as the Old Bastard would've called it. Feeling foolish, Chip realized all at once that at least in this case, the accusation was true.

All he had, after all, was Carolyn's word about the novel. For all he knew, Siobhan Walters thought Carolyn was only blowing smoke about writing one. Maybe Siobhan had just been humoring her star author about it, keeping Carolyn happy.

In any case, no contracts had been signed for any such project; if they had, Chip would've seen them. Contracts, like taxes and receipts for expenses, were the kind of boring, routine thing Carolyn always let him handle.

By tomorrow she might even have changed her mind about giving up true-crime writing, especially if things started going well here in Eastport. She'd talked about quitting before several times, and always for the same reason, but had never done it.

So things might not be as bad as he thought, he reminded himself sensibly. And anyway he'd feel better, he knew, when he got back to the city, to his own apartment with his own books, his own papers and music and his own computer.

His own bed. Thinking this, he stepped out of the shadows to look up and down the dark, quiet street for Carolyn. Probably by now she'd be wondering where he had gotten to.

But she wasn't there.

Carolyn Rathbone hadn't reached the top of *The New York Times* nonfiction bestseller list by being a pushover. But as she stepped out of the bar and looked around for Chip, who was nowhere to be seen, the man got the jump on her, clamping a hand over her mouth and yanking her back cruelly.

She thrust her head back hard, hoping to hit his nose with it. She tried to kick the heel of her boot backward at him, but he dragged her so fast that it was all she could do to stay on her feet.

He hauled her around a corner. No one else was in sight. He took his hand off her face. She sucked in a breath to scream out Chip's name.

But before she could, the man slapped tape over her mouth. Suddenly she was fighting to breathe.

A car stood with its trunk open. *No. No, I'm not*

getting in there. . . . She resisted as best she could, but he lifted her easily, shoved her in, and slammed the lid.

It had taken less than a minute. Pitch dark, smothering, and stinking in the car trunk . . . sheer panic boiled her thoughts down to a single phrase: *No, please God no, oh please* . . .

Something was in here with her, thick blankets or something, trapping her. She couldn't move, and she couldn't . . .

Breathe. Fear seized her as she battled to get air into her lungs. The drinks she'd had earlier rose like fire into the back of her throat. Desperately she forced them down, forced herself to pull twin threads of precious air in through her nostrils.

The reek in the trunk was of gasoline and stale sweat. Her own tears clogged her throat. She swallowed the salty taste and struggled not to sob.

Why? Her mind shrieked the question as the car started up, lurched backward, and swung around, then headed uphill, rolling her violently onto her side. Her cheek hit the trunk latch with a pain so explosive she saw stars, and the thick, heavy blankets or whatever they were rolled on top of her.

The trunk latch . . . hope pierced her. But when she tried to reach out for it, she found that he'd wrapped something around her arms, too, binding them to her body. The car accelerated, forcing her even tighter into the space between the trunk lid's edge and the weight of whatever it was, smothering her.

Tiny, shuddering trickles of air . . . with terrible effort, she made herself concentrate only on them. On each small, lovely sip of oxygen . . .

But even as she seized this bare triumph, her heart thudded madly, her mind filling with awful questions she already knew she didn't want to know the answers to.

Where is he taking me? And what will he do then? Whoever he was, he might let her out of the trunk when they got where he was going, but what might happen after that was too bad to think of.

Yet she couldn't help it. Even as she fought for breath, a slide show of crime-scene photographs flew past her mind's eye:

Girls tied in handcuffs, in blindfolds, in chains. Girls in rooms, alive but hidden from everyone, sometimes for years.

Girls in graves. It was the crime writer's dark burden, this knowledge—real, factual knowledge—of the terrible things people could do to one another. It was why she'd tried getting out from under it, by borrowing—all right, *stealing*—an idea from Chip.

At first she'd been proud of remaining unhaunted by victims of even the most depraved crimes. But by the time she and Chip finished the first book, they'd crept in, infesting her dreams.

And they haunted her now, the girls with their bruised eyes and limply curled fingers, their hair clotted with earth. Because as she lay there trying not to smother to death, she knew without any doubt that however much she begged, bargained, or pleaded, she was about to become one of them.

Because they'd tried all that, too, those girls. That and more, in the vain hope of escape. And yet there they all were in the crime-scene photographs Carolyn had pored over. And this right here, what was happening to her right this minute—

This was how they'd gotten into those graves.

The car drove on, rumbling along under her. This wasn't a nightmare. It was real. She couldn't believe it, but blood from her wounded cheek leaked down under her nose and she could smell it, like the taste of a copper penny.

Gradually, though, her breathing settled and her heartbeat slowed. *Think.* A man was taking her somewhere for a reason she did not dare imagine. If she did, she might just die of fear. But he was not doing anything to her now, was he?

Not right now, not yet. That meant she still had a chance to . . .

She tried moving her feet. They were weighed down by the heavy blankets, but they weren't bound. Which meant that if she got the chance, she could run.

She tried rolling partway onto her back and was able to. But as she did, something behind her shifted and fell with a metallic *clunk*.

Carolyn froze. A tire iron, maybe, striking the metal rim of the spare. Had he heard it? She held her breath, but the car didn't slow. She felt it turn again, realized it had done so several times.

It felt as if he was driving around in a circle, or maybe around the block. As if he was waiting for something—for the coast to be clear, maybe? Only . . . clear for what?

But from this thought her mind reeled back in terror. Her gorge rose chokingly, her eyes streamed tears, and a scream tore at her throat until she thought it would burst. Until . . .

No, she told herself with a terrible effort. *Stop. Breathe. Think.*

Probably those other girls had tried to command themselves, too. Tried, knowing they were facing death, to get a handle on their terror, at least enough so that they could function. And it had always failed.

But Carolyn had always felt herself to be an exception, the one who despite (or even possibly because of) a solid mountain of disadvantages—a mental picture of her childhood home, a two-room trailer hunkered at the edge of a one-horse town in the middle of rural Kansas, flashed into her mind—would succeed better than anyone else could.

Thinking this, she pushed the fear down again, stretched as best she could to force a larger space in the mass of blankets. Remembering to breathe slowly and shallowly, she began inching her legs around, pushing first with her back and then with her feet.

At last she lay perpendicular to the trunk, with her head toward the passenger compartment, knees drawn in, feet aimed up.

If her wrists had been tied in front of her, she could've worked on loosening the tape. But they weren't. They were bound flat to her sides.

He's done this before; it's why he knows how, she thought, then banished the realization before it could paralyze her. Her only chance was to wait until he opened the trunk, then kick out hard with both feet, hoping to surprise him and maybe hurt him.

Then, before he could recover, she would throw

herself bodily over the trunk's rim, get herself to her feet somehow, and run. . . .

The car slowed. Her heart slammed in her chest. Tiny whimpers, muffled by the thick tape, sounded as loud as screams inside her head.

Those girls . . .

Without wanting to, she saw them once more, lying in shallow holes . . . never deep, because the men who'd put them in there were so lazy and stupid.

And because they wanted to be able to get at them again. . . .

No. Don't think that, either. Or about how slim her chances were, slim bordering on none.

The car door closed softly. Footsteps scuffled around to the rear of the vehicle. The click of the trunk latch sent an electrical charge of terror through her.

She could barely breathe. The trunk swung up with a faint creak. *Not yet,* she thought as he leaned in at her, his big hands blotting out the light shining from behind him, making a massive shadow of him. . . .

Now. She kicked as hard as she could, felt her booted feet slam his chest. He let out a grunt of pained surprise and reeled backward as she lurched up, praying for the momentum to hurl her forward.

But her bound body was too clumsy and the blankets on it too heavy. . . . Just for an instant she saw the distant breakwater and the lights illuminating its empty concrete expanse, as she tried with every muscle and nerve to lift her torso off the floor of the car trunk.

Then a hand gripped her throat and squeezed. A fist punched the side of her head. Pain burst brilliantly behind her eyes like a million fireworks, and she felt herself go limp.

Felt the blankets wrap her tightly, felt the tape snugging the thick fabric around her head, waist, and ankles. A terrible sorrow overwhelmed her as she realized: *one chance.*

Just like the other girls, the ones in the pictures she had studied and written about, the girls in their graves . . .

One chance only. She'd had it. Had it and blown it. And now—

Now it was gone.

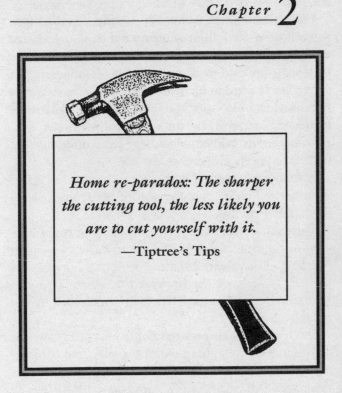

Chapter 2

Home re-paradox: The sharper the cutting tool, the less likely you are to cut yourself with it.

—Tiptree's Tips

I'm going to kill you!"

On the morning after Chip Hahn and Carolyn Rathbone arrived in Eastport, the voice on the phone was a high, disguised warble of malice.

The slim, dark-haired woman in jeans and a paint-speckled red sweatshirt put the receiver down. Her name was Jacobia Tiptree—Jake, to her friends—and it was the fourth such call she'd had in two days.

"Who was that?" asked Ellie White, coming into the old gold-medallion-wallpapered dining room of the big, ramshackle antique house on Key Street.

Model-slim and as deceptively fragile-appearing as an Arthur Rackham fairy princess, Ellie was in fact as tough as an old boot. Today she wore a chartreuse turtleneck, a turquoise smock with lime green rick-rack edging its bodice, black leggings, and gold flats with fake jewels glued onto the toes.

A yellow gauze scarf with a lot of sequins on it tied back her red hair; it was a habit of hers to raise each day's glitter quotient as much as possible.

"Just some jerk." Crossing to the dining room window in the thin, fleeting light of an early November morning in downeast Maine, Jake gazed out past the pointed firs edging the backyard to where a row of barberry bushes divided her lawn from that of her nearest neighbor.

She had not seen him tending to his own lawn or anything else lately; the time of planting and cultivating was over for the year. But the plot of ground over there was still a gardener's paradise, with dozens of low, pampered rosebushes neatly pruned, mulched, and—as of this morning—covered in tan burlap.

So he'd been out. Must have been; he never let anyone else touch the roses. She simply hadn't noticed him.

Just as well, she decided, that they hadn't run into each other. He'd moved in the previous summer and immediately gotten to work improving the property. But he'd never introduced himself and when she'd tried, he'd shut the door in her face with a snide glance at her unmowed grass.

Which was why nowadays even without his flat, disapproving gaze across the common lot-line, she felt each immaculately tended mound in his rose bed as a reproach. In her own yard, the fallen leaves still littered the lawn, and if the dahlia bulbs got dug up before they froze solid, it would be a miracle.

"Well, can't you find out who it was?" Ellie asked with a frown at the telephone.

"Probably not." Jake peered at the caller ID box. It listed the most recent call as having come from "undisclosed." That meant the caller, whoever he or she was, had blocked the ID function.

Just like before . . . "Kids playing a joke, most likely," she told Ellie, more annoyed than concerned.

When she first came to Maine ten years earlier, a telephoned death threat would've unnerved her. But nowadays she reserved her anxiety for true emergencies.

Such as, for instance, the fact that it was nearly winter and despite earnest promises from a succession of remodeling contractors, her old house still had no insulation in it. So she was doing it herself, a decision she dearly hoped would not end up making her wish the death threat were carried out.

She was only putting about a gazillion cubic feet of fire-retardant-treated cellulose into the old walls, though, so what could go wrong?

Nothing, she reassured herself. The whole thing would be a snap. But Ellie still didn't seem quite convinced.

"Are you sure we should try this?" she asked Jake

again when they had climbed the two full flights of stairs up to the third story of the old dwelling.

Most of this floor had been turned into a large, modern studio apartment a few months earlier. But a big, south-facing section was still Jake's carpentry workroom: a place to glaze antique windows, strip off layers of paint, and sand sections of old hand-carved woodwork laid out on milk crates.

"I don't see why not," said Jake. Much earlier that day, as dawn was breaking, the delivery truck had arrived and the big, bright room with its tall, bare windows and whitewashed walls had been filled by the delivery men with as many blue-plastic-covered bales of insulation material as could be stuffed into it.

Hoping yet again that she hadn't bitten off more than she could chew, or at least not without breaking a tooth, she added, "People do it, we're people, therefore . . ."

Also in the room were a forty-foot orange heavy-duty extension cord, a circular saw that in a pinch could've been used to anchor a barge, an iron pry bar, dust masks, and two plastic shower caps. A leak in one of the insulation bales had spewed a small volcano of impossibly fluffy-looking gray cellulose onto the floor.

"How's Bella doing?" Ellie asked, poking one of the bales experimentally and watching it spring back.

"Okay, I guess." Since the housekeeper's recent marriage to Jake's father, her relationship with Jake had gotten awkward, or so Jake felt. "We don't quarrel, if that's what you mean."

They never had. The trouble was, now Jake didn't think it was enough. At her insistence the third-floor studio apartment had been put in for the newlyweds; Jake thought that alone must signal to Bella her happiness at her father's choice.

But Bella had gone on behaving after the wedding just as before: kindly, even affectionately, yet with the faintest touch of distant formality. And surely, sooner or later, a person's stepmother should begin treating a person more as a daughter and less as an employer?

"She'll warm up," Ellie predicted, but Jake barely heard her as she looked around again at the room full of stuff. It was a lot of equipment, as befitted the installation of a lot of insulation, yet something was missing. A big something, an important—

"Oh, what an idiot I am." Standing at the window, she peered to the yard below, put a hand to her head in dismay.

Three stories down on the lawn stood an air compressor. Positioned on a wooden pallet, the compressor was for blowing the insulation material into the space between interior and exterior walls. About the size of the cab on a standard pickup truck, it had been delivered early that morning while she was still getting dressed.

And by the time she'd raced downstairs to ask them to move the machine upstairs, the delivery men had gone. Then the dogs, Monday the black Labrador and Prill the red Doberman, had begun dancing urgently around, indicating that they needed to go out.

So she'd taken them, even though it wasn't her job, being careful not to let them cross over into the precious rosebushes. She'd brought the animals in and fed them—not her job, either—and then the death threat had come in.

And in her annoyance over all these things, she had forgotten about the compressor. "Dumb, dumb . . ."

"What?" asked Ellie, but Jake was too vexed to answer. Even from this high above it, she could see that the machine the men had delivered featured a large metal intake hopper on one side and seventy-five feet of wide-bore, black corrugated plastic hose on the other.

A hose with a plastic nozzle on it, just as required. The trouble was, the compressor was way down *there,* but the insulation bales that needed to go into the hopper were all up *here.*

"Hmm," she commented thoughtfully, which made Ellie look cautious.

"Jake," said the pretty redhead in a warning tone born of experience.

Jake wasn't listening. The hose was plenty long enough to reach up here; she could still stick its nozzled business end into the third-floor walls to fill them with heat-saving material just as she'd planned, no problem at all.

But she was pretty sure she couldn't throw a bale out the window and hit the hopper with it, even if she could figure a way to get the plastic to come off the bale as it descended.

She could throw one out the window and *not* hit the hopper, though, and a bale of what was basically shredded paper couldn't do too much more than bounce at the bottom, could it?

Surely not. And then while she ran the hose, Ellie could just go down there and put the dropped insulation bale where it belonged, into the compressor's maw.

"Jake," Ellie said even more warningly, but Jake just waved her off, experimentally hefting a bale.

It was a foot square, three feet long, and surprisingly heavy. Solid as a brick, too, in its blue plastic wrapper, almost pressurized-feeling, as if the contents were trying hard to burst out at her.

Downstairs, the phone began ringing. Jake ignored it as, with the bale in her arms, she staggered over to the window and raised the sash with her elbow, and gave the bale a shove.

"Wow," said Ellie as the bale toppled out.

They watched it fall. As Jake had expected, it missed the hopper, dropping straight down to hit the ground just a foot or so away from the compressor.

But it didn't bounce. Instead, with a short, sharp *pop* that sounded like big trouble—and was—the insulation bale exploded.

Gray stuff spewed up from the burst blue plastic wrapper as if shot out of a cannon. An aerosol of pale gray insulation flew up past the third-floor window and just kept on going.

Jake felt her mouth drop open in awe as the stuff spread out over the neighbors' lawns, wherever it wasn't blocked by treetops. Where it was blocked, it snagged in the high branches and began fluttering in the breeze.

Fortunately, none of it landed on the rosebushes next door, because they were already burlap-wrapped. And that, as far as Jake could tell, was the only fortunate thing about the entire event.

"You know," Ellie said thoughtfully, "maybe that wasn't a good idea."

"Right," Jake said, as below, a familiar shape came around the corner of the house.

Thickly covered with a truly enormous amount of fluffy gray stuff, the shape strongly resembled the Abominable Snowman. Then, slowly, it looked up and saw them.

Jake recognized the figure. Under all the abominableness, it was her father, and despite his usual unflappable good nature, he did not look happy.

"Let's get out of here," she said.

"No kidding," said Ellie.

But then that phone started ringing again.

Jake had a husband, a father, a grown son, and a stepmother who was also her housekeeper living with her in the big old house on Key Street.

But, as often happened, when she wanted one of them, nobody was around.

Racing down the two flights of stairs from the third floor, she noticed in passing that her son Sam's bedroom door was wide open and that his bed was neatly made. Like the dogs' anxiety to go out earlier and their not having been fed, this was unusual.

Sam, who was doing this year's autumn college semester here at home, was ordinarily very responsible about his animal chores and casual about his bedmaking ones. But in her hurry she didn't pause to wonder about it.

That phone . . .

She took the last few steps at a leap, sprinted into the telephone alcove between the dining room and the kitchen, and glanced at the caller ID. *Undisclosed.*

Answering, she spoke fiercely. "Stop calling me. Do you hear me? You stop calling here, I mean it, or I'm going to . . . What? Say that again, please?"

Bella Diamond peered in, her grape-green eyes inquisitive. Tall and rawboned with henna-dyed hair skinned back tightly into a rubber band, she smoothed her hands over the front of her white bib apron, then returned to her morning's task of cleaning the kitchen even though it was already so spotless that in a pinch, organ transplant surgery could have been done in it. Bella was the teensiest bit devoted to household hygiene, if by that one meant obsessed.

"Sorry," Jake said distractedly into the phone, "but I was expecting . . ."

A death-threat caller.

"You are . . . Who did you say?" she asked, still perplexed. "And who did you say you wanted to—"

The caller pronounced his name again; the light dawned. "Oh, Chip Hahn! Of course I—"

Outside the dining room window, the Abominable Snowman had lost most of his fluffiness. He looked like Jake's father again, a lean, clean old man in faded overalls and a red flannel shirt, his stringy gray ponytail fastened back with a leather thong. But he still didn't look happy.

"Of course I remember you, Chip," said Jake. "But you're where? The police station? Here?"

She listened some more. Not much that came out of the phone sounded sensible, though. Mostly she understood that someone had gone missing; the rest was panicked babbling.

"Chip? Listen, you just stay there and I'll come

and . . . No. No, I'm not hanging up on you, I'm just . . . Stop. No. Chip, listen to me, now, I—"

She took a deep breath. "Chipper—Will. You. Shut. Up?"

So he did. And then she did hang up.

Bella Diamond watched Jake and Ellie hurry out of the house, then lifted a large wooden box down from a pantry shelf. Her own feelings of pleasure at the younger women's liveliness mingled with regret that she could no longer share in it.

Or so it seemed. She had celebrated her sixtieth birthday a few months earlier, not that sixty was old, especially nowadays. But with age and experience had come caution, and now she worried that caution might be hardening into timidity.

Lately she feared heights, spiders, snakes, even the pilot light on the gas stove. And darkness—especially that. Going down into the cellar after nightfall had become a trial, because the string used to pull the light on was located several paces from the foot of the cellar stairs.

Paces that had to be taken blind, with no idea what horror might be reaching stealthily out of the darkness at her . . .

Bella shuddered just thinking about it, at the same time as she made scornful fun of the thought. She was turning into a scaredy-cat, an idea she would have pooh-poohed vigorously only a few years ago.

Still, right now there was work to be done. Turning to it with relief, she peered into the box, where a whole pollock, split and cleaned, lay in a bed of rock salt. Its preparation, at which Bella was an expert, was a legacy from early Eastport, at a time when refrigeration was unknown and ice a luxury.

Once the large white-fleshed fish had absorbed all the salt it could—Bella knew just by looking at it when it was right—it would be hung out on the clothesline with two clothespins, to dry until it had a texture somewhere between leather and cardboard, at which point it could be stored for the winter.

Later it would be used to make dried-fish dinner, with boiled potatoes and fried pork scraps. Bella smiled, anticipating this; her new husband, Jacob Tiptree, liked hearty fare, plain cooking, and plenty of it.

She hadn't yet tried serving him what the old guard in Eastport still called huff-and-puff—potatoes and turnips mashed together with bacon fat—but sooner or later she was going to get her nerve up, she resolved, and do it. But that notion brought her thoughts around to her own cowardice, and to Jacobia again.

She closed the lid on the fish box and returned it to the pantry, wondering why she had always felt so comfortable with Jacobia before, but not anymore. Something about being a stepmother had thrown her off, Bella decided.

Of the two jobs, being a housekeeper was easier. And being a mother-in-law *and* a stepmother . . . well.

She just couldn't seem to get the hang of it. Returning to the big old-fashioned kitchen with its high, bare windows, pine wainscoting, and scuffed hardwood floor, she reflexively touched one of the small gold hoop earrings she wore.

Anne Dodd had given them to her as a birthday present, long ago. And Anne, who had been Bella's oldest friend in the world, would know what to do.

How to reach out to Jacobia, to signal a willingness to try—what? Anne would know.

But Anne Dodd was dead now and would not be offering any more opinions on anything. Fingering the earring sadly, Bella reminded herself to get safety catches for these, her most treasured possessions.

Well, aside from her wedding ring, of course. She'd been wearing the earrings for six weeks, ever since Anne's body was found, and they hadn't fallen out or gotten lost yet.

That didn't mean they couldn't, though. In fact, Bella had her hand on the phone to call the jewelry store in Bangor and ask about safety guards for the earrings, whether she could just go in and pick a pair or if there were other considerations.

But just then Jacob came inside with a few lingering fluffs of insulation material still clinging to him, and in her haste to remedy that situation she put the telephone down and forgot about it.

Although not about her own decision, that in the personal courage area—especially as it had to do with her new stepdaughter, Jacobia—she was going to have to try to do better.

Jake Tiptree's big old Eastport house was a white clapboard 1823 Federal with three full floors plus a two-story ell, forty-eight antique double-hung windows, each with its own pair of dark green shutters, and three tall red-brick chimneys.

The bricks needed pointing, the flashing around the chimneys needed tar, and as she backed the car out of the driveway she saw that the whole house needed painting again, too.

None of which came as a surprise. Moose Island, where Eastport, Maine, had been located for two-hundred-plus years, was a large granite rock sticking out of cold salt water. On it, an old wooden building was as tricky and difficult to maintain as a wooden boat.

The only difference was that if the house got a hole in it, the people inside wouldn't drown. Or anyway not immediately.

"Who's Chip Hahn?" Ellie asked as they pulled away down Key Street.

Jake sighed, eyeing the old green shutters in the rearview mirror. They looked as if they had a disgusting disease. *Paint, putty, scrapers,* she thought.

Plus someone to go up on a ladder and get the shutters and stack them in the workroom. But not until after the insulation material got used up. Until then, there wouldn't be space up there to put shutters or anything else.

"He was Sam's friend in Manhattan," she answered. "He lived with his family in our building."

It had been an Upper East Side penthouse with a doorman, a concierge, a private elevator, and a view, all so exclusive you practically had to show a pedigree to get in. That or a brokerage statement plus the deed to your place in the Hamptons.

"But I didn't know much about them, and anyway, that was what, a dozen years ago?"

In those days, she'd been a freelance financial manager to the filthy rich, many of whom turned out to be so crooked, they made the Soprano family look like the Brady Bunch. At that time she was the only money professional in the city with not one but two well-connected, high-octane criminal defense attorneys' home phone numbers on her speed dial.

Her neighbors in the exclusive building would no doubt have been horrified had they known. Or perhaps not.

Anyway, the kind of clients she'd had then plus long workdays, way more money than she could spend, and a brilliant neurosurgeon husband so chronically unfaithful that his nickname around the hospital where he worked was Vlad the Impaler hadn't done much for her neighborly instincts.

Or for her son's well-being. "Chip spent a lot of his time at our place," she added, "hanging out with Sam. Which turned out to be a blessing."

By age ten, Sam had quite naturally been spoiled, scared, and furious, a perfect candidate for membership in a gang of preadolescent boys even angrier and more disaffected than he was.

Also, he'd had not-yet-diagnosed dyslexia. If you want to make the child of a couple of high-IQ parents feel worthless, try that one. "Still, I'm a little surprised Chip even remembers us," Jake went on.

One day back then, Sam had gone missing, and when he finally came home, she learned that he and his pals had been riding the tops of subway cars for eighteen hours, in a contest to see who could stay on the longest. Sam had won, but in the process he lost six pounds and had to be hospitalized for severe exhaustion, dehydration, and an electrical burn that just missed being fatal.

Slowing at the foot of Key Street, Jake glanced to her right at the Motel East, a long, low wooden building perched over the bay's edge. A new, sleek black Volvo sedan with New York plates sat in the parking lot.

It was the only car there, since what there was of the tourist season in Eastport having ended a month earlier. "I'll bet that's his."

At the stop sign she turned left, then left again into one of the angled parking spots fronting the Eastport police station, across Water Street from the Happy Crab Bar and Grille. On the Crab's sign, a cheerful crustacean teetered gaily on the rim of a boiling kettle.

"But what's Chip doing way up here at this time of year?" she wondered aloud.

Once the Frontier Bank building, the Eastport police station resembled a red-brick wedding cake with its tall, arched windows on granite-slab lintels, gobs of ornately carved stone trim, and massive stone steps leading up to the front door. The bank's old alarm box, helpfully labeled *Bank Alarm* in large white letters, still hung beneath a front window.

"Anyway, I don't know Chip's whole story," Jake went on as she and Ellie got out of the car. "He was five or six years older than Sam. A real nerd, I thought back then. But he was very good to Sam."

And good for him, she added mentally, recalling

Chip Hahn's pear-shaped body, thick glasses, and earnest expression.

"If you needed to sum Chip up in a word, it was 'podgy,' " she said. "And you wouldn't think a kid like that would be good at sports, but he was, and that's how he took Sam under his wing. Played catch with him, took him to ball games and so on."

They climbed the police station's half-dozen granite front steps.

"Chip taught Sam to ice-skate down at Rockefeller Center one Christmas Eve, and after that he took him out for dinner at the Russian Tea Room. It was," Jake added with a half-wondering pang of nostalgia, "before it closed."

When his father and I were too busy working, she thought but did not add.

"Chip's family had a big resort cabin on a lake somewhere in upstate New York, too. One summer Sam learned to sail there, and water-ski."

At the police station's big glass front door they paused. "That's how he found out he liked boats."

Which for Sam had turned out to be a lifesaver; nowadays he was in school for an engineering degree and was already licensed by the Coast Guard to pilot any number of heavy work vessels. He wanted someday to own a tugboat fleet, which as an alternative to drinking himself to death, Jake thought was a fine plan.

"You know . . ." Ellie began as they entered the police station's cramped vestibule.

"Yes," said Jake, knowing Ellie's concern without having to be told. "Don't worry."

About what they might be getting into, she meant.

Over the past few years, together she and Ellie had enjoyed quite a career looking unofficially into local bad deeds, even clearing up a few when no one else could.

But a recent episode involving a kidnapping, a very bad guy, and a final, frightening twist that neither of them could quite manage to forget had spoiled their appetite for other people's business.

For a while, anyway. "No more snooping," Jake said as they passed through the vestibule and then a second set of glass doors. Finally: "There he is."

Inside, Chip Hahn sat nervously on a wooden bench, across from the high marble counter where once thrifty Eastport ladies had waited to deposit their savings into the Christmas club. The counter now held a display box of neighborhood-watch brochures.

Chip looked up when he heard the door. He wore a thin polished-cotton jacket over a tired-looking white shirt, no tie, and dark brown slacks. A pair of black wing tips were on his feet.

He'd lost some of his baby fat since the last time Jake had seen him, but his hands still made the anxious, automatic washing motions she remembered from a dozen years ago, and his round face looked guilty as hell about something.

Uh-oh, Jake thought as she spotted this. Chip jumped up when he saw her, his expression changing swiftly to one of relief.

"Hi. Thanks for coming," he began, sticking his hand out as he smiled uncertainly, looking from Jake to Ellie and back again. But Eastport's police chief, Bob Arnold, interrupted this greeting impatiently.

"Is everyone taking stupid pills around here today, or what?" Bob demanded from behind his desk.

He was pink, plump, and balding, with pale blue eyes, a few thin strands of blond hair combed over his shining forehead, and small rosebud lips that did not look at all as if they belonged on a police officer.

A child beauty-pageant contestant, maybe. "Because first I got a guy," he went on abrasively, "who said his car was stolen, and I drove around half last night looking for it."

He eyed Chip suspiciously, as if the young man now standing across from him might be responsible for the missing vehicle. "But then a couple hours later he calls again, he says the car's right back where he left it."

He took a breath. "So that's a mystery. Next, I got a bunch of middle-school kids hanging out on the breakwater, also last night, screamin' about a guy in a scary mask from a horror movie. They're sayin' he yelled at 'em and chased 'em."

Jake knew better than to interrupt. "Then," Bob went on, "I get this guy, first damn thing in the a.m. before I even finish my coffee."

He waved at Chip, then at his big green-and-white paper cup, still nearly full. The local grocery store's delicatessen did a mean hazelnut-mocha lately, and Bob was hooked on the stuff.

"And," Bob finished, "the guy whose car got stolen? He says there's a scary mask in the trunk; he never saw it before."

Chip opened his mouth to speak, which Jake could've told him was a bad idea. She motioned for him to shut up. Wisely, he did.

But she had a feeling that this sort of wisdom was not one of Chip's strong points. Or Charles, as he apparently wanted to be called now. She looked back at Bob.

"So now your friend here says his lady friend's run off to somewhere, he can't find her, and how come I don't hop right to it, bring in the FBI an' call out the National Guard?"

In Eastport, when lady friends ran off, their boyfriends did not often call the cops. More often, they felt lucky the cops had not been called on them. Not all the time, but still.

"She's not my lady friend," Chip protested tiredly and with the air, frustrated and beginning to be annoyed, of a person who has said this a number of times already.

"I told you, she's my boss, and she didn't run off. She's been missing since last night; she just disappeared right off the street. I'm afraid someone took her."

He turned to Jake in appeal. "We were coming out of a bar. The one at the end of the street overlooking the harbor, called The Artful Dodger? I was outside, a little ways down the street, waiting for her, but she didn't catch up, and when I went back to look for her—"

That there was more to this story Jake couldn't help seeing in Chip's expression, and Bob Arnold was even more familiar with the looks on liars' faces than Jake was.

It was one reason why he was not precisely leaping to Chip's aid, Jake realized. But she could get to the bottom of that later, she decided.

"Poof," Bob said, eyeing Chip skeptically. "Gone, like a fart in a hurricane."

"Wait a minute," Jake told Chip. Or Charles. They could get reacquainted later, too.

For now it just seemed clear that a young woman was missing. "Start over, Chip; tell me the whole thing right from the start. Why are you here in the first place, and just exactly what were you and this—"

"Carolyn Rathbone," he supplied. "That's her name. She's a very popular true-crime writer, two bestsellers, you must have heard of her. She wrote *Young Blood,* which is—"

"I know what it is," Jake said. She'd have had to be dead not to. Even here in Maine, the ads for the book had resembled an artillery barrage: TV, radio, Internet, the works.

"But that doesn't answer my question," she added. "What were you two doing here in Eastport?"

He flushed uncomfortably. "We're writing a new book—Carolyn is, I mean—on the Dodd family crimes. And the . . . the weird events that happened here."

Oh, brother, Jake thought. As far as Bob was concerned, Chip might as well have said they were planning to do a tell-all book on the Appalachia of the Northeast, which was what many people who didn't live in downeast Maine thought of the place.

Wrongly, smugly, and utterly unfairly, boyfriends and their lady friends' habits notwithstanding, and Bob resented it keenly. Now he leaned back and clasped his hands over his ample front.

"Weird events, huh?" He made a sour face. "Well, whoop-de-do. Now I can die happy."

Even without comparisons to Appalachia, Bob thought most media stories about Eastport ranked right up there with Charmin, in the what-are-they-good-for department. But he saved his deepest scorn for the ones created by persons from away—by which he meant anyone who wasn't actually born right here on the island—and that went double for stories about local tragedies.

Which the Dodd family misfortune certainly was. Jake and Ellie glanced resignedly at each other while Chip rushed on.

"You see, a couple of years ago, these two Eastport brothers married two sisters, also from Eastport. Rich girls, the last two descendants in some big local industrialist family."

"Yes," Jake said. The whole town knew the sad tale. Joseph Paducah Lang, the great-great-grandfather of the "rich girls" in question, had been a prosperous sardine can manufacturer back in the days when the sardine was king around here, in the late 1800s.

If you could call what they did back then "manufacturing." Putting things together one by one with your hands, however fast, didn't seem to quite fit the word's definition. Chip went on.

"Next thing you know, one of the Dodd brothers falls off his boat, body never found," he said. "Randy Dodd, his name was."

This wasn't news, either; the opposite, actually. The story had made the Bangor papers.

"And after that, both women got murdered," said

Chip. "Or," he added hastily as Bob made to object, "one did, for sure. Anne Lang Dodd, Roger Dodd's wife, was stabbed in her own kitchen."

Yes, just six weeks ago. By a person unknown, and it's too soon to be here trying to make money on it, Jake thought. Writing a book about it, or whatever.

But perhaps the timing hadn't been all Chip's idea. He had, after all, said the missing woman was his employer, and it was her name on the books' covers.

"The other one," Chip said, "Randy Dodd's wife—"

Cordelia Dodd, he meant. She'd been the pretty one; sweet-natured, too, by all accounts, if not terribly bright.

"Fell down stairs," Jake put in. "Yes, we know that, too. But I still don't see what that's got to do with—"

"Carolyn disappearing?" Chip frowned. "I'm not sure. But I think . . . I've just got a funny feeling maybe someone has lured us here."

At this Bob Arnold's white-blond eyebrows rose skeptically. Chip's next words came out in a hurry.

"Lured Carolyn and me, I mean. Someone who knew that she had taken an interest in the Dodd boys and their dead wives. And," he added, "someone who didn't like it."

Bob Arnold rested his chin on his shirtfront and gazed with interest at Chip. "Do tell," he said.

Chip either missed the sarcasm or ignored it. "See, I put out a few requests for information while I was first checking out the whole Dodd case just in general. I mean, to see if it really was anything Carolyn would want to pursue."

He looked around at them. "I have," he added, so modestly that Jake thought it was probably an understatement, "a couple of research contacts."

Bob's eyebrows shifted questioningly.

"People who know things, or people who know how to find them out," Chip explained. "I help them, and they help me."

Jake looked over again at Ellie, found that her friend had produced a small legal pad from her bag and was busily writing on it. *Stolen car, mask on the breakwater, miss'g woman,* the page read in Ellie's large, clear handwriting.

And on a separate line: SAM???

Ellie had noticed Sam's neatly made bed, too, Jake realized, as they'd rushed downstairs. And Jake had complained bitterly to Ellie about the untended dogs that morning.

A quiver of apprehension seized her as Chip continued: "After I put requests on a few of the members-only true-crime discussion boards, I started getting these strange e-mails."

Bob looked even more skeptical.

"E-mails," Chip continued, "from someone who said he knew more about the Dodds than anyone else." He took a deep breath. "He said he'd tell Carolyn what he knew if she met him, here in Eastport."

Bob cleared his throat, spoke to Ellie and Jake. "The person your friend here's been hearing from says his name's Randy Dodd."

"Chip," Jake said, "I hate to tell you this, but someone's been fooling around with you." It was the nicest way she could think of to put it. "Randy's the brother who drowned, remember? He's been dead for two years. Before his wife had the accident, even, he was already—"

"See, but that's just it," Chip said, undeterred. "Maybe he's not dead. Maybe he faked it and he just doesn't want Carolyn reviving any interest in the whole thing, and he knows she could, so he grabbed her."

Unaware of the disbelieving stares of his audience, or maybe ignoring them, he went on intently.

"See, Carolyn thinks the Dodd boys might've married the Lang girls for the money, and killed them for it. She thinks maybe Randy's supposed death was part of the plan. That he survived going overboard somehow. That he's here, now."

Silence followed this, until: "That's quite a theory you've got there," Bob Arnold said in disgust. For one thing, in the fact-gathering department, he thought websites were about as reliable as Ouija boards.

"It's also just about the dumbest thing I ever heard," he added, getting up from behind his desk.

"You've looked for her, right? Your little girlfriend. You checked her motel room, all that."

"She's not my girlfriend," Chip repeated, starting to sound impatient. "And of course I looked for her. The only reason I waited so long before I came in here to see you was that I still thought she might show up. I mean, what d'you think, I'm some kind of a fool?"

Bob's answering look said that early indications were not in Chip's favor on this question. "Son, I'm not sure what you are or what your problem is," he said.

"But," he went on, holding up an admonishing finger, "I do know Randy Dodd was out lobsterin' all alone one morning a couple years back, slipped on a piece o' herring bait, an' went over the rail."

Herring chunks were what the lobstermen used to get their prey to crawl into the traps. Bob's voice dropped.

"Drowned," he pronounced gravely. "Body never found. Left three torn-out fingernails, though, meat an' all still attached to 'em, stuck in his trapline where he must have got tangled in it. You get me?"

He held Chip's gaze. "I mean, that fella struggled. He tried but he died. Coupla men do it every year or so, tryin' to make a living. And I don't know how things are wherever you come from, sonny, but around here that's no joke."

Bob headed for the glass doors, grabbing his hat and duty belt and putting them on as he spoke.

"And that's what happened. So you can tell any tall tales you want to about how come your girl took off on you," he said. "I'll keep an eye peeled for her, and put the word out, just in case. That's my job and I'll do it, don't worry about that. But probably she went home."

He turned. "Unless by some awful coincidence, in the next day or two, she shows up dead, which you better hope she doesn't. Because if that happens, the first one I'm coming to talk to about it is you," he finished scathingly.

Which was a little tough on Chip, Jake thought. But she, too, felt skeptical about his story.

For one thing, if Randy Dodd had wanted people to think he was dead, why reveal otherwise to Chip? Or to his friend Carolyn Rathbone? Or his employer, or whatever? But . . .

"Bob? Where did you go last night? I mean, after you looked for the guy's stolen car?"

"Out on the causeway," he replied. The one that connected Moose Island to the mainland, he meant, linking Eastport to the rest of the world.

There was no ferry, except for a few weeks in summer. The rest of the time there were not enough people living in Eastport to support ferry service.

"Took the night shift for Howie Crusoe. He's on leave 'cause his wife's havin' a baby. Sat there like he always does, trolling for speeders. Why?"

"Oh, just something that occurred to me." She put the timing together: a stolen car, a disguised guy on the breakwater scaring everyone else off, and—

"So you saw everyone who came onto or went off the island, between—"

"Between ten and three," he finished for her. "Knew 'em all, too. All their cars, where they're going, what they're doing. All the same ones as go back and forth every night for their jobs and so on. No mysterious strangers," he added dryly.

"And the guy wearing the horror movie mask," she persisted. "Did he scare the bunch of kids right off the breakwater? I mean, completely off? They ran away?"

Which at that hour would've left the breakwater empty, most likely. Bob snorted.

"Sure did. Anyway, that's what all their moms said when they called me up to complain about it. Although where any of 'em got the nerve to do that, I don't know. Eleven-thirty's a good couple hours past when youngsters that age oughta be out on the street at all, you ask me." Bob shook his head. "Maybe I'll get myself a mask like that. Sounds useful. Anyway, is that all?" He eyed Chip balefully.

"Yes, Bob," said Jake. "Thanks very much."

The police chief slammed out. A silence followed. Then: "Is he always like that?" Chip asked shakily.

Outside, Bob's old Crown Vic started up with a roar, nearly stalled, and coughed back to stuttering life again a few times more before dying completely.

"Only when he thinks someone's trying to take advantage in some way," Jake said. "Stir up something people here would rather forget, maybe, just to make something for themselves out of it."

Which was how Bob Arnold would've viewed a Carolyn Rathbone book, even one that didn't happen to be about Eastport. He called people who wrote or made films about true crime "the blood-and-guts-ers."

"And by the way," she added, "the bar you two were in last night right before your friend vanished? Or boss, or whatever," she added quickly before Chip could correct her. "That's Roger Dodd's place," she finished.

Chip looked stunned. "Oh."

"Bought it right after he got married," she said. With his wife's money, she didn't add, though that was common knowledge.

"Before that, he was a paramedic on the town ambulance." A job, she also could've added, that he'd been happy to give up in order to buy his own business. With his new wife's cash.

But by all accounts the marriage had been happy. "He just reopened the bar a week ago. Word around town is he's still pretty torn up about Anne."

At first Roger had of course come under suspicion; husbands always did. Roger Dodd had an ironclad alibi for the time of his wife's murder, though, and ever since, he'd been walking around town like a grief-struck ghost.

People felt awful for him. "So if I were you, I don't think I'd be going on about how the Dodd boys killed the Lang girls for profit. Not around here, anyway."

Chip nodded slowly, frowning. "We didn't know the other Dodd brother ran a bar," he said. "What a blunder. All the research I did, how'd I miss that?"

As a onetime financial pro and longtime Eastport resident who heard what there was to hear—which in Eastport was plenty—Jake could have told him that for tax reasons, the Lang sisters and their husbands had been incorporated for business purposes. So none of their names were in the kinds of public records Chip would have had access to.

But Chip Hahn's problems were the least of her worries all of a sudden; she turned back to Ellie. "Sam was on the breakwater last night to help a fellow haul his boat."

Pull it out of the water for the winter, in other words, so it could be stored under a tarp or a roof from now until spring. Home from college on his independent-study semester, during which he hoped to finish many of his engineering-major electives in one fell swoop—

Or swell foop, as he would've called it; he was, despite his diagnosis and treatment, still quite severely dyslexic.

—Sam was learning Morse code, doing a biology experiment on seaweed, writing a research paper about the Spanish Inquisition, and auditing a class in electronic communications at the marine center in Eastport.

Still, he made time to do a lot of odd jobs around the dock and elsewhere in town, for spending money and because he enjoyed it. He'd put the brand-new karaoke system into Roger Dodd's bar, for example, and spent hours testing and tuning the equipment.

"But he didn't let the dogs out this morning, and his bed was made," Ellie said.

Outside, Bob Arnold's car stalled again.

"Right," Jake said. "That's why I'm starting to think he didn't come home last night at all, and I wonder if maybe . . ."

But Ellie was already on her way out the door, to catch up with Bob Arnold before the Crown Vic finally managed to get its backfiring, fumes-spewing act together.

When Carolyn Rathbone woke up, she couldn't see, speak, or move. Terror set her heart hammering again. Caught . . .

Gagged with tape and wrapped in a roll of blankets with even her head covered, she'd felt the man lifting her from the car trunk. Sometime after that, she'd passed out. But how long ago?

She couldn't tell. The faint clang of footsteps going down a metal stair had been followed by the creaking of a dock. Then she was falling, crashing into something hard.

She'd felt a part of her hand twist as it struck something, with a flare of pain that rocketed up her arm.

An instant later her head landed and bounced, knocking her unconscious.

Now the surface she lay on, whatever it was, rocked gently. The salty smell of the sea mingled with the harsh reek of diesel fumes, strong even through the blanket. *A boat . . .*

Despair clutched her. He was taking her out onto the ocean, where no one could hear her scream. But then . . .

"Mmgh." Her own voice, she thought it must be at first. Through the pain of her injured hand, her head's awful thudding, and the harsh agony of barely being able to breathe at all, she couldn't tell what sounds were coming from where.

The boat's engine started up, a low, liquid grumble not far from where she lay. Fright and nausea mingled as she remembered that she got seasick, and that the tape he'd stuck over her mouth was still there. . . .

Not that way, oh please, I don't want to die, but if I have to, please not like that, not strangling on my own . . .

Control of her limbs returned suddenly, as if a switch had been flipped inside her. From frozen in terror to wild with it, her heart slamming madly inside the cage of her ribs, she writhed frantically until the side of her face pressed the rough-textured blanket he'd wrapped her in.

Tears and sweat soaked the tape on her mouth. Rubbing her cheek back and forth against the blanket, she managed to peel the strip of sticky stuff—and most of her skin, too, it felt like—partly off. The rest of it came free when she wrenched her jaws apart.

She worked her mouth around, trying to get the

stiffness out of her jaw. Then she froze as from some-where nearby came that odd sound again. A groan of pain, it sounded only half conscious.

A man, she thought. *Or a boy. Not Chip.* She'd have known his voice. Someone else . . .

Gulping in huge, luxurious breaths, she tried think-ing about what the sounds might mean but could only get her mind to take in the present moment.

Now. For right now, I'm alive. . . . Breathing helped, and so did the realization that at least she'd done something about her situation.

Not that it would make a difference. Ninety-nine times out of a hundred, she knew, guys like the one who had her made sure in advance that no meaning-ful resistance was possible.

And they knew it, too. Because most of them had done it before. So fighting would achieve nothing. And yet . . .

Her cheek went on burning. Gradually, she realized that she was still rubbing it against the rough blanket. Back and forth . . .

And now the blanket was moving. With each mo-tion of her head it slid more, until the tightly wrapped hood loosened to a cowl.

A gleam of light penetrated it. Turning slightly, she pushed the blanket's fold past her right ear. Be-cause . . .

I want to see, she thought. *I want to see his face.*

Another low groan came from nearby; this time she ignored it. Coldhearted, maybe, but too bad. Carolyn did not believe herself to be a nice person, even in the best of situations. And anyway, what could she do about it?

She wasn't even convinced that she could save herself—the opposite, in fact. *Sorry, buddy,* she thought, *but you don't sound like help to me. So sayonara.*

Meanwhile, she did at least have a plan: get this blanket off her face so she could see the son of a bitch who'd grabbed her. Maybe he would end up killing her anyway.

Probably he would. She'd seen enough crime-scene photos and other evidence not to have many illusions about that.

Still, before he did whatever it was he'd brought her out here to do, she meant to see him.

To look right at him, not crying, if she could help it—

. . . she might not be able to help it . . .

—and spit in his eye.

"**Still got** that great right arm?" Back in the city, it had been Chip's ability to throw a baseball that first caught Sam's interest.

Beside Jake in the car, Chip managed to look pleased and discomfited at the same time.

"Yeah. I guess. Haven't used it a lot, lately. Few friends of mine, we get together in summer when we can."

He fell silent for a moment, then went on. "Listen, I'm sorry about this."

"Don't worry about it. Not your fault." Though whose it was she couldn't imagine, either.

She and Chip Hahn had left the police station an hour ago, and since then she'd been calling everyone she could think of who might know where Sam was.

But she'd reached only the guy who'd hired Sam the night before.

Down at the breakwater last night at about eleven-fifteen, Sam had finished cranking a twenty-two-foot Sea Ray onto a trailer, then signaled that the boat and trailer were good to go. The guy who'd hired Sam had pulled the trailer out of the water, stopped to pay Sam the twenty bucks they'd agreed on, and continued home.

He'd offered Sam a ride, he said, but Sam had his bike with him and said he'd be riding it. And that was the last the guy had seen of him.

Now it was late morning; beside Jake, Chip gazed out the car's passenger-side window at the north end of town. Moose Island was only seven miles long by about two miles wide, not much territory at all for everyday purposes. But it was vast if you were searching for someone.

A gravel turnaround edged the grassy bluffs overlooking the Old Sow whirlpool and the U.S. geological survey marker. From here you could see all the way up the Western Passage.

On the Canadian side, the distant hills rising up out of the landmass of New Brunswick had snow on them already, white between the dark stands of old trees. "I don't understand," she said.

They'd found Sam's old red three-speed leaning against the rear wall of Rosie's hot dog stand between the picnic tables and the trash barrels, not far out on the breakwater near the boat ramp.

"If he'd meant to ride his bike home," she wondered aloud, "why's it still there?"

"Someone could've picked him up in a car," Chip

said. "In which case he's probably still somewhere on the island."

She glanced sideways at him. "Because?" He'd been quiet for a while; now she recalled how smart he'd been, back in the city.

"Bob Arnold said he saw everyone who crossed the causeway late last night," he reminded her. "I suppose Sam could've gone somewhere on foot, then got driven to the mainland later."

"We'd still have heard from him by now," she objected.

It hadn't always been true. For the past ten years, Sam's life had been an ongoing battle against the bottle, with as many skirmishes lost as won.

But just two nights ago she'd stood out in the yard with him and the dogs, watching a vee of Canada geese whistle south across the full moon. Sam's face in the moonlight was bluish-white.

"I know why they fly that way," he'd said in that grown-up man's voice he had now. "What's that vee remind you of, those two lines they make?"

She'd been working with him on Morse code and reading with him about its science: how it got sent and received.

"An antenna?" she guessed.

He nodded. "Got it in one. See, geese navigate by magnetic field. That's how they migrate, and I think that vee shape they form when they fly is how they sense it."

She'd turned, amazed. "You read that somewhere?" It knocked her out, sometimes, how much he was like his father, Victor.

The late great. Victor at his best. "No," Sam said. "I just think so."

They had followed the dogs back to the house, calling them when they strayed into the adjoining yards. "Not that a goose isn't great all by itself," he'd added. "But it's when they get together that they can really do something special."

It was the last time she'd talked with him. Now she scanned to her right and left for him as she drove slowly on Water Street past the assisted living facility, a long, low waterside building that had once been a sardine cannery.

There'd been fifteen of them in the late 1890s when Joseph Paducah Lang made the cans to supply them all, she recalled, meanwhile trying to stay calm, trying not to think about what might have happened to Sam. Fifteen canneries crowded along the island shore, employing some eight hundred people, cutting the small fish and packing them. . . .

Sam, she thought.

"Bob Arnold also said there was a car stolen last night, but it got returned to its owner," Chip said. "Remember?"

"So?" The day had brightened, then gone sour again. Weather in Eastport in November was notoriously fickle. She hoped Sam was not out in the cold somewhere, as sleet spattered the windshield; she ran the wipers again.

Sam, where are you?

"So the only safe place to leave a stolen car," Chip said, "where the police won't be able to draw any conclusions about you from it, is back where you got it. Someone knew that, and cared."

She glanced again at him, surprised; he shrugged modestly in reply. "Hey, I told you I worked for a crime writer. I'm used to thinking about this stuff."

But not to living it. No one ever was. Out on the water, the Coast Guard's orange Zodiac and her crew practiced water rescues, tossing and retrieving a man-shaped dummy. Cold duty, but at least once a year they did it for real, so they rehearsed. At the wharf by the Chowder House restaurant, closed for the season, a few lobster traps were being put onto the deck of a tubby little wooden boat.

It was the season for lobster fishing now that the creatures were done with their yearly molting. Soon the boats would be out in force, no matter the weather.

Randy Dodd had gone overboard in November. If he had.

Funny thing about work in Eastport, that somehow the best season for it was always the worst weather for the people who did it. Warm day, though, she recalled, when Randy went over.

"A car you used to transport someone . . . or something?" Chip mused aloud. "To a boat, maybe? That's the only other way to get off this island efficiently, right?"

She nodded. "Which brings us to the guy in the mask."

On the dock the night before . . . Because if you knew from personal experience, as Randy would have, that local kids hung out on the dock at night, and if you wanted to be prepared to get rid of them if you needed to, so they wouldn't see something—or see you—that's what you'd bring along. A fright mask, or something like it.

"Maybe Sam did see someone on the breakwater," Chip said. "While he was helping to haul the boat, or afterward. Did he know Randy Dodd? Would he have recognized him?"

"He used to crew for Randy," she replied. "A few years ago, before he went away to school. So yes, Sam would know him if he saw him."

But then it hit her how ridiculous she was being. She wanted an answer to where Sam was, and in the absence of anything else she was fastening on to Chip's theory.

Trouble was, Randy being alive still didn't make any sense. The fingernails that had been found stuck in his trapline showed that, even if nothing else did.

She bit her lip hard, drew warm blood before she trusted her voice enough to speak. For almost a year now, Sam had been as sober and as reliable as the tides.

He could've fallen off the wagon again. But she didn't think he had. Something had happened to him, something bad. She wished her husband, Wade Sorenson, was home.

For a moment she pictured Wade, tall and solid with brush-cut blond hair and pale eyes that were blue or gray, depending upon the weather. Wade was calm and silent, a man prone to doing things instead of talking about them.

A native Mainer, he knew everyone in the county, too, and if he was here he would be calling them, thinking of more things to try, and trying them. And perhaps most usefully of all, they could lean on each other.

But he wasn't here. He'd left that morning to go on a deer-hunting trip, before she was awake. She didn't know if she could even reach him.

"Randy Dodd's dead, Chip. I don't know what happened to your friend, Carolyn"—*Sam, where are you?* she thought helplessly—"but Randy's not lurching around here like some zombie, kidnapping people."

When they were boys, Chip and Sam had been fans of all things horror-related: books and comics, films and video games. Probably one or both of them had owned a scary mask like the one the guy had been wearing on the breakwater last night.

"Zombies don't kidnap people," Chip said with a small smile, seeming to follow her thought. "They eat 'em. Vampires just drink your blood. Shape-shifters might kidnap you, or ghouls. But—"

She smiled back in spite of herself. "You haven't changed much, have you? Are you still interested in strange music, too, the way you used to be?"

"I am. I might even try writing about it," he added, clearly gratified that she remembered. "And I have a bigger project in mind to do, too." He hesitated. "But there are some things I have to clear up with Carolyn first." At this, he looked miserable again.

"What is it, Chip? No," she added, "don't bother denying it. I know you, remember? And I know that look on your face."

She'd last seen it when she'd tried asking about his family, years earlier in New York. He'd given her a brief, useless answer whose unspoken message was *Don't ask me again.*

So she hadn't. "Spill it," she said now.

Whereupon he broke down and revealed to her how much work he'd done on Carolyn Rathbone's books, and how little credit he had received.

"People want to think she does it all," he said simply, "so we let them. It's just good business."

They passed the massive granite-block post office on Water Street, and across from it the Moose Island general store. "Even those strange e-mails I got," Chip said. "I replied in her name, not mine. I'm supposed to be invisible."

"And you resented that?" She pulled over in front of the bar Roger Dodd ran, on the first floor of a two-story brick building a few doors down from the store.

With its side window overlooking the length of Water Street, the Artful Dodger had a view of nearly the whole downtown.

"No," Chip said. "That's what I signed on for, I knew what I was doing, so how could I have resented it later?"

He sighed. "But she's not an easy person, Carolyn. And right after we arrived . . ."

His hands made those washing motions again; the guilty look returned to his face. "She'd stolen an idea of mine. I found out last night. We argued about it."

"I see. And did anyone hear you?" The sleet had stopped, but the gray sky over the water was still wintry and the air damply penetrating.

"The bartender heard. I guess it must've been Roger Dodd," Chip replied.

She parked the car and they got out. "And there was another guy at the bar, too," Chip added, sounding as if he was only now recalling this. He zipped his thin cotton jacket, which was in no way adequate for the day's nasty weather. "Just some local, I think. I remember he had kind of a limp. But he had his own troubles, it looked like."

He paused. Then: "I thought about it," he blurted. "About hurting her. Just for a minute, she'd made me so angry, it felt like being rid of her would make things better."

He gazed unhappily at the asphalt parking lot adjacent to the fish pier. "But I'd never really have done anything to her."

Just then Bob Arnold drove by in the squad car, flipping one hand up in a curt wave as he passed. If he'd learned anything about where Sam was, he'd have stopped to say so.

"He was right, wasn't he?" Chip said, meaning Bob. "It was stupid of me to let Carolyn come here. And now Sam might be in trouble because of it, too."

But Jake was still mulling Chip's previous remark, that he'd thought about harming the missing woman. That admission, plus his being the last person known to have seen her . . .

"Do yourself a favor, Chip. Don't volunteer more information to anyone but me, okay?"

Because nothing good could come of it. She didn't think Chip had done anything dreadful.

But he could still get his name on a warrant by talking too freely; she sensed in him once more a kind of youthful naïveté, a too-honest softness about him that could make him easy pickings for a tough prosecutor.

Although of course she didn't really know what

Chip Hahn might've turned into in the years since he and Sam had played catch and tossed footballs around. Reminding herself that she shouldn't take anything at face value, she pulled the Artful Dodger's front door open, gestured for him to go in ahead of her.

"Meanwhile, let's just see what Roger Dodd has to say about all of this, shall we?" she told Chip. "You never know, he might remember something important."

Inside, the air smelled of stale beer and dish detergent. Roger was behind the bar washing glasses and placing them on the rinse rack in assembly-line fashion.

Freshly shaven and dressed as usual in a polo shirt and jeans, he turned the sprayer off and listened while Jake explained who they were looking for and why. After that, she let Chip describe Carolyn and ask about the fellow at the bar, the one with the limp.

Roger's face changed at that part of the conversation, but she wasn't expecting anything to come of it.

So she was amazed when, after giving them the old I-don't-know-anything-about-it routine for a few more minutes, Roger Dodd suddenly broke down.

"I didn't know. When he walked in last night after two years of me thinking he'd been drowned, I just about fainted," Roger babbled as they went out. He closed the bar's front door and locked it. "Anne said she knew Randy wasn't dead, that if he was, there would have been a body. But I told her no, she was crazy to think that after so long." He sucked in a hitching breath. "My God, it was like seeing a ghost. . . . I knew he was dead. He had to be. Anne and I, we even fought about it. We fought about it on the day she—"

"Shut up, Roger," Jake told him in disgust. Beside her on the sidewalk, Chip waited silently. He seemed to know he was out of his depth here.

Me too, Jake thought. "Let's go talk to Bob Arnold," she told Roger, and he came along obediently enough, still justifying and explaining.

"I didn't know," he insisted again as he got into the car. "I loved Anne. I'd never have let anything happen to her."

"Oh?" she retorted. "So that's why when your supposedly dead brother showed up here last night, you didn't tell anyone?"

She pulled out of the parking spot. "Or even before then? That he was still alive, that he'd killed her sister, Cordelia—his own wife—and that he intended to kill Anne, too?"

She felt like punching him, but of course she couldn't. "You kept your mouth shut on account of how you loved her so much?"

Because that, impossible as it seemed, was the gist of what Roger had admitted: that Chip's crazy theory was right and Randy Dodd was alive—though Roger insisted he hadn't known it until his supposedly deceased sibling appeared hale and hearty in the Artful Dodger the night before. But now Roger was convinced—

"I was about to go see Bob Arnold myself when you two walked in," he declared defensively.

—and Jake was, too: Randy Dodd was indeed alive, and as recently as twelve hours ago he'd been right here in Eastport.

And that meant anything could have happened. She gunned the engine, causing a couple of blithely jaywalking teenagers to jump back up onto the curb. She didn't quite give them the old middle-finger salute as they glared at her.

But it was close. In the back seat, Roger went on whining. "Cordelia could've been an accident," he insisted. "How was I to know that Randy had—"

"Yeah, sure," she cut him off sarcastically. "Her falling down those cellar stairs was just one of those things, huh?"

Sure it was. At the time, everyone had thought so. But now . . . She met his eyes in the rearview mirror.

"But Anne dying, and the way that she died—come on, Roger, don't tell me you didn't know then that something was up."

Stabbed to death in her own kitchen. Imagining it, Jake just barely managed to restrain herself from stomping the gas pedal again.

"But why am I even asking? You knew it all from the start. You had to. Because here's the thing, Roger."

What the brothers had done was falling together in her head now, like a disgustingly graphic picture puzzle. She might not have believed it at all if he'd been talking about some other motive.

But she did, because it was money-related, and money—plus what it could make people do, the wanting and getting of it—had been her bread and butter once.

In the bad old days, when she'd helped pirates of commerce stash their ill-gotten treasure in offshore accounts.

Chip wasn't comprehending it yet, though. Mostly he just looked frightened.

"Two things," she corrected herself. "First, you can't very well inherit any money or anything else when you're dead."

Roger's lips clamped together stubbornly. "And that's what it was about, wasn't it?" she continued. "That's why both sisters died. So you could inherit."

She thought a moment. "Probably there was a trust fund." It was how wealth stayed in wealthy families.

"The proceeds would go to the surviving sister. Once she was gone, you'd be a beneficiary. After the dust settled, you'd share the money with Randy."

Simple. And it had worked, or nearly. But Roger shook his head in denial.

"I thought Randy had drowned, just like everyone else did. I mean," he added shakily, "a long time ago he'd said something to me, to the effect of how if the girls died, we'd be wealthy men."

They passed Wadsworth's hardware store. *That insulation,* she thought as they went by. Bales and bales of it waiting for her in the attic.

No telling, now, when she might get back to it. In spring maybe. Or never. But who cared? A nice cold layer of ice sounded just right at the moment, like the perfect anesthetic.

"But I told him he was nuts, and to shut up and never talk to me about it anymore," Roger said. "I never thought of it again, either. It was an awful thing, repulsive, what he'd suggested, and I told him so."

He looked out the car window; she followed his gaze briefly. Out on the water the little lobster boat she'd seen earlier by the Chowder House pier puttered determinedly across the waves.

"But I guess he must have. Thought about it, that is," said Roger.

"So, what did he want?" Chip asked quietly. "In the bar last night?"

Roger laughed bitterly. "Money, of course. What he thought he was entitled to. He said he'd earned it. Can you believe it?" His tone was outraged.

Angling for sympathy. Jake parked in front of the police station, shut off the engine. Bob Arnold's squad car wasn't there in its usual spot.

Well then, they'd wait. Throwing her keys into her bag, she repressed the urge to fling them backward at Roger's face.

"Please," she ridiculed his story. "After what he said to you, first Cordelia has an *accident*." She put a scathing twist on the word. "And then some stranger just randomly picks your house to invade, your wife to kill?"

"It's not the kind of thing that would slip your mind, is it?" Chip agreed. "Randy hinting around about them dying, and then they do? That didn't, like, tip you off?"

He turned, eyed Roger accusingly. "But I still think the two of you plotted it together. Randy fakes dying, he sneaks back and kills both women . . . and man, that took some nerve, didn't it?"

He paused, considering this, then went on. "But

you got the money. You inherited, which makes you a perfect suspect right along with him. Lucky you had a good alibi, also twice. Once for his wife, once for yours." Chip frowned. "So, what I want to know is, how could that happen unless you knew in advance when Randy was going to do it?"

But for this Roger had an answer ready. "Because I always have that alibi," he retorted. "All I do is work in that bar. And the front and rear doors are in plain sight of all the customers and staff, so everybody knows if I go in or out."

He opened the car door. "I didn't do anything," he repeated. "I knew nothing about any of this."

Chip made a huffing sound of skepticism as he got out, too. "Yeah, you can say that. But I guarantee you the cops are still watching you and they have been all along." He grimaced at the chill outside the car. "Waiting for you to make a mistake. And now you have. The two of you have. That's what I think, anyway."

He looked back in at Jake. "Carolyn's book proposal, what she sent in to get a contract this time, was one sentence long: 'Two brothers in rural Maine marry two rich sisters, kill them for the money, and get away with it . . . almost.' "

Roger winced, listening to this.

"And they bought it," Chip said. "That's how obvious it is. One sentence, they took it."

Just then Bob Arnold pulled the squad car into his reserved parking space, got out, and marched up the station's granite-slab front steps. Jake slammed the car door, turned to Roger.

"Why?" she asked again. "If you weren't in on it

with him, why didn't you turn Randy in as soon as you realized what he must be doing when he showed up last night?"

But again, Roger had an answer. He gazed, stricken, at her. "Well. You know that unbreakable alibi I've supposedly got?"

The bar, the doors, his being in plain sight of everyone all the time . . . "What about it?" Jake demanded.

Roger hesitated. Then:

"Randy can break it," he said. "I was afraid to go to the police, because if he wants to, Randy can make it look like I did it all. Killed Anne, I mean, and Cordelia, too."

He looked around slowly, as if he thought this might be his last glimpse of freedom. "He can frame me completely. And if he doesn't end up getting away from here with his money, that's what he'll do."

Chapter 3

The blanket's edges parted at last and Carolyn's face poked out into the chill air. It was late morning, the sky threatening rain or snow, a sky she'd feared she would never see again.

But here she was. Everything hurt: her hand, her head. Her cheek, raw with so much rubbing, felt

sticky and hot, and she was thirsty. So very thirsty . . .
but alive.

Alive . . . She froze with fresh fear. Would he notice
that the blanket was off her face, that she'd somehow
found her way so far out of his restraint? If he did,
would he kill her at once?

All she could see was the boat's rough wooden deck
with a sort of bench sticking up from it, and the
round orange shape of a life preserver roped to the
bench.

But he is around here somewhere. Has to be . . .

She fought the cringing urge to duck back down
into the blankets again. She'd thought being able to
see what was around her would make her feel better.
But instead she only felt more exposed, like a little kid
who'd been hiding under the bedcovers. Hiding from
the monsters. Which in this case she really was doing.
But she wasn't a little kid and she couldn't act like
one. Not if she wanted to live.

Painfully, she inched herself up, craning her neck to
try locating her captor. *There . . .*

A dozen feet away at the front of the vessel, a man
stood in an open cubby with his hands on a steering
wheel, looking ahead through a curved windshield.
His back was turned to her, but she could see his pro-
file.

Something wrong with it . . . She couldn't tell what,
only that it looked odd somehow. Unnatural. But as
she'd thought when he'd first grabbed her, he was a
big man, and powerfully built.

Abruptly, the guilt she'd felt over not managing to
escape evaporated. He was at least twice her size; as
she'd suspected, she'd never had a chance.

Which meant beating him physically wasn't in the cards as an escape method, either. Not without a weapon, at any rate, and she didn't have anything like that.

A surge of despair threatened to swamp her, but she resisted, choking down sobs; better to know the truth than to try something that was doomed. And with her hands both still bound to her sides, there was no point even thinking about fighting him.

Not yet. She peeked over the blanket again, trying to spot anything that might help her get free. To the left of the wheel and the instruments near where the man stood, a small hatchway gaped, dark and forbidding-looking.

No one else was on the deck. The groaning she'd heard must have come from down there, but she hadn't heard it in a while.

The thought flew from her head as something struck the boat with a muffled *thump*. Her throat closed with renewed terror, but at the sound the man at the wheel only let out a triumphant bark of laughter.

He slowed the engine until it made a thick gurgling noise, the boat's lunging movement over the waves subsiding. Hurriedly he left the wheel, peered eagerly over the boat's side, then grabbed a long pole—the phrase *boat hook* popped into her head—and began poking around in the water.

He seemed to be trying to snag something. *One shove,* she thought bitterly, *and you'd be fish food.*

He went on straining with the pole. But whatever it was out on the water went on eluding him, no matter how he tried.

Then she noticed that each time he leaned out, a slip of paper in his shirt pocket slid up a little more. As if alerted by her thought, he jerked up suddenly, squinting suspiciously around.

Carolyn held her breath. If he turned his head toward her, he would see her face poking from the blanket. His eyes narrowed further as he listened, tipping his head.

He looked familiar to her, almost as if . . .

Satisfied, he returned to his efforts. The slip of paper in his shirt pocket now stuck out from it about two inches. He still hadn't noticed it.

"Damn," he muttered as a gust of wind caught the edge of the paper, fluttering it. Painfully, Carolyn worked her head around so that if she had to duck and cover quickly, she could.

She hoped. God, she was so thirsty. Her tongue stuck sourly to the roof of her mouth, and her broken hand felt like a flaming club at the end of her arm. But he hadn't killed her.

Yet. *Please,* she thought. *Please, if I get out of this, I'll be good for the rest of my life.*

The rest of her life being all she wanted now. All she could think of . . . That and that damned slip of paper poking out of the guy's shirt pocket.

A burst of sleet stung her eyelids suddenly. It hit the guy, too, causing him to wince and rear back slightly. Then a wave hit the boat, but he was sure-footed, even with that limp he had. . . .

He leaned over the side again. That limp . . . Where had she seen it? A gust of breeze lifted the corner of the paper. It was covered with something shiny, like plastic wrap.

The long pole bent; with a low grunt of satisfaction the man caught whatever it was he'd been fishing for and swung it into the boat. Some kind of a package . . .

It landed on the deck with a wet thud. He rushed to crouch over it, pulling at the soaked wrapping on it. But the wrapping wouldn't come free. He pulled a knife from his belt, slitting it open impatiently, then opened the plastic storage box inside.

Money fell out. Thick, rubber-banded slabs of money. The man gazed silently at them, picked one up and then another. He fanned one of them, as if making sure the interior of the pack held bills, too, and not just the outside.

Then he stuffed all the packets into a big plastic bag, sealed the top, and pushed the bag into a lidded bin that was built into the side of the boat, up near the wheel.

When he straightened, his shirt pocket was empty. While he'd been leaning over the side, the slip of paper must have . . .

Another muffled sound came from the dark hatchway. Next came pounding and thumping. Leaving the wheel, the man went down there and a smack rang out.

Flesh on flesh, a slap or a punch . . . Carolyn cringed as the man came back to move two levers by the steering wheel, one after the other. The engine revved and the boat began chugging forward once more.

No more sounds came from the dark hatchway.

·   ·   ·

Ten minutes after Roger Dodd entered the police station, Bob Arnold had broken down the last of his lies and evasions, and with them, Jake's remaining hopes that this might all be a mistake.

She sat very still while Roger spoke, meanwhile wanting to run out and start looking for Sam again: somewhere, anywhere. But first she needed to hear what else Roger said.

"Randy started talking about it before the four of us even got married," he began. The big double wedding—Roger to Anne, Randy to Anne's sister, Cordelia—had been the event of the year.

"He had it all worked out, about how if everyone thought he was dead, he couldn't be suspected. And if I had an alibi, then we'd both be in the clear," Roger continued shakily.

"That's not what you just told us," Chip objected. "You said *he* said that if the wives died, you two guys would get rich. Not that if he murdered them, you would."

Roger looked caught. "Yeah. Well. It was a little more than what I told you, what Randy suggested. A lot more, actually," he admitted.

Clearly he'd decided to throw himself upon the mercy of his listeners. But if so, he'd miscalculated; Jake didn't feel at all merciful, and from the look of him, Bob Arnold didn't, either.

"How did he do it?" Bob asked.

Strictly speaking, in a situation like this he should have been waiting for the state police, whom he'd already called. But Bob knew two people were missing, and that they might both now be in the hands of a double murderer.

And he'd never been a by-the-book guy, anyway. Way out here at the back of beyond, he called them as he saw them; if anybody didn't like it, they could . . .

Well, mostly they did like it. But Roger didn't. "Fake his own drowning, you mean?" Roger asked, looking increasingly uncomfortable.

Playing the innocent wasn't turning out to be as easy as he had expected, apparently. A line of sweat rimmed his hairline.

"Simple," he replied, but his voice shook uncertainly. "He set it up like he'd gone overboard. Cut himself, pulled a few hairs out, smeared that mess of blood and whatnot on the boat's rail." He frowned, remembering. "He had a dry suit and scuba gear on board with him, and he knew how to use them. It was the ripped-out fingernails that clinched it, though."

The ones found snagged in Randy's submerged lobster trapline, after he'd vanished off the boat . . . Jake recalled how this detail in particular had convinced everyone of Randy's demise.

"Even I thought it was real," said Roger. "The scuba stuff was missing, so I knew he must've at least tried the first part of his plan without telling me." His frown creased into a grimace. "But the fingernails made me think something had gone wrong, and he'd really drowned. . . ."

He shook his head regretfully. "I thought so until Cordelia died. When she fell down the stairs a few months after he went overboard, I had an awful feeling. Because if Randy were alive, still working a plan to inherit the money—"

"For you both to inherit it," Chip corrected.

"Yes," Roger admitted, "that's what he'd talked about. Both of us. But I never agreed," he added defiantly, glaring at Chip.

"Never mind that," Jake interposed. Every minute this idiot wasted explaining and excusing himself was a minute she could've been—

"All right, Jake," Bob Arnold said, putting up a big hand. "Just keep quiet and let the man tell what happened."

Bob had already put every law officer in the state on notice, along with the U.S. Coast Guard and their Canadian counterparts. So serious people were on the hunt for Sam and Carolyn, and for their possible captor.

But it didn't make Jake feel any better. Listening, she held her tongue as best she could.

"Okay," Bob told Roger, "so your brother's rich widow dies, by whatever means. Your wife inherits all the Lang family money, being as she's the last surviving member of the family. Then what?"

Roger sighed heavily. "Then nothing. Time went by, a year. Two years. I decided Cordelia really had just had an accident, that maybe Randy had tried the first part of the stupid plan he talked about but that was all."

He looked up at Bob Arnold. "I told him not to, told him it was crazy, but he did, and it killed him. The end. I mean, why shouldn't I think so?"

His voice turned pleading again. "And no matter what, even if he was alive, never in a million years did I ever think he'd come back and . . ."

"Okay, that's it," Jake said suddenly. Before Bob

could stop her, she stood up and grabbed a handful of Roger's sandy hair. It was assault just to be touching him. But she didn't care.

"Where is he?" she hissed, yanking hard. "Your crazy brother who was in your bar last night, where has he gone?"

She let go, shoving his head away roughly. "With my son," she added. Let him swear out a complaint against her if he wanted to.

"Jake," Bob began cautioningly, but she cut him off, bending to speak urgently into Roger's ear.

"He's got my son, that whack-job you protected. The one you didn't call the cops about even when he showed up in person. You knew, but you didn't—"

"I didn't even know who he was! Not at first . . ." He cringed away, glancing up fearfully at her.

She lowered her hand. "Go on," she commanded.

"He'd . . . changed," Roger faltered. "Once I saw him straight on, I realized who it was. But at first, when he walked in, he looked so different. He'd had surgery. His nose, his eyes . . ."

He looked helplessly around. *Poor baby,* she thought. And to think she'd felt sympathy for him. The whole town had.

"Anyone who knew him would've recognized him, close up. And when I saw those fingers of his, with the fingernails gone . . ." He made a face. "But just at a glance . . . and that limp he's got now. Even I would've walked right by him," Roger said.

"So, Sam might've known him, though?" she demanded. "Say, if he saw Randy in a good light?"

There were dark places on the breakwater, in the

shadows behind the barge-loading crane and the winch shack. But most of it was lit up like an airport.

Roger nodded sullenly. "He could've. But if it happened, it must've just been bad luck. He wouldn't have wanted to hurt Sam. Not unless he had to."

She laughed in disgust: *had to.* Right, like someone had his arm twisted behind his back. "You pathetic little piece of—"

"Get back to your story, Roger," Bob Arnold cut in. "Your wife, Anne, inherited the money. You thought you were home free. And—"

"Yes. And then Anne died." Roger spoke resignedly. His eyes filled with tears. "I was next in line for the estate. I didn't care, but I did what the lawyers said and the estate got closed. I thought it was all over, so you can imagine how I felt when he called me two weeks ago—"

"So you did know he was alive," Chip pounced.

"After he'd called, yes," Roger admitted defensively. "But not before. I suspected, like I said, but . . . anyway, Randy said I had to get his half of the money in cash. A million."

"Dollars?" Jake blinked. But of course he meant that. And no one in town knew precisely how much the Lang sisters were worth, only that it was a lot. So it was at least possible.

Roger nodded again. "I was supposed to put it in a waterproof container and float it on a buoy."

An anchored buoy like the ones lobster traps hung from, he must have meant. It would keep the container from drifting away.

Roger waved miserably in the direction of the bay.

"Out there. He gave me the coordinates, where to put it."

"Just leave it?" Chip asked. "And you did that?"

"Yeah," Roger replied defeatedly, his shoulders sagging. "I got it, and I did it."

Jake opened her mouth, but Chip got in ahead of her, tipping his head skeptically. "What size bills did he ask for, exactly? And how big was the package?"

Not bad, she thought. Roger looked annoyed at the obvious trap Chip was setting for him, but he answered.

"Hundred-dollar bills. Some small ones, too. Walking-around money, I guess. But mostly hundreds. For the package itself . . . I don't know, six by eight, maybe. Inches, that is. And what, about two feet tall, each stack? Or a little more. Twenty like that." He looked at his hands. "I put it in a big plastic storage box, the kind you store blankets in. And sealed it up tight."

Chip's face gave nothing away. "So Randy was the guy with the limp in the bar last night. You knew who he was by then. But you still let Carolyn shoot her mouth off in front of him."

Oh, come on, Roger's answering grimace said. "What else could I do? Just blab the whole thing to her, tell her to shut up because the guy she's all hot to catch is sitting right there at the end of the bar, listening to her?"

Chip got up. "It might've been better than just letting her walk into a trap."

He pressed on. "So, what do you know about him e-mailing her? Luring her here, promising her an interview, because he knew she didn't think he was really dead and he wanted to stop her?"

"Nothing," Roger said flatly. "But then, why would I? If he thought she was onto him . . . I don't know. It sounds kind of crazy. But I guess he is, too. So maybe. I guess it could've happened."

"Do you think he knew Carolyn and I were together in the bar last night?"

Roger shook his head. "From the way you two were acting at first, you could have just happened to walk in at the same time. You didn't start arguing until later, when he'd gone." He looked up. "Anyway," he added meanly, "you're not quite the kind of guy a woman like that would be with ordinarily, you know?"

Chip flushed. But he returned the shot swiftly. "Yeah, I do know. Last time I looked, she wasn't hanging out with wife killers, either, though. So we're sort of even."

"Never mind that," Jake said impatiently. "The co-ordinates where Randy said to float the money . . . I want them. Now."

Chip handed Roger a pen, Bob supplied a scrap of paper, and Roger scribbled hastily. When he was finished, she snatched the paper from him. "This had better be—"

"Tell me about the alibi now," Bob interrupted. "The one you told this young fellow here that your brother could break if you didn't do what he said."

Roger looked sly all at once. "You didn't read me my rights, you know. I've got rights. None of this stuff can be used against me. You know that, don't you? That nothing can—"

Suddenly, Chip was standing beside Roger. He'd taken a small black electronic device from his pocket.

He's still working on the book, Jake realized. *Even with all that has happened* . . . He waved the tiny machine in Roger's face. "If you don't answer the nice policeman's questions right now," he said, "I'll shove this thing so far down your throat, you'll hear your own voice every time you swallow."

Gulping, Roger looked at Bob. "Are you going to let him threaten me?"

But Bob only smiled. Maybe this kid had possibilities after all, his look seemed to say.

"All right." Roger gave in resentfully. "The house Anne and I lived in, the old Lang House."

On Washington Street, he meant, a block uphill from the bar. It had been the Lang girls' family home before they married, and Roger had lived in it for a little while after Anne's murder.

But then he'd moved out. He couldn't stand it anymore, he'd said, and people had understood: Poor Roger.

My foot, Jake thought as he went on: "After Randy married Cordelia, Randy liked coming over so he could go down to the cellar and see if he could find any things to sell. Antiques or whatever." Roger sighed heavily. "And you know the girls' great-great-grandfather, in the old days he had the factory on their property attached to the house?"

Jake knew. Everyone did. "Get to it," she said.

"Well, they needed a way to get the raw materials, the sheet tin and soldering stuff and so on, from the wharf to the factory, and then the finished cans down to the cannery by the water," said Roger.

He relaxed a little. "Even in bad weather, which back then was even worse than it is now," he went on easily, beginning to sound conversational, "they needed to—"

"Roger?" inquired Chip. "Do you think you'll like eating this recorder? Or is there some other reason you're stalling?"

Roger blinked nervously, seeming to remember why he was here. "All right, all right." He sat straighter. "There's a tunnel down there, okay? In the cellar, for the can factory. It goes down the hill a block and a half or so, to where the wharf was way back then, right underneath my bar."

He looked down at his hands. "It comes out in a room under my cellar. Randy found the tunnel, pried a bunch of boards off the entrance, and opened it up when he was hunting for valuables."

"So, you could've gone back and forth between the house and your bar without anyone ever seeing . . ." Bob Arnold began.

Outside, the clouds parted, sending a stray shaft of light onto Chip's face.

"I think what Roger's saying is that for his wife's murder—and his sister-in-law's—he has no alibi whatsoever." He put the recorder into his pocket. "And Randy threatened to remind everyone of it if Roger didn't play ball, didn't he?"

Roger nodded silently as Chip's voice turned confidential. "So, where's he going, Roger? Your dead brother, who drowned off his own boat and was never seen again—where's he headed now?"

Roger shook his head. "I don't know."

Chip was on him suddenly, one hand on Roger's

throat and his fist cocked in Roger's face. "You tell me, you—"

"I don't know!" Roger cried, shrinking back in alarm. "Don't you think I would tell you if I did?" He looked around desperately. "I'm afraid of him now, don't you get it? He's different, and not just his face. He's changed."

"What do you mean?" Chip demanded grimly. But he took his hand away.

"I'm not sure," Roger muttered, fingering his throat. "But the things he was saying last night before you two came in . . . all crazy, violent things."

A tear slipped down his face. "He killed Anne and Cordelia, I know that now. But while he was away, I think he got a taste for it. Maybe it started out being for the money, but"—his voice dropped to a whisper—"I think he got to like it."

A chill sense of foreboding invaded Jake, as if Sam's being missing wasn't the worst thing about this mess, suddenly.

As if maybe the worst thing about it was who Sam was missing with.

Bob got up. "All right, I think that's it for now," he said. "Roger, you'll say all this again for the record, right?"

Which made Jake wonder again, as the unhappy barkeeper nodded in reply: Roger was upset. But he wasn't stupid. So—

"Why, Roger? Why tell us all this now, and . . ."

He understood. "Incriminate myself? Not that it will." He turned sneeringly to Chip, then faced her again. "Please, that's the least of my problems."

A bitter chuckle escaped him. "I know Randy's alive, and what he's done. I'm the only one who has known, until now. So if anyone chases after him, *he'll* know who talked, won't he?"

His shoulders sagged. "So put me in jail, please. Maybe in there I'll be safe. Knowing Randy, though, knowing what I know about him now," he added bleakly, "I'm betting not." He put his face in his hands.

Chip gazed impassively at him. "Okay, Roger," he said. "Okay, thanks."

Chip walked out.

Jake caught up with him outside. "You'd better come on up to the house with me. There's no sense your sitting around alone in a motel."

No sense telling him the real reason behind her invitation, either. Because maybe he was a nice guy, as he had been when he'd befriended Sam, years ago. But maybe not, and his performance just now had convinced her she'd better keep an eye on him.

Chip looked balky, but he followed her to the car and got in. "What next?" he asked.

"Call my husband." She gripped the wheel; no question about it, she needed Wade's calm confidence.

"It might take me a while to reach him where he is, though. Meanwhile, I'll have to"—*What?* She had no idea—"figure out what else to do, and do it," she finished.

She backed the car out. "What difference does it make how big the money package was?"

Chip glanced sideways at her. "Because Roger Dodd's a liar. That sob story he's giving us is an act. On top of which, if you'd ever handled a million bucks—"

She had, actually. Back in the city her duties had included some interesting tasks for people who believed cash should travel incognito. But she'd never measured it with a ruler.

"Not that I've ever seen that much in one place," Chip went on, "but Carolyn was writing about a ransom demand once, so I actually had to find out how high a million dollars in hundred-dollar bills is. Roger's measurements were right."

She did the math in her head, another holdover from her old money-manager days. Chip must have a bit of a head for numbers, too, she realized, to recall such a thing. "Yup," she confirmed. "And that's not the kind of trivia he'd be likely to have just hanging around in his memory, is it? So he could be telling the truth about the money part."

"Maybe. How did he get his hands on so much cash, though?" Chip wondered aloud. "Because I don't care how rich you are, you can't just walk into your local bank branch and . . ."

This part she knew for sure. "He didn't. An estate like the Langs' has someone handling it, a personal banker. So a wealthy client doesn't have to stand in line with the riffraff."

It was cold in the car. She turned the heat on even though they weren't going far.

"All Roger had to do was make a call, say what he wanted and how he wanted it, and go pick it up or have it messengered. The banker might've had thoughts about how wise it was, and counseled Roger about it."

And good luck getting anywhere with that, she thought, *rich* and *brilliant* not being exactly synonymous, in her experience. "Also, there are reporting rules about withdrawing so much cash."

"To thwart drug dealers and terrorists, right?" Chip asked interestedly.

In the old days, he'd been interested in everything, too: surgical tools Sam's father had brought home, medical-text cross-sections of the human brain, baseball statistics.

Especially New York baseball statistics. She felt a burst of reminiscent affection for Chip.

"Uh-huh," she replied. "Bottom line, though, it's Roger's money. If the Lang trust's provision was that it be dissolved when the last family member died, and the proceeds delivered to a beneficiary, that's what happened."

It wasn't rare for a large family trust to provide for its own end. There were a few paperwork hoops, not particularly onerous if no one involved was fighting about anything, and once they'd been jumped through, it would all be fairly routine.

Roger would have had no real problem getting the cash, if he was insistent enough.

"What made Carolyn Rathbone believe Randy Dodd might not be dead in the first place?" she asked.

She turned onto Key Street, past the old red-brick Peavey Library with the arched leaded-glass windows and the antique cannon mounted out front, then continued uphill between rows of small white clapboard houses built close to the sidewalk, their hydrangeas and trellised clematis vines brown and dormant for the winter. Identical gray wisps curled from their chimneys, scenting the cold air with wood smoke.

"Before he ever started sending you any e-mails, I mean," she said. "And even afterward . . ."

"Why believe it was really him?" Chip nodded agreement with this question. "You're right, it could've been a crank. Online, anyone can say they're anyone, can't they? I mean, it's the whole principle of the chat room."

They passed the old Smith mansion, a three-story, mansard-roofed monstrosity with rotting trim, a sagging roofline, and more holes than stones in its foundation.

No smoke there—the chimney had collapsed into the yard long ago. Last year's shriveled Christmas wreath hung from a doornail.

"But the idea was originally Carolyn's," Chip explained. "She said until proven otherwise, a lot of money and a missing body meant murder, no matter how much it might look like something else on the surface."

"I see." Someone had slapped sheets of cheap white vinyl siding onto the rot-raddled expanse of the Smith mansion's façade, apparently in an effort to make the whole place look less like a tearer-downer.

The attempt hadn't worked. "But how'd she even know—"

"—that much?" Chip turned from the window. "She subscribed to an electronic clipping service. She got news stories about all kinds of crimes from all over the world, and I screened them for her."

Which explained how a writer of true-crime best-sellers had cottoned on to events in a place so remote that it might as well have been on the moon, especially now in early winter. Overhead the clouds thickened again; a spatter of rain hit the windshield and froze there in shining globs.

"Once her last book was finally done, she started reading the clippings I'd picked out for her," he went on. "She chose the Dodd story, and I started doing research about it."

"But—" she began. Surely the pair of them hadn't come all the way to Eastport just on a hunch?

"And what I found," he continued, "was one tiny detail that didn't make sense: a motor vehicle department record of a moving violation in South Carolina, issued to a driver by the name of Randy Dodd."

She glanced at him. "A speeding ticket? You can do that? I didn't know that you could just look up somebody's . . ."

Driving record. "You can't. But I can." He sighed heavily. "See, I've been a computer research geek for a long time."

Back in the city, pretty much the only other thing the then teenaged Chip Hahn had done besides hang out with Sam was spend time on the early online bulletin boards. Still . . .

"Trust me, if you know who to ask and they think you might be able to help them in return sometime, you can get just about anything from the people who run databases," said Chip.

She thought about this. "It could have been some other—"

"Somebody else with the same name?" He seized

the objection happily. Then—"But not with the same driver's license number"—he demolished it.

"But that means—" She was still trying to wrap her mind around the idea that Chip could get this stuff at all.

"Yup. I think Randy had his act together," Chip said. "He must have done a lot of planning. But then he made a mistake."

She looked questioningly at him.

"The ticket was dated just a day after he vanished," he explained. "I think maybe he had new papers stashed somewhere for a new identity. And he was going to pick them up, but on the way . . ."

"He was nabbed for speeding." She put it together. "While he still had only his real driver's license in his possession."

Chip nodded once more. "Which wouldn't have mattered. No one was looking for him then. But I was, later. I was trying to be really thorough before Carolyn and I put a whole lot of work into anything more. Otherwise, she would be unhappy about it. *Very*," he emphasized, "unhappy."

Jake slowed for a black cat dashing across the street.

"My heart nearly stopped when I actually found that ticket, though," Chip admitted as they crossed the intersection at the top of the hill.

Her own big old white house loomed ahead: white clapboards, green shutters, red chimneys, all wanting maintenance. And a pressing need for more insulation before the real winter arrived, she remembered again sinkingly.

"And then later hearing from someone who kept hinting at actually being him," Chip added, "that just topped it off. I was intrigued, and Carolyn was even more so."

"And that's why you came to Eastport. To meet this person, see if it really was him."

He nodded tiredly. It hit her that he must have been up all night. "I didn't want to. Finding the speeding ticket with his name, it didn't mean the guy writing to us was him, did it?"

No, of course it didn't.

"And anyway, why would he?" Chip said. "If he'd gone to all that trouble to be . . . well, dead to the world, I guess you'd call it. That was going to be our working title. But Carolyn said we had to come," he finished resignedly.

He stopped, seeming to hear how foolish the whole thing must sound. She turned into the driveway, pulled to a stop.

"You'd have to know Carolyn," he said finally. "If there was even a chance that it was true, it would make her next book another big success. And she wanted to check out the area, the background, too."

At this, the energy returned to his voice. "The place, the people. Mostly people—survivors, what they feel about it all."

He turned earnestly to her. "Carolyn always says it's not the crime that makes a book a big hit. It's the emotions."

Which both of you planned to exploit. Grief, guilt, revenge—the old saying "If it bleeds, it leads" was as true for books as it was for news coverage, Jake supposed.

Although maybe that wasn't fair. She'd never read a Carolyn Rathbone book. She decided to change the subject.

"Sam's dad passed away a few years ago," she said, turning off the car. "I don't know if you'd heard."

He stared out the car's side window at the big old houses lining this part of Key Street, where ship captains and lumber barons had built their homes in the early 1800s. The architecture ranged from vast, elderly Queen Annes to narrow Carpenter Gothics with pointy roofs and elaborate gingerbread.

The plain four-square Federals, like Jake's house, were the oldest, built right after the War of 1812 when the British had decamped from their loyalty-oath-demanding occupation and people decided it might be safe to come back.

"No. Dr. Tiptree died? I'm sorry, I didn't know," Chip said. "And . . . how's Sam?"

"He's okay. He's had a few bad times, in and out of alcohol rehab, mostly."

Ordinarily, she'd have hesitated about saying this. But Chip already knew Sam's life was no rose bed in the substance-abuse department.

Back when Chip started coming around, Sam's pals had been introducing Sam to the fun of aerosol-propellant huffing. Things had only gone downhill from there.

"The troubles didn't end when we moved here. For a while it was pretty grim. But it's better now," she added.

Fluffs of insulation lay on the lawn where they'd landed a few hours and a lifetime ago. She laid both hands in her lap.

"Why did you do it, Chip? Why were you such a good friend to Sam? I've always wanted to ask you."

His lips pursed. "I don't know. I just liked him, I guess. I'd always wanted a kid brother, and . . ." His voice trailed off, perhaps at some painful memory. "And you know, at the time I wasn't exactly Mr. Popularity myself," he added wistfully.

"Right. Well, I guess a lot of us weren't at that age." They sat in silence a moment. Then it hit her again why he was here.

"How'd you get yourself into this?" she asked.

He gazed at the huge white house with its wide lawn and big garden areas, the pointed firs widely spaced along the rear lot-line. It wasn't a mansion, but from the outside it could be mistaken for one.

"If I had it to do over again, believe me, I wouldn't. I told Carolyn it could be dangerous, but . . ."

They got out and walked toward the house. He kept looking up at it puzzledly. "But like I said before, she talked me into it, as usual. And I let her."

Also as usual, his tone said. For all their crime-writing experience—but none as victims, apparently—the two of them had been as innocent as Hansel and Gretel, Jake realized.

Which was how they'd walked into a trap, and yet another reason why she meant to keep close tabs on Chip. Who knew what further foolish things he might do otherwise, and how they might make Sam's situation worse?

Seeming to be thinking the same, he made a face. "This is all my fault," he said ruefully.

"Don't be too hard on yourself." Then, alerted by

something in his voice: "Chip, do you have feelings for this girl? I mean, more than—"

But to that he shook his head emphatically. "No, of course not. That is, we've worked together awhile, I think we know each other pretty well. But like I told you, Carolyn's . . . difficult." He craned his neck back, gazing up at the high front gable again. "A stone bitch, actually. Wow, this place is big."

Straightening, he peered around at the quiet street with its other huge old houses set far apart, all the stately gray-trunked maples lined up in front of them.

A few white flakes drifted down. The peace and quiet here was as loud and unnerving as any Manhattan taxi horn, until you got used to it.

Maybe more so. "So, you just came up here and started living like this?" he asked wonderingly.

An iPod stuck out of his shirt pocket. Everything in Eastport was very different from the city he was used to, she realized. The space, the pace . . . She hadn't heard a car horn in months.

And when she had heard one, it had been getting leaned on by a tourist. An iPod wasn't a common sight around here, either—too expensive. . . . Remembering all this, she made a mental note to take it easy on Chip Hahn, as much as she could.

"Why?" he asked. "Why'd you do it?"

He waved at the massive antique structure with its peeling paint and sagging shutters, its acres of clapboard and trim. She couldn't see the crumbling red brickwork of the three chimneys from this angle, but the porch steps needed painting again, too.

"Believe it or not, I thought it would bring order to my life," she replied. And in many ways, it had. But at the moment she couldn't remember any of them. *Sam,* she thought.

"Come on," she told Chip, starting up the steps. "We'd best get you situated. You should have something to eat and drink and maybe get cleaned up a little if you want to, and then we'll go get your car."

He'd given up the idea of a rental cabin when he couldn't find Carolyn anywhere, he'd said, and parked at the Motel East instead, without checking in. His things were in the car, too.

It struck her as odd that a fellow like Chip, who'd seemed so capable and confident just now at the police station, had apparently been getting pushed around pretty thoroughly by his writing partner.

But that also was a topic for later. "And we'll talk about what else to do about Carolyn and Sam," she added. Thinking, *Sure, right after I jump off a tall building and learn to fly.*

Because what the hell am I supposed to do when— On the porch she turned. He was nowhere in sight. "Chip?"

Inside, the phone began ringing. "Chip, damn it . . ."

The front door was unlocked. The kitchen shone spotlessly, smelling of soap and scouring powder. It meant her housekeeper-slash-stepmother, Bella Diamond, had been here recently.

But Bella wasn't here now. A mixing bowl and spoon stood on the kitchen counter. The dogs looked up sleepily from their beds.

"Hello?" she called out. "Is anyone home?"

The phone kept ringing. She dashed to answer, but as she did, it stopped.

The machine's red light winked at her, though, signaling that a call had come in earlier. She pressed the "play" button—

"I'm going to kill you!" a high, disguised voice promised cheerfully, followed by a giggle.

Click.

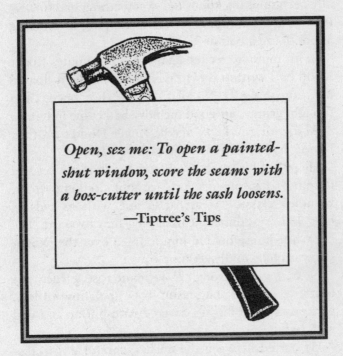

Chapter 4

Open, sez me: To open a painted-shut window, score the seams with a box-cutter until the sash loosens.
—**Tiptree's Tips**

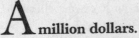

A million dollars.

Chip Hahn felt ashamed even to be thinking about it as he shoved his way through the shrubbery at the back of the Tiptree house. A million in cash . . .

Wincing as the thorns on some kind of red-berried bushes scratched at his hands, he cringed inwardly even harder at the kind of greedy jerk he knew he was being.

It was even worse than last night, when he'd actually been thinking about doing something bad to Carolyn. Only this time, he wasn't stopping at thinking about doing a bad deed. This time . . .

In his mind he recited again the coordinates Roger Dodd had written down, where he said he'd floated the money: *44.91 N, 67.02 W* . . . For once, Chip thought grimly, his good memory had come in handy.

And with any luck, maybe Roger Dodd's brother, Randy, hadn't gotten to the cash yet. *Hurry* . . .

He pulled his trusty iPod from his shirt pocket and thumbed his playlist on without looking at it, Blondie's classic "Heart of Glass" with its pulsing bass and crystalline vocals urging him forward. The big white house behind him loomed over the expansive yard like an observation tower.

Next, he cut through a dormant rose garden put neatly to bed for the season, row upon row of low, perfectly spaced bushes covered with burlap and tied with twine.

He darted between the bushes, careful not to disturb the loose mulch heaped around them. The house they belonged to was a low, white cape with two stone lions on the front steps, a wide center chimney, and a massive copper beech in the front lawn.

A curtain twitched in an upstairs window of the cape. A burl as big as his head seemed to stare ominously at him from the beech tree's rough bark. Chip hustled across the frozen lawn to the sidewalk beyond, looked up and down it.

One way led into a warren of small streets, frost-browned yards with boats on rusty trailers, and dirt driveways containing older-model cars and trucks. The other way, downhill toward the water, lay a stretch of larger homes featuring Andersen windows, prepainted siding, and red-brick front walks.

He recognized them, or at least he understood instinctively the impulse they represented:

Keep your things nice.

The banal phrase encompassed what he'd been taught from the time he was a very small child. Your house, your car, the parts that other people could see of your body . . . It was a class thing, he knew, this obsession with personal maintenance.

It said you deserved your wealth, that you had been born or had become the sort of person who was inclined to preserve and defend capital, and Chip knew that drill only too well. After all, he'd been rich himself once, and at a level that made the well-kept dwellings he was rushing past look like the most abject poverty.

But deciding to be a writer instead of going to Yale Law and joining the family's generations-old firm as an associate, wading in hip-deep, as his father had so delicately put it—Hahn & Associates was a global concern that hid its bloodlust for courtroom victory, along with its dodgier clients (of whom there were many), beneath a stodgy exterior—had taken care of that. In the Old Bastard's opinion, not wanting to be a lawyer in his firm was like wishing you had horns and a forked tail. Or actually having them . . .

Hurrying downhill toward the water that glittered

at the foot of the street, Chip recalled the night he'd broken the news. The Old Bastard had glared at him, all wattled and lizard-eyed, from the far end of the dining room table.

Between them, there had been about an acre of white linen covered with china, crystal, and silver. The meal had been roast beef, bloodily dripping. There was no one else in the room. A bell sat by the old man's right hand.

"Screw you," the Old Bastard had said, and, ignoring the bell, had thumped the table to demand more cabernet.

Chip had been only eighteen then, and had believed the Old Bastard might change his mind. He hadn't, though, which mostly accounted for Chip's financial situation right now. People who refused to do what he wished, the Old Bastard thought, deserved what they got.

Which of course had been nothing. At the corner in front of the long, low Motel East overlooking the bay, Chip made a beeline for the Volvo in the lot, grabbed his topcoat from the back seat, and pulled it on. Glancing around guiltily, though he wasn't sure why, he headed downtown, trying not to think about where Carolyn might be right now and what might be happening to her.

Serves her right, a mean little part of his brain said. But she didn't deserve this—whatever *this* was—and Chip couldn't go on pretending he felt that way for long.

Because even as the harsh thought died, the rest of his mind went on pondering what Sam Tiptree's mother had asked:

Do you have feelings for her?

Of course not, he replied silently again. Or anyway, not the kind Sam's mother meant. But he didn't hate Carolyn the way he'd thought, either. Instead, in her sudden absence he felt as if something sharply painful had stopped hurting, and he missed it.

He felt . . . confused. Which he wasn't a bit used to feeling. And thinking about Carolyn just made it worse. *A lot worse,* he thought. Painfully worse.

So don't. Think about the money.

He hurried on. Downtown in the old red-brick buildings some of the shops were open now: a hardware store, a pizza joint. An old, battered pickup truck went by—not the one he'd seen last night—hauling a load of firewood.

Late morning, and the day's business was going on all around him, as if he and Carolyn had never been here. As if somebody hadn't grabbed her.

But something might still be happening to her now, or might already have happened, that he didn't even dare imagine.

He stared at the space in the lot where the Volvo had been last night, willing her back unharmed. Suddenly even her thieving of his idea didn't seem so bad.

It was just Carolyn, trying to make something of herself and not wanting to go on doing what she had been. *Like me.* She could have his precious book idea, he realized suddenly, plus the money from the ones they'd already written together.

Anything she wanted. If only she was okay. To his horror, his lip began trembling. *A million,* he thought, swallowing the lump in his throat.

But it just wouldn't work. A million dollars, ten

million . . . Who did he think he was kidding, anyway? He might fantasize about being the kind of guy who would steal it.

Fantasy, though, was as far as that idea would go. Because if money was all he wanted, there were easier ways to get it. Like for instance sucking up to the Old Bastard.

So, what are you really doing, buddy boy? he asked himself. For that, though, he didn't have an answer, only a painful sense of urgency that made him want to writhe. Or run . . . but not away from anything. Toward it, rather, whatever it was . . .

The iPod finished Blondie, started on the Boss. "Born in the U.S.A." blared its anthem-like opening bars into Chip's earbuds. He'd accidentally pushed the oldies list, not what he'd wanted. But he didn't feel like fooling with it now, as from the parking lot he hurried along a path behind the old waterfront buildings overlooking the boat basin.

A riprap of pink granite boulders formed a low, slanting wall that continued down to the waves. Beyond, the breakwater was an L shape; inside were floating piers in a wooden maze, to which dozens of boats were secured by heavy lines.

Big, beat-up fishing vessels with lobster traps stacked on their decks bobbed cheek-by-jowl with broad-beamed rowboats, oars shipped and gear stowed neatly. Scanning the marina for any sign that Carolyn had been here, he made his way past the boat ramp, past the shuttered hot dog stand where Sam's bicycle still leaned lonesomely, and beyond, out onto the wide concrete breakwater itself.

As soon as he left the protection of the buildings, ·

the wind began biting at him again. And not just wind . . .

You wanted her dead, a cruel voice in his mind tormented him. *You thought about it, you wanted to . . .*

But he hadn't done anything. He'd been so angry, was all. The whole long, conflict-filled evening atop the tiring drive, his ongoing worry over who their mysterious next-day's interview subject would turn out to be . . .

It had all been too much. But he still felt just hideously bad about it, as if he'd willed something to happen to Carolyn and then it had. And if he hadn't stepped out of sight between those buildings, he might've seen it, been able to stop it.

Now, though, maybe he could make up for it. As he stepped onto one of the metal gangs leading down to the finger piers, an even more elaborate fantasy than the one about money rose in his mind: rescuing Carolyn. Sam too.

And then maybe the million, which would come to him in some hazy but completely justifiable way that he couldn't yet imagine. As a reward, sort of.

Not that any of that made sense. The icy wind, high waves, and unfamiliar waters around here put any such notions into the realm of impossibility.

Yet here he was, walking out along a wooden dock section. Half a dozen smaller, plank-built finger piers branching off from it were each home to three or four boats floating alongside, all rafted together by more lines.

Mostly they were diesel-engined working vessels. He'd have had no notion of even how to get one of them loose from its neighbors, much less how to pilot one. Fifteen minutes aboard and he'd accomplish a shipwreck, most likely, get himself towed in by the Coast Guard, but nothing more.

That little whatever-it-was, there, though, all by itself at a finger pier of its own . . .

He crouched to examine the craft. It was a homely little wooden vessel, broad and beamy, with a newish thirty-five-horse Evinrude and what appeared to be a pair of decent life jackets. The open boat had only a coffee can for bailing, too, which meant she didn't leak.

And . . . there was a key hanging in the ignition. *Don't even think about it,* he told himself. *Don't be an idiot, make things worse, get into trouble.*

But he knew how to run this boat, how to start the engine and how to handle the tiller. The Old Bastard had owned one just like it up on Saranac Lake, and as a young teenager Chip had taken it out plenty of times, alone and with Sam Tiptree.

So, how could it be a problem? Why shouldn't he just hop in? Other than the fact that the boat didn't belong to him, that is, and there didn't seem to be anyone around here to ask if he could borrow or rent it.

Hesitating, he scrutinized the craft more closely. Thick orange rubber gloves and what must be a chart folder wrapped in plastic were stashed under the boat's bow.

Not only that but the faintly visible dark line on the red plastic gas can stowed in the stern said there was plenty of fuel. Finally, there were oars set in decent oarlocks, so if worse came to worst he could always row.

Someone will stop you. And if not, someone will catch you. You can't just . . .

But no one was even in sight. Looking around again, ready to jump back and stutter out an apology at the slightest hint of trouble, he stepped into the boat. It felt reassuringly familiar, and no one shouted at him.

He sat and push-buttoned the ignition. The Evinrude fired up on the first try, with a low, confident rumble, and still no one made any protest.

He couldn't believe it. He wondered what it was like, living in a place where no one would steal a boat like this, where you could leave things out unlocked.

Or at any rate, no one but Chip would steal it. . . . He spared a moment to switch his music playlist. David Byrne and Brian Eno's "Strange Overtones" began coming out of his player, the electronic harmonies and a dreamy, faintly ominous vocal just strange enough to calm and energize him at the same time.

It sounded . . . intelligent. Like not everyone in the world was stupid and brutal.

Listening, Chip huffed a few breaths in and out. Maybe he would just sit here, and if anyone came along and yelled at him he would climb out, act like he was just some dope who didn't know any better.

But even as he thought about this, he was already getting up, shedding his topcoat and pulling on one of the life vests with its thick canvas straps and heavy-gauge metal buckles, and moving forward toward the gear in the bow. Hat, gloves, charts—rapidly he sorted through all the stuff and decided what to do with it.

He put the hat and gloves on. They wouldn't keep him warm forever, but—

But what? a voice demanded suddenly in Chip's head. *Just what the hell are you planning to do here, pal?*

Got an idea? Or are you just muddling stupidly along with no plan at all, as usual?

Chip didn't know the answer to the questions that the voice in his head kept asking. He did notice, though—and not for the first time, actually; he'd had quite a lot of interior monologue going on lately— that the voice sounded like Carolyn's.

He thought that if you wanted a critical voice, hers was the one to use. Harsh, nasal, and much like the cry of the seagulls now clustering on the breakwater . . .

What a mean thing to think, he scolded himself. He squelched the unkind comparison, atoning for it with the knowledge that he would have given plenty to hear Carolyn's voice for real right now.

But for the first time since he'd discovered that she was gone, he noticed also that he didn't have that scary, untethered feeling, like a balloon whose string someone had let go of. Here in the wooden boat that he was about to steal—

Borrow, he corrected himself. *I'm bringing it back—*

Here, he still didn't know what had happened to Carolyn or what to do about it. But he knew how to do something, and he had to, or he would go nuts.

And this was it. So he would go out there and cast his eye around. After all, from what little he knew, it seemed logical that both Carolyn and Sam might've been taken away by water, and that they might even have been taken together.

Sam's abandoned bike, Roger Dodd's guilty admissions, and Eastport Police Chief Bob Arnold's report of a stranger on the breakwater last night, one who'd used a fright mask to scare away potential witnesses and who might briefly have stolen a car—

There must've been one when Carolyn disappeared, Chip thought. There'd be few other ways to make her vanish right off the street like that, so suddenly and silently, other than by bundling her into a vehicle. He pulled the chart envelope open and unfolded the chart.

Passamaquoddy Bay, it said, and at the number of tightly packed curving lines drawn on it, he paused in dismay.

Channels, ledges, ridges, and peaks . . .

That wasn't a bay out there. It was a mountain range with a thin layer of water on top of it. There were a million things in it that a boat could hit, all made of granite.

And to judge by the speed of the chunks of driftwood and clumps of seaweed scooting along atop it, the currents must be murder.

You could die out there, warned the voice in his head.

Because this wasn't Saranac. If he got in trouble, the Old Bastard wouldn't be calling out the cavalry, or a mechanic to fix things if the engine should fail.

Not that the Old Bastard ever had done any such thing, but Chip had depended on the marine mechanic in Saranac more than once, when the outboard had suddenly crapped out. And there were a dozen other things Chip should be doing on land, anyway.

Calling Siobhan, and possibly Carolyn's parents. Keeping Sam Tiptree's mother company, maybe finding a photograph of Carolyn so the police could . . .

But he couldn't imagine what to say to Carolyn's editor or to her parents, either, even if he did get in touch with them.

Hi there, just wanted to let you know your girl's been snatched by a killer. . . .

No, he couldn't call them. Not yet. A sick, drowning feeling swept over him. And there was a picture of Carolyn on the back of every one of her books; the police could use that.

So nobody needed him. No one but Carolyn and a guy named Sam Tiptree, who was older now but who once upon a time had thought Chip was the greatest sports expert in the world, because he could tell an inside fastball from a high curve, and throw one.

He looked down at the chart again, and then back out at the choppy water. From here to the little island almost due north . . . It wasn't far, really.

Only a couple of miles, and he'd be within sight of land all the way. If worse came to worst, he could stand up and yell, and wave his arms. . . .

Someone would see him. And the idea of sitting around Sam's mother's house waiting for something to happen was unendurable.

He couldn't do it. It was as simple as that. So he would have a look, just go out there and have what Carolyn would have called a "peekaroonie" at the situation.

Do some research. And while he was at it, keep an eye peeled for a solitary buoy, right about—he squinted at the chart and then out at the waves—there. A buoy with money attached should be floating, right on that spot. Chip could just go out there and check.

As he imagined it, the only useful thing the Old Bastard had ever told Chip popped into his head. Standing in his paneled study looking out over the skyline, Central Park, and the gauze of light spreading to the north and west, the old man had sipped bourbon contemplatively and said:

"Ninety percent of everything, boy. Ninety percent of this whole damned shootin' match is just showing up."

He'd knocked back the rest of his drink and glowered darkly. *"And the rest,"* he'd slurred, *"is pure dumb luck."*

Chip looked around a final time for someone to stop him. He debated leaving a note, decided an undamaged, promptly returned boat and a hundred bucks would probably soothe any hurt feelings that developed.

He pulled the iPod out again, chose another playlist of cuts he'd assembled himself. Hercules and Love Affair, Fleet Foxes, Vampire Weekend . . .

He resettled the earbuds in his ears. He centered himself on the boat's transom seat. Then he slid the line off the dock cleat and reversed out of the slip.

Finally he shifted forward and began motoring out of the boat basin, still expecting to hear someone yelling at him to stop. But no one did.

•   •   •

"I don't know where he is. He just walked away when I wasn't looking."

Hours after Chip Hahn vanished out of the yard, Jake stood in the phone alcove clutching the phone, trying to make Bob Arnold understand that yet another visitor to Eastport had gone suddenly missing.

Or rather, Bob got the missing part all right. It was the part about her not having anything to do with it that he seemed to be having trouble absorbing. And it was driving her nuts.

"Bob, when I got up this morning, all I needed to do was put enough shredded cellulose to insulate a battleship into my house, and now Sam might be with a murderer."

She took a breath. "I can't reach Wade, and in a situation like this it might be nice to have my husband around. Ellie's got her hands full, because her husband is with my husband, so she's on full-time parenting duty."

Ellie had gone straight home from the police station after they'd found Chip there. After that, she had called every twenty minutes to be updated on what was happening.

But at age four, Ellie's little daughter, Leonora, was a handful; whenever George was away, the mornings when the child attended prekindergarten were just about the only waking hours that Ellie didn't spend dashing after her offspring. So when Ellie had Lee, Jake didn't have Ellie—not for snooping purposes, anyway.

"And as if that weren't enough, I've got some idiot

prankster calling here, saying he's going to kill me," Jake said. "So, Bob, if you could just stop—"

Pestering me to tell you things I couldn't possibly know, she wanted to finish. But of course he wasn't doing that. He was trying to help, she told herself firmly.

Which gave him a chance to talk, but he didn't say that Sam had been found. And since that was the only thing she wanted to hear, it just made her furious again.

"How'd Randy even get hold of a boat, anyway?" she demanded.

"Seems Roger helped him out there, too," Bob replied. "A few days ago, Roger called the marine store and asked them to get it out of storage, put it in the water."

In the boat basin, he meant. Bob went on: "Roger rented a slip for it, said he was going to sell it and wanted it out where somebody could try it out. So," he finished, "we think Randy's on that."

"Oh, that's just great," she began, but Bob was talking over her. Or trying to. Exasperated, she interrupted Bob's well-meant advice to stay calm, sit tight, and—

"Bob, I've been babysitting this phone for hours now. I'm losing my mind here, just doing nothing. Can't I even—"

Drive around some more. Walk up and down the street calling Sam's name. Give one of the dogs his sock to sniff, and let them go roaming around trying to find him.

But Bob just kept talking. In his voice she heard the same reassuring tone that in the past she'd heard him use while telling recent automobile accident victims that they weren't seriously injured, even when they were.

In other words, he was handling her. The thought frightened her badly. "All right," she said, chastened. "And I appreciate it, Bob, you know I—"

In the kitchen, Bella Diamond went on scouring the sink. Any minute now she would polish through the enamel, right down to the steel beneath.

Jake thought about taking up a useful activity, too. Putting in all the insulation material using a teaspoon instead of an air compressor sounded about right at the moment.

"Yes," she told Bob Arnold again. "I know someone's got to be here to answer the phone, in case—"

But at the thought of what exactly she might need to answer it in case of, her throat closed.

"—and if Chip gets in touch, I'll let you know right away," she finished.

"Yeah, do that," he agreed dryly. "I'll get in touch with the wardens up north, too, see if they can get hold of Wade and George Valentine."

Wade's hunting partner, he meant: his best friend, and Ellie White's husband. "And, Jake, one more thing. Right now it seems like maybe Randy Dodd's got himself some hostages. That's bad enough. But—"

"What?" Because what could possibly be worse? But he sounded very uncomfortable, so something must be.

"Randy had to be somewhere all this time while we thought he was dead—when he wasn't here, that is—

and now Roger says it might have been South Carolina that Randy went to. I mean, after he supposedly
drowned."

That traffic ticket, she thought. The one Chip had
found a record of. She'd forgotten all about it. She
told Bob about it now.

"Yeah, well. Seems Randy'd been there before,"
Bob continued, "and Roger thought that maybe he
might've gone there to work construction."

"What?" she demanded again. "What are you trying to say?"

"Jake, the thing is, some things happened down
South." Bob sounded sorrowful. "Women went missing. Three of 'em. While maybe Randy was around."

He liked it, Roger had said when they were with
him in the police station. *I think he got a taste for it.*

Killing, Roger had meant. Her knees went watery.

"Of course, we're not sure of anything," Bob said.
"Maybe it was just a coincidence, but—"

She sat down. It was not a coincidence. There was
no such thing as that much coincidence. She told Bob
about the speeding ticket again, meanwhile trying
very hard to keep her voice from quavering and her
hands from shaking.

But Bob already knew; cops, as it turned out, could
check records better than even Chip Hahn could. And
doing so was the first thing Bob had thought of, as
soon as Roger Dodd mentioned his rogue brother's
possible hiding place.

"So," she said, "maybe we should try wrapping
our minds around the idea that Sam's in real—"

Trouble. Bad trouble. The kind he wasn't going to
get out of without help. But Bob knew that, too. He

was just trying not to scare her. Or no more than she already was.

"Yeah." He sighed resignedly. "I'm just saying, Jake. Don't do anything dumb. Because Randy's got his money, probably. That means he's happy. But maybe he's also got Sam and this girl who's missing. One good thing, he doesn't know yet that his plan's gone all to hell. So let's not do anything to make him feel—"

Worse. Like he's got to kill them right away.

Unless he decides to do it for fun. She bit her lip.

"Okay, Bob," she managed, and after that he reassured her some more: State cops, Canadian authorities, local law officers, and marine enforcement, including two coast guards on both sides of the water, were on the job.

The coast guard services were most familiar with possible hiding places and ways to get out of the country, Bob added. That last being what fugitive Randy Dodd would want most if he knew people were onto him.

And Randy was very familiar with the water and coastline, too, from his fishing days. All the little hiding places, inlets and coves . . . There was no guarantee that anyone, even marine law officers, would be able to find him.

"So let's not any of us tell Randy, by word or deed, that he needs to get any sneakier than he already is," Bob finished, and hung up.

"Yeah, right," Jake whispered to no one. Around her the big old house seemed to hold its breath, as if just waiting for Sam to return and bring life back into it.

• • •

In the dining room, the gold-medallion wallpaper glimmered in the thin light of a November afternoon. In the hallway, the stairs were silent, no young-man feet thudding energetically up and down them.

In the kitchen, the dogs sniffed around restlessly, hunting for their pal. At this time on any other day, Sam would've had them out for a walk.

"Drink this," Bella Diamond commanded as Jake wandered in there and sank down at the kitchen table. The room smelled like kitchen cleanser and lemon-scented spray cleaner, but the cup of tea the housekeeper handed her—her stepmother, Jake corrected herself impatiently—smelled suspiciously like whisky.

Tall and rawboned, Bella wore her white bib apron over a navy blue sweatshirt, blue jeans, and loafers with white socks. "Your father'll be back soon," she said. "He's just out walking around. Just in case."

Looking, Bella meant. Hunting for Sam. Jake felt a pang of envy for her father, who could at least be out there trying to do something, instead of sitting here just—

She gulped the spiked tea. Bella's face creased in sympathy. "Here," she said, and held out a paper bag. "A little chore I've been waiting for someone to have time for."

In it were a half-dozen antique cut-glass doorknobs. All were coated in thick white paint, the result of some previous house owner's ham-handed attempts at interior decoration.

"You might as well be doing something," said Bella,

handing over an X-Acto knife to go with the paint-coated doorknobs.

Jake looked at the doorknobs, and at the knife, and then at Bella, who had of course known Jake's usual method of coping with problems, or at least of thinking about how to cope with them.

But Bella had gone further, apparently taking some trouble to put together a sort of kit for this purpose. Touched, Jake looked down at the items again.

The X-Acto knife consisted of a metal handle with a small, arrowhead-shaped blade sticking out of one end. She tested the blade with the tip of her finger and found it so sharp that she could've used it to split atoms.

Perfect for paint-peeling. But it was no use. "Thanks, but I can't just sit here and—"

Bella wasn't listening. "Finish that tea," she said. "And a cup more, if you can. And while you're working there, you just tell me about whatever it is."

Sam's vanishing, she meant. And Chip Hahn's collaborator on the true-crime books, Carolyn Rathbone. Plus Randy Dodd, and—

Fifteen minutes later Bella had finished scrubbing the sink and wiping down all the kitchen counters and polishing the stove top, and had started on the old woodwork. Jake looked down to discover that she'd already peeled all the old paint off three doorknobs.

And it had helped. Her hands weren't shaking, and her heart didn't feel as if it were about to jump out of her chest. She was still very frightened. But her mind didn't feel as if a bomb had gone off in it, blasting her to bits.

I thought it would bring order to my life, she'd told Chip Hahn, of buying and fixing up the antique house. And it did.

It had. Outside, the sky had taken on its afternoon-in-November look, which was indistinguishable from dusk. *Sam,* she thought. *It's getting dark wherever he is, too.*

"So there's a tunnel," Bella said, scrubbing at a stubborn finger mark on the pantry door.

"Yes," said Jake. "Seems that's how Randy kept Roger quiet, by threatening to tell about it."

She started on another doorknob, pausing to sip cautiously at another cup of tea. "Roger used being in the bar as an alibi, but in fact he could've gone back and forth between the bar and his house without anyone knowing."

Roger had since moved into a small apartment upstairs from the bar, leaving the house empty. The Dodd House, it was called now.

"The house where the two of them lived. So he could've killed Anne," said Bella.

Her voice gave little hint as to how she felt about this, but if she rubbed that area of finger-marked woodwork any harder, Jake thought smoke might begin rising from it.

"He could have," Jake agreed. She got up and rinsed her cup.

"But according to Roger, Randy planned the crimes and did them by himself, then came back for the money he thought Roger owed him. It sounds as if Roger might've suspected, but that the whole idea was horrible to him. So he didn't dare examine it very closely until he had to."

And by that time, Anne was already dead. "It would've worked the way Randy planned it," she said, "except for Chip and Carolyn Rathbone's interest complicating it for him. A well-known writer, raising questions."

"And except for Sam," Bella pointed out. "Even without them, Sam would still have run into Randy on the breakwater last night and recognized him. If that's what happened," she added. "So—"

Bella was right, it was probably good luck that Chip and his writer friend arrived just when they did. Because otherwise, Jake wouldn't have known about any of it.

Sam would just be gone. If that was what had happened . . . A thought struck Jake. "Bella, you didn't by any chance make Sam's bed this morning, did you?" She turned hopefully. "I mean, we really are sure this isn't all just a—"

Mistake. Because Bella adored Sam and would've made his bed every morning of his life without complaint if Jake had allowed her to, and Sam felt the same way about Bella. He'd even gone so far as to call her "Grandma" a few times, although mostly in jest.

While I, Jake thought guiltily, *am still trying to wrap my mind around the concept of my dad's new wife at all.* "Bella? Did you?"

Bella touched her gold hoop earring distractedly. "What? Oh, no. I didn't make it for him. How could I? He hadn't slept in it, had he?"

Jake's heart sank; of course he hadn't. "Has anyone looked in that tunnel?" Bella asked, cupping her hand to sweep crumbs off the trash bin's top before wiping it down thoroughly for the third time that day.

Jake put the X-Acto knife down. "Not yet. The state police don't have a key to the house or to the Artful Dodger."

Bob Arnold had told her this, too, apparently feeling that since he couldn't give her good news, he would at least give her what news he did have.

"They'll need to get them from Roger, and he's refusing any searches until he's spoken with an attorney."

After Roger went all tearfully blabbermouth on them that morning in the police station, Jake thought his caution belonged firmly in the locking-the-barndoor, horses-gone category. But it was what Roger wanted, Bob said, and he had a right to want it.

For now. "Hmmph," said Bella expressively. "Can't they get a warrant?"

"Well, yes. But . . ." If Roger didn't change his mind, there would be one, but it would take time. Search warrants didn't get handed out like candy in Washington County, where a person's home was still his or her castle until a judge heard something very convincing indeed, and ruled on it.

Even then, the whole thing sometimes had to be forced to a conclusion, certain householders tended to feel that they might've lost the argument but they hadn't lost the battle, not until the sheriff got inside.

Bella wrapped a spray-cleaner-soaked paper towel— she made the cleaning solution herself out of white vinegar, lemon oil, and some other ingredients that she wouldn't divulge—around a faceted glass cabinet doorknob, twisting the paper towel—she'd have made those, too, if she could have—vigorously back and forth. "You know, I've been thinking about that phone of yours, too."

Jake considered yet another cup of spiked tea but rejected the idea. She had things to do, people to see.

She just didn't know what or who. "Listen, Bella, I really appreciate—"

"And," Bella went on imperturbably, finishing the cabinets, giving them an assessing look, and moving along to the front of the refrigerator, which of course was already spotless, "I do realize you probably feel you have to stay here, to answer it yourself."

The telephone, she meant. "But I know something interesting about it."

She put her sprayer down. The kitchen now smelled sweetly of vinegar-and-whatever, like a well-dressed salad.

"It has call forwarding. Which I think means you can jigger it to send—"

It occurred to Jake suddenly what Bella was getting at; she jumped up. Sam had mentioned it once, also, but she'd never felt the effort was worth it.

Fooling around with electronic gadgets just wasn't among her interests. Until now. "Calls from one telephone to another," she finished for Bella. "So, if somebody called on that one—"

She pointed at the instrument in the telephone alcove, whose number was in the book and could be dialed by anyone. By unknown death-threat callers, for instance.

Or by Randy Dodd. "The signal would be forwarded to—"

"Your cell phone," agreed Bella. Whose number

hardly anyone knew. But Sam did. "If you did it right, I think so."

So if Sam or Randy Dodd should try to call here . . . or Chip Hahn, she thought excitedly. Anyone who currently was missing. Even Wade . . .

"I want to see that tunnel," said Bella.

"But . . ." Jake began. In answer, Bella pointed at the bottom right-hand drawer under the kitchen cabinets.

"I want to," Bella repeated flatly. "And I'm going to."

In the drawer, along with a few other books that Bella kept there for her exclusive use—a DeLorme atlas, a first aid book, and a book of home remedies that could be made out of common household ingredients— were stored the instructions for every electronic device in the house.

Despite her initial doubts, minutes later Jake had the phone's call-forwarding ability enabled; it was surprisingly easy. Next she called Ellie, to ask her to call back. "To test this thing," she explained.

It worked. "And Jake?" Ellie added after dialing the house phone and being answered on Jake's cell. "Your dad's over here. He wanted me to tell you so."

"He is? But I thought—"

Jake looked around. In the hall, Bella was already putting on her coat and hat. She pulled Jake's jacket off its hook, held it out, and stood there waiting not very patiently.

"And he says he's going to stay here with Lee," Ellie went on, "to take care of her while I'm out. Which is fine with me, but I don't understand—"

Jake caught on suddenly. "I do. He and Bella must've talked this all over."

Because while Jake was stripping paint off old doorknobs and bringing Bella up to date on all that had happened so far, Bella had twice interrupted her for trips outdoors, where Jake's dad had returned and been patiently picking bits of insulation material from the lawn and garden surfaces.

And during those visits, Jake guessed, the newly-weds must've figured a few things out. Such as what Bella wanted to do—was in fact hell-bent on doing, actually—as soon as she'd learned about a secret tunnel in the cellar beneath her old friend Anne Dodd's house.

Anne, who'd been murdered in her own kitchen.

Jake carried the phone to the front door, where Bella waited. "Meet us in front of the Dodd House in five minutes," she told Ellie.

Sam, she thought. *Sam, I don't know how what we're going to do might help you, or even if it will, but—*

It occurred to Jake fleetingly that this whole enterprise was way out of character for Bella, whose desire for adventure ordinarily equaled her desire to get anthrax.

But right now, Bella seemed both confident and determined. Touching one of the gold hoop earrings she wore as if it were a good luck charm, she hurried ahead of Jake down the front walk in the late-afternoon gloom, then called back over her shoulder.

"Ask Ellie to bring along another flashlight," she said. "I don't know if the power's on over there."

Her tone turned grim as the shadows seemed to swallow her up; full darkness came unbelievably early in downeast Maine in autumn. Bella's flashlight snapped on, its beam wavering ahead of her on the sidewalk.

"It might be dark down in that cellar," she said.

The front steps of the Dodd House on Washington Street might as well have had a sign on them: *Get Your Broken Ankle Here!* Half the risers leaned one way, half sagged the other, and the rest of the place was no better. Cracked siding, poorly installed and now with vines growing into it, a broken window covered with a sheet of cardboard, rucked-up shingles . . .

Everything in Eastport looked better in summer, of course. But in the few short weeks since Anne Dodd had been murdered, her once-pristine home had begun looking as if it wanted to fall right into the grave with her. Jake took another step up and felt her right foot crunch suddenly through the step riser.

Her right leg followed. Bending her other knee swiftly to avoid toppling over, she sank to an upright crouch while the leg extended straight down through the splinter-edged hole her weight had put in the rotted plank.

One of the splinters had gone through her pants leg. "Ouch," she said, but this didn't begin to cover her predicament. She was in up to her thigh, and her femoral artery suddenly felt as if it had a neon arrow pointing to it, flashing *Poke Me*.

Cautiously, she straightened her left leg, with Bella

at one side and Ellie at the other, helping her to rise. "Careful. That splinter is . . . Oof."

As the flesh on the inside of her right thigh slid upward, the splinter in it slid out, still attached to the porch step by sharp, woody fibers. By the glow of Bella's flashlight, red blood painted the splinter's thin, wicked tip.

But not a lot of it, and she'd had a recent tetanus shot after a nail-gun incident, the less said about which, the better.

So, she let herself be hauled on until she was out of the hole, and once Bella and Ellie were convinced that Jake was really none the worse for wear—or not too much worse than usual, anyway—they confronted the house again.

"How do we get in there?" Ellie asked. Early evening had thickened to night very quickly as usual, and around them a light mist was falling.

The street shone like wet licorice in the lights of the few cars passing by only a few feet away; the houses on this part of the street were all built right up close to the sidewalk. A block distant, the centuries-old bell atop the Seaman's Church slowly struck five.

"I don't know," Jake began, then stopped as Bella marched up the remaining rickety steps with the calm bravery of a sherpa confronting Everest. When she got to the top, she produced a key chain, thrust the key on it into the front-door lock, and—

Viola, as Sam would've said. "Anne gave me this," Bella answered Jake's surprised look. "When she married Roger, I tried giving it back to her. But she said to keep it because you never knew, someday I might need it."

Bella looked downhill toward the granite-block post office building, and beyond that the row of brick storefronts on Water Street. In the farthest one—past two art galleries, a souvenir store already closed for the winter, and the Moose Island general store—was Roger's bar, the Artful Dodger.

But they couldn't see it from here. "I guess she was right," said Bella, turning the key.

As far as Jake knew, Bella hadn't been in the house since then. But if the skinny woman in the knitted wool hat and navy peacoat felt nervous about entering now, she gave no sign of it.

Jake followed her in, with Ellie behind. She hadn't been in many houses older than her own, but she saw right away that this one was special, even through the uniform layer of grime that seemed swiftly to have settled in it.

The hot water radiators had never been repainted, retaining the thin gold-colored finish they'd gotten at the factory, now aged to a rich bronze. Etching as thick as frosting whitened the fragile glass globes on the gaslights, whose fixtures remained intact.

The same well-to-do family had lived in this house for over a century, and it showed. People had loved it and taken care of it. But now the house smelled of dust and animals; the cardboard on that broken window wasn't enough.

Ahead, a hardwood-floored hall leading to the rear of the house was already festooned with cobwebs; in Eastport, autumn was spider season.

"Wow," Jake breathed into the stillness.

To the left, the dining room was decorated with olive green satin curtains at the windows; the antique furniture in there was gray with dust. A living room, littered with dirty dishes and *TV Guides,* was on the right.

Jake recalled that Roger had tried staying here for a while, before giving up in—what, grief? Guilt? Whichever, he hadn't bothered cleaning up after himself when he left.

Bella led them to the cellar stairs, averting her eyes as they passed by the kitchen, where Anne's body had been found. "Watch out," she cautioned as they went down the steps.

But the warning didn't prepare Jake for the mouse that ran over her foot, squeaking. "Gah," she said, and then "Oh!" as a large gray cat streaked past with a banshee yowl.

In the cellar, Jake stepped from the shaky staircase, whose support posts looked rotted and whose railing had apparently been put on with chewing gum. Ahead, Bella strode past the furnace, which chose that moment to go on with an explosive bang, its old machinery rattling and grinding.

"Oh, good." Ellie's laugh did not sound convincing. "We'll be able to wash our hands in hot water."

Jake thought that if the misfiring ignition device on that furnace didn't get replaced soon, the availability of hot water would be the least of anyone's troubles. Eyeing it nervously, she sidled past the massive old oil burner; from the sound of it, the ancient flue was clogged with soot.

No wonder everything was so dirty upstairs. . . . "Over here," called Bella, pulling off her wool hat.

Waving away more hanging cobwebs, they followed her into one gloomy, granite-block-walled corner of the old foundation. In it were a wooden desk, an antique wooden office chair on wheels, its leather seat long disintegrated to mouse-chewed shreds, and a row of wooden filing cabinets.

The small yellowing cards in the slots on the fronts of the filing cabinets were labeled in faded ink by an ornate hand. The oldest said *1893*.

"This must be the stuff out of old Mr. Lang's office, from when he was running . . ."

The sardine can factory, Jake would've finished. There were old, curled-up photographs on the desk, too, of shop-aproned men with heavy mustaches in front of primitive-looking machinery.

But then she saw it, half hidden behind one of the wooden file cabinets, which had been pulled away from the wall just far enough to reveal—

"A tunnel," breathed Ellie, shining her flashlight at it. "So it's true."

"Seems like," said Jake, eyeing the opening mistrustfully. It was a brick archway, five feet wide, maybe seven feet tall. In the light of Ellie's flashlight, it gaped like a dark, open mouth.

"Roger was telling the truth about that much, anyway," she went on. "Did Anne know about it?" she added to Bella.

But Bella just shook her head, tight-lipped. It struck Jake suddenly that Bella didn't like being down here at all.

Nor did she appear to want Jake to notice this; Jake turned her attention back to the tunnel, and the huge piece of furniture half blocking it. Experimentally, she leaned on the thing. "You know, there must be a way to move this. . . ." she began.

Whereupon it did move; the cabinet was on wheels, and despite its weight it slid easily. Once she had rolled it farther away from the tunnel, they could see that a pair of old rails led into it, like train tracks but thinner and set more narrowly together.

At their near end a chunk of old railroad tie was secured to the cellar floor with two huge spikes. It was a stop block for the rail car, Jake realized. A pulley was bolted into the bricks above the arch.

For pulling the cart back up, she supposed. "They brought the finished cans down here from the factory that was at the rear of the house, back then," she said, imagining it.

Nowadays, the factory building itself was only a memory. But there were photographs of it in Peavey Library, of long, shedlike sections built onto one another as the business grew.

"On a conveyor belt, maybe. Or on carts. The cans went on a car, probably, down to the wharf."

There they would be filled with small, silvery fish. "They could bring the pallets of tin up here that way, too. The tin to make the cans with."

The raw materials, as Roger Dodd had put it. Jake thought about the domestic life of the house going on upstairs, of the starched white curtains, cooks and scullery girls, and maids in caps, with all that industrial rumbling going on below and behind.

"Everything they needed came in here."

Not the pleasantest sounds to live with, probably, but maybe they thought of the commotion as the sound of money pouring in. Still, why put the tunnel here at all?

"I suppose since they already had a cellar here," she began doubtfully.

"Ledge," said Bella, understanding Jake's puzzlement. A wish for domestic peace was one thing they had always shared.

"This is the only place on the property where they could put a tunnel," Bella went on. "The rest is granite ledge, like the whole island. Anne wanted a garden, but you can't dig six inches without hitting rock. Except right here."

Here Jake could see far enough into the tunnel to note that its walls were of earth, braced with enormous timbers. And digging was cheaper than blasting, as well as less likely to damage the house.

Drawing back, Bella made an unhappy face. "Dark."

"Over here," called Ellie. Jake turned from the tunnel's mouth toward another part of the basement.

"Look," said Ellie as she emerged from a small room under the cellar stairs. "I think Randy Dodd's been here. I think he's been—"

The tiny, granite-block-walled room looked as if it might once have served as a bomb shelter. "Back in the fifties a lot of people around here built rooms like this," Bella told them. "Stocked them with supplies. But I didn't know the Langs had one."

They went in. The room had no windows, just one thick, heavy wooden door, and many wooden wall shelves loaded with water jugs and old, unappetizing-looking cans, their once-bright labels now faded, mouse-chewed, or absent altogether.

But it also held a low iron bed, a bedside table with a lamp on it, a wooden chair with a denim jacket thrown over the back of it, and a card table with a spiral notebook open on it.

Tattered paper bits in the notebook's wire spiral said that pages had been torn out of it. Otherwise the room was bare—no books or newspapers, no radio or TV. It was more like a cell than a room where anyone actually lived.

A place where the life of the mind had been extinguished, or had never existed at all . . . but then, Jake guessed Randy Dodd didn't care much about what went on outside his own head. On the other hand, what went on inside his head creeped her out very thoroughly, never more so than now as she took in the undeniable fact that he was real.

Not an imaginary bogeyman, one others had seen recently but not her. A living man, who slept in a bed, wore clothes, and ate—she looked into the small metal basket by the table—Ritz crackers and Campbell's Chunky soups.

"Do you think Roger knew Randy was down here?" Ellie asked as she lifted the denim jacket and stuck her hand in each of its pockets.

Jake shook her head as Ellie's search came up empty. "If he was." But as a hideout it made sense. No windows down here, so no light spied by anyone outside . . .

Jake recalled Roger saying that Randy had found the tunnel while scavenging the cellar for valuables. So he would have known about the room. "I'm betting it was him, though," she finished.

She snapped on the bedside lamp, its bulb casting a weak yellow glow on the room's dingy walls. "I wish

I knew what he wrote in this," she said, eyeing the notebook.

Bella plucked it up, angling it this way and that in the sallow lamplight. "Hey," said Jake, "what're you—"

Bella put the book down again and left the room hurriedly, returning a moment later with her hands extended in distaste. It was the way she held them at home, Jake recognized, when they had gotten filthy and she wanted to wash them, pronto.

But this time, the stuff on her fingers was furnace soot. Brushing past Jake and Ellie, she positioned the spiral notebook on the table under the lamp. Something had been written in it, and urgently, too; with the light at this angle, grooves showed where someone had pressed down hard with a pen or pencil.

Lightly, Bella smoothed a finger across the blank top page. Sooty smears appeared, but not in the grooves. Whatever had been written on the torn-out page showed as faint white lines in the blackened soot marks.

Around them the Dodd House seemed to hunker down for another evening of lonely misery. Another mouse squeaked, cousin no doubt to the one the cat had dispatched. A timber settled; a floorboard creaked.

Bella's hand trembled, resting on the sooty page. Suddenly, Jake was again aware of the silent kitchen upstairs and the happy hours Bella had probably spent there with her friend, before Anne Dodd was found stabbed to death on the linoleum floor.

She looked down at what the touch of Bella's hand had revealed.

It was a map.

•   •   •

"So you're awake."

Hours after he'd grabbed her off the street and bundled her into the trunk of a car, the man who'd taken her crouched beside Carolyn Rathbone on the deck of a boat bound for who knew where.

By now it was dark again; twenty hours or so, she thought, since her old life had ended and this new, terrible existence had begun. The boat had sat idle for a while, she did not know where or how, but now they were under power once more.

She fought to keep her eyes open, her mind clear. But it was no use; the damp, cold hours she'd spent lying there injured on the hard deck, weeping and suffering and fearing she was about to be killed at any moment, had taken their toll.

Everything hurt: her head, her hand, her neck, her legs. No physical part of her had escaped the constant battering of the boat's *bump, bump, bump* across the waves. As for her mind—

Better not go there, some tiny surviving part of her sanity instructed. No siree, best not lift the lid of that particular booby hatch, or what flies out at you—

He put the point of his knife to her neck. That woke her up, all right, that tiny sharpness in her vulnerable flesh.

What flies out at you might scare you to death. A whimper forced its way up her swollen throat; on top of everything else she was thirsty, so thirsty . . .

Now she knew what those other girls had endured, the ones whose pictures she'd seen, whose case files she'd read through, while writing her first book. She licked the salty mist from her cracked lips, knowing it would make her feel worse but unable to stop herself.

The man touched the tip of the knife to her throat again, drawing it lazily across her skin and then, suddenly, moving it to her eyelid. "Here," he murmured. "Or . . . here."

She cringed, holding her breath. Something in his face said he wanted to kill her, wanted to very badly. His weird, worked-on face with its tiny white scars and odd, lumpy places . . .

Right now, he wanted to do it. Right this minute. She looked past him, up into the sky at a white seagull sailing on a sea of darkness.

She hadn't known the birds flew at night. Maybe they didn't, maybe it was a hallucination. Or a sign: that if he did kill her, she might sail away, too.

Her spirit, maybe. Or maybe nothing. But she didn't find out which, because as he leaned over her with the knife in one hand, his other hand patted his shirt pocket unthinkingly, then froze.

A puzzled look came into his eyes, replaced at once by one of consternation. He straightened, patting both shirt pockets and then his pants in urgent succession.

Turning away, he searched the dimly lit deck with his eyes, then began pacing, back and forth, peering into and under everything. His left foot dragged slightly, but it didn't slow his search.

Where? His whole body seemed to be saying it as he lifted the life ring from its hook, raised the lid on the wooden bench, patted himself all over again anxiously.

Carolyn cringed at the sight of three mutilated fingertips on the man's right hand, the nails gone and the tissue there all scars that hadn't healed right. That paper, she thought as he went on searching himself, the one he'd lost overboard and hadn't noticed. Maybe he'd been too distracted by the thrill of having captured her.

It gave her a brief moment of grim satisfaction to think she had spoiled part of his plan. But he *had* gotten . . .

The money. She'd forgotten all about the money. Now, as the memory of it flooded back to her, another low groan came from the hatchway. Someone down there.

She'd forgotten that, too, but now she realized she'd been hearing the sounds all along. The man came back and stood over her.

Maybe he was thinking about whether he should just kill them both, get it over with. Carolyn, and whoever it was down there in the cabin beyond the hatchway, too.

Probably he was considering it. After what he'd already done, he couldn't very well leave them alive, could he? Because for one thing, she'd seen his face.

So if she lived, she could testify against him. And he knew it. She could see it in his eyes, that for his purposes . . .

—*Whatever those were, no don't think that*—

. . . she was already dead, and so was whoever she'd heard groaning down there.

Dead and gone; the only question was when. A pair of bodies he'd need to dispose of . . .

—When he was finished with them, oh dear God when he was—

All he needed was the right time and place.

But not right now. Not yet.

Please. Just not quite yet.

Shivering in the chill of a November afternoon on the water in downeast Maine, Chip Hahn blinked astonishedly at the object in his hands. It was a hand-drawn map, he could see even before he got done peeling the plastic wrap from it.

The thing had come bobbing by, very different from the half-submerged chunks of driftwood and matted clumps of seaweed that Passamaquoddy Bay was full of. Curious, he'd leaned out from the motorboat he'd stolen and grabbed it.

Stolen. Oh, he was going to be in so much trouble. What, back on land, had been explainable now seemed much less so, with the shore a mile distant and the streets and houses of Eastport fast diminishing to toy-town miniature.

On the other hand, a little thing like a stolen boat was not going to matter if Carolyn and Sam Tiptree didn't get back okay. You couldn't find money that might be floating on the bay without going out there, either.

Could you? No, you couldn't. And anyway, the deed was done and it was too late to worry about it.

He unfolded the sheet and squinted through the mist at it, through the chill drizzle that was developing. *X marks the spot,* he thought. Only there was no

X, just an outline of a something or other that he didn't recognize, blue ballpoint ink marks pressed in hard, as if someone who felt very urgent about something had drawn it.

In the bluish-gray light of the fast-fading autumn afternoon, Chip reopened the chart he'd found in the boat and tried comparing it to the markings on the paper. There . . .

A little rock called Digby Island was the same tiny comma on the hand-drawn map as on the printed one. It was surrounded, too, by the same dangerous-looking periods and parentheses, asterisks and exclamation points.

Which if he was not mistaken meant that Digby Island, a tiny hunk of land sticking out of the northern end of Passamaquoddy Bay, was surrounded by submerged spurs, ones that would munch the bottom out of his small vessel like so many sharp teeth.

Local boaters might know how to pick their way through them, but he didn't. He didn't even know if that was really where Randy Dodd was going, or if this was even Randy's map.

Why, after all, would a guy like Randy need one? He'd been fishing these waters for years, and must surely know his way around them competently. He probably knew all the places to hide in or escape through, and how to navigate by sight wherever he wanted to go.

So, why would he need this? The bit of paper could've been dropped in anywhere, by anyone, Chip realized with a bad sinking feeling.

Maybe it was some kid's science project, or a joke.

Maybe it had blown out of a car window, or the back of an old pickup truck on its way to the dump.

Or it might be a trick. Huddled in the open boat, Chip considered the many unpleasant possibilities this bit of paper could offer if that were true: shipwreck, drowning, being marooned.

Or . . . capture. Suddenly the prospect of venturing off to save Carolyn and Sam seemed worse than foolhardy. The smell of the sea, pleasantly exciting back on the breakwater, now tickled an anxiety nerve Chip hadn't even known he possessed.

Big icy droplets leaked down his neck, soaking his jacket collar. The steady collision of the boat's keel with the waves made his rump sore.

If only he could run parallel to them for a while . . . but when he tried, the boat wallowed dangerously, the chop rocking it back and forth violently until the craft threatened to swamp, bucking and rolling.

So he eased away again, turning the bow so it angled at the rollers and cut through them. By now they were the only things he could see, as evening kept coming on and fog thickened around him with shocking suddenness.

The shore he'd left so confidently (*stupidly,* the mean voice in his head commented) had long ago vanished into the equivalent of dark gray cotton balls, and the Canadian island of Campobello, only a mile or so off, according to the chart, might as well have been on the far side of the Atlantic.

A bell buoy clanked somewhere. He couldn't see that, either. It was getting dark so fast, and now it occurred to him that the massive freighters he'd read about before coming to Eastport—it was, he'd learned, the deepest undredged U.S. port, second only to Valdez—must navigate through this passage.

One of those freighters, he realized with an inward shiver, could cut him in half without anyone on it even noticing. All he would know of it himself was the deafening blast of the horn as the ship plowed through him on its way to the freighter terminal.

Whichever way that was. The open boat had been stocked with a lot of gear, including a compass. But in the fog he couldn't see it. For a moment Chip wished heartily that he was in Central Park again, running a shiny toy boat on the pond with a remote control, instead of sitting on a real one here.

He'd have turned back, given up, and admitted this foolish effort was doomed, taken his lumps for stealing the boat, too—at least the Evinrude was still rumbling along well, fortunately—but by now he was fairly sure he wouldn't find his way back to land at all.

Certain of it, really. Or find his way anywhere; until this fog lifted, the lights of the shore, no matter how nearby, might just as well not have existed.

Suddenly the fear he'd been trying to hold down got free with a vengeance, climbing from the pit of his stomach right up into his throat. He looked down at the map that he'd plucked from the water again, but he couldn't see it, or the chart, either.

Or even his own hands. Panic invaded him as he realized he should turn the running lights on. But he hadn't noted where the switch for them was back when he could see it, and now he couldn't even find that.

He was lost, and in planning this little adventure it now seemed he'd left too much to chance.

Way too much to chance.

Like, a hundred percent too much.

Yeah, he thought. *You're an idiot, is what you are.*

He was still thinking this when the engine quit.

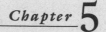

Chapter 5

Chip figured it could only be about five in the afternoon, five-thirty at the latest. But around him it was pitch dark. Steady drizzle kept falling. He was wet through and through, and so cold that his teeth had begun chattering uncontrollably. He got the outboard started again with some difficulty and aimed the boat toward what he thought must be the shore.

But the Evinrude coughed hard and died once more after only a minute or so. And this time the engine's death was permanent, the starter button producing only a brief *clickety-click,* then silence.

So here he was. The map he'd found was in his pocket, but it wouldn't do him much good if he couldn't see. He didn't think he could get through the rocks it showed anyway, and besides, he had much bigger problems now.

He never should have come out here. Knowing how to run a boat, thinking that just because it looked the same, the water along the downeast Maine coast was as friendly and easy to be on as it had been up at the Old Bastard's resort place . . .

Idiot, he berated himself as a foghorn's low *whonk!* came out of the thick fog-billows from somewhere off to his right. To his left, a buoy clanked. Briefly, he wondered if he might somehow be able to orient himself from them.

But since he didn't know where they were, either, that idea soon revealed itself as hopeless. *Like you,* he told himself again harshly. After that, all he heard besides his own scathing self-criticism was the water lapping the boat's side as the current carried him along fast.

He had his cell phone with him, but when he'd opened it no bars came onto the display and no calls would go through. He'd read once somewhere about being able to get emergency help on a cell, even if no other numbers would connect.

But he hadn't retained the information, not thinking that he would ever need it. Still, he decided to try the phone again now. At least it had a live battery, and maybe by now he'd drifted to within reach of some sort of signal.

Hunching forward, he slid it from beneath the life jacket. The screen's faint glow was momentarily comforting, until he saw that there were still no bars. He was starting to put the phone away again when a new sound caught his attention.

It was a sort of . . . rippling sound, coming from ahead and to the left somewhere, as if he were approaching some deep, fast-running stream. No such thing was possible out here; the entire bay was a stream, running in and out with the tide.

But there it was. The sound grew louder. He tipped his head, trying to imagine what could make that unusual, hissing kind of a noise. It still sounded to him like fast water rushing along a—

Then he saw the wave coming at him, about three feet high, white and foamy and rolling. He squinted at it, still not quite able to believe what—

It was a bow wave, he realized with a shock of horror, and behind it was the bow of a big freighter, rising up at least three stories over him. Mountain-sized, from where he sat frozen in his little boat—

A blast of a horn erupted out of the darkness at him, a massive, world-cracking, elemental explosion of sound that blew him back off the boat's seat and slammed him whimpering into the transom. Reflexively he clapped his hands to his ears, but that was laughably useless. The sound was inside him, battering him like the shock wave of a bomb blast, his ribs vibrating with it.

Stunned, he lay helpless. Something up there, a huge shape forming above him, emerging endlessly from the fog . . . *Oh jesus.*

The curving bow of the enormous vessel bore down on him out of the streaming darkness. He couldn't see the top of it through the fog, only a hazy glow from the deck lights far above.

But what he could see was coming right at him. Another heart-stopping, brain-hammering blast of the great horn exploded all around him. Not because anyone on the ship knew he was here, though. Or if they did, it was too late to do anything about it.

Huge, inexorable, the thing just kept coming. Desperately, Chip scrambled up, pounded the outboard's starter button again and again, to no avail. The wave alone would swamp him. . . .

The wind hit first, thick as a fist, a vast blowback off the ship's flat moving side. It lifted the spare life jacket and carried it away. Then the high white wall of rolling water struck, lifting the tiny vessel he was on like a stick of driftwood, and him an insubstantial bug clinging to it.

Wrapping his arms around the Evinrude's console, he hung on, grateful for the life jacket he was wearing but knowing it wouldn't do him any good, either; that ship's towering bow was going to slice him in half in another second—

He stared wonderingly at it. For an instant it was so close, he could count the rivets in the glow from the lights above. . . .

Hey, he thought, *I'm down here, look at me. . . .*

But of course they didn't. And then it hit him: *Row, you idiot, row!* He leapt forward, seized the oars, and flung their blades into the water. Hauling on them, he felt that his heart might burst out of his chest with the effort and his terror.

Row . . . The churning sea yanked his shoulders. Every stroke felt like his joints might dislocate. But nothing was happening; his tries were nothing against the massive waves and the giant thing bearing gigantically down on him.

Oh jesus oh mother of god oh jesus . . . He closed his eyes and hurled himself backward, pulling and pulling, again and—

Suddenly something smacked one of the oars with the force of a train locomotive, snapping his arm back and shattering the oar itself; he had only its grip in his hand. At the same moment the opposite oarlock jumped up out of its sleeve; the wind hit the oar's blade, and then the water did.

And then it too was gone, and he was powerless. Sitting there stunned and helpless, he gazed up open-mouthed at the size of the freighter, its skyscraper height looming above him and its lights hazily brilliant, like a massive city afloat in the fog.

Its bow wave hit him. His own ridiculously small craft rose up sharply, the bow pointing heavenward as the stern spiraled around, rolling one way, pitching another . . . and then everything beneath him suddenly slid down the side of the great, gleaming wave cascading off the slanted bow of the huge ship.

Away he went, zooming into the roiling darkness, surfing sideways, then headfirst, in a boat now so near to rolling over that small objects in it showered past him like change out of an upended purse.

And then . . . then it was gone, the freighter's massive bow shining for an instant before the fog made it all into a glowing blob. As his breath came in spasms that became sobs, the blob diminished hazily, faded, got sucked into the fog . . . and winked out. The ship's horn sounded again, the sound drifting back to him, lonesome and small. Then nothing; he was alone once more, spinning in the churning wake of the big boat.

Chip leaned over the rail, lost whatever was in his stomach, and fell back, drained. His heart still stuttered ineffectively, weakness flooding him and his breath subsiding to short, defeated huffs.

Relief washed waterily over him as he fell back against the Evinrude's solid bulk, but then came despair. If he'd had any idea that he might still survive the night out here, that notion was gone, blasted to smithereens by the departing horn of the great container ship.

Because maybe he'd escaped it, but what was next? Squallish gusts buffeted his boat, which had taken on water in the violence of the recent encounter and was now listing badly. He'd lost the oars, and the cell phone, if not overboard, was somewhere at his feet, drowned and ruined under several inches of icy brine.

Miserably, he calculated his chances of getting out of this alive and found them skimpy in the extreme. Probably he would never see his apartment again, his books and CDs, the collection of posters from indie music groups hanging framed in his hall.

Sadly, he wondered who would arrange his funeral. Not the Old Bastard, now so pickled in bourbon that he would probably not even understand the bad news.

Assuming he thought it was bad. And not Chip's mother, now an aging, made-up, and bejeweled drama queen happily ensconced—he continued to hope—in a mountainside commune in New Mexico, where she'd gone to escape the rigors of Chip's own early childhood, and never returned.

Occasionally he'd had a card from her—one at Christmas, usually, and once in a while there'd be one on his birthday. Sometimes the card had a hundred bucks in it.

But nothing for several years now. And otherwise, no one. Surprised, he searched his mind; could it really be that he'd become so alone, so isolated, that if he died, no one would . . .

Siobhan Walters might miss him. For a few minutes, anyway. Long enough to send a short, somber e-mail to the marketing and publicity people, and the handful of others in the office who'd known him distantly.

After that, though, she'd be on to the next new whoever, a new writer with new ideas who could show up with the stuff, on time and in shape. It was why Carolyn had always been so driven, he understood now, so intent on not letting anyone steal even an ounce of her thunder.

And on stealing any she could get her hands on, herself. Because once you were out there, alone in the cold and dark, you might never get in again.

Wretchedly, he leaned back against the boat's transom, trying to find a position where everything didn't hurt. He was still moving right along, the boat riding a fast current, or so it seemed from the way the wind stayed constant in his face and the water chuckled faintly against the boat's side.

Riding to disaster; he just didn't know what kind or when. Yet . . .

Something hit the bow with a dull thud. He lurched up, his heart suddenly hammering again and his ears ringing loud in the silence. But nothing else happened. Driftwood, maybe.

He fell back, bones aching with fatigue and chill. The rain, at least, had stopped for the moment. But he had a bad feeling that pretty soon now it would get even colder.

A lot colder, and his jacket and the slicker, even with the life jacket under them, weren't nearly enough. He stuffed his cold hands in his coat pockets and closed his eyes.

After a while he thought of shouting. So he tried that, but the wind snatched his voice and swirled it out into the fog, where it was swallowed up instantly. No answer came, and when his voice was only a harsh croak, he stopped.

Maybe when morning came, the fog would lift and he would at least be able to see again. Maybe then some other boat would be out here, too, and somebody would find him.

Thinking this, he fell into a sort of trance; of darkness and fog, the water moving beneath him like a great unseen beast. He couldn't tell how much time went by, nor did he care; what difference did it make? He found his iPod and put the earbuds in again; k.d. lang began asking what his heart concealed.

But for once even her lush, languorously articulate voice failed to revive his spirit. All he knew was that he was cold and frightened, that he never, ever should have tried coming out here alone, and that it was dark.

His bravado in the Eastport police station, confronting Roger Dodd, now seemed a cartoon-like bit of playacting. *Big man,* he mocked himself bitterly, *when there's a cop to protect you in case somebody sees through you.*

And all the things he'd been thinking and feeling the night before were even worse, his silly I'm-going-to-do-this and you-can't-have-that.

God, had he really ever thought he could hurt somebody? That he could harm Carolyn, that there was something important enough? Had he been that stupid?

Well, now he knew better. He missed Carolyn, her abrasive, demanding way of looking at everything, her self-absorption, and her instant, reflexive belief that people were going to arrange things the way she wanted them.

Or else. Chip sniffled, not caring anymore how pathetic he was. Maybe if he'd been a little more like Carolyn, he wouldn't be in this trouble.

But it was too late to worry about that now, too, wasn't it?

And anyway . . . a sob racked him and he let it, unashamed, as this last thing occurred to him:

That anyway, Carolyn was probably dead.

When the three Eastport women came out of the Dodd House on Washington Street, it was full dark. Fog like a thick, damp sponge muffled all sound, and in the glow of the streetlights the pavement gleamed wetly black. A few cars passed, their dashboard lights tiny beacons and their wipers smearing the drizzle.

Jake picked her way down the wrecked front steps. The weird forbidden-thrill feeling of exploration and discovery had faded fast as they came down the dusty hall toward the front door. Now behind her the lovely old house stood silent, as if too proud to acknowledge the fact that it was being abandoned again.

Sam, she thought. A foghorn moaned distantly. "I've got to get back," Ellie said. "Your father's waiting for me, and George might call."

There had been no word from the husbands—Jake checked her cell phone again, without result—but if the wardens Bob Arnold had promised to alert had found the hunters, they might be out of the woods by now, perhaps even on their way home.

She nodded, hunched up under her jacket against the damp air. Another car went by downhill, its tires spinning crystalline droplets that vanished as they flew off into the darkness.

Bella tucked the sheet of paper with the map on it into her coat. Its delicate, revealing smears of soot wouldn't survive for long, but she knew what it had showed, and she would remember.

"I'm going downtown to see Bob Arnold," she said.

"Bella, we can call him from home. It's awful out here—"

The housekeeper turned. In the gloom her long, hard face was like an antique wood carving, deeply grooved. "I'm going," she repeated, and when she got like that, there was no point arguing with her.

"All right," Jake gave in. "Tell him—"

"I know what to tell him," said Bella flatly. What they'd found, where they'd found it, what it was . . .

Well, that much was obvious. Even Jake, no expert marine navigator, recognized Digby Island. The barest, most unappealing and inaccessible little spur of jagged stone for a hundred miles, it lay about halfway between the north end of Deer Cove and the Canadian port of L'Etete, just barely on the Canadian side of the line. Its nickname was Nothing Rock because it had no place to put ashore and nothing on it to put ashore for.

According to Sam, who had once gotten stuck there with a crapped-out bilge pump, the only reason anyone would try was if they were already sinking, and even then it was even money if they'd get to the shore alive, because the channel around Digby was so deep in some spots and rock-infested in all others.

Drown, smash, or get hung up at low tide and capsize later at high: those were your choices in the waters around Digby, Sam had reported. He'd survived the episode, but Sam was so expert on the water that he practically had gills.

So, why had Randy drawn a map of the place? So he could avoid those rocks? To put people off his track? Or for some other, even worse, reason?

Bella's final comment cut into Jake's thoughts. "If that miserable Roger Dodd is around, I'll know what to tell him, too," she declared as she marched off.

Ellie put her arm around Jake and then released her. "Listen. It looks bad now. But this is going to be—"

All right. "I know," Jake said. But it wasn't. She managed a weak smile. "Sam's pretty capable. I'm sure if there's anything he can do, he'll be—"

"Of course he will," said Ellie, and with that they parted, Ellie heading downhill toward the thinly shining lights of Water Street and Jake turning into the dark, dripping alley beside the nursing home, toward her own house on Key Street.

By the time she reached the porch steps, the need to go out and find Sam for herself felt like a toxic compulsion; it was all she could do not to get into the car at once. Even driving around aimlessly would be better than this awful waiting and fearing.

Instead she went inside, let the dogs out and fed them and petted them, and then put coffee on. She reset the phone, and turned the lamps on, pausing in each of the empty rooms in case their silence should have something to communicate to her.

But none of them did. At last she ventured upstairs to Sam's room, where the sight of his neatly made bed struck her anew with the force of a well-aimed blow. On the dresser his Morse code notebook lay open. His seaweed experiment grew in its aquarium.

His penknife wasn't there, nor the compact emergency fire kit—flint, steel, and a dozen strike-anywhere wooden matches—she'd given him the previous Christmas.

So he had those, anyway. And his textbooks stood in a pile on his desk like a mountain he had not yet finished climbing. But he would.

Surely he would; looking out his window to the dark street below, she promised it to him. Yet she had no idea how she would manage this, and after watching the silent street for a while she went back downstairs to the doorknobs and the X-Acto knife.

She poured coffee, sat at the kitchen table, and opened the bag of doorknobs. They were really very pretty ones, and fully salvageable. She looked at the X-Acto knife, at the paint on the old china knobs, at her hands, and at the knife again.

And then it hit her, what else Sam had said when he'd returned from his unpleasant adventure on Digby Island:

That not only was it wild, inaccessible, and protected by rocks so sharp you might as well jump feet-first into a bag of razor blades.

He'd said that at low tide, it had a sandbar. No problem at high tide, he'd allowed, expanding on his adventure, when twenty feet of water lay between it and your boat's hull.

But at low tide it could catch you up and strand you, put your vessel on its side quick as a wink, and when the tide came back in again you'd go swirling straight to the bottom.

A sandbar, Sam had said, so wide you could walk across it. She dropped the X-Acto knife and dashed into the parlor. On the mantel stood a device like a clock but with just one black hand.

It was a tide clock. Sam had given it to her last Christmas. *High, Ebbing,* and *Low,* said the words on the dial, then *Flowing* and back to *High* again.

At the moment, the hand pointed at *High.* So, right now the sandbar Sam had described didn't exist. But in a few hours the tide would be going out again from Passamaquoddy Bay. Then for an hour or so there would be a land bridge over to Digby Island.

Only . . . from where? Sam hadn't said. She flew to the right-hand bottom drawer under the kitchen cabinets, yanked it out, and rummaged in it, tossing all the many electronic-equipment manuals out onto the floor while the dogs sniffed curiously around her.

Because beneath the electronics manuals, Bella kept other books, including a DeLorme *Maine Atlas and Gazetteer*. The information it contained was very detailed. . . .

She found it and pulled it out, laid the large paperbound volume open on her lap as she sat on the floor, and began paging hurriedly through it. Randy Dodd knew the water around here, the tides and currents, coves, inlets, and islands. Whoever he'd drawn a map for, she felt certain, it had not been for himself.

And who it had been for was a question for another time, as well, because for now it didn't matter. For now, all she knew was that she needed to find her way to where a cunning fugitive might be holding Sam captive.

Bella would give the soot-smeared map tracing they had found to Bob Arnold. Bob knew the waters around here as well as Randy Dodd or better; if the map turned out to be useful, he would use it.

And that was all well and good. But if she didn't try, too, and Sam didn't get found, she would never forgive herself.

So she had to. She just had to. And the DeLorme—

"Come on, come on . . ." she murmured impatiently, flipping to the next page, and the next.

—the DeLorme was a whole book of maps.

•   •   •

Carolyn dreamed of water. She woke with a strangled shriek that came out a painful croak to find the man standing over her. An empty plastic quart jug was in his hand; he'd emptied it onto her.

Desperately she licked at the moisture on her face, felt the cool liquid relief spread like a blessing onto her parched lips and tongue . . . only not enough.

Not nearly enough. Pleadingly she gazed up at him, her eyes like two hot stones, aching and burning.

He kicked her. "Get up." Then he walked away, the plastic jug with a few precious droplets perhaps remaining in it hanging loosely from one big hand.

Aching, she shifted tentatively and found that while she'd been out cold, he'd taken the tape off the blanket she was rolled in. Pains shot from her joints as she tried to move, to get up; with a groan, she fell back onto the deck.

He was at the wheel of the boat, his back turned to her. "You don't get up and I'm gonna just shoot you where you're lying there."

She didn't believe him. It was not a part of his plan. She recalled very clearly the look in his eyes as he'd held the knife to her throat. A look of longing to push the knife in. Now . . .

But something had changed. His face when he'd found that the slip of paper he'd had was missing . . . He'd been afraid.

So she thought he wouldn't kill her; not yet. And not with a gun . . .

He stomped down through the hatchway. First loud thumping, then the ugly sounds of choking came from it. Next came cursing and barked orders. *Quit whining. Get up, on your feet.*

Or the man would . . .

Killyoukillyoukill . . . Shivering uncontrollably, she fought to silence the murderous refrain, as constant now in her mind as the low thrum of engine from the boat's diesel shack.

It was still dark, and so cold she could see her breath. She tried getting up again, put her weight on her hurt hand and nearly screamed with the onslaught of pain that roared up her arm and shoulder.

In the dim light from the boat's control console, her swollen hand was a fat blue club. She couldn't move the fingers, could barely even lift the arm, as she struggled to sit.

She looked around, saw nothing. Where were they? And . . . what was he planning to do now?

As if in answer, he returned. "Get up."

Gasping, she tried to obey. If she tried grabbing the gun, she would only drop it, one hand unusable and the other so cold she couldn't feel it.

She made it over onto her side, caught her breath as another stab of agony pierced her hand. She got both her legs underneath herself and pushed.

There . . . She struggled to a shaky crouch, prayed that would satisfy him for now. But he seized her bad shoulder, ignoring her croaked shriek, and dragged her up the rest of the way.

Then he shoved her against the boat's rail, where she clung, too frightened even to weep.

Too scared to fight. *This was how they felt,* the old Carolyn thought clearly from somewhere inside her, the part that could still think at all.

The part who'd seen photographs of crime scenes

and burial sites, and in her spoiled, safe stupidity had thought that she understood them.

Pictures of girls in graves. Well, she understood now, all right. She couldn't have known better what they were all about if they'd opened their eyes and looked at her, parted their ruined lips and spoke.

Here we are, those broken girls seemed to say to her now. *We had lives, too, like you. Blonde, brunette, redhead, students and cocktail waitresses. Soccer moms, nurses, doctors, lawyers, even a few priests, and whoever we were, we were . . . special.*

All of us were. This couldn't happen to us. To other girls, maybe. Not us.

But it did. It had. And now . . .

The man grabbed her hair. He'd stuffed all the money into a bag like a doctor's satchel, but he couldn't get the top closed. The money stuck out like a funny illustration in a cartoon about bank robbery.

But it wasn't funny. She staggered and nearly fell as he hauled her along, a grunt of pain escaping her as he pushed her ahead of him up a low step stool to the boat's opposite rail. She perched there, nearly losing her balance but not quite.

"Don't you move." He backed away, toward the boat's wheel again. From where she stood now, she could see down through the hatchway to a rough below-deck cabin furnished with a plastic lawn chair and a table made of a plank laid on two sawhorses.

Something had changed; it took her a moment to realize what. It wasn't dark anymore down there. Instead, in the sallow yellow light from a dangling bulb, a man stood bent over with his hands braced on the tops of his thighs.

He was bleeding, fat red droplets falling from his lip onto his hands. He was young, in his early twenties, she thought, with dark, curly hair and a long lantern jaw.

Tall, athletic-looking but not muscle-bound, he took slow, deep breaths as if trying to steady himself. She understood this just by looking at the young man, that he was trying to follow their captor's orders, trying to catch his breath and get hold of himself.

Trying to survive. He turned his head very slowly and saw her. He tried to straighten, grimaced as a spasm of pain hit him, then straightened some more.

Still looking at her, as if the sight of her was helpful to him. She wanted to say something to him, something encouraging, and once, she could have.

Back in that other life. Back when she didn't belong surely and completely to the company of the girls with dead eyes, when a silent scream wasn't the only thing she could think of.

He moved toward the hatchway. His cheek had a bruise on it and his lip was still bleeding, but otherwise he didn't look bad. She wondered why he'd stayed down there so cooperatively, not trying to escape.

Then she spotted the chain around his leg, fastened with a padlock and attached to . . . she squinted, trying to see through the gloom. An anchor.

His leg was chained to an anchor. Stiffly he put one foot out, pulled against the chain with the other. The anchor didn't budge. He looked at it, bent to it.

Lifted it, heaved it up out onto the deck with a groan. The anchor hit with a dull thud and a rattle of chain. The man at the boat's wheel looked over impassively.

The guy with the chain around his leg climbed the steps on his hands and knees, crawled out onto the deck beside the anchor, and struggled to his feet once more.

"You throw that thing at me and I'll slit your throat right here and gut you like a fish, you understand me? Now get over there with her."

The man at the wheel spoke calmly, jerking his head in her direction. But he didn't sound calm. Something had gone wrong, it was why she was still alive, she could tell by the way he held back, didn't let himself get outwardly excited.

Didn't let himself do what he wanted to do, only on account of having something more crucial to deal with first. Because on the inside, he was very excited. When he looked at her, when he'd touched her . . .

Shuddering, she concentrated on not losing her balance, poised at the rail. Beneath her the boat bumped and rumbled. The air all around smelled of salt water, fish, and diesel fuel, a mix that now made her feel nauseated.

A bird flapped by invisibly, very near, with a wet-sounding rush of wings. Reflexively she flinched away, caught her breath, and nearly fell.

The chained man had made it to her side; he reached out and caught her. His accompanying grimace of pain said it had cost him something to do it. She felt a rush of gratitude for him, warmth suddenly replaced by fear as she noticed that his lip wasn't the only place he was bleeding from.

His light blue chambray shirt collar poked out over a forest green sweatshirt with the word MAINE lettered on it in white. Between the N and the E, a small slit oozed. The cloth around it was sodden-looking and nearly black.

Blood. He grinned weakly, then staggered as his face went abruptly pale and his eyelids fluttered. Putting out a hand, he fell against the rail and leaned there.

"Okay," he whispered. "You're gonna be okay now. Just hang in there."

Talking to himself, as well as to her. And that was good, that was . . .

But then he coughed; white foam flecked with darkness came onto his lip. He wiped it away with the back of his hand, dragged in a breath that sounded like wet cloth ripping.

Their eyes met. His look, amazingly, was apologetic, as if he knew his being hurt was terribly inconvenient for her.

From somewhere inside herself she managed to produce a weak smile. "You don't look so good."

His eyes smiled back, though his face wasn't quite able to go along. "You're no oil painting yourself."

The man stopped what he was doing, strode over to them as if to confront them, hands on hips. "Sam, meet Carolyn."

He turned. "Carolyn, meet Sam."

She wondered with a fresh burst of fright how he knew her name, then realized that she knew his, the face she'd seen in old newspaper photographs popping clearly from behind all the clumsy work he'd had done somewhere on his features.

Panic made her heart flutter, because with the realization, she knew something else, too: He didn't just want to kill her. He had to.

Because seeing his face and knowing what he'd done to her was one thing. But knowing why he'd done it was another, and now she understood that he hadn't just taken her off the street at random, or because she was a long-haired brunette, or for any of the other crazed, obsessively personal reasons men like him did things like this to women like her.

No, this time he'd targeted her specifically, because he knew she knew—or suspected, which as far as he was concerned was nearly as bad—that he was alive at all.

It was Randy Dodd there at the boat's wheel, she was certain of it. "Now," he went on, "unless you want me to tie the both of you to that anchor and drop it overboard . . ."

He looked levelly at them. "Shut the freak up," he said.

Chapter 6

*Tool rule: If the extension cord
gets hot, you're running too big
a power tool on it. Get a heavier-
duty extension cord.*

—Tiptree's Tips

It was two in the morning when Jake heard
Bella come down the hall stairs in the dark, in the big
old house on Key Street. Jake lay on the parlor sofa
with the dogs dozing beside her on the floor and the
TV turned on, the volume set very low.

She didn't speak as Bella passed by in the hall.

The dogs looked up, then went uneasily back to sleep.

Wade hadn't called, and there'd been no word at Ellie's house, either. That meant either that the men had spent the night in the woods and didn't know what was happening here at home or that they did know and they were still trying to get here.

Neither theory accounted for their silence, or why not even a guide or warden had sent any message from them. Jake tried not to worry, instead lying there being tortured with it.

Enduring it, and waiting for the time to go by. An hour or so before low tide, she figured, was about when she should leave. She'd readied her supplies: flashlight, rain gear, warm gloves, an extra pair of sneakers since the first pair would surely get wet.

She'd thought about asking Ellie to go along, then decided against it. There was no one to care for Lee without going to some trouble about it, and anyway, Ellie had a child's life ahead of her now, and a responsibility to make that life good.

So, Jake would do it herself. She rose and padded into the hall, then paused vexedly at the sound of Bella moving around out in the kitchen. She hadn't bargained on Bella being up and about. Now it would be a project, trying to get out of here unnoticed.

She didn't want anyone trying to dissuade her, and in any case she hadn't left time for an argument. The tide paused for no man, and no woman, either, and in an hour it would be just right.

Much after that would be too late. She didn't want to get stuck on the far side of the sandbar leading to

Digby, assuming it appeared at all; even now she had only Sam's casual word that it would.

She made her silent way to the cellar door, moved the light switch quietly, and for once got the door open with no betraying squeak of old hinges. The steps were bare wood, steep and liable to creak, but at least she wouldn't put a foot through one.

The memory of the rotten step over at the Dodd House sent a pang through the deep gash she'd found on the inside of her thigh when she got home. A half-inch higher and she would be in the hospital now, but if that was all the injury she ended up suffering tonight, she would count herself lucky.

In the cellar she remembered to keep her head low so as not to smack it against an old ceiling beam. Crossing silently to the northwest corner of the old foundation, she paused.

A stream of water trickled down the drainpipe passing by her head: Bella, still busy in the kitchen. To the right of the pipe, a foundation stone was loose.

Bracing herself, she lifted it with both hands and set it on the cellar floor, then reached into the hole it had covered. A wooden box met her searching fingers.

Inside were two handguns: a .32-caliber semi-auto and a .22 pistol. In happier times, she'd handled them both enough on the target range to feel comfortable with either of them; it was yet another benefit of her marriage to Wade, being okay with guns.

She chose the .32 and two boxes of ammunition for it. If all went well, she would not have to touch the weapon. If not, she meant only to wound the man who'd taken Sam, to slow him down so that she could get her son and Chip Hahn's friend, Carolyn, away from him safely. And maybe Chip, too; she wondered again where he had gotten to and didn't like the possibilities she came up with.

So if she had to use a weapon . . . well, best not finish that thought now, she told herself, tucking the weapon and ammunition boxes into her sweater pocket.

It had always been this way, through the snooping she'd been doing with Ellie White in Eastport and surrounding towns, and sometimes on her own. A few of those episodes had ended badly.

Not many, but a few, and in those she'd had to face what she faced now, without liking it a bit. She replaced the loose stone and turned back to the cellar stairs, then gasped in startlement.

Bella stood there. "Good morning," she said.

Jake leaned against the cold stone wall. "Bella, you—"

Scared me. More startling, though, were the clothes Bella wore, and the look on her face.

Bella approached, ducking automatically under the ceiling beam, and reached past Jake to push the loose stone into the wall a little farther.

"No sense letting anyone notice what's there. Hidey-holes should be hidden," she told Jake with a complicit glance.

She wore thick pants made from the kind of heavy-duty stuff men put on for cold-weather construction jobs. Over them she had on a gray sweatshirt, a blaze-orange quilted vest, and the shirt from Jake's dad's new set of white insulated underwear, peeping out from the sweatshirt's heavy ribbed collar.

Her face in the dim cellar light was like a gargoyle's, long and bony and without any friendliness in it at all, her eyes flat with purpose. "Let's go," she said.

Jake followed her upstairs. Bella had hiking boots on her feet. Jake hadn't known that Bella even owned hiking boots. In the hall the smell of fresh hot coffee floated.

In the kitchen Bella poured two cups without asking, thrust one at Jake, and began drinking the other herself.

"I figure it's about an hour from here, where we need to go," Bella said without preamble. "And low tide is in about an hour."

She put her cup down. "I didn't wake your father." Because he wouldn't have liked this, either, and Bella knew it.

She plucked a pen from the mug full of them on the kitchen counter, a pad of paper already on the table. "If he gets up, or if Wade comes home, they'd better know where we are, though."

Or if we don't come back. "Bella, now listen to me. I can't be dragging you into—"

Bella's hand paused on the notepaper. "If I'm not going, then you're not, either. I can still wake him, you know."

The words sounded implacable but her tone didn't, her voice faint and shaky. She was frightened, and forcing herself to do this, Jake saw. Only that she felt she had to.

Me too, Jake thought. *I don't know what will happen, and I'm as scared about it as she is.*

Still, going alone wasn't the brightest idea in the

world. She just hadn't been able to think of anyone else; at least, not anyone who wouldn't try stopping her.

Bella finished the note and propped it against the sugar bowl. "So, which is it?" asked Bella. "Me or us?"

"All right," Jake gave in. "It's getting late."

In the car, Bella settled in the passenger seat. "I set your cell phone on vibrate."

Jake glanced over in surprise. She hadn't examined the phone before tucking it into her bag.

"You don't want it ringing at the wrong time," said Bella matter-of-factly.

But the look on her face was anything but matter-of-fact. She looked like a Christian getting ready to meet the lions, her head high but her eyes wide, anxiously determined.

"I put some food in a bag, just snacks to keep our energy up, and the rest of the coffee in a thermos," she added, as if she were in the habit of sneaking up on murderous men hiding on desolate islands every day of the week.

"Thank you," Jake said, trying to keep the smile out of her voice as she backed the car out into the dark street.

Maybe this expedition was just as crazy as Bob Arnold would say it was, if he knew about it. Maybe it was insane.

But she was suddenly very glad to have Bella riding shotgun on it with her. "What's your plan?" Bella asked as they drove out of town.

"We'll drive up to where Sam said the sandbar to

Digby is at low tide," she began. Her own voice was as shaky as Bella's.

Bella didn't notice, or if she did, she decided to make no comment. "We'll get as close as we can, maybe even right out onto the island," Jake went on.

In the predawn hours, Eastport's streets full of antique mansions and small wooden bungalows slumbered peacefully; only the fog and their own vehicle moving through them.

"The rocks there are probably very slippery, and it'll be dark, so we'll have to be careful. We can't turn on a light, and we'll need to be very sure we don't—"

Slip, fall, cry out, make a commotion, or in any other way get injured or react to an injury, she did not finish. But Bella just nodded once, her hands clasped tightly together in her lap.

They passed the bank and the IGA, took the long turn in the foggy murk past the Mobil station and Quoddy Airfield, its runway lights pinpricks in the streaming dark. Bella spoke again when they'd crossed over the causeway to the mainland and turned onto Route 1 headed north.

"I'll warn you if need be," she said calmly, as if Jake had been inquiring as to Bella's job description on this trip. "Or I will bonk someone, if that needs doing."

She reached into the back seat and came up with her bonking tool, which she'd apparently placed there while Jake was down in the cellar. "With this."

It was an iron crowbar from Jake's workroom, curved at one end, flat at the other. As a bonker, it could not have been more satisfactory. Still . . .

They sped between the trees and thickets lining

Route 1 on both sides. "You know we're probably just reconnoitering, though, right?" Jake asked her.

The headlights were flat white cylinders in the fog ahead. Jake slowed, trying not to drive into what she couldn't see. But it was no use going so slow that it felt safe.

"That even if we find them—"

On a night like this, the only safe thing was staying home, huddling under the covers.

"All we can do if that happens, probably, is call Bob Arnold and tell him."

"Hmmph," said Bella communicatively.

Bob hadn't been impressed by the soot smear she'd delivered to him, or by their invasion of the Dodd House. He'd warned Bella not to do such a thing again, though he'd promised to follow up.

According to Bella, who'd been quite indignant about it when she got home from the police station, Bob said that if it was a map they'd found, there was no proof Randy had drawn it.

Nor would their romping around down there clarify matters, he'd added. "Bob said if Randy did make it," Bella declared now, "it could just be part of a plan that Randy had thought about and then given up on."

Which Jake had to admit made some sense. Digby Island was about the least likely refuge in the bay, with not one single easy place to get out onto it by boat. Even helicopters couldn't land there, Sam had said, because of the trees; also, there was nowhere flat.

And anyway, tracings from the pen grooves of a

map—if it was one—weren't much evidence of anything. This could be just a goose chase. But:

"If I were Randy Dodd," Bella went on, "and I needed to find a hideout, I'd pick the one place that no one would expect me to go. If it were infested with poisonous snakes that would bite you to smithereens—"

Jake was pretty sure poisonous snakes only needed to bite you once, and that the result was rarely smithereens. But never mind; Bella continued:

"That is where I would go. I know Bob wouldn't, but that boy has the failing of too much common sense."

The other news Bella had brought home was that the Coast Guard had called back its search vessels until morning, and air traffic was grounded, too, on account of too much fog.

Shedding tamaracks' gold needles made a slick, wet carpet of the winding two-lane. Twenty minutes later they entered Calais, the border town between Maine and Canada.

The officer in the border-crossing booth looked sleepy and uninclined to think they were either smugglers or terrorists. After rattling off his questions— where they were from, where they were going, what they would do there—

"My sister's sick," said Bella with a straight face.

—he let them through without a hitch. Coming out of customs into the small town of St. Stephen, New Brunswick, they turned right onto the main street, past the dark, silent duty-free shop and the currency-changing storefront.

It was still several hours before dawn; only an occasional car moved in the streets. "When I was a girl, we used to come up here for parties now and then," said Bella. "We'd have bonfires on the beach. The boys brought beer and the girls . . . well, the girls brought themselves," she added.

Jake hadn't ever linked Bella with the notion of parties, or of being a girl. "Turn here," Bella said. "It's a shortcut."

The narrow, rudimentary road was of pale gravel, angling in between old fir trees that crowded up on either side. The car's tires on gravel made loud crunching sounds, and the headlights's glow made Jake nervous.

More nervous, even, than she already was. Bella frowned. "Pull over and park. That's what we used to do. It's only another half mile or so to the beach."

Jake tried imagining Bella with a gaggle of girl-friends, out late at night for a party featuring boys, a bonfire, and beer. Not being able to picture it at all made her feel sad, and what Bella said next didn't help.

"You new people around here think you know what it was like back then, when no one had a penny and we were all we had. But you don't," she added as she got out. "You really don't."

In the pine-smelling darkness, the silence all around them felt huge, Eastport and home very far away. The only thing that kept Jake from turning back was the knowledge that Sam might be out here, too.

"All right," said Bella. Her voice shook only a little bit. She began marching forward into the darkness. "Lets the two of us just get this over with."

After a moment, Jake followed.

*   *   *

Carolyn Rathbone lay flat on her back on the deck of the boat Randy Dodd had put her on some unknown number of hours and a whole long lifetime ago.

They had motored along very slowly through the fog for what felt like forever. Now with the sky clearing and her eyes fully adjusted to the dark, she could glimpse that the boat was pulled up against the side of a cliff rising out of the water.

Above her, very near, spread a canopy of dead branches, made, she supposed, by a tree that had toppled off the side of the cliff as erosion took the edges of it.

Or something like that. Not much about her situation was certain, was it? she thought ruefully; only that she was in bad trouble.

And that Randy was gone . . . for now. She didn't know where. But she knew that sooner or later he would return.

And then the trouble would get worse. She turned her head. Nearby, the young man whose name was Sam sat with his back to the rail.

He didn't look good. "Hey," she said.

His eyes opened. Grimacing, he held a hand to his side. It was still leaking blood. As the moon emerged from the thinning overcast, the blood's dark wetness shone in the bluish light.

"Hey," he said in reply, and managed a smile. But his lip trembled as he did it.

Hell, she thought. He didn't even look able to get up, much less get off this stinking boat and walk.

And especially not with that anchor still chained to his leg. Which meant that as she'd suspected right from the start of this whole nightmare, she was on her own.

Still taped tightly in the blankets Randy had wrapped her in again, she wiggled to a sitting position and began straining against the tape strips. But it was no use. He'd wrapped them around and around her so no matter how much she twisted and flexed, nothing gave.

"Inch over here if you can," said Sam. "Closer to me." His voice sounded awful, like two pieces of sandpaper being rubbed together. But she had no good plan of her own, so she obeyed.

"Ouch," she said as her hip bones bumped the deck. After a long, painful slog across the damp, hard boards, finally she got to within an arm's length of him. "Now what?"

"Get . . . your back close to my hands."

She squinted doubtfully at him, then saw something gleam in his trembling fingers. It was a tiny penknife.

A thrill of hope went through her at the sight of it; maybe she wouldn't die after all. A shaky grin creased Sam's face.

"He was in too big a hurry," said the young man who held her salvation in his not-very-steady grip. She recalled Randy's rough, almost panicky rush as he'd seized her. . . .

You bastard, you made a mistake, she thought exultantly, and in the back of her mind she could hear the girls in their graves cheering about it, too.

Eagerly she bounced herself closer to Sam, angled her stiff, tape-wrapped torso near enough for him to reach it. Freedom . . .

He dropped the knife. It clattered to the deck. In the pale moonlight she could see it was bloodstained.

Sam's blood. "Ouch," he whispered softly, and let his head fall back. Or maybe it fell back without him realizing it.

"Sam?" Please, no, not now when she was so close . . . "Sam?"

His eyelids fluttered open. "Sorry. Maybe you can . . ." His head moved slightly.

Get that. Oh, yes. She definitely could get that.

She let herself fall onto her side, then inched like a worm toward the fallen blade, heedless of the pain the movement cost her.

Eyes on the prize, damn it. Because this was it, she had a strong feeling that this was her very last chance. She could get out of this tape somehow, get out of it and live, or stay in it and . . .

No. She shoved the thought from her head. The knife lay just inches away. Craning her neck, she touched her lips to it, tasted the blood on it, clamped her teeth around it, and pulled back.

It stayed between her teeth, though the blood taste made her gorge rise. Aching and feeling half dead with fatigue and terror, she began wiggling her way back.

"Hurry," Sam whispered weakly.

Yeah, tell me about it. A little more . . . there. She thrust her chin up, poked the knife toward his searching fingers . . .

"Okay." This near, she could hear the harsh hitching of his breath, smell the blood soaking his shirt. "Sit up, I can't—"

Biting back pain-sounds, she struggled to comply and at last got herself turned around and sitting so he could reach her. The first shaky cut went through the blanket into her arm.

Startled, she cried out. "Shh!" he warned, and pulled the knife back. But the next cut was no less vigorous. "I'm sorry," he gasped. "But there's no time for—"

"Just get the damned tape off me," she grated out. "I don't care if you cut my arms off. It surprised me, is all."

At last the blankets fell away. Next he slit the tape from her arms, which produced an unpleasant surprise in a night that had already been full of them: She couldn't move.

And the man—Randy, his name was, Randy Dodd—could appear again at any moment.

Suddenly she began sobbing, hating it, hating herself, but unable to stop, because she'd gotten so far, she'd gotten free, and now none of it was going to make any difference.

"I can't move," she wept. "They're all . . ."

"Hey," said Sam. "They're asleep, that's all. Your arms and legs are just . . ."

A cough cut his words off as he slid down, tried to sit up again, and gave up the effort, collapsing with a hand pressed to his middle. Creased with pain, his face went even whiter. In the moonlight, his lips looked nearly black.

The sight shut her tears off abruptly. Was it just a few hours ago that she'd written him off because he wouldn't be able to help her? Yet now, suddenly, keeping him alive felt almost as important as surviving herself.

Because they were together against Randy, and an ally in that fight seemed desperately required; she didn't see why that should be, but it was. It just was. That Randy shouldn't win. "Sam?"

The feeling was coming back to her arms and legs, ferocious prickling and tingling that was much worse than not being able to feel them at all. But they moved.

Tentatively she lifted one arm and then the other, flexed her fingers as much as she could, tried getting her feet under her. *Up, big fella,* Chip Hahn used to say whenever he hauled himself out of a chair after a long session at the computer. Chip . . . She hadn't thought about him in hours, not since she looked for him outside the bar.

A fine assistant you turned out to be, she thought at him, with a flash of the old irritation she used to feel when he screwed up. Which, she had to admit now, he almost never did.

But that thought seemed so irrelevant, she dismissed it almost at once. Because wherever he was, he wasn't beat up and captive, held by some guy who would kill you as soon as look at you.

Another burst of resentment made her lips tighten, then all thought of Chip was gone, along with everything else back in her old life, the one she'd been snatched out of.

Because now everything was different. "Sam?" she said again, then got to her feet and managed to totter a few steps.

The boat moved gently in the water, the wind had gone down, and the sky, fully cleared now, spread overhead thick with stars.

Still no sign of Randy. What he might be doing, she had no idea; digging graves, maybe. The thought sent her to Sam's side again, where she crouched urgently.

"Sam? Listen to me. Do you know how to run the boat? How to start it?"

No reply. She shook his shoulder gently, drew back with a little gasp when even that slight motion produced fresh blood on the front of his shirt. He roused with difficulty.

"Can't go . . . now. Tide's too low. Can you . . . water?"

She got up. Everything hurt, her wrist most of all, but now she thought maybe it wasn't broken, because she could move it and the swelling at least wasn't getting any worse.

And water was a good, a wonderful, idea; her tongue felt like a dry bone. "Cabin . . ." Sam muttered.

Turning, she confronted the dark hatchway. The notion of going down there at all repelled her; if he returned and shut her in there . . .

But of course that's where the water would be. Food, too, although the idea of eating was disgusting. The thought returned that if Randy came back while she was down there, he could trap her there.

The fear of what he might do with her then made her stomach roll lazily and her throat close with fright. On the other hand, there might be more than food and water down there.

Randy might've stashed a weapon, maybe even a

gun. Carolyn didn't know how to shoot a gun, had in fact never even held one. She was afraid of them.

But he didn't know that. Swallowing past the cottony-thick terror that was so all-consuming it felt like it might smother her all by itself, she put both hands on the frame pieces around the hatchway opening and started down quickly, before she could lose her nerve.

The cabin was a tiny, low-ceilinged enclosure with a small filmy plastic window, a low cupboard, and the table on sawhorses. Moonlight through the square of window plastic showed a crumpled bag of Cheetos and a half-eaten pack of Ring Dings on the table.

Despite her belief that she wasn't hungry, she crammed one of the Ring Dings into her mouth. Chemical-tasting fake sweetness clogged her throat, but she forced it down.

It gagged her, but she made it stay there. The stink in the cabin was hideous, even with the hatchway door open. Squinting around, she saw why:

A plastic bucket on the floor was coated with ancient fish scales. Unidentifiable stuff stained the rough table. Cleaning and gutting tools, some with toothed blades and others with edges so sharp they glinted even in the thick gloom, hung from nails.

A plastic gallon jug stood in one corner; she grabbed it and cautiously sniffed its spout. Water . . . She drank greedily, then spied a quart bottle of Wild Turkey by one of the sawhorse legs.

Thank you, God. . . . She tipped the bottle up and took a long, warming swallow, felt the alcohol hit her and spread out through her nerve endings, and took another.

Then she caught sight of the scrapbook. Sticking out of a large canvas duffel, its corner looked at first like a sheet of cardboard; she almost missed it.

Even as she approached the bag, she thought only that it might contain a gun, or perhaps a cell phone. Her own phone was missing along with the rest of her bag's contents, and the bag itself.

Still in the car trunk, maybe, or in a trash can somewhere. She didn't care. Hastily she rummaged in the duffel.

A tattered sweater came out, some socks and underwear, a can of mosquito repellent. A few T-shirts, threadbare jeans, sneakers, and . . . a black official-looking folder.

She opened it, found papers in an envelope. A Canadian passport, the name on it unfamiliar, the photograph recognizably Randy Dodd.

There was a driver's license, also Canadian. And a bankbook in French, which Carolyn neither read nor spoke.

She tucked them away again, not wanting Randy Dodd to know she'd been down here, and reached out for the scrapbook to put it back where she'd found it, as well.

As she did so, it fell open. A clipping slid out. Stapled to it was a photograph.

Not a newspaper photograph. Carolyn glanced at it and felt her gorge rise; reflexively, she grabbed the Wild Turkey bottle again. The alcohol made her eyes water, blurring the face of the girl in the picture.

Unfortunately, it didn't obscure the rest of her body. Or what was left of it . . .

Hideously, Carolyn felt her working instincts kick in with a cold surge of excitement. The clipping was a year-old story from a small-town newspaper in Georgia, detailing the disappearance of a local girl.

FAMILY IN LIMBO AS VANISH ANNIVERSARY LOOMS, yelled the headline. Carolyn didn't bother reading the rest. She didn't have time, and anyway, she knew what it would say, so much so that she could have written it herself.

It said what they all said. It said everyone still hoped the girl had just run away, that after all this time she was alive.

Even though they knew she wasn't. Carolyn flipped through the rest of the scrapbook, knowing what she would find: girls in graves, girls who were about to be in graves, girls who had been in graves but who'd been removed from them.

Six in all. Two in Georgia, three in South Carolina, one in Alabama, all vanished over a period of eighteen months. The last one had disappeared in a Walmart parking lot, in broad daylight.

All had long black hair like Carolyn's, except for one whose hair color could not any longer be determined by anyone who hadn't already known her.

Not from the photograph, or in any other way. Carolyn closed the scrapbook with hands she would positively not allow to tremble, put it back in the duffel, picked up the water jug and the Wild Turkey bottle.

She stumbled back up on deck and crouched by Sam, tipped the jug to his lips. In her mind's eye, all those dead girls watched her carefully, waiting to see what she would do.

For them. For herself. Sam drank thirstily, then gasped and signaled enough. She broke off a piece of the chocolate snack and showed it to him.

"Can you eat? Maybe you should . . ." But to this he shook his head firmly; she hesitated, then ate the other Ring Ding herself.

"Do you want some of this?" She held up the Wild Turkey.

He hesitated, licking his lips, but refused this, too. "Maybe I shouldn't," he said with a strange little laugh. "I might have something kind of . . . important to do."

She didn't like the sound of that. She took another sizable swig herself, capped the bottle, and put it aside. "Sam, we've got to get out of here."

He frowned, said nothing. "While he's gone, Sam," she said urgently. "We've got to move the boat out of here, or get off it before he comes back."

It had been maybe an hour now that Randy had been gone, though she had no way of measuring time. Her watch had smashed when she landed on her wrist, and Sam wasn't wearing one.

She inspected him again. He was breathing, and his color—at least as far as she could tell—seemed better, his lips not so bluish-black and his cheeks less papery-looking.

Though that could be the growing moonlight, as the fog thinned and the sky cleared. She picked his wrist up and tried to find his pulse, but she didn't know how to take it, and what would she do about it anyway, whatever it was?

"Sam." His eyelids flickered, but there was still no reply, and she had to hurry.

"Sam, I've got to leave here, I've got to try to find someone to help us, I can't—"

The water would be frigid, and all she could see of shore was dark, the big old trees and whatever lived in them. A person could die out there, especially in this cold, and she was not so stupid as to think she could survive just by wishing it so.

But staying here . . . It just wasn't possible. Not if she wanted to live. "Sam, I'm going. I'll try to come back for you, I'll find someone and tell them . . ."

The boat rocked gently in the dark waves. She shook Sam's shoulder gently. Muttering, he woke. "No. You can't . . ."

Leave me, she thought he meant. "I'm sorry, I don't want to, but—"

It was only thirty feet or so to shore. Wincing, he opened his eyes. "Tide's running out," he whispered. "Too fast. It'll take you. . . ."

A terrible suspicion struck her. Rising, she hurried to the rail and peered over. In the moonlight the water's surface was a bright, ruffled expanse, like aluminum foil smoothing and then crinkling again.

Not too bad-looking, really, and there were plenty of rocks sticking up out of it. So even if it turned out to be deep, she could stagger from one to the next. . . .

"Don't do it." His voice was an anxious whisper, followed by a cough.

You just don't want me to leave, she thought rebelliously. *You just can't stand it, that somebody else might get to . . .*

But then she looked straight down, saw the water

against the boat's side rushing along . . . racing along. On the surface, it was flat. But . . .

No, she thought. *Oh, please no.*

Because Sam was right, she'd never make it. Not that it was so far, and the rocks were there, all right. But the water . . . the water was running like a river. A fast river.

"Rocks . . . too slippery," he whispered. "Don't . . ."

Wildly she looked around for something to help her, to hold on to, the tree that the boat was hidden under, maybe. Grimly she managed to climb onto the rail, straining up hard with both arms, trying to reach one of the thicker branches overhead.

But when she grabbed it, it snapped crisply off in her hand, knocking her off balance. Arms windmilling, she fought to stay upright, then sidestepped crazily and fell off the rail, tumbling to the hard deck.

Ouch. No more Wild Turkey for you, missy.

But even being stone-cold sober wouldn't make those branches any sturdier. They were as brittle as old bones.

Like yours will be . . . She struggled up, bolts of panic invading her at the thought that any minute now, he would return.

For one thing, as Sam had pointed out, that tide was moving. On its way out now, but when it came back in, the water would be too deep for Randy to slog through it.

And he must know that, too, that he had only a window of opportunity, that the water would be too . . .

Squinting into the darkness, she spotted a thin, pale line running across the water to the shore. A rope.

She hadn't noticed it earlier, but now she saw one end of it was tied to a cleat on the boat's front end. So if she untied it . . .

He wouldn't be able to follow it back. She scrambled back up onto the rail, inched along until she was nearly to the rope. The boat's rocking threatened to push her off the narrow board she perched on, as with stiff, numb fingers she fumbled at the knot, tearing at the rope looped tightly and, worse, so unfamiliarly in the metal cleat.

The knot didn't budge. Carolyn kept at it, nearly weeping with frustration. How, how were you supposed to untie this thing? She fought with the loose end, pulling and pushing it.

Still the knot held, and though she went on battling it, in her heart Carolyn Rathbone began to know it was hopeless. That she hadn't quite yet joined the company of girls in graves but that she would, soon.

That it was only a matter of time.

Trudging along the gravel road in the dark, Jake tried to keep up with Bella, who had apparently been running marathons and taking fitness classes from Arnold Schwarzenegger when not busy scouring the kitchen sink.

"Just . . . wait up a minute, will you?"

Bella turned impatiently. "Low tide," she said quietly, "is nearly over. It's just about finished running out."

And after that, the tide would begin coming in again. . . . It had taken longer than Jake expected to get here, up thirty miles of Route 1 in the fog.

Which was now clearing. "So if we want to get there—" Bella went on.

"Yes, yes, we want to get there," Jake interrupted. But she also wanted enough strength left to lift a weapon, if necessary.

"How much farther, do you think?" she asked, then stumbled headlong over a hunk of driftwood onto a stony beach.

"Shh," said Bella. They'd emerged suddenly from the trees. Jake saw the sky opening up overhead, and the sharp scent of the evergreens dissolved all at once into the smell of the sea.

"Now what?" The sky was nearly clear, but mist still lay along the beach and on the water's surface. Behind them, droplets pattered from the branches, the fir boughs rustling and sighing.

Suddenly the fog's curtain parted at ground level. Islands appeared, their shorelines dark edges of rocks and seaweed. Jake crept up beside Bella.

The sandbar should be showing now, a trail leading to Digby Island. But there wasn't one, only dark water. "Are you sure this is the place?"

"Oh, yes." Bella began walking again, striding away down the narrow strip of beach. "But there's no sandbar, is there?"

Jake followed. "So, what happened? It didn't just—"

Disappear. They didn't do that, did they? It was indeed low tide; most of the beach was covered in slippery, slimy rockweed so treacherous that they had to pick their way.

Through the weed mats, huge granite slabs stuck up, jagged obstructions alternating with smooth, gleaming platforms that were even more dangerous. Slip on one of them, crack your skull on another, and bingo, that's all she wrote.

"Look." Jake followed Bella's gesture to where a patch of paler sand spread out. Overhead, the moon pushed through, making the patch glimmer.

It was a sandbar. They'd just missed seeing it at first. But once spotted in the gloom, it was as clear as a marked trail.

Small, chaotic waves broke on it, lacy white. Jake lurched forward excitedly toward what looked to be easy walking, unbroken by rocks or weeds. Maybe this wasn't going to be such a difficult project after—

"Wait." Bella's hand stopped her. "Here's what we should do."

What? Jake thought, irritated. *You're going to tell me—*

Bella went on quietly. "We make sure they're out there. We try to make sure they're okay. We use your cell to call Bob Arnold. Then we sit tight and let the people who do this kind of thing for a living take charge of it." She eyed Jake calmly. "All right? Because we should agree in advance on what we're doing."

Which made sense. "Well . . ." Jake began uncertainly. What she wanted to do was charge out there, guns a-blazin.'

Well, one gun, anyway. Biting her lip, she stared across the sandbar. If he was here, Randy Dodd had been smart. But just as he had when he got the speeding ticket Chip Hahn had found, Randy had made a mistake.

Two mistakes, really: he'd left a blank notebook

page in the Dodd House, not a map but the ghost of one, brought to life again by Bella when for once in her life she'd spread some dirt instead of cleaning it up.

And you took my son, she thought at him, staring into the night. *That was your biggest mistake.*

"Fine," she said. "But if they're not okay, then we're going to plan B, and I'll be in charge of it."

With that, she took a step forward, tripped over a chunk of driftwood, and fell headlong onto the stones again. The satchel she carried, with her phone and a flashlight in it, flew from her hand, landing with a tinkling crash.

The flashlight, she thought as her cheek smacked hard stone. But it wasn't the flashlight smashing, she realized in the next moment; it was the phone. Meanwhile . . .

Pushing up painfully from the wet, cold rocks, she grabbed the cell phone and raised her head just in time to see the flashlight rolling toward the water. "Bella . . ."

But Bella was busy grabbing up the satchel with one hand and Jake's arm with the other. "Come on," she hissed. "If he's nearby he could've heard that."

The flashlight kept rolling, a small dark tube moving down the sharp slope to where the waves lapped. But not all the way—a rock stuck up from the water's edge.

The flashlight smacked the rock with a small, sharp *click* and went on, its yellow beam like an arrow shining directly at the sandbar.

Or if you looked at it from Randy Dodd's point of view, at Jake and Bella.

"Get it," Jake whispered, struggling to rise. But something was stopping her, something around her ankle. It burned. . . .

Bella scampered down the beach, crouched swiftly, snatched the flashlight up, and snapped it off in one quick motion. But too late; an answering light appeared on the far shore of one of the islands out there.

Bobbing and bouncing, it proceeded swiftly toward the pale, shining path of the moonlit sandbar, then snapped off. A dark shape where it had been started across the bar toward them.

"Quick," said Bella, tugging at Jake's arm. "Get up."

But whatever was tight around Jake's leg wouldn't let go. She twisted to try getting a glimpse of it, then wished very hard that she hadn't, because the driftwood she'd tripped over wasn't merely a chunk, she realized now.

It was an entire waterlogged tree trunk. Washed up here by the tide, it must have been leaning precariously, propped up on a thin stick of branch now lying a few feet away.

And when Jake tripped over the branch, she'd broken it, so the tree trunk had rolled right onto her ankle. Sitting up, she strained forward, pushing with both hands against the massive old tree's dead white corpse.

It didn't budge. The shape across the water bobbed nearer. Now it was halfway across. "Bella, I can't—"

Bella bent beside her, saw the problem. "Here. Dig. Do it fast."

She shoved the cup top from their thermos bottle into Jake's hands, crouched, and began digging furiously herself. Jake gouged sand and pebbles from around her trapped ankle, flung them away, and dug up the next cupful.

A depression formed. But there was her whole foot remaining to be unearthed. . . . It struck her that this was serious.

"Go," she said, thinking about the gun in her sweater. In reply, Bella just grabbed Jake's pants leg and pulled.

But the chunk of tree might as well have been an anchor, as meanwhile a new sound came from the sandbar: boots, releasing one after another from each wet step with an awful sucking sound.

A low, scrubby screen of sea grass still hid them from that direction, but soon whoever was approaching would reach it. Bella gazed around wildly, then snatched up an old plank, part of some dock or collapsed boat shed that had floated or blown here.

It was about six feet long and not sturdy-looking at all, but it was something. She shoved one end under the tree trunk. "Lean back. Out of the way . . ."

Then she jumped on the other end with both feet. The tree trunk lurched up a scant inch.

"Now," Bella said urgently as Jake scrambled back, kicking with one foot and dragging the other. The instant her ankle was free, the old board snapped, hurling Bella backward and letting the tree trunk fall again.

Backpedaling, Bella reached out and snagged Jake's collar as the massive, waterlogged thing slammed down with a thud. Half crawling, Jake let herself be hauled along across the wet stones toward the relative shelter of the trees.

Scooting into the brush, they hustled back from the exposed beach area until Jake fell into a mucky depression full of wet leaves and slimy washed-up masses of rotted seaweed.

"Shh," Bella whispered, crawling into the depression, too.

"Get down," Jake whispered, yanking Bella's sleeve. Through a scrim of weeds between the beach and the trees, they watched as a man stepped from the sandbar onto the beach itself.

He stopped, peering around, then spotted the tree trunk and hurried toward it. Leaning down to examine it, he picked up half the broken plank, swung it experimentally a couple of times, and flung it away.

Jake felt a moment of relief at the thought that she wasn't about to be bludgeoned to death with a hunk of wood. But then—

Then she saw what was in his other hand: an iron boat hook. *The better to bash you with, my dear . . .*

"Bella?" But Bella didn't reply, staring at the man who now came closer, following their footprints. Swinging the boat hook.

Jake dug in her sweater pocket. She hadn't wanted to shoot Randy at all, since if she did he might not be able to lead them to Sam and Carolyn.

Now, though, things were really getting serious. She put her hand in her pocket.

No gun. Disbelief flooded her. She'd put it there, and she hadn't taken it out, so—

Fifty yards distant, Randy Dodd paused, looking down at his feet. Seeing something. Picking it up, he peered around slowly, tucked it into a pocket of whatever it was that he was wearing. An army jacket, it looked like.

The .32, she realized. It must've fallen from her own pocket when the tree trunk hit her or when she was writhing on the sand, trying to get free.

And now Randy Dodd had it.

He began walking toward them again, taking his time, making sure he didn't lose sight of the footprints they'd left for him. He had a slight limp but it didn't impede his progress. Still swinging the boat hook, he reached the far edge of the sea-grass meadow.

Close enough now for Jake to see the confident smile on his face. Confidence, mingled with anticipation . . . But then a sound came suddenly from above and behind them, a low, guttural roar that rose very fast to a sharp *whap-whap-whap!*

It was a helicopter. Coast Guard, probably; the minute the sky cleared, they'd have begun sending out search crews by water and air.

Bob would've told them about the map tracing from the Dodd House even if he put little confidence in it himself.

But Digby Island was on the Canadian side of the border, and like it or not, the Coasties weren't going to provoke an incident. They couldn't chase bad guys to Canada any more than Los Angeles cops, say, could follow their own suspects into Mexico.

Randy's shape vanished as he crouched by some boulders at the water's edge. From above, motionless, he would seem to be one of them and nothing more, or so he obviously hoped.

Still, Jake's heart lifted hopefully as the craft came

in low. She didn't know where the international line was, precisely, but they obviously did, and for an exultant moment it seemed they were coming straight at her, wind from the copter's rotors ruffling the water and searchlights crisscrossing on it.

Minutes passed, and then more of them, as the craft swept back and forth. But it never came near Digby. And even if it had, an air search at night on the water was no guarantee of anything being found.

The strobing lights stabbed the night again and again. But they showed nothing but waves and the roiling, river-like rush of the racing currents. At last the near-deafening sound faded, the helicopter and its hoped-for salvation whapping away back toward the west.

Staring, Jake couldn't believe it. *Come back,* she wanted to shout, but of course she couldn't; Randy still had that gun. Once the aircraft was gone, he resumed his progress, slapping the boat hook he still carried into the palm of his free hand.

Something about the helicopter must've spooked him, though, because after only a few more steps he stopped again. Then he turned and went back toward the shore and the sandbar he'd come from, as if he'd suddenly thought of something.

As if, pleasurable as it might've been, he'd realized that it just wasn't worth it to find them and kill them. Watching him go, Bella let her breath out. "Now what?"

Jake shifted painfully. "I don't know. I guess he must think the helicopter might come back."

Another thought prickled at the edge of her mind, but she was too cold, scared, and hurting to be able to concentrate on it. "He's got my gun. And I think my ankle is sprained."

Also, they were sitting in a muck pit. "Let's try to get out of here," she said, feeling heartsick. Because the helicopter had probably saved their lives by stopping Randy's search for them, but it hadn't done anything for Sam.

In fact, for him it had probably made things worse, because now Randy knew people were after him, and that they had at least a general idea of where he might be.

Not that we've helped in that department, either, Jake told herself bitterly as she and Bella clambered up the side of the gunk-filled hole in the beach. With the copter gone, the night felt empty and desolate. The moon shone down coldly, turning the beach to a silvery sheet.

The car was half a mile away and no more help was coming anytime soon; not for them, not for Sam or for Carolyn Rathbone. Or for Chip Hahn, wherever the hell he'd gotten to.

Jake pulled her smashed phone out and tried it. But nothing happened when she opened it. She hurled it away. *Sam, I'm . . .*

"Sorry," she began aloud. "Sorry, sorry . . ."

But Bella didn't let her finish. "If your ankle really is sprained, and not broken . . ."

"Oh, there's a happy thought," said Jake as regret went on flooding her. In retrospect she could think of a dozen things she should have done differently, but now it was too late for any of them.

"If it's only sprained, then what's good for it is a soak in cold water."

Bella wiped her muck-smeared hands on the front of her jacket. Jake put her weight testingly on her bad foot. The result was not good in either case.

"Bella, you've got to get to the car. Get out of here and get help, send them . . ."

Bella just looked at her. "He knows we are here and he knows we're not just kids looking for an isolated place to park, have a party. To drink and fool around, and so on."

"Yes, I realize that. He found my gun, heard the helicopter. He knows pretty soon people will be back, that even though they didn't find him this time . . ."

"Daylight will come," Bella finished for her. "He needs to be away before then. And if he has Sam and that girl—"

She didn't need to finish. Two hostages would only slow him down. Bella bent and seized Jake's arm. "Just come on along with me now. You need to soak that ankle."

Jake let herself be grabbed hold of and urged forward. If she didn't, she thought she might just sit again. "Bella, I'm not sure I—"

"We've got to." Supporting most of Jake's weight, Bella put her shoulder under Jake's arm and took a step, and then another.

Toward the sandbar. "The tide's turning," she said. "It's why he started back. We've got to get over there, too, before the water's too deep to walk across."

In the moonlight, her bony face was terrified. But her words didn't match her look. "Once we're there, I'm not sure what we'll do," she said.

She's still scared to death, Jake realized. *Like me.*

"But if we don't go," Bella continued, "you know as well as I do he's going to kill them."

It was enough to get Jake moving. Letting go of Bella, she tested the ankle once more, winced, and sucked in a breath as it signaled its determination not to function, or at least not without torturing her.

Screw you, she thought at it, and at any other body parts that thought they could run the show just because they happened to be attached. Then she took another step. It wasn't quite so painful this time. *Probably because I've already severed all the important nerves in there,* she thought.

Moments later she stepped into the cold salt water, now already lapping at the edges of the sandbar. As Bella had said, the tide was coming in.

Soon it would cover the temporary land bridge leading to Digby. But an icy bath, just as Bella had also said, did indeed make Jake's ankle feel better. And . . .

Sam. She couldn't leave him here. She just couldn't. Not without at least trying . . .

"Fine. Let's take it a step at a time," she gasped to Bella, who went on struggling along beside her.

So they leaned on each other and did.

The helicopter woke Chip Hahn out of a frozen half-sleep. He'd been drifting out here for hours, it felt like, in the cold, fogbound darkness, just letting the tide and currents take him where they wanted to go, in the engineless boat.

He'd had no other choice. Even waiting for daylight wasn't a great bet, he'd figured out, since when it did come he might find himself in open water.

On the ocean. Far out on it, since for all he knew, that was where the current he was riding went. It sped him along as if an engine were pushing him, he just couldn't tell to where. When the copter came, he'd thought for an instant that he was rescued.

But no such luck. The searchlights had come within a few hundred yards of where he'd stood in his small, disabled vessel, yelling and waving.

But that few feet might as well have been miles, for all the good the searchers had done him. They simply hadn't quite seen him, hadn't quite been close enough.

He sank back against the transom. The jagged rocks and arrowhead-shaped trees he was beginning to be able to make out in the moonlight now that the fog had cleared were all he could see. He was in a cove, surrounded on three sides by a pale shoreline, here and there a few feet of beach studded with indistinct shapes and a lot of trees behind them.

The shapes were probably rocks. With the life jacket on, he might be able to swim to them. What he would do then, he didn't know. Getting to the shore would be hard enough, but getting from there to any kind of help could be an even more difficult task.

He didn't know how far it might be, or in which direction. He wouldn't even know which way to try. *Useless,* he berated himself bitterly, *just a freaking useless little . . .*

Then he saw the fishing boat. It floated very nearby, tucked under a dead, fallen tree whose matted branches formed a sort of awning over the water.

No light, no sound came from the vessel. Just a dark shape in a dark place. The waves lapping at its side made a faint gleaming line in the moonlight.

Soundless, ghostlike. Chip wasn't making any sound, either, and he resolved to go on not making any for as long as he could. The current kept rushing him toward those branches and the boat.

And because his engine was dead and he couldn't steer at all without it, there was nothing he could do about that. Or . . . *Wait a minute,* Chip thought. He was under power. Just not engine power.

Even as he thought this he was lifting his rump and planting it on the transom seat, gripping the Evinrude's throttle arm in his cold, stiff hand. Turn to the right, the boat's nose veered left, powered by the current. Turn to the left . . .

Oh, hell, he thought miserably, *I can do something.* Which meant he had to; for one thing, impact would occur in about five seconds if he didn't. Noisy impact . . .

Desperately he hauled on the tiller; obediently, the little boat swerved around the thick, white, dead branch hanging down in front of him like a road-block.

Holding his breath, Chip felt it go by with inches to spare. *Thankyouthankyouthankyou,* he thought. But it wasn't over yet.

Ahead hung a thick, dense curtain of thinner branches. *I'm not the right guy for this. Plump and bookish. And timid . . .*

A stump rose out of the water at him. He pulled hard again. This time he was rewarded by a patch of clear water. Chip gasped inwardly as his little craft slid silently up against the larger vessel.

All silent above, too. Chip wanted to call out, to find out this very second if Carolyn was up there and still alive. Sam, too, maybe. But he didn't dare make a sound. Any instant now, he expected Randy Dodd's grinning face to pop up at him from the fishing boat's stern.

Randy, whose own brother, Roger, said Randy was a killer. That while Randy was away, he had gotten a taste for it . . .

Chip shivered as the current wedged his small boat tighter against the stern of the larger one, between it and half a tree trunk, broken off like some massive white bone slanting down into the water alongside him.

He swallowed hard. He had no plan, no weapon, and no way to call for help. Also, he noticed tardily— but there was not much he could've done about it earlier, was there?—no way to run.

Which was the option he would certainly have chosen had it existed. As it was, however, a metal ladder hung from the fishing boat's transom like an invitation.

Not quite close enough . . . but a line ran from a cleat on the fishing boat's rail, extending toward shore. If Chip could grab that, he could pull himself . . .

Here I am, the silent boat seemed to be saying to him. *Here I am, kid. . . . Wanna come aboard?*

No, Chip thought. *I most definitely do not want to.* But his hand reached out anyway. His fingers grasped the line and pulled his own craft nearer to the ladder.

Hand over hand, he worked his way along the line. It bounced tautly each time he grabbed it. At last he pulled his body over onto the ladder and began climbing.

He was about halfway up the ladder when he heard something.

Carolyn lay exhausted and beaten, one rubbed-raw hand still on the rope knotted in the cleat, when she felt it tighten. It began quivering rhythmically as somewhere out in the darkness some other hand gripped it and began moving along it.

Randy. Randy was coming back . . . now. With her breath coming in harsh sobs, she rushed to crouch by Sam and tell him.

Sam's eyes opened. "Below. Get below . . . find . . ."

His words snapped her to alertness, finally; she knew he was right. This wasn't over; not yet. Help hadn't come, though she'd screamed her lungs out as the helicopter flew near.

Just not near enough. Still, if she followed Sam's advice now, she might not need help at all, because if Randy was coming onto the boat and she couldn't get off, she would just have to . . .

Ambush him. Go down there in the cabin and wait. He would climb aboard, notice her missing, and . . .

Stick his head through the hatchway, maybe. Or lunge through with his entire body.

She would have to be ready. And now, as the quivering of the taut rope grew stronger, she thought that possibly she could be. After all, booze and junk food and a rancid-tasting jug of stale water probably weren't the only things stowed down there.

No, whispered the girls. The girls in graves, their voices a whispered chorus of trembling eagerness . . .

So long denied. So coldly silent. Until now.

No, there are . . .

Knives. Fish knives. Big, sharp ones.

Chapter 7

By the time they'd gotten halfway across the sandbar, Jake was having second thoughts. But when she voiced them, Bella shook her head stubbornly.

"We're all the way out here. We might as well get a look at him," she said as she trudged grimly ahead.

We are insane, Jake thought. But she went on slogging through the wet sand, too, since for one thing if Bella wouldn't back out of this, she couldn't, either.

"Yeah, well, what I'm worried about now is that he's going to get a look at us," she whispered. "And then he's going to take a shot at us."

"We're here. He's here. Sam might be here," insisted Bella. "I'm not going back."

It was still dark, a couple of hours yet before sunrise, and as cold as the grave out here. Jake told herself firmly to think of some other comparison, but she couldn't.

"You," she told Bella, "have even less sense than I do, did you know that?"

As she spoke, she stepped into a foot-deep hole that she had not seen because it was underwater. This put her soaked-to-the-skin-and-chilled-to-the-bone line right up around her hip.

"Oof," she said, catching herself just in time to keep the line from rising swiftly above her head. Bella seized her arm and held it.

"Yes, I do know that. You're the one who hadn't noticed until now. But never mind. That's it, over there."

Digby, she meant. Moonlight slanted across the expanse of water, picking out the shapes of the trees on the island ahead. To the left they were pointed firs, cut-out black arrowheads against the sky.

To the right the vegetation looked thicker. Jake imagined tangles of brushy softwood, mountain ash and sumac mingled with blackberry vines; that's what wild land grew around here. With a machete, the going might be difficult.

Without one, *difficult* was a mild term for what

bushwhacking through it would be. And that, of course, was the direction Bella was aiming toward.

But the trees and brush weren't what she pointed at. "Boat," she said quietly.

Jake nodded silently as she spotted it, too, half hidden in the gloom. It was a squat, blocky shape like a kid's drawing of a fishing boat: wheelhouse, rail, a few bright, sloppy little waves running along its side.

It was pulled in under a long-ago-fallen tree, which made a canopy over it. Nothing moved on it. Bella stopped, staring at the dark, silent vessel sitting there motionless.

Bad ankle or no, the sight of the boat banished Jake's pains. She shook Bella's hand off her arm. "Sam could be on there." She started forward.

Bella caught her. "Probably he is. Maybe the girl, too."

Carolyn Rathbone. "But unless you're planning to get them both killed and us with them . . ."

On the boat, a dark shape moved briefly. Jake kept her eyes on it, but it didn't move again. Maybe it was just a shadow, the light changing as the boat shifted in the tide.

Which, she noticed nervously, had now risen to mid-calf on her frozen legs, running fast. Its pressure was an insistent shove whose ripples sent regular stabs of frozen pain all the way to her backbone.

"We've found them," Bella went on. "We can tell people where they are now. That's what we came here to do, and—"

"Are you kidding?" Jake turned in disbelief. "I thought you wanted to do something about this.

We're all the way out here, we've got them in our sights, and—"

"What sights?" Bella demanded fiercely. "We don't have any weapons, we're soaked and half frozen, what do you suggest?"

Jake said nothing. Bella went on: "I said we should see. We have. But, Jacobia, that man has *nothing* to lose."

Jake felt her body slump in defeat. But then she took stock of her surroundings again, and disappointment changed to something else.

Anxiety, maybe. Or . . . fright. Because in the few moments that they'd been standing there, the water now rushing over the sandbar had quickened to a torrent. Deeper, too. Much deeper . . .

"Come on." Bella had turned her back on the boat. "We've got to get somewhere that has a phone, so we can—"

"Right." Jake pulled one foot out of the sandbar, which had become less solid and more . . . liquidy, sort of. It sucked at her shoe, nearly pulling it off, when she took a step.

And then another step, even more difficult, as if something down there was pulling hard in its own direction; harder, even, than Jake was pulling in hers.

"Bella? I think we've got a . . ."

Situation. Because the tide had turned, and as it came in, it wanted to pull everything in its path along with it. To that implacable surge of water, she and Bella were pieces of flotsam, just stuff to be hustled along with the rest that was lying along the shore.

The word *futile* popped into Jake's head as she made yet another attempt to haul a foot out of yet another ice-cold, salt-water-based, ferociously sucking sand pit. Then everything else left her thoughts except trying to escape.

Trying and failing. The tall, bony woman beside her fought also to make some sort of headway. With each step, her foot made a sound like . . . like the top of a sealed jar of something glutinous being opened.

Ahead, the dark shore they'd come from beckoned. Half a mile or so past that, the car waited. Five minutes after they reached it, they'd be in St. Stephen.

From there they could call help: cops, ambulances if necessary.

Please don't let ambulances be necessary.

But for right now, the task was to get to shore before the tide got too much higher. And at the moment, the tide was winning.

"Listen, I think we'd better—"

"What? Take a rest? Pray for deliverance?" Bella gasped. The ropy-armed old housekeeper, who could haul a full-sized vacuum cleaner up and down two steep flights of stairs without seeming a bit inconvenienced, sounded winded.

The water was up to their waists. Jake's feet were so numb with cold, she couldn't even tell anymore when they were stuck in sand-muck and when they were being released. The sucking, slurping sounds had also vanished, replaced by the gurgle of surging water; only a few inches of forward motion every so often told her they were making any progress at all.

And the shore, as best she could estimate in the dark before dawn, was still a good hundred yards or so distant.

"No," she said with what little breath she could spare. "We don't have time to rest."

As for getting saved, previous life experience had clued her in pretty thoroughly to the likelihood of that possibility: i.e., not very. "How deep do you suppose the water gets here at high tide, anyway?"

"Twenty feet," Bella exhaled. She seized Jake's hand, tried pulling her forward again, then stumbled and nearly fell into the waves herself.

Waves, thought Jake. And water, twenty feet of it. Walking, at that point, might not be appropriate. Or possible.

But swimming wouldn't be, either. Bella slogged forward once more, making pretty good headway until another, bigger wave hit her amidships, nearly capsizing her.

Uh-oh, Jake thought. "Bella, I want you to listen to me."

"I'm listening." Bella got her feet back underneath her on the submerged sand, tried another step, and stopped dead, water swirling around her waist.

"What is it you'd like to suggest, Jake? That we walk some more? Because I'm sorry, but I—"

"Yeah, me neither." Walking had indeed dropped off the list of options available.

"No, we're done with that." Overhead, the stars had begun fading. The sky, without becoming any lighter at all, had changed from indigo to a charcoaly hue that meant dawn would come soon. A line of pink edged the eastern horizon.

Jake tried stepping forward again, noticed that her feet were instead making little paddling motions.

Now, too late, she understood why Randy Dodd had turned tail so suddenly.

It wasn't the helicopter that had spooked him, she understood now, though that might've been enough to get him moving all by itself. It was the tide. He'd seen it turning. And he'd known he had to get back across the sandbar while he still could.

The water rose to her armpits. "Bella, we've got to swim for it." A driftwood chunk swirled past. Jake grabbed for it, missed.

"Hah," Bella replied. "Just one small problem."

"What's that?" Another chunk, larger; missed again. But if an even bigger hunk came along, they might be able to—

"I can't swim," said Bella.

Oh, fabulous. "I mean, I don't know how. If you must know," Bella added reluctantly, "I'm afraid of the water."

"Oh. Well. That is unfortunate." A large wave rolled in, and then another. The shoreline looked farther away. Jake's own toes now barely touched the dissolving sandbar.

She tried to keep her voice calm. But it was hard to do with the water all around them getting suddenly so much . . .

Deeper. "Okay, then, maybe you can just hold on to me, and I can—"

A section of tree trunk appeared, bobbing around as it raced at them. Jake let go of Bella, reaching out with both arms for the impromptu life raft. Only at the last moment did she realize:

It really was a tree trunk. A whole one, roots and all, its huge bulk looming menacingly, charging toward them in a blur of churning water and jagged wooden daggers.

"Bella!" Jake grabbed for Bella's arm, too late. The tree trunk rotated lazily, one big broken-off stump section aimed out at them like a battering ram.

Desperately Jake dove, found Bella's legs and wrapped her arms around them, and kicked out hard. Water and sand rasped on her face and arms, filled her ears, and made a gritty, salty mush that forced its way up her nose and between her lips.

In her embrace, Bella's body went horrifyingly limp. Chunks of wooden stuff charged by overhead, as if a whole lumberyard had been emptied down a sluiceway up there. Rocks, gravel, and slick seaweed, all with the consistency of thick pudding, cascaded endlessly.

Or so it seemed. Something hit Jake hard from behind, jolting Bella away from her. Any instant, her lungs would burst. They would, or the water would fill them, unless—

Her foot found a rock, then another. Found it and pushed . . . Her face broke through to the surface. "Bella?"

No sign of her anywhere. "Bella!"

She didn't dare shout. Only a few hundred yards off in the other direction, the dark boat still sat like an evil omen.

"Bella!" Jake's feet found a steadier purchase and balanced on it, her hand dragging something it had found floating beneath the waves . . .

Hair. It was Bella's hair. Jake hauled on it. Bella's bony face popped up, dripping and wheezing.

"Shhh. He might be—"

Listening. Or creeping up on us, right this minute . . .

Bella nodded wordlessly. "Thank you," she gasped when she got her breath back. "That was very resourceful of you."

"You're welcome." Besides nearly drowning them, the rushing water had pushed them nearer to shore. So when they emerged, it was just possible for them to stagger, limp, lurch, flounder, and in places flat-out crawl on their hands and knees back to the beach where they'd started.

So they did that, and all the while Jake thought for sure that Randy Dodd might appear any instant, grinning and shooting. But he didn't, and at last Bella collapsed to the wet sand.

Her henna-red hair, ripped out of its rubber band, hung around her face like a nest of snakes. "I never thought we'd—"

Make it. "Me neither," Jake said, yanking on Bella's arm to get her moving again.

But they had, and they'd found Randy's boat. Sam might be on it. And Chip's friend Carolyn.

Maybe even Chip himself. So all they had to do now was . . .

"I'm so glad you're with me," she told Bella humbly as they stumbled back under a paling sky to where they'd left the car.

"I'm not." Bella's teeth chattered audibly. "I'm cold, I'm wet, and if I don't catch pneumonia, I'll be amazed. I wish," she finished earnestly, "that I was home in my own bed."

With that, she yanked open the car's passenger-side door and fell in. Jake got behind the wheel and pulled the keys from under the seat, hugely glad she hadn't stuck them in her satchel, which she'd lost back on the beach somewhere.

"All I want to do," said Bella, "is put the heat on."

"Me too," agreed Jake, and turned the ignition key.

"Oh, that'll be elegant," said Bella.

Jake turned the key again.

Hauling himself up over the stern of the fishing boat in the thin light of near-dawn, Chip thought he heard stealthy movement again and knew for a certainty that any second, Randy Dodd would appear with a gun in his hand and murder in his heart.

Or a knife. Something. Chip's own hand slipped on the rail and he nearly fell backward, flailing wildly. Then his searching grip latched onto a cleat fastened to the rail . . .

The cleat with the line knotted to it . . . Clinging to it, he clambered past the engine, smelled diesel and the stink of fish. Ahead, the open wheelhouse gaped vacantly, its instruments dark.

A man lay on the deck, his hands clasped over his middle and his back propped against a storage bench set starboard along the rail. Even in the deep gloom, Chip could see that the man's hands were stained with something dark.

Something . . . *unpleasant*. The man didn't move. Chip couldn't even tell if his eyes were open or closed. Tiptoeing forward, he tripped over a bunch of blankets, barely caught himself, stumbled again as a loop of tape stuck in the blankets snagged his shoe.

What's in those blankets? he wondered coldly, not

liking the shape of them. His chilled skin felt suddenly as if extra nerves had sprouted from it, all tuned to something nasty going on here, all bristling with unease.

He made his way to the man on the deck. If it was Randy, then Chip could relax a little.

It wasn't. It was Sam Tiptree: older, larger. A man now. "Sam? It's me, Chip Hahn."

He crouched by the slim, bloody shape. Sam's eyes opened in puzzlement that changed to recognition. "Chip. What're you . . ."

Sam smiled weakly, but then a grimace of pain wrinkled his face. The last time Chip saw Sam, he'd been waving through the back window of a car on its way to Maine.

Sam had been a kid then, with problems that Chip's lonely efforts at friendship couldn't fix. But Sam had still been good company. Hunkered down by him, Chip remembered Sam's standard greeting, when Chip would show up at Sam's door with a couple of skateboards or a new pair of catcher's mitts.

"Yeah, it's me, your old pal the Chipster," Chip said now, trying to sound reassuring. Trying as well to wrap his mind around the change that had happened to Sam while he, Chip, wasn't around to see it. He'd never known anyone as a kid and then seen them as an adult, before. It meant . . .

It meant time was passing, that was all, his mind told him sternly. Which was not exactly an original observation, and by the way, it was passing now, too. *So hop to it, buddy, before . . .*

"Sam, the guy who took you . . . do you know where he is?"

Sam shook his head minutely, biting his lip. The blood on his shirt looked fresh, thick, and shiny. Chip thought briefly about opening the shirt to see what was under it, decided not to. He wouldn't know what to do about it, and the sight of it would only scare him.

And he was already scared enough. *Radio,* he thought. If the boat had one, and he could get the power on, he might be able to get help.

Assuming Randy Dodd wasn't in the cabin right now, waiting. When Chip looked down again, Sam had passed out. His chest rose and fell regularly, but he still didn't look good, and you didn't need to be a brain surgeon like Sam's dad to know so much blood was a bad sign.

Sam moaned faintly. How long, Chip wondered, beginning to feel panicky again, before things really got bad? An hour, a few minutes? Less?

He turned toward the roughly framed doorway to the boat's cabin. No sound came from it. Everything he needed might be down there. First-aid kit, maybe. Some kind of equipment to get help with, a radio, or even some signal flares. And possibly even a gun.

Or his next few steps might be his last. Holding his breath, he straightened. "Sam, I'll get you out of this," he promised, though Sam couldn't hear him.

Sure, his mind added mockingly. *Sure I will.* But Chip wasn't listening anymore, either, so intent was he on spying any flicker of movement from the cabin below, any hint of sound.

Silently he approached the opening. The stealthy sounds he'd heard had been coming from this area of the boat. He wanted to peek past the doorframe, but the best way was surely to just charge through it, shouting and swinging. Maybe he could get a lucky punch in.

Or maybe Carolyn was down there, dead. . . .

But he didn't dare continue to think that way. Instead he looked around at the dark water and the lightening sky.

Small birds swooped batlike near the shore. A humped form, and then another, slid through the waves a hundred yards distant in the other direction.

Porpoises, or the small, graceful minke whales that while doing his pre-visit research he'd learned were numerous in these waters. Too bad the articles he'd read hadn't mentioned killers.

Overhead, the stars were going out as the day came on. There was still no sign of Randy Dodd anywhere. *All right,* Chip told himself. *One, two . . .*

"Yearrgh!" He flung himself at the opening and through it, fists clenched and arms windmilling. As he hurled himself through the hatchway something thudded into his scalp with a hot stabbing pain, dark blood spurting out in a curving arc.

He flung a hand up, grabbing at whatever was stuck there. A curtain of red fell over his eyes, warm and thick. Fear made him strong; one thrust-out foot connected with something soft, while his free hand seized a fistful of something else and—

"Chip! Oh God, Chip, stop, it's me—"

Carolyn. She was alive. He'd have wept, probably, just sat right down and bawled like a baby in a combination of startlement and relief. But he didn't have time. And—

Blinded by the blood streaming into his eyes, he tried again to grab the slippery handle of the thing stuck in his . . ."Gah."

He pulled it out, feeling a shudder of revulsion go up his spine at the sound of bone on metal as it came free. With his breath coming in great, tearing sobs, he swiped an arm over his eyes and peered at it: a knife, a great big thick serrated one.

"Jesus, Carolyn," he managed, and dropped the thing.

She stood a few feet away in the cramped cabin, staring at him through eyes wild with fright, a thin runnel of snot mixed with tears leaking down her lip.

"Sorry," she babbled. "Sorry—oh, Chip, I'm so—"

Grabbing a filthy towel from the low table at the cabin's center, she flung herself at him and began madly dabbing at his bleeding head. "Sorry, sorry . . ."

"Okay." He seized her arms and held her away from him. She was alive. But then he saw what else was on the table.

It was a scrapbook open to a black-and-white snapshot of a woman. A newspaper clipping was pasted in beside the picture.

The woman was dead. Staring, Chip felt his guts shrivel up into themselves as if they, too, wanted nothing more than to be as far as possible from what the photograph represented.

The woman's pose had been carefully, even lovingly, arranged. Her face had been made up and her hair curled inexpertly.

He got to like it, Roger Dodd had said frightenedly of his brother, and now Chip understood. Roger might have been lying about a lot of things, but not about that.

Not about Randy. The woman's eyes were open. Tearing his own gaze from the photo, Chip scanned the filthy cabin for anything they could use. But . . .

No radio, no first-aid kit. "Carolyn."

He grabbed her by the shoulders again. Her whole body was trembling and her eyes looked unfocused, smeared makeup making them raccoonish. Without wanting to, he contrasted the way she looked now to the dead woman in the photograph.

She burst into tears. "Chip, he just grabbed me, I couldn't breathe, I couldn't—"

Suddenly, to his horror, she was hyperventilating. He took her in his arms awkwardly, then wrapped them around her tight.

"Okay," he said into her wet hair. "Okay, now. We'll get out of this, Carolyn, I promise. I'm here now and we'll figure this out. We'll figure it out together."

She drew back, still gasping and shuddering. He pulled some wadded tissues out of his pocket and handed them to her, waited for her to wipe her face.

"Where is he?" Chip asked when she was finished. "It's Randy Dodd, right? And he's alive, just like you said."

She didn't speak. Or couldn't. "Carolyn, do you know where he is?"

"Out there somewhere." She gestured tremulously at the cabin's murky oblong plastic window.

"He's been gone awhile. He'll come back. Chip, can you get the boat started? Can you get us out of here?"

"I don't know. I might be able to start the engine."

Or not. He'd never run anything with a diesel on it. "But we're jammed in here and there're rocks all around. Even with the tide rising . . ."

He peered out the small, cloudy window. The huge, dead limbs of the fallen tree blockaded one whole side of the boat.

"We'll get stuck on the rocks if we don't know what we're doing. He must know a channel in and out of here, but I don't."

Carolyn's face threatened tears again. "But we've got to get away, we can't just sit here and wait for him to—"

Kill us. It was lighter outside, the sky pearly gray. Real sunrise, Chip thought, would be in half an hour or so. The cold light of day would make it easier to see Randy Dodd, when and if he returned. But he would see them, too. Chip put a hand to his head and felt the wound there, still oozing.

Not bad, really. Just messy. But up on deck, Sam Tiptree had a larger hole in him, one that had not stopped bleeding.

"Let's go." Chip put a hand on Carolyn's shoulder to guide her ahead of him through the hatchway. Once on deck, he gave his immediate surroundings a thorough scan in the growing light.

Carolyn crouched by Sam, who wasn't moving. But he was still breathing.

"Did you look around downstairs?" Chip asked her as he opened the lids of storage bins on either side of the deck behind the life rings.

"Yes, I looked everywhere for the best thing to . . ."

Stab you in the head with. "I didn't know it was

you," she added defensively at his look, which he had not been able to hide. "Chip, are you sure you know what you're doing?"

He didn't. But this was no time to worry about it. "I've got a boat. We're going to put Sam in it, okay? Start trying to wrap him in that blanket."

He went on hunting for a weapon. The knife would be fine at close range, but he didn't want to get any nearer to Randy than he had to.

About a thousand miles would be good, and so would a guided missile, he thought as he rooted through the boat's contents. A Styrofoam chest contained crushed beer cans. The cubbies by the wheelhouse were empty.

As he rummaged, Carolyn stared at him in confusion and the beginnings of her old scorn showed. "Chip, what do you mean, you've got a—"

She wasn't doing anything. He abandoned his search, helped her spread the blanket and roll Sam onto it.

Sam roused and tried to help, too, which Chip thought was a positive sign. Not great, but something.

"How do you think I got here?" he asked Carolyn while they tied Sam's belt around the blanket to try keeping it on. "Do you think I swam?"

He waved at the fishing boat's stern. "It's back there. We can get in it and get away."

I hope. There was still the little matter of the stone-dead engine to deal with. "So get moving."

She bridled at his tone. Starting to get her wind back, he realized, and that was a good thing, too. But somehow she seemed to think that just Chip's being there was all she needed.

"Move," he commanded. "We haven't got much time."

"Okay, okay." She knelt alongside Sam again. There was a lot of thick, sticky tape still on the blankets, and she used some of it to secure more of the covering around Sam.

"I don't see why you have to—"

This time he didn't bother answering. The sky was trending rapidly toward full day. And the tide was high again, or nearly. "Let's get him overboard."

Which was going to be a good trick all by itself. Chip looked past the big diesel engine of the fishing boat, over the transom. It was only about a five-foot drop to the smaller craft, but that was plenty far enough to have to try lowering a guy, especially one who seemed to be bleeding to death.

Still, they didn't have much choice. They dragged Sam down the deck, hauled him around so that he hung over the transom feet-first. "Now what?" Carolyn demanded.

"I'm not sure." What did she think, that this kind of a situation came with an instruction booklet?

"Well, it was your idea," she began. "You should—"

He whirled on her, suddenly near tears. "I don't know, okay? I don't know what to do; why should I? You're the one who got us here, you're the one who got so loaded you didn't pay attention to what was going on around you."

Fists clenched, he went on. "I'm the errand boy, remember? The one you can bully and boss around and steal from. But now I'm trying to fix it, as usual, and you are not helping."

His voice was shaking. He didn't bother trying to control it. "So unless you want to end up like that one—"

He pointed at the hatchway. Beyond it in a scrapbook lay the evidence of Randy Dodd's handiwork, what he'd done while he was away. A mental picture of the girl in it—what remained of her—popped back into his head.

Along with something else. "Stay here," he ordered Carolyn as he strode past her, ignoring her shocked expression.

It wasn't fair, what he'd said to her. It hadn't been her fault, and it was mean of him to suggest that it was. Randy Dodd would've found a way to grab her one way or another, the way he'd grabbed the other ones.

Blaming Carolyn was the easy way, was all. The way to make it all make sense. Which it didn't. And never would. He glanced back at her as he ducked down through the hatchway.

"Carolyn," he began. "I'm . . ."

Sorry, he would have finished. But she was crying again and refused to look at him.

In the cramped, stinking cabin he snatched the scrapbook lying on the fish-cleaning table and riffled through it. The faces of Randy's previous victims flipped by: blonde, redhead, brunette.

A real equal opportunity sicko, he was. But even full of clippings—and, dear God, some of these pictures were Polaroids—the book was a lot heavier than it should be.

And the pages were thicker. Hurriedly, Chip pulled one of the clear plastic page covers apart. Inside were two sheets of paper, each with clippings and photographs mounted on it, their blank back sides placed together so they formed a single page.

The scrapbook was made that way so you could re-arrange just one page at a time, Chip realized. You could move the front side without moving the back, or the back without moving the front.

Biting his lower lip, he parted the sheets of paper to look between them and found . . . money. Five hundred-dollar bills to a page, four laid horizontally top to bottom, one more vertically.

On each side. So a thousand per page, basically. With sweat-slicked fingers he inspected more of them. Each page was fattened with money. A hundred pages or so . . . a hundred thousand right here in the book.

So Roger must have put the money out on the water just as he'd said, and Randy found it. But this wasn't all of it. There should be more somewhere.

Almost a million more, most likely hidden on this boat. But as he examined the ones he'd already located, he realized that there was no point looking for the rest of the cash. Because the bills were identical, and that meant . . .

He stuck one of the hundreds into his pocket, stuffed the scrapbook down his jacket front, his fingers coming unexpectedly as he did so upon the map he'd found, floating out on the water.

A hand-drawn map scrawled in blue ballpoint on a torn-out sheet of notebook paper, the paper wrapped in clear plastic. Soon after he'd found it, he'd gotten so busy avoiding a watery death that he'd forgotten all about it.

And there was no time for wondering about it now, either. Shoving it down with the worthless bill he'd taken, he turned for a last glance around the cabin in case there was anything more in here that they might be able to use.

There wasn't. Time to get out of here . . .

"Looking for something?" The voice came from behind him. Not Carolyn's, and definitely not Sam's.

"Or maybe you think you've already found it."

Randy Dodd's big hand seized Chip's shoulder, spun him, and went into Chip's jacket front. The scrapbook landed on the table alongside the knife Carolyn had used on Chip.

The hand came back clenched into a fist, and when it arrived all the lights went out.

Dawn was breaking when Jake and Bella finally stumbled to the end of the gravel road and onto the pavement; the first passing vehicle, a bread truck, gave them a ride.

The driver, an apple-cheeked young guy wearing a Yankees cap, wanted to take them directly to the cops, but they argued him out of it, and with difficulty persuaded him to let them out at the customs station between Maine and New Brunswick.

Cars were already lined up at the border crossing in the thin morning light as Jake stood at a pay phone just inside the building, talking to Bob Arnold.

"Bob, we saw him, okay? Never mind how we did it, he was in the water, he's got a boat, and—"

Dripping and shivering, Bella sat on a bench wrapped in a coat one of the clerks had lent to her. Bob was talking again, explaining to Jake what a fool she was, and that when he saw her in person he would go into even more detail on the subject.

But right now he had questions to ask her, and based on her answers, urgent tasks to accomplish, and had he mentioned just how risky, how dangerous, how reckless, she had . . .

Jake waited until he was finished. The swelling around her ankle had progressed down into her foot; soon she might have to cut the shoe off.

"Someone'll be up to get you," he concluded when she'd told him all she could about where she and Bella had seen Randy Dodd. "So sit tight."

He hung up, not gently. Turning from the phone, Jake watched a customs officer walk up to Bella with a paper cup of hot coffee in his hand and an interested look on his face. He offered the cup to Bella, then sat and began asking questions.

Apparently two women, one half-drowned and the other with an ankle the size of an elephant's, required some investigation before they could be allowed to cross back peacefully into their own home country.

Bella opened her purse, which was when Jake remembered that she did not have her passport with her, and no birth certificate, either, because they also had been in the lost satchel. Her ankle now felt like the elephant was stepping on it.

Across the room, the border official had stopped smiling at Bella and begun looking grim. He stood and beckoned to another much less pleasant-looking fellow wearing a badge. Bella had not had the required paperwork, either, it seemed.

And from the look on her face, she had not appreciated being reminded of this. Meanwhile, through the lobby window, Jake saw two U.S. customs guys hustling out of their own building, on the far side of the bridge.

Judging by the customs guys' expressions, Jake knew she and Bella must've interrupted something crucial, like making sure a carful of nice blue-haired Canadian ladies bound for a day of stateside shopping plus lunch wasn't also secretly smuggling in an improvised nuclear device.

The U.S. customs officers entered the Canadian building and looked around suspiciously. "Look," she began to tell them, "this can all be—"

Straightened out, she'd meant to finish. But suddenly it was all too much; her throat tightened and her eyes prickled.

"Ma'am?" The two U.S. officers stood over her. They wore the kind of all-purpose smiles apparently issued nowadays by the U.S. government. "Ma'am, could you please come with us? Your friend here, too?"

"Sure." She sighed, straightening. No passport, no driver's license, no birth certificate . . . oh, this was going to take hours. Maybe days.

At least Bob Arnold already knew where they were, and where Randy was, too. "Come on," she told Bella, who was already up and knew the drill as well as Jake did.

Jake and Bella had been on—gasp!—foreign soil, and they wanted to—gasp!—come back. So now a

decision had to be made: Should they be allowed to?
Or had the foreignness infested both of them, like
bedbugs?

It was only about five hundred feet between the
Canadian building and the U.S. one, but to Jake the
distance looked like ten miles. Felt like it, too, on her
bum ankle.

A truck roared by, spewing foul exhaust. The U.S.
customs building had a muck-tan exterior and a low
concrete portico. Inside, they were left to wait in a
room about as charming and hospitable as a gas station restroom.

The chairs were hard plastic. Bella sneezed. They
were both still in their wet clothes. Jake unlaced her
shoe, tried pulling it off her swollen foot but couldn't.

Bella got to her feet. "Stay here," she said, and disappeared down a hall made of cinder blocks painted
yellow. She looked angry and miserable, and in danger of coming down with double pneumonia.

But as she paused before an unmarked door, her
look changed to one of mild-mannered reasonable-
ness tinctured with a drop of pathos. Only the glint of
purpose in her eye betrayed what an act this was;
even now, Bella was about as pathetic as your average
steamroller.

Her act must have worked, though, because when
she returned she had two pleasant middle-aged clerks
with her, one carrying dry clothes and the other bearing a lot of rough cotton towels. An hour later Jake
and Bella were warm, dry, and dressed in outsized
U.S. customs sweatshirts and huge pairs of regulation
trousers.

But still they were waiting. Jake leaned back again

in the hard plastic chair, sighing with impatience, then looked at the clock whose minute hand had refused to move since the last time she'd looked at it.

"What d'you suppose is happening?" Bella asked tonelessly.

Jake just shook her head. *Purgatory,* she thought, *must be like this.* But then through the building's front window she spied a familiar face.

Square jaw, blond brush-cut hair, eyes that in this early-morning light were a pale bluish-gray—

It was her husband, Wade Sorenson.

Chapter 8

*Who, me? Humans can do it, you
are human, therefore et cetera.*
—Tiptree's Tips

In the next moment, Wade's arms were around her. Jake pressed her face into the rough fabric of his heavy blaze-orange hunting jacket and felt his embrace tighten.

"Hey," he said into her ear. Not until then did she realize how much she'd needed his presence, that doing this all alone was, of course, possible . . .

But it was dreadful. "Hey, yourself." He smelled like soap, lime shaving cream, and the sharply herbal scent of the bag balm he used on his hands to keep them from cracking in cold weather.

"Is there any news about Sam?" Because in the hour since she had talked to Bob Arnold, anything could have happened.

But Wade only shook his head. "I got home just as Bob was hanging up the phone from talking to you. So I heard him out, and then I turned right around and started up here."

Half an hour later, the U.S. Customs and Immigration people accepted the copied documents Wade had brought with him. Wade had been on the phone again with Bob meanwhile.

"He sent a boat over to where you said you saw Randy," Wade reported as they left the customs building.

"And?" she said, steeling herself.

Because if the news had been good, he would already have told her about it. Bella sneezed again and wrapped the wool blanket Wade had brought along more tightly around herself.

"He said they found the fishing boat, but Dodd was gone. No Sam or anyone else on it, either."

They drove through the market town of Calais between tire shops and convenience stores. As they pulled out of town, Wade reached over and turned the heat up even higher, then let his arm fall around Jake's shoulders.

Along the road old maples and cedar trees screened

barns and farmhouses from traffic noise. A little snow dusted the north sides of the tree trunks. As well as she could through a haze of fatigue and fear, Jake brought Wade up to date on the events of the night, until at last he steered the truck through the final pair of downhill S-turns before the turnoff to Eastport.

In the distance, the leafless white maples on the hillsides looked like stands of soft paintbrushes. "Randy was hunting us, back there on the beach. If something more important hadn't come up, I think he might've found us and . . ."

Beaten us to death. Or shot us. "He's got some plan in his head," she said. "But I don't know what. And if he's not where Bella and I saw him . . ."

He'd already proven he could hide, that he knew the coves and inlets as well or better than anyone around here. So by now he could be anywhere.

Then she saw in Wade's face that there was something more. Something worse. "Sam's old friend," he answered her unspoken question. "Chip Hahn is his name?"

She nodded.

"When they found the fishing boat, they found a life jacket floating nearby. Bob Arnold's pretty sure it's one from the dory Chip stole out of the boat basin yesterday. Guy it got stolen from, he says he'd left two jackets on that dory."

Wade went on. "But the dory's gone. Bob thinks maybe Chip's with them now. That maybe he's on the missing dory with Sam and the girl."

And Randy Dodd, Jake thought, chilled. Her ankle felt huge, and as sore as a boil. "But how would Chip have—"

"Found 'em?" Wade slowed for the speed trap just inside the Passamaquoddy Indian reservation.

"Drifted there, maybe. There was a slick on the water by the fishing boat, a gasoline leak. So maybe a fuel line came loose, Chip lost power? And that's right where you would end up, if you just let the current take you."

Just before the causeway sat the Indian police squad car, waiting for drivers who didn't know or had forgotten that the speed limit sign meant business. Wade lifted an index finger from the wheel as he went by, and the cop returned the salute.

"None of this is in any way your fault," he added evenly. "If Randy Dodd hadn't seen you, he'd still have seen the copter and hightailed it."

"Yeah," Jake said glumly, hoping her dad felt that way about it, too. Keeping Bella out all night, putting her in danger, and soaking her to the skin . . . oh, he was not going to be happy about this.

"We'll just get home, get that ankle looked at and everybody present and accounted for again, and then see what happens," Wade said comfortingly.

But the expression on his face wasn't comforting. It said things were bad, and that they might be about to get worse.

"Bob's sending a car up to Saint Stephen," he added. "To check your vehicle."

In case of evidence, he meant. In case Randy Dodd had made it that far inland before returning to his boat.

"It's a big ocean," Wade added quietly.

As if he was thinking it, too: that all Randy wanted

was to get away with the money. That his simplest, best move was to kill all three of his captives.

And that he could dispose of their bodies most easily just by throwing them overboard.

"I can make you famous," Carolyn Rathbone said quietly to Randy Dodd. She sat near the stern of the small boat Chip Hahn had come in. The dory, he'd called it.

Up front, Sam Tiptree lay crumpled and motionless; Randy had gotten Sam from the larger boat into the small one by the simple method of dumping his limp body over the transom.

Chip sat near Sam, sullenly silent. A huge purple bruise was swelling on his cheekbone where Randy had hit him.

Randy himself looked straight ahead, one hand on the tiller of the engine he'd gotten started simply by tinkering with it and one on the little gun he'd gotten from somewhere. It was daylight now; as he piloted the boat, he kept scanning the shore.

But nothing moved there. They'd heard engines for a while, and voices; Randy had tucked the dory into a cove between high boulders and a deadfall, dark as a cave, and from outside just as invisible. When the voices went away and the engine sound faded, they'd emerged.

And now here they were. Rocks, trees, cliffs . . . once she saw an eagle swoop, seize a fish out of the shallows in its talons, then sail away with its silvery prey still wiggling and gleaming.

And once, only a dozen or so yards distant, a whale

breeched, its vast, dark, gleaming shape like something in a science-fiction movie. But since then, nothing.

"I mean it," she said, keeping her voice low. The sound of the engine probably covered it, she thought, but there was no sense letting Chip hear.

No sense in depending on him to save her. "I write crime books. I sell millions of them. You could be in one, and then—"

Then everyone would know how smart you are, she'd meant to finish. Because they all wanted it, didn't they? Everyone did. To be famous. To be *special.*

As if being a bloody monster wasn't special enough. It was all she could do just to talk to this guy at all without throwing up or screaming. The girls, though; the girls in their graves.

You're one of us, they seemed to intone yearningly as they gazed at her with hollow eyes. *You're one of us . . . almost.*

The girls sounded confident. She wanted them to be wrong. She took another breath of the salt air, let it steady her, and tried again to make what they were saying untrue.

"People would understand how important you are," she said to Randy. "How . . . interesting."

Right. Like a tumor is interesting, she added silently. She tried keeping those thoughts off her face, though. Because if she was going to get out of this, she had to offer him something.

Something he wanted. And he would have to believe her, that she could deliver. "I'd let you talk to my editor," she bargained. "You'd stay entirely hidden, though. Completely anonymous. They might," she added, struck by a burst of inspiration, "even help you get out of the country."

Not bloody likely. The only thing Siobhan Walters would do if she heard from this creep would be to hire security guards, and with her next breath she'd demand her own bazooka. Because Siobhan was no fool; she knew she didn't need the real people that most nonfiction got written about. And especially not the criminal ones; a photograph, maybe, just to show readers he really did exist and wasn't the product of some fool's fake memoir.

But nothing more. Most nonfiction subjects were nothing but trouble anyway, with their new prima donna attitudes and their demands to have their pasts fixed up to their satisfaction, their good deeds magnified and the bad ones papered over like so much rough plaster. And it was the same with true-crime books.

Forcing herself to gaze at Randy Dodd's surgically altered features, she knew for a fact that she could bring his dead body home strapped to the hood of the Volvo, write about him as if he were alive, and barely anyone would even know the difference.

Dead guys didn't open their big yaps to contradict anything the writer said about them, either. They didn't give interviews, or sue.

In other words, he'd be perfect, and for Carolyn herself it would be a coup. "You'd be famous," she said confidently again.

Interviews with a serial killer that the author had escaped from herself . . . God, it would be beautiful. All just as a way of getting free from him, and saving Chip and Sam, too, of course.

She told herself that once more as the dory pulled between the shore and some more large rocks. "Famous, huh?" he said.

Tonelessly, his eyes still roving back and forth. In the pale morning light, she examined his face, the scars at his temples and in front of his ears where some clumsy surgeon had made a tuck here, loosened a little there.

Reddened ridges revealed where stitches had been. *What a botch job,* thought Carolyn, who had done a teensy bit of preemptive research into cosmetic surgery herself, just to be ready when the time came.

Still, what he'd done had been enough to let him venture into Eastport, to pass for a stranger as long as it was dark and no one looked too closely.

"Yes," she said, forcing herself to sound enthusiastic when what she wanted was to puke on his shoes. His bloody shoes . . .

She looked away. "You could be," she went on, keeping her voice even, "a star. Go on TV. They'd probably make a movie about you."

Randy Dodd laughed humorlessly. "That what you think I want? Lots of people knowing about me?"

He turned his gaze on her. The surgeon had gotten something about the corners of his eyes wrong. His nose, too, trimmed to a hawklike beak, looked like a plastic piece stuck above his lips, which had been plumped out cartoonishly.

"Well," she amended smoothly, sensing something going wrong but not knowing quite what, "not really about you in detail. Not so anyone could ever—"

Find you, the girls chorused spookily. *Find you and catch you and—*

"Kill you," he said flatly, his eyes searching the shore for anyone who might be watching from there. "That's what I want."

Anyone who might see her and save her. "That's the plan," he added. "And there is no other plan."

He met her gaze, which was when she realized how hopeless it was, talking to him. Arguing, trying to persuade.

Because there was nobody in there. He might have been a real person once, with rational thoughts, feelings, empathy for anyone else.

But not anymore. Now he was just a walking, talking, deadly compulsion. Sick, twisted, and getting more grandiose—convinced he could do anything and get away with it—with each passing minute.

"That's what I want: That's what I'm going to do," he said, his voice calm and hideously matter-of-fact. "I'm just waiting for the time to be right. So do yourself a favor: Don't get your heart set on anything else."

Carolyn probably thought Chip Hahn wouldn't be able to hear her trying to bargain with Randy Dodd, but he could. Typical, he thought. She would try to get herself out of this first.

Not that it would work. Wherever Randy was going, it would be a place he could hide three bodies and get away.

Out of the country, carrying a million bucks, or so Randy still thought. It wasn't all in the scrapbook, but Randy had the rest somewhere, and that was all he wanted: freedom and cash.

And the pleasure of doing with Carolyn whatever bad deeds he could devise. Chip thought there were probably plenty.

Beside him on the floor of the boat, Sam Tiptree breathed in and out. His color wasn't too bad, and from the way the stain on his shirt had stopped spreading, he wasn't bleeding the way he had been.

But overall he still looked terrible. Lips dry and cracked, his face drawn and creased deeply with pain, the young man who in his childhood had thought Chip was the next best thing to a comic book hero now hovered close to death.

A doctor, preferably a surgeon, was what he needed. And if he didn't get one soon, Chip thought Randy might as well have dumped Sam into the waves and been done with it.

Sam opened his eyes. "Hey, guy," Chip said, trying to sound encouraging.

Sam didn't look fooled. "Check my pockets," he managed, and when Chip did, he came up with a small leather case containing a fire kit: matches, flint, and steel.

He tucked these into his own pocket. Sam watched, nodding approvingly.

In the stern, Carolyn was still trying to sell Randy on the idea of being famous. With her indispensable help, of course . . .

A burst of impatience flooded Chip. Didn't she know they were past that now, that if something didn't change soon, it was all over?

Because it was daytime, and even a big risk-taker like Randy wouldn't want to be out here where anyone could see them for very long. He had some destination in mind, and it wasn't far. And when they got there . . .

Sam was trying to say something more. Chip leaned in so he could hear, caught a sweet, familiar whiff of something chemical on Sam's breath. Searching his memory for where he'd smelled it before, he realized: The Old Bastard had smelled like that after his kidneys started failing, and he'd had to go on dialysis.

True to form, the Old Bastard had refused to be treated at even the finest Manhattan clinic. Instead, he'd had a guest suite in the Fifth Avenue apartment turned into a dialysis treatment room complete with full-time professional staff, and repaired to it three days every week to have his blood cleansed in patrician splendor.

Chip wondered worriedly if Sam's organs were failing, too, on account of all the blood he'd lost. Sam's head fell forward. He was asleep again, or unconscious; Chip didn't know which.

Then he felt the boat swerve as Randy pulled hard on the Evinrude's tiller arm. It had taken him about ten seconds to find and fix the loose fuel line Chip hadn't been able to diagnose. Now he turned the small boat into a narrow inlet and cut the engine.

Dry reeds and beach roses suddenly pulled up close on either side of the tiny waterway. The rose thorns hung into the boat, tearing at Chip's scalp. A branch appeared, low enough to knock Chip's block off; he ducked just in time and shot an angry look toward the man in the stern.

"Hey," he protested, unable to help himself. And what did it matter, anyway? Randy couldn't kill him any deader than he already meant to. "Can't you call out a little warning when—"

Randy didn't answer, or even bother to look at him. Carolyn, either, slumped over with her head against the transom seat. She had given up trying to talk to their captor, apparently.

Trying to convince him that she would be more useful to him alive, that he should let her introduce him and his exploits to the big world.

Like Jack the Ripper, or the Boston Strangler. Because if he let her do that, then he'd be Somebody.

And she'd get to live. But Carolyn had misjudged. Chip could tell by the look on her face, thwarted and petulant, as if someone had just told her that Chip Hahn wouldn't be lugging her satchel around for her anymore.

Or writing her books, or schlepping her carry-ons through airport security. *Funny how clear things get when you're out here in trouble,* Chip thought. *Alone and at the end of your rope.* He'd have done those things in a heartbeat now; all of them and more. He wondered if he would ever again get the chance to.

Probably not. He shivered inside his topcoat, glad for even the minimal protection that it and the life jacket he still wore provided in the icy autumn weather.

Randy let the boat drift up the channel, the brush on either side giving way first to small saplings and leafless bushes, then to massive trees. The biggest one, an enormous old white pine, stuck up from the rest like a giant peering over the shoulders of the smaller trees, from deep in the forest.

A tan carpet of pine needles spread between the tree trunks. Here and there a massive, moss-encrusted boulder jutted. No bird sang. Everything was silent.

Chip thought that if it wasn't for Sam, he would jump out and run, take his chances on Randy being able to catch him. He'd let Carolyn try some more to make it on her own, let her see just how well her powers of persuasion worked when push really came to shove.

But Sam was here. Chip couldn't just leave him. And anyway, Chip wouldn't have any idea which direction to go, even if he did get out of the boat before Randy shot him.

The boat bottom scraped rocks. Randy pulled the outboard up and stood. "Get out."

He had the gun in his hand as he stepped past Carolyn and over Sam, then across to the stony shore where small waves moved. He waved the gun at Chip.

"Out," he repeated flatly.

Chip bent and shook Sam's shoulder, trying to rouse him, while Carolyn hesitated. *Do something,* he thought at her. *Put that supposedly fabulous mind of yours to work and—*

Drop the engine, push the starter button, ram that sucker into reverse, and get us out of here, he urged her silently. *Try, for God's sake, just do it.* But she didn't know how.

"Sam," Chip said softly. But Sam didn't rouse at all, only muttered something Chip couldn't make out, and then Randy stepped back aboard.

Blank-faced, he lunged at Carolyn, grabbed her, and threw her out into the shallows. Carolyn uttered a breathy scream and began struggling clumsily up onto the stony bank, weeping.

Then Chip felt himself being lifted. The world turned upside down and when it stopped he was on shore, too, flat on his back. Stunned, he lifted his head. He spotted Carolyn scrambling away on her hands and knees as fast as she could.

But not fast enough. Randy fired a shot past her head. The sound clapped itself to Chip's ears, deafening him. Granite bits flew as Carolyn fell facedown, covering her head with her hands.

Randy took Sam by his collar and belt, heaved him overboard into the water, stepped out and took Sam's hair in his fist, and dragged him up onto the beach, dropping him there.

He walked over to Chip and looked down at him. Chip had the sudden unpleasant realization that he was about to be shot. This cold beach, water, and sky were the last things he would see.

Looking up, he met Randy's gaze. The gun didn't waver. Time seemed to stretch out as Randy's finger tightened.

Do something. . . .

Chip kicked out, hard, connecting with Randy's knee. At the same time he glimpsed Carolyn, miraculously on her feet, rushing at Randy. She leapt, hurling herself onto his back, her red nails clawing at his eyes.

Those eyes . . . blank and empty, like there was nothing in them but smoke. Randy howled, whirling around on one leg in an attempt to dislodge Carolyn, but she hung on tight as Chip struggled up to try to help. Grabbing a rock, he hurled it at Randy's head and missed. He found another and flung that, too.

It connected just above Randy's left ear. Blood streamed down the side of his face as he battled to get rid of the furious woman who had attacked him so suddenly, clinging to him like a mad thing.

Which she was. *Hang on,* Chip pleaded silently as he advanced on Randy through the stones and seaweed. Both Randy's hands were on the gun now, but he couldn't see to fire it.

Don't let go. . . . Over Randy's shoulder, Carolyn's face was a mask of pain and terror. Her hands, even the one that was swollen and discolored, scratched like savage talons. Even in his terror she reminded Chip of someone, and then he realized:

The girls, the ones in the first crime that he and Carolyn had ever worked on together, for their first book. Their faces, so hurt and ruined they hardly looked human. Their eyes . . .

Chip snatched up another rock and charged Randy, raising the rock over his head as he ran. Aiming for the nose, because he knew that would hurt the most—

Gripping the gun in both hands, Randy Dodd brought his fists straight back over his right shoulder, slammed the barrel of the weapon into the center of Carolyn's forehead. Her arms loosened abruptly on impact; she dropped off him like an empty sack.

Turning, Randy Dodd swung his arms like a scythe, his fists smacking Chip's head as if it were a baseball, Randy the cleanup batter. Chip staggered backward, his legs suddenly insubstantial and his vision gone blurry.

He tried stepping forward again, thought about the boat. He could get it running, he could . . .

Randy yanked Chip upright. Carolyn lay still. Sam too. Chip felt his legs moving as if from a great distance as Randy marched him roughly up a short, steep embankment.

At the top Randy let go and began urging Chip forward with short, sharp jabs of the gun into his back. Once, Chip nearly fell but caught himself; once, he thought he heard a cry from somewhere behind him.

He hoped it was Carolyn, hoped she could get into the boat and get away. But he knew she wouldn't.

Randy jabbed him again, painfully. Chip kept putting one foot in front of the other, sure each time that this step would be his last.

Because Randy was just waiting for a good place to kill him. Chip didn't know what kind of spot it would be. Soft earth, to dig a grave in, or by a fallen tree trunk that Randy could roll on top of him.

But whatever it was, when it came, that would be it. The end.

All done. And no one to save him. Randy poked him once more as Chip stumbled, caught himself, and resumed walking.

Nothing more to be done about it. In this way they proceeded together into the woods.

Chapter 9

Chip kept on walking until Randy told him to stop at the edge of an old pit that looked as if it had once been mined for gravel. A rickety-looking old superstructure hung over it, built of timbers with a metal wheel bolted to it.

A fraying rope still hung down from the wheel. For

hauling the gravel out, Chip imagined, as he peered down into the pit. Its steep sides were sandy, with a few dead, dry weeds poking up at intervals from the tan soil.

Pockets of stones interrupted the sand, extending downward in a flow pattern as if the stones had come out as a liquid, then frozen. Last summer's grass bristled yellow and brown in a narrow long-ago-cleared area all around the top of the pit.

A rough trail had led here, barely visible now, twin narrow tracks recalling the passage of wheels. Chip noticed each separate thing in a sort of hyper-vision, the colors brighter and the edges of everything sharper than normal.

It was freezing out here, even more than on the boat. He was getting tired under the weight of the life jacket, heavy with its straps held tight by thick metal buckles. And it was damp; it had rained here sometime in the recent past, and he could smell the cold water at the bottom of the pit.

He supposed he should feel afraid, but he was long past that. He felt angry; he felt as if he had nothing to lose. So he said it as soon as he thought of it.

"The money's fake."

The words hung in the cold, clear air as if printed there. Chip felt Randy stop short right behind him. They'd reached the huge old white pine—a sentinel tree, that kind of big, solitary evergreen was called, he remembered irrelevantly—that he'd been able to see from shore.

Around it, the breeze made a rattling sound in the few brown leaves still remaining on the smaller maples and birches. About twenty feet up, a thick dead branch stuck straight out from the pine like the lowered arm of a railway crossing: *Stop*.

"How'd you know that?" asked Randy with what Chip knew was deceptive mildness. But he answered anyway.

"I looked. On the big boat, in your book." The memory of it sickened him: clippings and photographs.

"Between the pages where you'd hid it. Though I guess there must be more of it somewhere. Because . . ."

"Shut up." Randy poked him in the back with the gun barrel. There was a long silence while, Chip supposed, Randy thought it over. Then:

"I don't believe you." But it was clear from his voice that he did. Chip could practically hear Randy thinking now, trying to come to grips with it.

With how he'd been fooled. Chip was still trying to figure it out himself, how it had happened and what Randy might do when he knew: That his brother, Roger, had screwed him.

That, somehow, that was what the map had been all about. Not for Randy, but for someone else, and who would it be but Roger? And besides, something had always been wrong with the story.

No matter what Roger Dodd or anyone else said, there was no million dollars. Chip's belief in it and his attempt to get it had, like Randy's, been doomed from the start.

"How do you know?" Randy's voice, asking it, was as calm as if he'd been asking the time of day.

Keep him talking, Chip thought. "I looked at the bills. And they look real." Felt that way, too.

Someone had gone to a whole lot of trouble printing them up. "But they've got identical serial numbers." And that meant counterfeit; there was no getting around it.

In as few words as possible, Chip explained this to Randy, felt him taking it in and believing it, finally: That it had all been for nothing. That the money had never been real.

That he'd been had. "You were supposed to bury it out here." Chip was trying it all out in his own mind by saying it aloud. "If things went wrong, you'd need someplace to stash it, where Roger could find it. And this was it." He looked down at the sandy soil at the foot of the sentinel tree. "Roger was supposed to come here later and check. That's what the map was for, to let him know where you'd put it. He'd go out to the buoy where he'd left the money; you'd have hung a map on the buoy for him."

Which now that he'd said it actually sounded straightforward enough so that Chip thought it was probably true: There'd been a bailout option. "But you lost the map and I found it," he said.

Randy kept listening. "If the money was here, Roger would know you'd had to leave it. He would take it back and you could try again to make the transfer later."

When, for instance, alerted border officials weren't looking for a guy with bad surgery, bad ID papers, and a satchel full of cash. The whole bailout option was a smart move on Randy's part, since lots of other things could have gone wrong besides the pair of them that had: first Carolyn, then Sam.

Carolyn had given Randy another chore to accomplish in Eastport: shutting her up, vanishing her off the face of the earth. Then, just when Randy must've thought he had her taken care of, Sam had showed up at the wrong moment.

And finally Chip himself had arrived, yet another glitch in the plan. Still, Randy had handled it all well; was handling it now, even, by deciding whether to kill Chip or do something else.

Chip hoped the unexpected worthlessness of the money would nudge Randy toward the "something else" option, since whatever it turned out to be, it was probably not as terminally disastrous as a bullet in the head.

Meanwhile the moments dragged on as Randy stood there thinking about it: *Which?*

The gun was at his side. His face, in the thin morning light a map of scars and stitch marks, wore no expression at all. But his eyes . . .

His eyes, empty of emotion, inspected Chip clinically. Chip thought that under the circumstances this represented progress, until a grim smile curved Randy's misshapen lips. They resembled the fake wax lips Chip had gotten as a kid around Halloween, too big and red, as if they were already melting a little on the inside.

As if Randy's whole mouth were collapsing and his face might follow. Around them the forest brightened, daylight filtering in through the trees.

"How'd he do it?" Randy asked unexpectedly.

Roger, Chip guessed he meant. "Fake the money?"

Randy nodded.

"Easy," Chip replied. "All you'd need is a few real bills, plus a good scanner and a really good printer.

But, I mean, most of them *are* really good now. Or good enough, anyway."

He was trying to fill the silence. "You'd scan in real ones. Then copy them, get a few on each sheet."

It wasn't quite that simple. Getting the right paper would be more difficult than it sounded, and getting the page set up to make the fronts and backs of the bills line up correctly would take some skill as well.

But it could be done. In fact, he'd researched a case where someone had, before Carolyn decided that counterfeiting wasn't a sensational enough crime to be worth a whole book.

"And there's another thing," Chip said.

Because as long as Randy was listening, he wasn't shooting. Also, maybe the way to keep Randy from feeling murderous about Chip was to get him feeling that way about someone else.

Roger, for instance. "See, floating the fake money out there was bad enough. But—"

Chip described in detail how at the very first opportunity, Roger had blamed everything on Randy, how he'd drawn himself as a victim in the whole scheme.

"So what I think is," Chip concluded—persuasively, he hoped—"I think if Roger hadn't gotten dragged in to talk to the cops, he'd have gone on his own."

The more he presented this theory, the more likely it began sounding, too. "I think he was gearing himself up for it, getting his story squared away so it sounded good, but his whole idea all along was to save himself by nailing you."

That's why Roger had cracked so quickly. Chip took a breath, hurried on before Randy could decide to shut him up. "Because he never meant to give you any money. So he had to get rid of you, right? Turning you in was one option."

"Okay," Randy said, nodding, and his voice still sounded so calm and reasonable that it gave Chip some hope.

"But here's the thing," Chip said. "You're not entirely screwed. Even counterfeit money is worth something. And I happen to know somebody who—"

Will buy it from you, he meant to finish. Ten cents on the dollar, but hey, a hundred grand. Better than nothing.

And he did know someone. Years of research, both online and otherwise, had turned up a lot of interesting characters, many of whom had nontraditional ways of earning a living.

But he didn't get a chance to say so because just then Randy raised the weapon and shot him.

It felt to Chip as if the massive pine tree had swung down and smacked him in the chest. He took a step back into thin air, over the edge of the pit.

As he fell, the sky and trees sailed in circles up and away from him, spinning and shrinking until they winked out.

Carolyn heard the shot from where she lay on the stones by the water's edge, trying to crawl. Sam lay a few yards away, where Randy had dropped him.

The boat, she had to get—

Then came the sharp crack through the chill morning air. *Chip,* she thought, seeing his face so clearly that it was as if he were still right there with her.

But he wasn't. A dagger of grief pierced her. *Gone . . .*

Out on the water, a flock of seagulls swooped low, crying excitedly. Then they settled again. Nothing else moved or made a sound.

A blurry line on the horizon might've been Eastport, its wharves and brick business buildings crowded along the bay and the white wooden houses rising behind, uphill from the water.

Or it might have been a trick of light. She pushed herself up on one elbow, then onto her two hands. Her nose was bleeding.

But every minute she was still alive was a minute to the good, she thought as she got her knees bent, sat up, and put a testing hand to her head where Randy had hit her with the gun.

Chip, she thought again, then realized with a jolt of terror that Randy Dodd would be coming back at any instant. It was what he had gone to do, kill Chip and put his body somewhere. So now . . .

Now it was her turn. Suddenly she was so scared that she couldn't even feel any of the various parts of her that hurt so much. Only the fear, freezing her where she sat . . .

The boat Chip had come in was a dozen yards off, pulled up onto the shore in front but with its back end floating. She'd seen how Randy had pulled the engine up, seen him start it, too.

She hauled herself clumsily into the icy water, so cold it made her whole body ache with a deep, dangerous throb that said this wasn't just uncomfortable. It was deadly, and she had to get out of it as soon as possible.

But not yet. She cast a terrified glance at the place where weeds and sea grasses gave way to the edge of the forest. No one appeared, but now she thought she heard heavy footsteps crunching nearer.

Hurry . . . She pulled herself up, gripping the boat's rail in both trembling hands. Up and over . . .

One hand slipped off; she fell back. Flailing, she clutched at the rail again and missed, then clamped her fingers around it. Her shoulders felt as if they were coming out of their sockets, and the awful cold made both hands numb.

But her fingers, even on the injured hand, finally locked on. Gritting her teeth, with a terrible effort she forced herself to her feet. The water sucked the sand from beneath them as she dragged herself higher, until her hips were on the boat's rail.

Crying as she did it. Weeping with fear. Only a little more now, though, just one solid push . . .

A wave made the boat lurch, sending her tumbling forward. She let go and rolled, and crashed out of control into the boat's bottom, panting with terror.

Still no one stopped her. But the crashing sounds through the brush on shore were louder now, and she could hear Randy Dodd's voice approaching, spewing a low harangue of profane complaining and cursing.

He sounded very angry, which was new for him. Something must have happened. Chip had done something, or said something. . . .

She peered over the rail just as Randy appeared from between the trees with the gun in his hand, his strange face convulsed with fury. As he approached she fought her way up from the boat bottom, then got her chest up onto the transom seat in front of the engine.

His presence behind her, coming nearer, felt like a black, sucking hole, pulling her down into it. Lunging up, with both hands she raised the engine and got the propeller back down into the water, thinking, *Where, oh God let me find the starter button, where—*

She found it and pushed it. The engine grumbled to gurgling life. *Now the throttle, how do you work the throttle . . .*

But it was easy, there were arrows on it to show you how to do it. *Go,* the girls in her head chorused sweetly, their voices a dead choir. She turned the sleeve on the throttle.

Yes, she thought exultantly in the instant before the engine revved with an agonized whine, shooting the boat forward a dozen feet or so to where it beached itself with a scrape of metal on rocks. Something in it banged once, then it stopped dead.

She hadn't thought to put it in reverse. And now . . .

Randy stopped also, raising the gun. *Fish in a barrel,* she thought as he aimed it lazily, cocking his head slightly to one side as if wondering how many shots it would take.

Or how few. Carolyn held her breath and it seemed everything else did, too: the water, the sky. Her heart. Even the dead girls were silent as he stood there, seeming to consider: Kill her now? Or later?

This isn't happening, Carolyn thought as the small

dark eye at the end of the gun barrel gazed flatly at her. But it was, and as she realized this she saw his arm move and his eyes narrow. He was adjusting his aim a little. *No . . .*

Before she could even think about it, she was rolling to the left, hurling her body over the side of the boat, hitting the icy water and choking on it. *No,* she thought, *no, no—*

Under the boat. If she could get under there, maybe there was a chance for her still. Her hands felt around blindly in the cold water, now thick and gritty with stirred-up sand. Maybe there was an air pocket under the boat—

Maybemaybemaybe, the girls sang. She opened her eyes, heedless of the way they stung in the salt water, fought her way past the propeller, a silvery clover shape turning loosely in the current.

And then she saw them, their drowned pallid faces and dark dead eyes all turning toward her at once. Their hair streaming, their mouths moving. Their long, graceful fingers beckoning.

Their broken fingernails. And their smiles . . . mocking her. Terror worse than any Randy Dodd had ever inspired went through her. Because they weren't encouraging her, were they?

Those girls in her head, the ones she'd earned her bread and butter on, whose agonies had brought her a fortune. Made her . . .

Famous, they all whispered gleefully. *Don't forget that.* They weren't helping her. They were luring her. Suddenly she knew why: They wanted her to be one of them. . . .

She wouldn't be able to hold her breath for much

longer. Suddenly a hand reached down in front of her, fingers searching.

Fright punched the breath out of her. Bubbles rose past her face, and in the next instant he grabbed her hair, dragging her up and out of the water. She coughed up bits of seaweed, heard a voice shrieking.

Her own voice. He shoved her back into the boat. Not even bothering to keep an eye on her while she lay there gasping and shaking, he found a small plastic box under the transom seat and selected some small parts out of it.

Swiftly he pulled the engine up, removed something from the propeller and tossed it aside. He'd done this before, she could tell, as he replaced it without hesitation with the part from the plastic box, then lowered the engine again.

She'd broken something on the engine, hitting those rocks with it. But he'd fixed it. Whatever he'd done was routine, easy if you knew how.

When he had finished, he seated himself by the tiller, facing her. "Change of plans," he said, and started the engine.

Back in Eastport, Jake sat in the medical clinic waiting room until her name was called, then let her ankle be x-rayed, pronounced unbroken, and wrapped in a pressure bandage so tight she thought her toes might pop off.

Wade waited outside, then drove her home. It was nine in the morning, and up and down the Eastport streets the daily routines were well under way: in and out of the post office, the hardware store, and the IGA, normal people and their ordinary chores.

All present and accounted for; all but Sam. At home, Jake's father was in the kitchen cooking oatmeal.

He wore denim coveralls, a plaid flannel shirt, and beat-up work boots. He'd been dressed since five that morning, when he'd woken to find Bella's side of the bed empty.

No stranger to disaster, he'd gotten up immediately to start making phone calls. But first he'd shaved and dressed, since at that point he still didn't know who he might end up talking to: a ransom demander?

Or maybe a coroner's deputy. All this she'd learned from Wade; her dad still wasn't talking much.

"He'll settle down," Wade told Jake when they got inside, putting a gentle hand up to push her damp hair off her forehead.

"I hope so," Jake replied guiltily. She still felt ashamed, as if she and Bella had chickened out instead of getting out of the water because it—or Randy—had been about to kill them.

An impulse seized her, to skip the shower she'd planned and instead crawl into Sam's bed and stay there. But:

"You can't try again if you're dead," Wade said, pulling a set of fresh towels out of the linen closet for her.

And in the end it was this remark that got her through the shower, the rewrapping of her ankle, and the putting on of clean clothes, even the application of a little makeup.

When Sam came home, she would want to look decent. Back downstairs, she found her father still in the kitchen stirring steel-cut oats.

"Don't you dare blame her," Bella said.

Jake's dad's gaze remained on the oatmeal.

"I made her take me," Bella said. "I was the one who decided to go."

The oatmeal spoon stopped moving. "You might have both said something to me."

Bella got a coffee cup from the cabinet and filled it for Jake. "Why, so you could make a fuss? Try talking me out of it? Forbid it?"

Before he could answer, she went on. "I'm too far along in my life to start letting you tell me what to do, old man." Her big green eyes flashed with anger. "So if you were thinking that, you can stow it." She passed Jake the cream. "We're sorry we worried you. But I married you, and I can unmarry you."

His lips pursed. But there was no hiding the smile twitching at their corners. Seeing it, Jake knew why he'd married Bella.

Exactly why. "Eat," he said, putting two bowls of steaming mush on the table.

The women looked at the bowls, and at each other. Neither of them felt anything like eating.

"Unless," he added, "you both want to lie around all day on fainting couches, sighing and weeping. 'Cause that's what you'll both be doing if you don't get some food into you."

So they dug in, mostly just to placate him. But it turned out that bowls of hot mush slathered with cream and maple sugar were just what the doctor ordered.

Jake was working on a second bowl and Bella was

drinking another glass of orange juice when Bob Arnold came in and laid a hundred-dollar bill on the table.

"I just had a talk with Roger Dodd," he said. "Turns out he bought a lot of electronic equipment not long ago. Copier, and a scanner."

Just then Wade came in with the dogs. Behind him came Ellie White and George Valentine. They'd all heard what the chief said.

"Why?" asked Ellie. "I mean, why would he buy . . ."

But Jake understood. "He copied it, didn't he? The money, he faked it up."

It was, she realized, the thing that had been bothering her all along. "He faked Randy out with it."

Bob turned to her. "Somebody wants a million from you, and you don't want to give it, it stands to reason you might try and fool 'em."

She got up. Cooked steel-cut oats, her father had once told her, put hair on your chest. She thought that if it ever came to a choice between the way she felt now and low-cut blouses, she'd take the oats.

Thank you, she mouthed at him, and he nodded in reply, not unkindly.

"Why?" said Ellie suddenly again.

She'd dressed in a white blouse, black wool slacks, and a red sweater, plus stockings and loafers. Even her hair was pinned up in a neat, reddish gold braid.

"I mean," Ellie said, "why would Roger try to pass phony cash off on his brother?"

No sequins, no glitter were anywhere on her. Wade and George were cleaned up, too: George in clean, pressed jeans and a blue chambray work shirt with pearl buttons, Wade in corduroys, a good collar shirt, and a navy crew-neck sweater with the words *Maine Fish & Game* embroidered on it in crimson.

A thump of fright hit Jake as she realized why they looked so respectable, all of them: Like her dad, they didn't know who they might be talking to. A police detective, a reporter . . .

An undertaker. "He knew," Bella said. "He knew Randy killed both those women—his own wife, Cordelia, and Roger's wife, Anne. And he knew that Randy would be coming back for the money."

Bob nodded in agreement. "Turns out that two days after Anne died was when Roger went online and bought all that equipment." He scowled communicatively. "Hadn't even had Anne's funeral yet. So you're right, he knew the score. Or he was an awful good guesser. But he says it was all for menus and place mats, for the bar."

A likely story, Bob's face said.

"Where is he now?" George Valentine wanted to know. "I'll go ask him a couple of pointed questions of my own."

Ellie looked warningly at him. Small and compact, with hard, work-toughened hands that clenched readily into fists, George was the type of fellow who, if he asked a guy a few questions and the guy didn't answer fast enough, would speed the responses pretty effectively.

"Okay, okay," he relented. "I just wanted to help."

"He's in custody now, though, right?" Jake asked Bob. "Roger is?"

But Bob shook his head. "For what? Getting

threatened and blackmailed by his brother, who by the way we also haven't proved anything against?"

His tone said that, left to his own devices, Bob would have locked Roger Dodd up permanently just on general principles. But:

"No. He's got a date with the state cops later today. And I guess someone'll be wanting to talk about that fake money with him."

Bob moved toward the door. "But as of now I've got nothing. I wouldn't have even known about the copying equipment if Roger hadn't been trying to fast-talk me about the cash. First he said he went to Bangor and got it, then that a courier delivered it. . . . I guess he never thought anyone would ask. So he had no story."

He looked at Bella and Jake. "That got me thinking, and the fancy copier and so on are right there in his office."

With the result that, as usual, small-town cop Bob Arnold had put two and two together, then pulled a rabbit out of a hat. Jake felt a burst of gratitude for him.

But it didn't last. "Anyway, I just came up here to make sure you two were okay," he went on, "and tell you the Canadian Coasties're on the way to where you think you had a sighting."

She stared in disbelief. "We *think*?"

Wade stepped in front of her. "Okay, Jake," he said. "Bob, has Roger said anything more about where he thinks Randy went?"

Bob frowned. "No. I went back down to the Artful Dodger and asked him again just now. But since this morning he's hooked up with an attorney and now he says he won't be making any more comments about Randy or anything else."

Bob pulled the back door open. "Also, he says as far as he's concerned the statements he's already made were under duress."

"Fine," Jake managed to reply when she found her voice again; the nerve of the guy. "Let's leave it like that, then."

She stepped up to Bob. "But tell him this from me."

Because maybe she wasn't a money person anymore, and maybe her days of cash clients so crooked that just talking to them was a prosecutable felony were over. But she remembered the important parts of that old life, where what you really needed was a cool head, a keen eye, and the ability to make good on your threats.

All of which she'd also had. And Roger Dodd wasn't the first barefaced liar she'd ever dealt with.

Not by a long shot. "Tell him I know he's mixed up in this," she whispered. "And if Sam doesn't come home—"

A sob blocked her throat. She swallowed it angrily and went on, feeling the bad old days pulling her back. And not caring.

Like in the old days. "Tell Roger that if that happens, his lawyers won't save him. Nothing will. You tell him from me."

Startled, Bob hesitated. Then, "You got it," he said.

Then he went out. But when he was gone, she sank into a chair again, because if vengeance for Sam was the only thing left to her, she could get it. She hadn't been bluffing about it.

But she wouldn't want it; not that, or anything else. Ever.

"How's the ankle?" Wade asked half an hour later when she'd retreated to her third-floor workroom and the insulation project.

"Fine." It hurt like hell, actually. They'd given her pills for it at the clinic.

But she didn't want to take any. "Wade, I was this close. I could practically touch him. But I gave up."

Furious, Jake flung old floorboards toward the holes they'd been pried out of. Her father had been keeping his hands occupied while he awaited word that morning, and had gotten a helper to run the insulation blower, too.

The result was that the floor up here had been insulated, although at the moment she wouldn't have cared if the whole place froze solid, maybe even forever.

Wade stood by the door watching. "I gave up and ran away," she fumed, seizing a claw hammer and some nails.

"Jake, you didn't. Where you were, you had maybe another minute. After that, the tide would've washed you off your feet."

She fit one of the boards back into the floor, realized she had it upside down and backward, flipped it angrily, and slammed it down again.

"You don't know that. We might've made it. I just got too scared, that's all."

Refitting floorboards was about the last thing she felt like doing. But she had to do something or her feet would find their way downtown, straight to the Artful Dodger, and then without any delay her hands would find their way around Roger Dodd's neck.

"So, what if we'd had to swim a little?" she went on. "We were both already wet. Maybe we could've . . ."

"Drowned," Wade said flatly. "And we'd be searching for the two of you now, too. For," he added quietly, "your bodies, yours and Bella's."

Silence. Then: "Yeah. I'm just mad, that's all. And scared." She looked up. "Wade, what the hell is Randy Dodd doing out there? Why didn't he just take the money and run? He doesn't know it's fake."

Wade shook his head. "I don't know. Maybe there's something else he wants. Something he didn't know he wanted, until—"

Which was when it hit her. She put the hammer down. "That's it, isn't it? There's something else now, there must be. Randy must have thought he'd just show up, get his cash from Roger, and vanish again. But then Chip Hahn and Carolyn Rathbone stuck their oar in, and he had to do something about that. Because Carolyn suspected that Randy was still alive, and if she said so publicly she might be listened to. And Randy couldn't have that."

"And then," Wade agreed, "Sam showed up unexpectedly on the breakwater and maybe recognized him. Talk about bad luck."

Right, she thought. For both of them, Randy and Sam.

Wade continued, "Which still doesn't explain why Randy didn't . . ."

Kill them all right off the bat, he would have finished, but instead he stopped short, not wanting to voice the thought.

He'd changed his clothes, she noticed suddenly; now he was dressed for boating, in heavy cargo pants and layers of shirts. An oilskin slicker topped the bright red sweatshirt she'd given him for his birthday.

"Right." She said what he hadn't wanted to: "Grab Carolyn, kill her, get rid of the body. Simple, right? But when he grabbed her, he must not have realized Chip Hahn was with her, that he's her partner. So, why not?"

She put a nail into one of the repositioned floorboard's old nail holes, grabbed another one, and slammed it home with the hammer. Hitting something felt good. She placed two more nails, positioning them carefully.

Wade crouched by her, put a hand on her shoulder. "Don't hit your thumb."

She managed a smile. "Right. But seriously, Wade, he should be out of the country by now."

She placed another board, hammered it down. "But maybe he's onto the fact that the money is no good? Or maybe—"

He's got a taste for it, Roger Dodd had said of his brother. And . . . *missing girls,* Chip had reported of Randy's time in another state.

Jake voiced her worst thought. "Maybe he just wants to kill them his way. His own time and place. Maybe it's worth the risk to him, waiting until he can—"

But this time she was the one who stopped before finishing the thought, because the end of this one was so unacceptable, just absolutely unthinkable.

Wade crossed to the doorway. It struck her that he wasn't just going out on the water; he was going now.

"George and I are taking his boat out to have a look," he answered her questioning glance. "A lot of the guys from around town are going; we're just going to stay out there until—"

She stood. The bad ankle protested strenuously; she told it to shut up. *Stupid body parts,* she thought angrily.

"Now that Randy knows someone might've spotted him on the New Brunswick side, he might decide to go in the other direction," Wade said.

"Through the Lubec Channel. He could make it out to Grand Manan," she mused aloud. "I hadn't thought of that."

The large island between Maine and Nova Scotia was thinly settled and even more thinly policed, especially off-season. "He could lay low there," she said.

Or he could circle on back to the coast of New Brunswick and disappear into the warren of brick rowhouses and narrow alleys of the industrial city of St. John.

She crouched once more, slotted the final loose floorboard into its place, and nailed it down.

"He's making it all up as he goes along now, and that makes him harder to predict."

Wade nodded. "On top of which, he knows the territory, all the isolated hiding places he can hunker down in. He can keep to the shoreline, not go too far out on open water, so he can take cover if he hears a boat or a plane. But improvising means it's also likelier that he'll make a mistake." He paused thoughtfully. "There would be that last long open stretch he'd have to cross, heading for Grand Manan. He could make it, though, I guess. Just get lucky. Small boat, it's not as easy to spot from the air as you might think."

But then he shook his head at himself. "But we'll still get him sooner or later," he said. "There's going to be a lot of guys out there all day, and into tonight if need be."

He straightened, impatient now to get going. "If we don't find him downriver, we'll come back up this way, keep on looking until we do."

He didn't suggest she might go along, and she knew better than to do so. Between a bad ankle and her tendency to lose her lunch at the slightest ripple, she wouldn't be an asset.

To put it mildly. "Thanks," she said, meaning it. "Tell the other guys I said so, too, will you?"

He shot her a grin that she knew was meant to help keep her spirits from collapsing completely. "Yeah, well. You just keep your chin up."

She forced an answering smile. But as she heard him go down the stairs, she knew Randy Dodd still held all the cards: three hostages (*please, God, let there still be three,* she thought) plus the willingness—possibly even the eagerness—to do very brutal things.

Topped off by a lot of what looked at least to the casual eye like genuine money. So the questions now were (a) what else did Randy Dodd want, and (b) what would he do to get it?

But they were so far unanswerable, she knew, and Wade did, too. Which was why he hadn't promised they would find Sam alive.

Thinking this, she hammered the last nail, then

swept up enough stray fluffballs of insulation material to stuff a mattress.

After that she picked up all the tools and cleaned
them, collected up all the empty blue plastic insulation bale wrappers, found a trash bag and filled it
with them, and dragged the trash bag downstairs to
the cellar.

In this way, what remained of the morning passed.
At noon, she let Bella force a bowl of soup on her,
looked at the bottle of pain pills again, and ignored it
again.

No call came to say that Randy Dodd had been
captured or that Sam had been found. Jake haunted
the house, fixing a wobbly doorknob in the front parlor and some loose carpet on the stairs.

Later on she got a new pane of glass from the hardware store and installed it in a cellar window, and
oiled the bulkhead door hinges. At two in the afternoon she checked the phone line and found it working. Still no call.

She took the dogs out, forcing herself to let them
romp while she threw a Frisbee for them until her
arm gave out, once having to retrieve it herself from
among the rosebushes over in her neighbor's yard.
The curtain twitched there, but as usual no one came
out to complain, or even just to chat.

By the time the animals got tired, lolling and panting ahead of her up the porch steps, it was past four
in the afternoon and already getting dark.

Bella was in the kitchen pouring kibble into their
metal dog dishes. The phone rang. Heart pounding,
Jake ran to answer.

By the time she did, whoever was on the other end of it had already begun speaking, the tone one of high, manic glee threaded with malice:

"... *kill you!*" it burbled out at her.

Hot rage coursed through her, demolishing all her careful defenses. "You do that," she snapped to whoever it was. "You come right on over to the house here, right this minute. And give it your best shot."

Shocked silence greeted this outburst. She could still hear someone breathing. She slammed the phone down.

Then, alone in the tiny alcove with the old gold-medallion wallpaper reflecting the evening light through the dining room windows, she sank to the floor and wept.

Chip Hahn woke flat on his back in a puddle of water, gazing up at the massive old sentinel pine looming far away, at the top of the pit. Everything hurt. A leaf floated down toward him. He turned his head to watch it landing a few feet away. Strange ...

But then he shot to a sitting position, hot pain knifing at his injured shoulder, as full consciousness returned.

Sam ... where is he? Struggling up, Chip remembered the rest of it: walking with Randy, being shot, going over the pit's edge.

Now he was at the bottom of it and what had been early morning was late afternoon, the sky darkening swiftly through the bare branches overhead and the pit filling with shadows. Getting colder, too ...

Chip shivered, pulling his coat and the life vest beneath it tightly around him. *Randy must have thought he killed me.*

But he hadn't, somehow. Chip didn't know why. The life vest wouldn't have stopped a bullet. And then . . . *Sam,* he thought again.

The last time Chip saw him, Sam had been lying unconscious near the water's edge where Randy had flung him. Bleeding . . . and the tide had been rising.

Had Sam been alive? If he was, then was he still? Had he been able or even conscious enough to drag himself away from that rising tide?

Chip had a sudden very clear mental picture of Sam Tiptree a dozen years earlier, age ten or so, falling into the pond in Central Park. They'd been racing a pair of brand-new, radio-operated model sailboats, laughing and yelling and having a fine time bashing into each other's remote-controlled vessels, trying every dirty trick in the book to cross the finish line first.

Until Sam slipped on a wet spot, hit his head on a paving stone, and fell in. Chip recalled flinging himself into the murky water, sure he'd never reach Sam in time and that he, Chip, would be responsible for his young friend's death.

Now the same fear made him charge the steep, sandy slope, scramble up it in a frenzy, dig in with his fingers and push with his feet, not caring if his fingernails broke until they bled. Which they did, and he kept climbing anyway, grabbing onto weeds where they grew and onto nothing where they didn't.

At times, it even seemed that he might make it.

But the sand kept slipping, and the stones flew from under his shoes. The weeds, pulled easily out by their dead roots' good-looking handholds, turned out to be deadwood, no more substantial than sawdust.

Finally, just as he was about to fling his hand up over the edge of the pit, the whole side of it cascaded down with him on it, all the way to the bottom, where he landed gasping and weeping in frustrated exhaustion.

Some kind of big bird flew over as he lay there, its cry lonesome and harsh. A breeze rattled the branches. Pulling his shoes off and emptying them, he felt a liquid trickle of weakness go through him, and that was the scariest thing of all.

Because with it came the idea that not only did Randy think he'd killed Chip, but that Randy was right. That Chip would never get out of here, just keep trying and failing until he filled up with weakness and eventually quit.

And that someday, somebody would be digging around down here and find his bones.

Or not.

Carolyn Rathbone lay motionless in the little boat Chip had stolen, watching the daylight drain out of the sky. Every once in a while a white seagull sailed overhead, crying.

She cried, too, but not on the outside, because she was way too scared to do anything but breathe carefully. She didn't know where Randy was taking her now, but when they got there something bad would happen, she knew that much.

So she just lay there, hoping they wouldn't get to that part for a while yet. Hoping and freezing, because now that the sun was going down it was getting cold again.

Very cold. After leaving Sam and Chip on the island, he'd taken the boat across a narrow channel and into a sheltered cove at first, and for a long time they'd sat there.

Waiting for it to get dark, she supposed. Or dark enough. For what, she didn't want to imagine.

Now in the gathering gloom they were motoring again. Waves thumped the boat, spray splashed in, and fog started thickening all around them once more, just as it had the night before.

Fog tasting of salt. She licked her lips thirstily. She hadn't drunk anything since much earlier, on the big boat.

And that seemed like ages ago, back in another life where there were things to eat and drink and people who didn't want to kill her any minute.

Randy Dodd's dark shape at the stern loomed in silence. The boat's engine roared monotonously. Lulled, she drifted woozily, hearing the girls singing in the engine noise.

Singing and sobbing. A wave slapped the boat's side hard and sloshed over the rail onto her, waking her with a start. Coughing up salt water, she lurched and froze, remembering:

Sam, Chip. The sharp, popping sound of a gunshot.

Randy was staring at her. Behind him, dozens of tiny red and white lights bobbed on the dark water.

Boats. They were the running lights of a lot of little boats, she realized with sudden hope. And behind them were the lights of Eastport. The breakwater, the streets full of houses . . .

She drew in a deep breath, opened her mouth to scream, then met his dark gaze again.

He was holding the gun. "Lie down. Put that blanket all the way over you. We're going to cut engine, sit here in the dark, and let them go right on by. But if you move or make a sound . . ."

Carolyn hesitated. The other boats drew nearer. Their lights did, anyway. But he was right: in the dark, those lights were the only thing visible. So his plan could easily work . . .

Everything in her said scream. Scream and scream, until the world ends, until the stars fall out of the sky.

And the girls, all the dead girls . . .

They said something, too. *We love you,* they sang.

But they'd been with her for a long time now. So she knew something important about them. Their darkest secret . . .

They loved her, all right. So much that they wanted her with them.

Down there in the dark. But she wasn't dead yet; not like them. Not quite. So she lay down obediently on the deck, pulled the blanket up, and waited for her chance.

Or for the sweet-voiced girls to welcome her home.

Curled up in a ball at the bottom of the sand pit, Chip thought about dying. But he just couldn't seem to get his mind wrapped around the idea of actually doing it.

Right off the bat would have been one thing, he figured. But by some accident of fate that he still didn't understand, he wasn't injured enough. No, this was a long-term project, one that even here in the freezing cold would probably take hours.

A shiver went through him, then another. He felt like the meat in a refrigerated sandwich: cold ground, cold sky. A sound of teeth chattering came from somewhere.

After a moment he realized it was his own teeth making that sound. A low, sad laugh came out of him, then: *God, what a mess*. All that trying and failing to make something of himself for all those years, and now here he was.

Miserably, he felt around in his coat pocket. The kit he'd taken from Sam back when they were on the boat was still in there, and maybe he could at least build a warming fire with it. He'd noticed some dry branches earlier, fallen from the trees growing at the top of the pit.

Maybe he could use them. The old sentinel pine he'd seen as he'd walked to the pit, especially, had dropped a lot of burnable material. He felt around in the dark, hoping to come upon some of it.

His hand closed on some twigs, on what felt like a scrap of old rope—he dropped it fast before realizing it wasn't a snake—then on a larger chunk, an entire pine branch. The dry needles clinging to it might make decent kindling, Chip thought.

Not that it was going to make a difference in the long run. No one would see his fire down here in this hole. But if it made him feel better for a little while, why not?

At least it was something to do. He opened Sam's

emergency kit, unwrapped the packet of stick matches inside it, and struck one. Its sudden, bright flare was just about the most beautiful thing he'd ever seen, and when he touched it to the sticks and pine needles he'd gathered together, they didn't just burn.

They flared, the pine pitch still in the needles sizzling and popping like gasoline. A giddy laugh escaped him as he warmed his hands over the blaze, which small as it was lit up the whole bottom of the pit.

Which was when it hit him: gasoline. If he had some of that, maybe he could signal for help with a bigger fire. Or maybe if he used . . .

Pine boughs. The sudden, vivid memory of the sentinel tree looming over the pit's edge came back to him once more. Tall, dead, and . . . well, not quite dead. With all those live pine boughs still waving all the way up there at the top, the old tree was probably visible for miles in daylight.

And at night, if it were on fire . . . At the thought Chip felt a surge of energy go through him. It made his pain explode back to life, too, as if somebody had just stuck a hot poker through his rib cage. But . . .

The hell with it. If he didn't do something, pain would soon be the least of his problems. He scrambled to gather more fallen pine boughs before his fire went out, grabbing any twig and stick he could find, especially ones with pine needles still on them.

By the time he had enough of them, he was gasping in agony, a slick of pain-sweat making his clothes stick to him. Sweat and a lot of blood, because now in addition to the pain in his ribs, he could feel a stealthy but steady pulse leaking warmly from his shoulder.

But before he could think too hard about that, he forced his bad arm out of his coat sleeve, letting himself groan aloud. Next he wrapped the coat around the pine boughs he'd collected and tied the sleeves in a tight knot. The boughs stuck bushily out of the coat's top like a bouquet, just as he'd hoped they would.

A bouquet—or a torch. But another wave of serious weakness washed over him as he thought of this and he sat down hard, very frightened again suddenly. Because maybe this dying business was not quite as time-consuming a project as he'd thought.

Maybe he was going to do it now, or in the next few minutes. The blood-pulse seemed abruptly very convincing, and meanwhile Sam might very well still be down there on the beach.

Maybe even still alive. If the tide hadn't washed him away, if he wasn't already floating . . .

So there was no time to waste. Tiredly, Chip got up, began feeling around the slope of the sand pit for the rope he'd seen dangling, back when there was light to see it with. He imagined it must be from where some out-of-work fisherman, long ago reduced to the grim labor of humping sand out of a pit, had built a pulley and hung it from a branch of the sentinel tree, so at least he wouldn't have to haul heavy bags of sand uphill on his back.

Chip tripped over a stone, landed hard on some more of them, flat on his face in the dark, and as he lay there found both ends of the pulley rope by accident.

When one end went down, the other would go up. With both rope ends in his hand, he sat again on the cold wet sand with his brush-filled coat in the crook of one arm, the match kit in his other hand. There were only six matches left. The kit did contain a flint and steel, but in this dampness he doubted he could do anything with them.

So: six matches, rope and pulley, and a bunch of pine boughs with his coat wrapped around them, instead of around himself. He shivered convulsively, gritting his teeth until the spasm had passed. Now all he needed was a counterweight, something to make one end of the rope go down so the other would go . . .

Up. Chip sighed heavily. All the activity was making blood pulse out of his shoulder thicker and faster; possibly that alone would kill him, especially if he tried climbing the pit's steep, unstable side yet again.

But what the hell, he thought. Probably it would kill him anyway. That or the cold. *Screw it,* he thought, understanding on some deep level that he was thinking a lot less clearly now.

Feeling worse, too. But . . . clumsily, he began to work, tying one end of the rope around his branch-stuffed coat. Then he struggled uphill through the shifting sand, gathering the slack in the rope as he went.

Sweating and bleeding, cursing and sometimes weeping, he fell several times and each time had to make up the ground he'd lost doing so. But he managed it. One step at a time. It was yet another of the lousy platitudes he'd inflicted on Sam, back in the city.

But to his surprise, it actually worked: step by step, he climbed the pit's side. After what felt like hours but was really only about twenty minutes, he reached the top.

Panic had made him fail earlier, he realized. The beliefs, simultaneously held, that he couldn't do it but that he had to. Plus Randy, shooting at him with a gun . . .

The memory made Chip giggle, which scared him again quite a lot. It convinced him that he really had lost a lot of blood so he'd better get on with it. Because this next part would be the worst:

Going back down into the pit again. Fast—

Everything in him said that instead he should find Sam, then stand at the water's edge, yelling for help. But the truth was, nobody would hear him. It might make him feel good, or as good as he could feel while freezing and bleeding to death.

But that was all. That, he realized bleakly, was absolutely the only benefit he or Sam would ever get out of it.

Hauling on one end of the rope wouldn't work, either, to make the other end rise. It would have, earlier. But now his hurt shoulder had stiffened up so much, he could hardly move it. So:

Climbing up the last few yards out of the pit, he took one end of the rope in both hands, letting the slack fall to the ground by his feet. Above, the rope hung over the pulley wheel; the other end was tied around his pine-brush-filled coat.

So when he went down, the coat would get hauled up to where the pulley wheel was bolted. . . .

Hoping the pulley itself wouldn't just crash down on his head, he tied the rope's free end around his waist. His fingers felt thick and unwilling; his body was urging him to lie down.

In a minute, he thought, then wrapped the rope around himself a few more times and knotted it. *Then you can rest.*

Funny how your hands went on moving even after your mind had let go, he thought. *And how after a while being ice cold made you feel warm . . .*

Oh, just get on with it. He pulled out Sam's emergency fire kit. Another giggle escaped him, but this time he didn't bother worrying about it. He was losing it, and he knew it.

At last he stood at the edge of the pit with his coat in his hands. One end of the rope was around it, the other around his waist. The middle still hung unseen, high above.

Where the pulley was . . . where the pine boughs were. The very flammable pine boughs . . . like the ones in his coat. A final task remained, but first Chip stood a moment looking down into the pit.

Big mistake. All that dark nothingness . . . for an instant, he didn't think he could do it. *It's this stopping to think about things all the time that's got you messed up,* he realized. *Hell, the worst it can do is kill you.*

And that, he was pretty sure, Randy Dodd had already done. Just a matter of time . . . Thinking this, he struck another match on the side of Sam's emergency kit.

The match flared yellow and red. Chip touched it to the pine boughs in his coat. They burst into flames, singing his eyebrows, and almost at once his coat caught fire, too, the stink from its melting fibers and plastic zipper stinging his nose.

Reflexively he flung the flaming bundle away, saw the arc it made, flaring as it swung at the end of the rope.

Then, with a calm inward smile that astonished him more than anything else so far, he hurled himself over the edge. Falling and falling . . .

From above him came a brief, harsh crackling sound, like a sudden intake of fiery breath. Next, the sky exploded, so that as he fell he was chasing his own dark, out-of-control shadow.

And after that, very suddenly so he didn't even have time to be afraid, he knew nothing more.

Out on the water, Carolyn Rathbone watched the eastern sky fill with light. The few remaining clouds glowed sullen orange, as if the fire came from within them.

But even from where she lay, she could tell that it didn't. Tall flames licked the sky over there, as if some giant torch had been set burning.

All the other little boats on the water had nearly gone by, while the one she was prisoner on waited silently in darkness for them to pass, only a hundred yards or so distant.

Randy Dodd crouched with his knife to her throat. He'd shut down the engine and disabled the running lights.

"Don't make a sound," he'd whispered, and she hadn't. So his ruse had worked, and as the fire over there rose higher she heard men's shouts, and the other boats' engines revving.

They were going away. The knife's pressure on her skin eased slightly. But, peeking up, she saw Randy Dodd's face contorted in a snarl of frustration.

He seized her hair, pulling her head up out of the blanket she'd been huddled in. Her breath came in shudders of fright that she couldn't control, as he scrutinized her face.

She thought he might kill her right then, but instead a new thought seemed to occur to him. As he considered it an eerie calm came over him, his expression smoothing and relaxing suddenly.

He flung her away from him, then cast another glance at the departing flotilla. They were headed toward the now-diminishing firestorm on the other side of the water. When their running lights were little more than sparks afloat on it, he restarted the engine and they motored slowly toward the lights of Eastport, so distant a moment earlier but looming rapidly now.

Brighter and nearer, but at low tide under the wharves by the harbor, no light shone. Down there, the gloom was complete. He aimed the boat at the nearest one, confidently and with the air of a man who knew, now, just exactly where he was going.

And what he would do there.

She knew, too. That it was over, that like the other girls' final moments, her own had arrived. Or would very soon. But unlike the others, she didn't wonder about them. She knew. Evidence, trial testimony, photographs . . . Oh, yes, Carolyn Rathbone, true-crime writer, knew only too well what was in store for her.

And she wasn't having any. *Come with us,* the girls in their graves crooned seductively, but she ignored them, scrambling up toward the boat's rail, full of sudden decision.

Up and onto it, where she stood for a glorious instant under a dark sky, looking out at the dark water. Startled, Randy Dodd lunged the length of the boat at her, but too late. She balanced on teetering tiptoe there, laughing and weeping.

Maybe I'm going to die now, she told the girls. *Maybe I am. Or maybe not.*

But that bastard . . . he's not going to kill me.

The smell of the sea was so intoxicating, it made her feel she could fly. Spreading her arms, she did.

Chapter 10

> *Home-ly: All old houses have age-related imperfections. So remember: It's not a flaw— it's a feature!*
>
> —Tiptree's Tips

By five-thirty in the afternoon, it was pitch-dark outside, and Jake had exhausted her list of immediately doable household repairs. A feeling of panic rose in her as she contemplated the washing machine that no longer boiled the laundry no matter what temperature its control knob was set on.

Ditto the leakless faucet in the upstairs bathroom, the old doorknobs that now turned without falling off in her hand, four non-creaky stair treads each cured by the application of a single well-placed grooved ring-nail, and a carpet whose dinginess had been eliminated by the simple method of throwing the damned thing out.

She searched her mind for yet another useful project, found none, and sat down in the telephone alcove in dismay. Just doing nothing while waiting for word about Sam was impossible, and so was calling someone—anyone—for updates.

Or just to talk. She'd already called everyone, and Ellie was the only one who hadn't made her feel that tearing her hair out was a viable option.

"I'll be here," Ellie had said. "Call any time you want. A dozen times, if you need to."

Which Jake had needed to, but she hadn't done it, because how many times could you tell even your closest friend that you were going crazy with worry, and even crazier with the inability to do anything helpful in the search for your missing son?

"They'll find him," said her father, coming in briefly to put a hand on her shoulder. "They will. Every boat in the area is out there on the hunt for him. You just concentrate on that."

"Right," she said, putting her own hand up to grasp his in gratitude. But the only thing she wanted was to be out searching, too, and she couldn't be. She would only be in the way.

"I'm going to take a ride down to the breakwater," he told her. "Just have a look around."

She nodded and let him go, then wandered aimlessly around the house until she recalled that the damper flap on the furnace flue in the cellar needed replacing, and that she actually had the replacement part.

Which was why she was down there, hands coated with black, greasy soot, when the phone rang.

"Bella?" she called up the cellar steps. "Can you get it? I'm all covered with—"

But Bella didn't reply, nor did her quick-step sound on the floor overhead. The telephone kept ringing.

"Bella!" she called again, hurrying toward the stairs. Still no answer.

Jake hustled up the cellar steps, grabbed a fistful of paper towels as she dashed through the empty kitchen, and tried fruitlessly to get the grime off her hands before picking up the receiver.

Apparently, furnace soot stuck much better to hands than it did to a wad of paper towels. The caller ID box said *Undisclosed*.

"Listen, you," she began angrily, but then a voice broke in.

"Jake? Jake, this is Roger Dodd. Sam's here, I've found him, Randy must have—"

"What?" Relief coursed through her, as strong as a drug.

"He's here," Roger repeated. "I found him in the cellar, I don't know how—he's hurt, I called an ambulance and the county dispatcher's trying to find Bob Arnold right now."

Sam. She leaned against the wall of the telephone alcove.

"Can you come down here? He's asking for you,"

said Roger. "He's conscious, but I don't know how long he can—"

Another voice came on. "Hello?" Faint but recognizable; her heart leapt. "Hello, can you hear me?"

"Sam," she managed. He sounded awful. "Yes, I can hear you fine. You hang in there, now, honey, I'm on my—"

Roger came on again, his tone urgent. "He's losing blood, Jake; I don't like the looks of him. Maybe you'd better—"

"I'll be right down," she said, and hung up. Then, pausing only to call Ellie White and let her know the astonishing thing that had just happened—

"I'll meet you there," Ellie said without hesitation.

—she rushed from the house.

In the dark yard, she yanked the car door open and hurled herself in, key in hand. She'd thrown the car into reverse and was halfway out of the driveway when Randy Dodd sat silently up in the back seat and put a knife to her throat.

Bella was coming down the hall stairs from the third floor, where she'd been running a dustcloth over the old floorboards in Jacobia's workroom—you could vacuum all you wanted, she felt strongly, but until you got down on your hands and knees it just wasn't clean—when she heard Jake leaving the house.

So now was her chance. Two minutes later, she strode down the dark street toward the Dodd House with fear and determination warring in her heart.

She wasn't supposed to go there. Bob Arnold had been very clear about it. When the search warrant was finally obtained, the whole place would be gone over by people who were authorized to do so.

Until then, everyone else was to Keep Out. But . . .

It simply was not possible to let the earring Anne Dodd had given her remain lost. Not without even looking for it. And the only place she'd been recently that she hadn't yet searched was . . .

The old cellar. She'd noticed that the earring was gone on the way to St. Stephen with Jacobia, her reflexive touch for good luck to it finding nothing but her own earlobe. Since then, she had retraced her steps to the Dodd House and back, and had gone over her own domestic territory with the grim intensity of a prospector hunting for even the tiniest gold speck.

Without result. A seed pearl, two pennies, and a whole clove that had rolled away while she was sticking them into oranges for pomanders a week earlier had been her only discoveries.

So this was her last chance. If the earring wasn't somewhere in the Dodd House, she would probably never find it. And although a lost earring was not the worst tragedy, she would never be able to replace it.

Never mind that the very thought of entering the place alone made her feel small and quavery. *You can quiver when you're back home,* she told herself brusquely.

Because sometimes if you wanted things a certain way, you had to make them that way. And if you didn't . . .

Well, if you didn't, you deserved whatever you got. Telling herself this, she emerged from the dark alley that ran alongside the Eastport Nursing Home onto the slightly less dark and shadowy thoroughfare of Washington Street.

Across it, hunkered down among the leafless over-grown trees, the Dodd House seemed to sulk behind shade-covered windows reflecting the yellowish street-lights. In the damp, chilly breeze, a patch of shingles on the sloping roof made a wet *flap-flap* sound.

No light showed from within. If it had, she might've turned tail and run. But—

There's no one in there, she told herself firmly. *And I'm only going to find what's mine.*

At nearly suppertime there were few cars on the street. She waited until none were in sight, then crossed and hurried up the old steps, careful not to put her foot through any rotten ones. She was so intent on not being seen, she forgot for a moment how nervous she was about being inside.

But she remembered once the door closed behind her and she stood alone in the dark. With trembling fingers, she snapped on her flashlight and forced herself down the hall, past the old staircase, whose carved mahogany banister, polished with beeswax and lemon oil until it shone, had been Anne's particular pride.

Now it was hung with cobwebs. A gritty scrim moved under her feet as she crept on; the whole place smelled like a sour mop. She scanned the kitchen floor with the flashlight but found only a few hollowed-out acorns, brought in by squirrels through some hole that hadn't been patched, she supposed.

It was hideous in here, and sad. She wished heartily that she hadn't come back. Still, almost done. A few minutes more and she would know whether or not she'd lost her earring for good.

She started downstairs, to the cellar.

The great, fiery wind of the tall sentinel pine's exignition sucked the air up out of the pit where Chip Hahn lay. Waking in horror, he forced his face in under some rocks and clasped his hands over his head, struggling to breathe.

As the initial roar faded, a rain of fire began, burning embers and sizzling sticks showering all around him with a sound like hail clattering on a tin roof, the reek of smoke filling his lungs. A massive flaming branch thudded down, inches from him.

Everything burning . . . a swarm of hot coals bit through his pants and attacked his legs. He jerked up and swatted them off frantically, then doused the remaining ones with handfuls of the damp sand, heedless of the tiny burning bits in it, blistering his hands.

A sound made him look up just in time to see a ball of fire plummeting at him, a ball the size of a house. . . . It was the huge pine's flaming top, broken off and falling to earth like a fiery comet. *Run . . .*

Gasping, weeping, shoeless and burn-flecked, he scrambled in terror halfway up the side of the sand pit. The massive fireball struck the ground with a concussive *whoomph* of renewed flame that hurled yet another spark-storm stinging and burning over his exposed skin.

But then it fell back. What remained collapsed into itself, burning more sedately as if, having demonstrated its unearthly power, the fire was content now with snapping and popping. A few remaining flaming branch fronds floated lazily down into it.

But the big event was over, Chip realized as he watched it. Already the yellow flames were subsiding to a mass of red coals, glowing in the dark.

He steadied himself as best he could on the unstable slope of the old sand pit. His streaming tears made the blisters on his face and hands sting like acid burns, and the smoke and hot gases he'd inhaled turned his breathing into torture.

And he was still bleeding, possibly a lot. He didn't dare to check, but the waves of light-headedness he felt washing over him were probably not all from the fire and his terrified flight from it.

His ears rang like gongs. Gagging, he hacked up sour gobbets of soot. His voice was gone, only a faint croak emerging when he tried it, and his throat felt like pins were being stuck into it.

Christ, what a mess. But under all his pain was the exultant realization that he'd done it, he'd lit the damned thing on fire. Someone would see. . . .

Someone would come. Now if he could just get to the top of the pit, find Sam, and try to help him until their rescuers got here. . . . He dug his stockinged feet—where had his shoes gone? He couldn't remember—into the sand slope. But when he did that, it started sliding again and he couldn't hang on, to stop himself. So he slid with it all the way down to the bottom again.

And again. On his third try, or maybe his fourth, he was no nearer the top than before. His fingers bled stickily from digging into the stony, shifting earth, and every so often an ember from the fire still sulking at the pit's bottom sailed up and zinged him; by now the exposed back of his neck felt like—and probably was, he realized—cooked meat.

He collapsed onto his face, spread-eagled on the steep hill. Again, he had to try again. Because the whole tree had exploded, for God's sake—somebody would've seen it. Surely they'd be curious.

But not about Chip, because no one knew he was here. No one but Randy Dodd, and he sure as hell wasn't going to tell anyone. So people might come to find out about the fire, but they wouldn't be here to save some poor injured fellow from out of this pit.

For all Chip knew, they'd never get anywhere near it. If they approached what remained of the sentinel tree from its other side, they might not even realize the sand pit existed.

And with his voice gone, he couldn't even yell to alert them. So he had to try to climb. Cold, hungry, thirsty, bleeding, burned—everything hurt now, banging and crashing with pain, so he had no way of knowing which parts of him were severely injured and which were just beat to hell—

Climb, damn it. It's easy. Put a hand out, dig in. Push with the foot. Again. Up, big fella.

Chip smiled in the darkness, remembering how he used to tell Sam Tiptree that same thing whenever Sam fell—running for a fly ball or a long, spiraling pass—on the lawn in Central Park. Or when Sam tripped over his own feet trying to make an easy layup or return a marshmallow serve . . .

Back then, Chip had been the athlete, not Sam, and the clear admiration in Sam's eyes when Chip knew how to throw a curveball, tie a slipknot, or get them both into a video game emporium with just one ticket had been, in Chip's pathetically lonely, solitary adolescent life, worth a million bucks.

He'd have given a million to see it again, too. But he was never going to, he realized bleakly as a cascade of stones from above showered down on him, loosened by his efforts at climbing. Sam was dead, either from the gunshot wound he'd had or drowned by the rising tide.

And I'm the only one who knows. The thought triggered a fast mental snapshot of Chip's mother, before she'd walked out on the Old Bastard.

Walked out on Chip, too. He grabbed another handful of sand. Walked, and never came back. His fingers seized a root clump as he went on thinking about when the cards from her stopped coming.

The Old Bastard's sourly delivered explanation was that she'd gotten tired of them, but Chip never believed it completely. He feared something bad had happened, that something had simply erased her from the face of the earth.

Chip thought that if only he knew what specific disaster had befallen his mother, which terrible event out of the many that capered in his imagination—if indeed any of them had happened at all—he might not feel so bad about it.

The way Sam's own mother was going to feel about Sam: just a big hole full of awful questions that would never get answered. Just nothing. Which plenty of people would say was probably for the best. Easier not to know the details.

But Chip knew better, and so did all the families of all those girls he and Carolyn had written about.

So maybe he wasn't going to make it; the funny, thready feeling he had all over his body now made him think that probably he wasn't.

That the bleeding he was doing might not be reversible, even if he got found. He'd probably be dead now if it weren't for the life jacket, the thick metal buckle all smooshed from a bullet's impact, flat and misshapen when he put his fingers on it.

It must've deflected the projectile just enough, he thought, when he finally felt it and understood what had happened. But the darkness all around him still kept shrinking and expanding with an effect like the wah-wah pedal on an electric guitar.

Another bunch of big stones clattered downhill at him. When they'd gone by, he stuck his hand up into the sand slope above him and dug his feet in again, and was rewarded with yet another six or eight inches of upward progress.

Reach, dig, pull. Repeat. He was beginning to feel now that it didn't even matter if he died, if only he got to tell someone first what had happened. So that someone—Sam Tiptree's mother, especially—would know.

And for that to happen, he had to reach the top of this pit.

Velvety blackness expanded all around him. It took all his will not to let himself relax into its warmth, to lie down in the all-encompassing, utterly forgiving, and welcoming dark.

But he knew how it felt, not knowing. So he kept pushing and pulling and bleeding, sliding down and crawling up again. After a while he didn't even realize anymore that he was doing it.

That his burned, bleeding hands and feet moved, twitching in the sliding sand but accomplishing nothing. That his raw, cracked lips twisted and his parched throat spasmed urgently with what he had to tell, making no sound.

Until he heard something, and did something. He wasn't even sure what. Then suddenly everything was blinding light.

The knife point snicked in just under Jake's right ear. A hot, liquid drip began trickling down the side of her neck. Not a lot of blood. But even a little felt like plenty.

She drove slowly down Key Street with Randy Dodd hunkered behind her in the back seat, past the small white wooden houses lined up on either side of the pavement like silent observers.

Silent and dark. Most were vacant at this time of the year, their original families long migrated away for better economic prospects or more pleasant climates, the current seasonal tenants now taking their ease at their winter places in Florida.

The few houses with any lights on inside shone like beacons in the gloom, but their shades were drawn and their porch lamps turned off; there would be no help from them, either.

At the foot of Key Street, Randy jerked his head to the left. "Park downtown, near Roger's," he said as she waited at the stop sign.

The late school bus rumbled by, taking the high-school kids home from club meetings and basketball practice.

"Okay," she managed, nodding while considering a variety of possible strategies. Gun the engine, shoot straight out across Water Street into the bay, for example. Lean on the horn until—

The knife point dug in again. "Don't try to be smart."

His voice was expressionless. She turned left past the library, the Happy Crab Bar and Grille, the glass-doored police station with its lights on inside but no squad car idling in the angled parking spot Bob Arnold reserved for himself out front.

"Pull in," Randy said after another few hundred feet, past Wadsworth's hardware store and the Commons Gift Shop, both closed for the evening. The pizza place was still lit, but no customers were inside; as they passed, someone turned the sign in the door to *Closed* and the lights went out.

Jake pulled the car up under the tall fisherman statue that loomed over the parking lot in a plastic-composite yellow slicker and sou'wester, bearing a plastic cod in his arms. Ellie White's car was already there, but there was no sign of her.

Out on the water, the lights of a lot of small boats showed faintly like a swarm of distant fireflies, away toward Canada. On the horizon beyond, an orange glow flickered, diminishing as she looked at it. "Why are you doing this?" The question came out a tight-throated whisper. "You could have gotten away. Why are you still—"

Here. Like a nightmare she couldn't wake from. *Sam,* she thought. But Randy Dodd's answer was no answer at all, or not one she understood. "I just want what's mine."

Out on the breakwater the sodium arc lights shed tall cones of swirling yellow-tinted mist. She turned off the ignition.

"So I came back for it," he said. Then: "If you scream or run, I'll catch you and cut your throat."

Getting out of the car, she believed him. And now it occurred to her what he meant about wanting what was his.

He must've found out the money was fake. Which meant that despite the coincidence, Roger's call might have been genuine and Sam might still be inside the bar.

She quickened her step. On the sidewalk he moved up beside her, put his arm casually around her, knife in hand. No one else was on the street.

The front door to the Artful Dodger was open. Randy stayed right with her as they went in; she heard the door lock behind them.

A lamp burned low behind the bar. Small red lights glowed on a few of the sound system's electronic components in the room with the dartboard and the karaoke stage, with all the gear Sam had worked so hard setting up and testing.

The system's ready lights were all on, the control panel a bank of red and green LEDs. Seeing them, she knew the call from Sam had been a trick.

Roger had cued up one of Sam's test recordings and played it into the phone, and she'd fallen for it. Simple as that, she realized bleakly as Randy urged her toward the rear of the small stage.

At the back of it, stairs led down. When she hesitated, he shoved her. The stairwell was lit by ceiling-hung fluorescent tubes. At the bottom, a concrete-block-walled hall with a green linoleum floor stretched away.

He hustled her along it. The linoleum gave way to unfinished planks. At the hall's dead end, the concrete blocks changed to rough wooden paneling, and a massive trapdoor with an iron ring in it was set into the planks.

The trapdoor was open. At the sight of it, a doomed, drowning feeling came over her, but it was too late to do anything about it. Randy shoved her toward the opening and the wooden ladder sticking up through it.

With trembling hands she seized the ladder and stepped onto it, noticing the slide bolt in the trapdoor as she proceeded down the rungs. He followed, kicking out with one foot as she reached the bottom to knock her off balance and away from him while he finished descending.

The room was about ten feet square, with a low stone ceiling reinforced by massive old beams, and stone walls carved out long ago from the island's bedrock. One whole side of it facing the bay was a massive old wooden door held shut by a rusted iron bar; it was obvious even at first glance that the door might've moved at one time to gain access to the water.

But not anymore. Time and rust and the settling of the old building had rendered it permanently shut. More iron bars cross-hatched two high window openings in the door; through them a cold breeze blew in off the water. She could hear the waves out there, slopping against the granite riprap that protected the shore side of the boat basin from erosion.

A kerosene lantern hung from a hook in the ceiling. Ellie White lay beneath it, bound with cord. Unconscious, her red hair the color of flame in the lamplight. Jake rushed to her and checked her pulse, which was strong but slow.

At Jake's touch Ellie opened her eyes, tried to get up but couldn't. Jake tore at the cord around Ellie's arms and legs, looked around for something to cut it with.

Randy wasn't even bothering to stop her, seeming to know there would be nothing here that would help her. And there *was* nothing, only a few heaps of discarded junk: an old mop bucket with an ancient mop in it, a heap of broken vacuum-cleaner parts, plus the vacuum attachments and piles of old stained rags.

Jake's searching gaze fell in horror on the small stream of water leaking across the stone floor. Each time a wave hit the shore outside, some splashed in through the window openings. And it wasn't even high tide yet. . . .

She scanned the stone walls, saw no high-water mark . . . which could mean only that when it was high tide, this chamber would be filled. Entirely filled, not even an air space at the top . . .

Silently, efficiently, Randy grabbed Jake's arms, yanked them back, and wrapped a length of cord around them, pulling it tight. He leaned down and tied more of the stuff around her legs.

Then he surveyed the room again as the trickle across the floor widened to a rivulet. This was where the Dodd House tunnel must come out, she realized suddenly, the one Roger hadn't wanted revealed because it spoiled his alibi. Its opening must be way back in the shadows somewhere, where the lamplight didn't reach.

Once upon a time a lot of cans had come down that tunnel, on a cart or wagon. Probably it had been some poor guy's job to haul the cart all the way back uphill again, too, to the Dodd House.

Long ago . . . She looked around the grim stone room again, its floor slimy and its walls greenish with algae. When the place wasn't being used for a distribution point, probably someone cut fish down here, or did some other hard, filthy work. And then the tide came in, to clean the mess up and wash it out to sea.

As it was doing now. Jake's throat closed on a hard lump of anguish. "What did you do to Sam?"

The nylon cord he'd used to bind her didn't stretch at all, the way cotton or hemp would have. It bit in, cutting her. But that could be a good thing, because blood was slippery. . . .

Trying not to let him see her moving, she rocked her wrists back and forth. "Hey, you didn't answer my question," she prodded as Randy approached the ladder again.

"Coward," she taunted. "You did something to him. And you're too chicken to tell me what. Big man," she mocked him abrasively.

Deliberately. She had to keep him here somehow. Because when he was gone . . .

"Scared," she accused. "Scared of a woman you're going to kill. What a loser."

Risky, like teasing a wild animal . . . but if he left, it was all over. Soon this room would fill with water, and that would be that. So, she had to keep him engaged, keep him—

Anger whitened the scars around his eyes and tightened his artificially plump lips. Glancing around, he spotted a loose rock on the floor under one of the window openings, and crossed to it.

Now all she needed was to actually have an idea of what to do next before he picked that stone up and bashed her with it.

"Now, now," she temporized. "Let's not be . . ."

Hasty, she'd have finished; getting knocked unconscious with a rock before drowning might ease the latter predicament.

But neither of them was on her wish list. Before she could figure out just what was on it, though, two more events occurred swiftly, one after the other:

First, Randy Dodd bent to pick the rock up, turning his back on the doorway to do so.

And second, Randy's brother, Roger Dodd, appeared suddenly and without warning, slipping expertly and silently down the ladder with a huge iron skillet in his hand. He raised his hand . . .

Without a word he crossed the room in two long strides and swung the skillet down hard onto Randy's head. Randy collapsed, sinking first onto his knees, then falling face forward into the rivulet crossing the floor.

Jake let her breath out. So she'd been wrong about him. . . . "Thank you, Roger. You had me very worried, there. Now get me out of this so I can . . ."

She held up her bound wrists. But Roger wasn't looking at them, or turning to Ellie. He wasn't doing anything helpful.

"Roger?" she ventured. "Are you . . . ?"

At last he turned, dropping the skillet. "I know you

aren't going to believe me," he said. "But I'm sorry about all this."

Oh, hell. "Roger, I want you to listen very carefully," she began. "You're upset. I understand that. But—"

The rivulet on the floor grew to a stream. The sound of the waves outside grew louder.

Nearer. And still Roger wasn't doing anything. "Roger?"

He returned to the ladder, scrambled up it with the ease of long practice. He hauled the ladder up behind him. The trapdoor thudded shut. She heard the bolt in it slide home.

Trapped . . . "Roger!" she shouted. "Damn it, Roger, you—"

Come back here. But the only reply was the distant sound of his footsteps going up the stairs; after that, only the crash of waves and the gurgle of water sounded in the stone chamber.

Water coming in. The lantern flickered yellow, reflecting a pool spreading across the floor. Ellie had passed out again; her breathing sounded harsh, like a person deeply under the influence of some strong sedative.

Jake wondered what Randy had forced down Ellie's throat, but it probably didn't matter. "Roger!"

No answer. Ellie took a deep, sighing breath. She'd have expected to get home again before George did, most likely. So she probably hadn't left a note.

Me either, Jake recalled bleakly. The only one who knew they were down here was Roger.

And he wasn't telling.

The kerosene lantern flickered and went out.

. . .

In the Dodd House cellar, Bella Diamond found a light switch, then began scanning the packed-earth floor for the earring she'd lost. Around the furnace, near the opening of the tunnel leading downhill to the old wharf . . . That's where she'd been, earlier.

That was where the earring must be. But when she searched the floor there, it wasn't. So she proceeded to the awful little corner chamber where Randy Dodd had been bunking.

Perhaps the earring had fallen in here. In a corner, or possibly under the makeshift bed. Cringing, she lifted an edge of the tattered blanket in case the earring had rolled underneath.

When she did, a curled photograph fell from it. Hesitantly she picked it up, then nearly dropped it in reflexive horror at what it showed: a dead girl. A color shot, in hideous close-up, of half-open eyes, slack lips, and fingers vulnerably curled.

Her stomach rolled. Her mouth felt dry, and her breath came in uncontrolled gasps. She had to get out of here, had to—

Cross the cellar. Climb the stairs, then down the hall to the door. *All right, now, one foot in front of the other,* Bella told herself mechanically.

But at the foot of the stairs, she heard a voice raised in anger or fear, distantly but unmistakably. Jake's voice. From . . .

Not upstairs. Right down here somewhere. Right over . . .

There.

It came from across the cellar, past the furnace in

the far corner of the foundation where the tunnel opened. An instant later Bella stood at the tunnel's mouth, peering across the stop block made of an old railroad tie.

Probably there was a block at the other end of the tunnel, too. But that wasn't her big worry now. What worried her was what might lie between the two stop blocks. Down there in the dark . . .

"Help!" The cry came again from the darkness that smelled of sea salt, damp earth, and rotting wood.

Bella tried shouting back, but no sound would come from her throat. The tunnel looked ready to swallow her. But then Jake's cry for help came again, and Bella knew she had no choice.

None at all. Which was why, standing there in the old Dodd House cellar, lip trembling and hands shaking, fear twisting like a cramp in her stomach, Bella Diamond squared her shoulders and lifted her head.

She settled herself firmly on her feet, bit her lip, and clenched her hands into tight fists, the better to punch somebody in the nose if she had to. Then she closed her eyes and ran at the tunnel, keeping her hurrying feet close to the center as best she could so as not to trip on the iron rails the old cart once ran on.

Just a minute or so, she told herself as she sprinted along in the gloom. *Then I'll come out into the light and find Jake and be able to—*

Help her, Bella would have finished, but instead she smacked suddenly into something unyielding, exactly at knee level, and flew headlong onto it. Clinging on in terror, she felt whatever it was lurch forward, slowly at first and then faster.

Much faster . . . the smooth thrum of rails vibrated

beneath her, and dank, chilly air rushed past her head. *The cart,* she realized as the slope she was traveling on angled sharply downhill.

It was the old tin-can cart, freewheeling down the tunnel's tracks. "Oh," she moaned, feeling the walls zoom by.

There was nothing to hang on to, nothing to try to stop with, and she didn't dare raise her head or put her hands out for fear they'd be knocked off. Faster and faster . . .

That other stop block, she thought suddenly. There would be one at each end of the tunnel, so the cart wouldn't roll right out onto the floor. . . .

Gasping with the unwelcome realization of what was about to happen, she yanked in her arms and legs, ducked her head into her arms, and in general squinched her whole self into as tiny a ball of tender, vulnerable body parts as she could.

Then she waited. The cart went on freewheeling beneath her. Astonishingly fast . . .

Flying in the dark.

Think, **Jake told** herself firmly when she'd given up yelling, her throat sore. But as soon as she'd begun thinking, she wished heartily that she hadn't, because the result was so discouraging.

Twenty feet in six hours was the rate at which Passamaquoddy Bay filled with salt water as the tide rose. And once it rose up past the windows in that old door, she realized grimly . . .

Then she heard it: a high, keening exhalation, like

air being let out of a balloon. Breathless screaming was what it was, actually.

Next came a thud, followed by a thump like a sack of wet laundry hitting the floor. Something heavy collapsed for a while, like stones sliding down a chute. And then . . .

"Oh!" said a woman's voice. "Oh, good gracious!"

Shocked, uncertain, as if its owner was checking for broken bones. It was Bella Diamond's voice, coming from the rear of the chamber in an alcove where no light shone.

The voice was muffled, as if it came from behind a door. *The old tunnel,* Jake realized. *She's come down the . . .*

"Bella, over here!"

The creak of seldom-used hinges sounded. Suddenly an image of the slide bolt on the trapdoor above her flashed into Jake's mind. Lockable, so no intruder could find his way upstairs into the Artful Dodger.

The inhabitants of the Dodd House would no doubt have felt the same way, and their safeguard would have been more than a simple slide bolt. "Bella! Don't close that . . ."

Door, she meant to finish, but another loud hinge creak and a solid-sounding thud cut her off. Too late . . . A flashlight beam appeared, wavering uncertainly around the chamber. Behind it was Bella, looking stunned but miraculously undamaged as far as Jake could tell in the gloom.

"Bella, I'm trapped. Get me out of these ropes, can you? Ellie's here somewhere, too. . . ."

Sounds of sloshing filled the room as Bella's flashlight approached; the water in here was becoming very deep indeed.

Too deep. "Oh," Bella breathed in consternation when she got to Jake's side. "Now you lie still. I'll get you out of here and . . . hmm," she finished, tugging at the cord around Jake's wrists.

"Bella," Jake managed, "the tide's coming in. We've got to get Ellie out of the—"

By the flashlight's beam Jake saw worry growing on Bella's face. "It's going to fill up, isn't it?" Bella asked. "This room is, I mean."

She always had been quick on the uptake. "Yes. Yes, it is. In fact, it's filling up right now, so I really do very strongly suggest that you—"

Hurry. "Too bad I didn't bring scissors," Bella remarked.

Yes, that is regrettable, Jake thought. But before she could say so, Bella had both hands on Randy's motionless form. Patting him down . . .

"Maybe he's got a knife."

With a mighty heave, Bella hauled hard on his jacket collar with one hand and on his belt with the other. Randy Dodd rolled over, head lolling hideously and sightless, half-open eyes aimed upward.

But then without warning, awareness came into them and he surged up, roaring and swinging. Jake flung herself at him; Bella had already found the knife on his belt and removed it.

Snatching it from her, he raised it and brought it down.

Trying to roll out from under it, Jake knew she was not going to be fast enough. Bella backed away hard as the knife, an unpleasantly large and sharp-looking specimen, continued to descend.

Until suddenly Randy's hand fell open, his eyes unfocused, and his mouth formed an O of unhappy surprise as Bella swung Roger Dodd's cast-iron skillet at his head and connected solidly. He dropped bonelessly on impact.

It was a lovely sight, but Jake didn't waste time gawking at it. "Get the knife, cut these ropes, do not slit my wrists while you're at it," she instructed.

Bella complied, then turned to Ellie. "We'll haul her onto that cart," she said. "Then the two of us can—"

"No, we can't," said Jake as Bella sat Ellie higher against the wall and began patting her cheeks gently.

Bella rubbed Ellie's bound wrists. "Why not?" The water on the floor was nearly a foot deep now, and rising fast.

"Because the door you came through is locked."

Jake made her way up the sloping floor to it, grasped its iron handle and pulled. But just as she'd expected, it wouldn't budge. Like the trapdoor, it was meant to let people in.

Not out. The people who lived in Dodd House hadn't wanted any menial laborers getting ideas about making their way up the tunnel, into the rich dwelling of their employers.

So they'd prevented it, and as she'd feared, they'd left nothing to chance. Whatever lock they'd installed, it engaged whenever the door was shut. Jake yanked again, felt the rusty antique iron of the old handle flaking under her touch. The years and the salt water had taken their toll.

Just not enough of one. And now water surged
through the two high, barred window openings on
the bay side of the room, foaming and churning. On
the floor, it had risen to Ellie's waist.

Jake looked down at the iron door handle. It had
been strong and new a couple of centuries ago,
but . . .

Then it hit her, that the bars in the window openings were probably iron, too.

Old iron. Rusty iron. She peered up at them.

"Bella, come over here and help me a minute," she
said. "I'm going to try something."

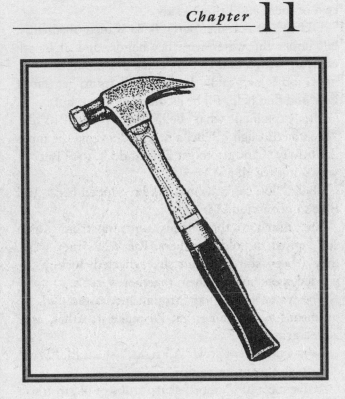

Chapter 11

Bella," said Jake as salt water went on filling the old stone chamber. "What do you call that
thing on a vacuum cleaner, with a brush at the end
of it?"

"A wand," Bella said promptly. She was crouched
by Ellie's slumped, still-unconscious form.

"Right. Feel around under the water. You'll need two of them and I think I saw . . ."

Old vacuum-cleaner parts. Bella waded obediently, felt under the water with her hands, and at length came up with a pair of long black plastic tubes.

"Good," Jake said. "I'm going to try to get out of here and find help. I'll be as quick as I can, but . . ."

She explained what Bella would need to do. "Breathe through it," Bella repeated, eyeing the tubes doubtfully. "And try to get Ellie to do it, too? But . . . why don't we all go?"

"Bella, you can't swim," Jake reminded her. "And Ellie's unconscious."

She turned to the window opening from which she'd pried the old iron bars. Rusted as they were, they'd been sturdier than she expected; luckily the welded spots holding them together weren't.

The water surged icily around her calves. "It's by no means a sure thing that I'll make it, either," she added gently.

Bella's face went still. "All right," she said. "What else do you want me to do?"

"Give me a lift." Short, sharp stubs of old iron still stuck out of the window opening. But she had hammered each one down with a rock until she thought it might not take out her appendix when she wiggled past it.

She placed her foot in the step formed by Bella's two hands. *Please let all this work,* Jake thought shakily.

"Once I get out there, I'll scramble across the rocks onto dry land, come back in and call help from

Roger's phone, upstairs in the bar. Then I'll be down for you."

Please, God, let the ladder still be up there. She didn't add that the rocks were always slippery or that by now most of them were already underwater. Bella knew. But . . .

"Bella, just in case I run into some kind of trouble . . ."

Bella's green eyes softened briefly. But then her bony face hardened with resolve. "Don't run into it. Run through it."

She glanced over at Ellie, then shoved the flashlight she held into Jake's jacket pocket.

"Take this. And hurry up about it, please; that tide's not getting any lower while we're gabbing here."

She braced herself with her hands under Jake's foot. "One, two—"

Jake sucked a breath in.

"Alley-oop!" Bella called from behind and below her, and shoved upward hard as Jake thrust her arms out through the opening.

Her head and shoulders, followed by her torso, went through, too, all the way to her hips.

Which stuck there, firmly and painfully. She wiggled one way: no result whatsoever. She wiggled the other as a huge, icy green wave rolled in and engulfed her.

"Bella!" she choked, coughing out sand and seaweed. "Bella, I'm—" Suddenly something poked her viciously from behind. Not just hard but sharp, like a needle in her right buttock.

That knife. "Hey!" she yelled, squirming away reflexively. And then—

She was out. In the icy water, drowning.

Flailing and drowning.

Gasping and struggling, Jake felt the seawater chill her body down in an instant, her blood thickening and all her muscles cramping at once.

A mass of thick seaweed surrounded her, trapping her. The water wasn't knee-deep, as she'd hoped, or even waist-deep. Shivering uncontrollably, she forced her legs to straighten but couldn't touch bottom.

The lights of town gleamed beyond the breakwater, impossibly distant. She'd have tried yelling for help, but when she opened her mouth water poured in, choking her. A wave swamped her as she surfaced again, gagging.

No one on the breakwater, no cars on Water Street . . . A chunk of driftwood slugged her, opening a cut over her left eye.

Another, much larger collection of flotsam nudged her. She heaved herself onto the mass of branches and vegetation, but her legs sank through at once.

Spread your weight, she thought, frantically paddling with cold-numbed arms. A hard, sharp something hit her shoulder; she pushed against it. It was a rock, a great, big . . .

She clung to it and reached out for another one, and found it. Hauling her body through water so cold, it felt like dry ice burning against her, she got herself up onto a jagged surface.

Waves crashed somewhere nearby, which meant

more rocks. But if she obeyed the strong urge to try swimming toward them, it would be all over for her; she would not survive another intense chilling.

Then she remembered the flashlight, checked her pocket, and found it. Not that it would still work. Or that it would do any good, even if it did.

She fumbled it out, thumbed its switch. To her astonishment it went on, just as she spotted the lights out on the water.

Running lights, red and white. She swayed, nearly losing the flashlight, but caught it just in time and aimed it out at them, praying that whoever was on the boat out there would see. . . .

And that they knew Morse code. Spasms of shivering palsied her hand over the flashlight's lens as she covered it.

And uncovered it. *Dot-dot-dot. Dash-dash-dash. Dot-dot-dot.* SOS, the universally known distress signal . . . but only if they saw it. She sent it again.

Each time she let go of the rock, she nearly slid off into the waves. But it took two hands to hold the flashlight and cover the lens.

A wave rolled in suddenly, its bulk blocking the light beam, its rogue height first confusing her, then pinning her in terror. In the next instant it was on her, spinning her, twiglike. Up and down, time slowing to a stretched-out instant . . .

Impact. Like slamming a wall. Everything in her stopped. No pain, just an astonished feeling . . .

Alive. She lifted her head. Blood smeared the rock beneath her, thickly gleaming in the light from . . .

No pain yet. Cautiously, she peered around. The wave had carried her shoreward, toward the tall bank of granite riprap along the shore at the edge of the boat basin.

And there it had dropped her. Saved her, really.

So far. Slowly, drenched and iced right down to the center of her bone marrow and feeling her wits still engaged in the very uncertain process of gathering themselves together, she got her arms and legs straightened out underneath her and began pushing herself up.

Clambering painfully up and over the granite riprap to the walkway between the harbor and the boat basin, Jake made herself forget everything except making it that far.

Next came a short, steep path between two of the old brick buildings that fronted on Water Street. She took it on hands and knees, at last hauling herself upright on the sidewalk directly in front of the Artful Dodger.

Still no one on the street. She could try to find someone, but the moments she would spend doing that and then explaining might make all the difference to Bella and Ellie.

If there was still any to be made. The Artful Dodger's door stood open; gazing wildly around for a passing car once more and seeing none, she went in.

The light behind the bar was still on but the cell phone was gone from its stand under the mirror. In the alcove by the restrooms, the pay phone's receiver lay with the cord yanked out.

She hurried through the darts area and past the

karaoke machine, snatching one of the darts from the dartboard as she passed, gripping it in her fist. Across the small stage to the stairs . . .

Silence. And if he had any brains at all, Roger would be far away from here by now.

But then, good old Roger hadn't demonstrated a lot of brain power recently, had he? He'd gotten himself neck-deep in all this already. So he could still be in here somewhere.

With the dart raised to eye level, ready to jab with it, she hurried down the stairs. "Bella? Bella, if you can hear me—"

No sound came from the end of the hall. She raced to the trapdoor; the ladder lay beside it. By now the room below must be flooded. . . . How long had she been on the rocks?

She didn't know, but now a terrible suspicion struck her that it was longer than she'd thought— maybe a lot longer. Flinging herself at the trapdoor's lid, she yanked up on the iron loop.

The heavy lid rose. At last it swung high. A strong smell of seawater rose from the open hole. No sound came from it.

She shouted, still heard nothing, wrangled the ladder's legs into the hole and lowered them, then clambered down into the dark water.

The chamber was flooded, the water over her head. No voices, no cries for help, came from anywhere in it. But there had been nowhere else for the trapped women to go.

So they were still down there. And Bella couldn't swim. Holding her breath and with her eyes clamped shut against the gritty, acidly burning salt water, Jake swam to where she thought she'd left them, fingers searching blindly ahead.

Stuff swirled around her in the cold water, the seaweed and unidentifiable slimy bits clasping themselves horridly to her. Tendrils of vegetation poked at her eyelids and explored her lips as if seeking a way in.

A convulsive shudder went through her as something curled briefly around her wrist and then was gone. *Gah,* she thought, but it was too late for disgust.

Too late for anything. The utter foolishness of what she was doing struck her. But she couldn't just leave them, she just . . .

The clasping thing grabbed her again, hung on tight. A hand, clinging . . . at the same instant the plastic tube she'd given Bella to breathe through floated up, smacking her on the forehead.

Feeling around desperately, her hand found a mass of hair; she dug her fingers into it, trying to raise it. But it wouldn't come, and with her last scrap of panicked energy, she let herself sink, bent her knees, touched the floor with her feet, and pushed.

Whatever she'd grabbed was stuck. Caught on something. Or it was dead weight . . . But then as her lungs were about to explode she felt her body surging upward, still dragging a hank of hair. . . .

Jake found the ladder by chance, grabbed onto it with one hand, and dragged the hair along with the other. At the top she couldn't climb anymore, with one hand still clutching Bella, but then Bella began moving.

One pale hand waved like a seaweed frond, then grasped the ladder rung in front of it purposefully. Jake hauled herself up out of the hole; right behind her, a wet mass of henna-red hair burst through the water's surface.

Bella's face followed. Jake seized Bella's shoulders, heaved her up and out of the hole the rest of the way, sucked a breath in, then plunged down through the hole and under again.

This time she opened her eyes, and the hell with how it hurt them. Ellie sprawled bonelessly, clothes billowing out around her like laundry in a tub.

Jake wrapped her arms around the cloud of fabric and pushed off again, dragging dead weight. Weeping, sure she had been too late. She reached the ladder, but as she tried to shove Ellie up ahead of her she felt her lungs rebel, sucked in a big breath of seawater, and panicked.

But from above came Bella's hand, searching and finding. She pulled Ellie from the hole, then reached down again and grabbed Jake, who let herself be pulled until her face felt breathable air, then battled the rest of the way herself.

Ellie lay by the trapdoor. Coughing and choking she gagged up an enormous gush of ugly water, rolled over onto her stomach with a groan, and finally spoke.

"You cut it a little close," she said, gasping through the sick, wet-sponge sound of her lungs reinflating.

But she actually smiled when she said it, or at any rate it was as close to a smile as a person could get while regurgitating half the bay.

Jake crawled between the two exhausted-looking

women. "Come on. You can finish being sick later. Right now we need to—"

But neither of them were listening to her, staring in horror instead at a ripple appearing suddenly on the murky water in the trapdoor opening.

Randy Dodd's face lunged up out of it, eyes narrowed into a glare of murderous fury and teeth bared. The rest of his big body followed; roaring, he heaved himself up at them.

"Oh, shut up," said Bella tiredly, and stuck her fist out at his nose; it flattened like a tomato. His eyes rolled up whitely as he submerged again, the water closing around him.

Bella slammed the trapdoor shut. "Nice one," said Jake, and would have laughed bitterly. But she was already crying, because all of it was for nothing: *Sam.*

By now he must be dead; Carolyn Rathbone and Chip Hahn, too. Randy had taken them, and she doubted he'd set his captives up comfortably somewhere to wait for him. She would probably never even find Sam's body, never know—

"Come on," she said again, eyeing the trapdoor unhappily. "Let's just get out of here before that jerk decides to try using up another one of his nine lives."

Bella helped Ellie as they struggled up the stairs, pausing to rest sometimes, and sometimes to weep. At the top, the rooms were as Jake had left them, dim and silent. The mingled smells of chlorine and stale beer hung in the still air.

Through the back window overlooking the breakwater, the bay spread out darkly. Some men were unloading something from a small boat, but from this distance she couldn't see what it was and she didn't care anymore, anyway.

She turned from the window. Bella and Ellie were in the bar area, on their way to the front door. Jake could hardly move her feet anymore, she was so exhausted suddenly, the taste of blood on her lips nauseatingly pungent.

Ellie looked back over her shoulder questioningly.

"Give me a minute," Jake began, but then Ellie's expression changed. Turning slowly, Jake faced Roger Dodd, who stood behind her with a gun in his hand.

He put it to her head.

"I want Ellie and Bella to walk outside and get in Jake's car," he said. "Both in the front seat, Ellie driving."

He nudged Jake's scalp with the gun. "Toss her the keys."

Jake found the car keys at the bottom of her pants pocket, tossed them. Ellie caught them as Roger went on, "I'll be right behind."

He marched Jake forward a few steps. "If you do anything but what I tell you, or if you see anyone and try to talk to them or signal them, I'll blow her head off. Then I'll kill myself."

So this was it. The endgame . . . "You and Randy were together on it all along, weren't you?" she said dully.

He didn't reply. "Chip Hahn was right about you. I should have seen it, too. But you'd done the grief thing so well. Faked it, that is. And I got snowed by it, just like everyone else. Especially when you faked Sam's call."

Because she'd wanted to believe . . .

He nudged her again. "It wasn't all fake. I loved Anne. But my brother, Randy . . . well." A humorless laugh escaped him. "You may have noticed that he can be persuasive. Could be, rather."

As was the gun to her head. "He came up with the plan. If I went along with it and helped him, fine," Roger explained. "But if not—"

"He'd kill you, too." She felt his nod of agreement in the movement of the gun barrel, now cold at the base of her skull.

And knew he was still lying. "Do it, please," she told Bella and Ellie. "Do what he says. And, Bella, no heroics."

Bella looked rebellious, but as it sank in that Roger Dodd was in control now, she nodded grimly; she and Ellie went out.

"They'll call help," Jake said when they'd gone. "The minute they get out there, they'll try to—"

Roger reached over the bar to the open cash drawer, scooped out the contents. "Nobody's around. They're all out searching."

He stuffed the money into his jacket pocket. "And anyway, if anyone tries to stop me, I'll do what I said."

Kill her, he meant. "You don't come back from a thing like this," he said, marching her forward.

She spoke again. "So you helped Randy disappear. You knew he'd come back to kill his wife, and then yours, so the two of you could inherit. That's the way you'd planned it."

"The way *he'd* planned it," Roger corrected her. "I told you that already. My plan was to let him do the dirty work, then get rid of him."

Keep talking, she thought. "So the map, the fake money, they were all just—"

He laughed again. "Window dressing. To give him something to think about, make him believe I was still on board. I told him if he got in trouble to leave the money where I could retrieve it."

"So he made a map and planned to float it on the same buoy where you left the cash. The fake cash," she said. "So you'd know where he put it."

"Right, so he could get out of the country without trying to smuggle it past customs." He pushed the door open ahead of her. "We'd try again to make the transfer sometime later, I told him."

Outside it was dark and silent. "But you double-crossed him, had the fake money all ready in advance?"

"Oh, for Christ's sake, of course I did. My plan was, he'd either get caught—if that happened I'd play victim, of course—or he'd figure it out about the money and when he came back for me, I'd be waiting for him, kill him in self-defense."

He shoved her outside. "I didn't know he'd turned into a nut job. A freaking girl-grabber, the kind you only read about in the paper. Who the hell would expect that?"

Glancing up and down the empty street, he kept the gun at her head. "And I didn't know those two goofballs from the city would show up at the wrong moment, wanting to interview him."

Chip and Carolyn, he meant. He kept close behind her as she crossed the dark parking lot to her car. But as they neared it he slowed uncertainly.

No one was in it. No Ellie, no Bella. *Sam,* she thought, and then, *Oh, the hell with it.*

They'd be here or they wouldn't. Swiveling on one foot, she ducked hard away from the gun, punched out at Roger, and felt her fist sink into his midsection.

Ellie, hunkered down in the darkness at the rear of the car, jumped out as if on signal and landed a solid jab to the side of his head as he doubled over, wheezing in pain.

Bella jumped out, too, caught the gun he dropped, and pointed it at him as he collapsed. "Think I won't shoot you if you move?" she asked him. "Think I'm scared to?"

But she obviously would and wasn't, so he didn't.

"Jake," said Ellie. "Look."

A man was approaching, running toward them down the street as fast as he could. It was her husband, Wade, and as he ran he was shouting something. When he got nearer and she heard what it was, her knees went wobbly.

"Jake! Are you all right?" He sprinted up to her and threw his arms around her. "We were on the water, we saw the—"

Distress signal. SOS. On the rocks with the flashlight; it felt like forever ago. "Yes," she managed, leaning on him.

Stupid to be this way, so weak and . . .

"What did you say?" she demanded, letting him hold her up. A stiff breeze would've knocked her over. "What was it about Sam?"

She'd heard it. But she still couldn't believe it. Then in answer he held her away from him and said the best, loveliest two words in the English language:

"*He's alive.* Jake, they found him alive; he's on the way to the hospital right now and that Chip guy is with him."

She looked around wonderingly. The world wavered in and out. Just then her father drove up behind Wade in his pickup truck.

He slowed. There was someone beside him in the passenger seat, wet and bedraggled-looking.

He peered at them all, rolled his window down, and spoke: "Anyone missing a girl?"

Later, after the hot shower, hot toddies, and hot chowder thickened with Pilot crackers, Jake lay on the couch in the front parlor with the dogs gathered around her and let Wade tell the rest of the story.

"George and I split up," he said. "George took his own boat south, in case Randy Dodd tried for Grand Manan."

Sam was in surgery, doing well so far: pulse, check. Blood pressure, check. Breathing, A-OK.

All the minimum daily requirements. In a few minutes she and Wade would be on their way up to the hospital to see him.

"I went with some other guys, up toward New Brunswick, where you'd seen him," Wade went on.

She managed a smile. Of course Wade had taken her sighting seriously. That was Wade in a nutshell.

"And on the way, we saw this humongous fire start up on one of the islands up there. Big old tree burning. Christ, but it was amazing. Went up like a damn torch."

Sam, she thought as Wade went on.

"But by the time we get there, the fire's out, it's dark, sky hadn't cleared yet, and we can't see a thing past the flashlights."

He swallowed some coffee. "So I'm stumbling around out there in the woods with the other guys, I turn around, this thing comes flying out of the dark at me."

Wade wrapped his hands around the mug. "It's a rock, came flying up out of this pit. So we look down there, and there's a guy. Lying down there—I thought he was dead."

The guy being Chip Hahn. "But when I get to him, I can see he's still crawling. Or trying to. He gets one hand uphill, digs in with it. Other one just flops. Then he digs again. We had to fight with him, get him to lie still so we could carry him."

He shook his head, remembering. "Finally one of the other guys had the brains to ask why he wouldn't quit struggling and just let us get him the hell out of there."

Meanwhile down on the breakwater Jake's dad had been pulling Carolyn Rathbone out of the water. Like a dead rat, he'd said.

Carolyn was at the hospital now, too.

"That's when he told us where Sam was," Wade said. "Said he was trying to get to him."

Wade stopped, swallowed hard. "He said he wanted to be able to tell you where the body was," he added quietly.

But when they found him by following Chip Hahn's directions, Sam had been alive. "They found the boat, too," Wade added. "The one Chip stole from the fish pier. Down behind the Motel East."

Where Randy must've put it . . . "Oh," she said. "Well, that's good, then." Because it would be a shame if Chip were prosecuted for theft, after all he'd been through.

She got up, steadied herself with an effort. "Okay, let me just go get ready." *Sam.* She still couldn't quite believe it.

Upstairs, she ran a swift hairbrush through her hair, then climbed to the third floor, where she found Bella in her own room, sitting up alertly in bed with her hands folded on the coverlet.

"Ellie all right?" Bella's voice was like a rough stick scratching across an old violin.

"Yes," said Jake. "She's at home. I asked if she wanted to come, but she says she'd rather be tucked up in her own bed."

Bella nodded judiciously. "Where she belongs. Family around her. Like," she added, "me."

"Yes," Jake said, feeling her throat close. She sat down on the edge of Bella's bed, wanting to say something.

But she couldn't. So the two women sat in companionable silence until Bella piped up with something surprising.

"Our backyard neighbor got arrested this afternoon."

"What? The guy with the rose garden?"

Bella nodded drowsily. She'd had several of those toddies urged upon her by Jake's dad.

Not that she'd argued much. "Yes. For making threatening phone calls. Lots of them. He didn't like it when the dogs got into his yard. Cats, either. Or children."

Bella sighed. "Or even a pet ferret one time, from what I understand. So he found out who they all belonged to, and—"

I'm going to kill you!

"So then I wasn't the only one? Other people had—"

"Complained," said Bella, closing her eyes. Just resting them, of course. "Yes. Your father was here when it happened; he told me all about it," she finished, yawning hugely.

Jake thought about that, and probably would have said something more about it, too.

But Bella had fallen asleep.

Chapter 12

*Water hazard: In an old house,
there is no such thing as a minor
leak. To avoid paying triple
overtime later, fix 'em before
the Great Flood. . . .*
—Tiptree's Tips

A week later, **Chip Hahn and Carolyn Rath-**
bone got out of Eastport at last. Or at least, that was
the way they thought of it. Carolyn was driving.

"That's what they mean about guys like him getting more grandiose as they get sicker," she said,
meaning Randy Dodd.

After five days in the hospital, the doctors had asked Chip if he wouldn't mind sticking around town for yet another day, for a final neurology checkup.

Considering the importance of the equipment that they wanted one more look at, he'd complied. He'd hit his head pretty hard somewhere along the way.

But now they'd pronounced him fine. Or as fine as he ever was, he thought ruefully.

"Thinking they can do anything they want and get away with it," she said. "And that they're allowed to."

She glanced at Chip. "He was saving me, you know. To kill me later. Like, to have for a treat."

Randy's body had been found in the flooded cellar of his brother's drinking establishment, the Artful Dodger. His DNA was being matched with evidence gathered from the remains of women down South.

"Yes," Chip said. "I know. I mean, I'd figured it out, that he was keeping you around for a reason."

He let his gaze stray over to her again, enjoying the luxury of being able to look at her at all. She'd had her hair cut in the little salon across the street from the Eastport breakwater, and she wasn't wearing any makeup.

With a lot of little black curls clinging tightly to her head and her blue eyes washed clean, she looked wonderful to him.

Alive, he thought. Just . . . what a pleasure it was.

"So, who do you think really did it?" she asked. "Killed the Lang sisters, Roger's and Randy's wives?"

The causeway off the island was a curving concrete band, the water and sky spreading blue on either side of it. But even the beauty of downeast Maine had a horror-show quality to it now, as if any minute something bad could still fly out at them from it.

He thought it might take a lot of miles to lose that gun-shy feeling. "That's obvious," he said as they drove off the causeway onto the mainland.

"To me, anyway," he added. "First Randy Dodd killed his wife, Cordelia. He had to get the ball rolling."

Once she'd been checked over and pronounced okay herself, Carolyn had stayed with Chip day and night all the time he was in the hospital. He'd thought at first she just felt obligated to, but then he'd remembered that Carolyn believed obligation flowed only one way.

And it wasn't outward. "But Roger killed his wife, Anne," he told her.

"Why so sure?" Carolyn asked as they slowed for the speed limit in Pleasant Point, then accelerated west toward Route 1. At the intersection, she waited for a highballing log truck to go past, then turned left.

By that time Chip had his answer ready. "If you and I were in a murder conspiracy, would you let me push you into doing all the dirty work so I could testify against you later if I had to?"

She shook her head. The black curls bounced prettily. Chip thought again about her staying with him day and night.

He'd been glad for the company. "Nope," she said. "I'd make you do some of the bad stuff, too. So we'd be equally guilty."

Around them now on either side of the road were only trees; they continued speeding south. "And there's another thing. Those fingernails," he said, still thinking about it.

"What about them?" Carolyn pulled out around a slow-moving pickup truck with a load of lobster traps piled in the bed, sped past it, and tucked the Volvo back into the right lane again.

She was a good driver; a little fast but accurate and very efficient. Chip relaxed in the passenger seat.

"Randy had to remove them somehow. His own fingernails. Can you imagine how painful that would be? But they had to be found stuck in his trapline so it would look as if he drowned trying to get free. Now, how do you suppose he did that?"

She made a face. "Knowing him, I'd say he just yanked them out with a pair of pliers. But no one could, so . . ."

"Right. He'd have needed help. Local anesthetic would be the best. Injected. And Roger Dodd used to be a paramedic."

She looked over appreciatively. "So he could have stolen the painkillers Randy would need. But only if he already knew . . ."

Chip nodded. "That he needed them. Which meant he'd have had to be on board with Randy's plan from the start."

Evergreen forest spread out on either side of the road, dark and deep. "But even with a busted alibi, he still has the perfect guy to blame it all on. His brother, Randy."

"Roger threatened those three women. Held them at gunpoint after they got out of that cellar," Carolyn objected. "He was why they were down there in the first place; he lured them there."

"So they say. He tells a different story. He says he called Jake Tiptree only to warn her that Randy might be around. He also says he never harmed or threatened them, that they misinterpreted all that because they were so distraught. He denies everything."

They drove for a while in silence. Then: "They'll get him for being part of it," Chip said at last. "But it all makes me wonder whether maybe Roger was really the one who planned it from the start, and not Randy at all."

Carolyn looked questioningly at him. He could see her mind working behind those blue eyes of hers.

"You mean, maybe Randy just thought it was all his idea?"

Chip shrugged. "Roger ended up with all the money."

"There's that." She frowned, changed the subject. "Listen, I want to talk to you about something else."

She looked at her hands on the wheel. "When we get back, I'm signing the rights from the first two books over to you. And I'm not writing the one about Eastport. About Randy and . . . all that."

She paused to pass another slow-moving vehicle, this one an old Ford sedan with a dead deer lashed to the hood. Its eyes were open, and its antlers reminded Chip of a crown of thorns.

"You can write it, though, if you want to. I'll fix it with Siobhan," Carolyn went on.

Shocked, he stared at her. "I don't want anything from any crime victims anymore," she explained. "Money, or anything else. Like I said before all this happened, I can't. And especially not now. Know what I mean?"

It sounded crazy. But he did know. He heard the words come out of his mouth. "Yeah. I guess I can't, either. But . . . listen, Carolyn. If we did write it, all about what just happened, we could give the money we made on it away. To a victims' organization. Or to something else entirely."

He took a deep breath. But what the heck. Might as well say it. "We'd keep just enough to live on. Say, for a year or so. And we could write the novel together. The one you—"

"The one I stole from you," she finished for him. "That I told Siobhan Walters was my idea, that I was going to do it."

"Well, yes," he admitted. On the face of it, that sounded like the craziest thing of all.

But he'd been thinking about it, and what she'd said a week ago—*God, was it only a week ago?*—was true:

That he'd never get anywhere with it by himself. Not for the reason she'd thought, though. But because he didn't want to do it without her.

Excitement coursed through him. "Look, I've got the research chops, what little we'll need. The organization skills and the outlining thing . . . I've got that down, too."

She laughed bitterly. "And what've I got, a good face for the jacket photograph?"

"No, no." He turned to her again. "Carolyn, you've got the heart."

It had always been true, he realized. What she'd said about the most important thing being the emotions . . .

Until now he'd never understood that, never felt it. And she always had. That's why writing true crime had gotten to her, had burned her out, finally.

That's why she was so good. "Look, Carolyn. I've got some of the skills, you've got the others and more. I just don't see why we can't put all that together and come up with something great."

She didn't say anything. He thought he'd made a mistake. Then he saw her lower lip quivering.

"Maybe," she whispered. "But . . . I don't deserve it."

It was probably the closest thing to an apology he'd ever get. But somehow, it felt like enough. Sliding a new CD into the player and turning it up—

"I don't know why I love her like I do . . ."

It was one of his favorites, Talking Heads's cover of "Take Me to the River"—

". . . all the changes you put me through . . ."

—Chip felt as if he might just possibly be enough, too.

For now. Which, come to think of it, was all they had.

"I'll be the judge of that," he told her.

And then the last thing happened:

It was just past four in the morning on the day after Chip Hahn and Carolyn Rathbone left Eastport when Bella Diamond woke suddenly, slipped out of bed, and padded from the room.

Her husband slept peacefully on; downstairs in his own room Sam slept, too, still sore but already remarkably recovered.

She continued on to the kitchen; even the dogs barely stirred while she made coffee and a slice of toast. She took her coffee to the laundry room, where she put on the clothes she'd left there, then in the back hall donned boots, a warm hat, and her winter jacket.

Outside, it was not yet light and the motionless hush was like a spell. She stepped quietly to avoid breaking it, along the dark sidewalk.

By the time she reached the Dodd House, she was tempted to turn back, but soon the door would have a new lock on it and it would be too late. A whiff of wild-animal stench met her nose in the front hall. Closing the door behind her, she lit her flashlight, then continued to the cellar stairs and down them.

At the bottom she paused; the habit of fear died hard, and if a sound had come she might have run back upstairs and out the door again, and all the way home. But no sound did.

And the earring was down here somewhere. She felt certain of it. Anne's last gift to her . . . She couldn't just leave it here.

She had to give it a chance. At the cellar's far end gaped the tunnel's mouth. In trepidation, Bella approached it.

The smell of the sea coming out of it like cold breath set her heart hammering. At the other end, so much had happened. She didn't even like thinking about it.

But she wasn't going to the other end, was she? Only here, where in her rush to find where Jake had been calling from . . .

Calling for my help, she thought with a quiet little

moment of pride. It buoyed her for what came next: a few steps into the darkness along the rails.

That was where she'd glimpsed a gleam of gold. Just a spark, but . . . Her flashlight's beam found it, centered on it.

Bending, she picked it up. A farewell gift, as it had turned out; not for the first time, Bella wondered what Anne might have known, especially at the end.

But she supposed she might never find out. Or not for a long time . . . Closing her hand tightly around her friend's final gift to her, Bella glanced around the cellar, not fearing it anymore.

Goodbye, goodbye, she thought. *To Anne, to all of it.*

Until we meet again . . . if we ever do.

Then she went back up the stairs and along the hall to the front door of the old house, and stepped out into the light.

If you enjoyed *Crawlspace*,
please keep reading for a preview of the next
Home Repair Is Homicide mystery,

KNOCKDOWN

Coming soon from Bantam Books

THEN

Jacobia. Come on now," said Victor. "Be reasonable."

Her husband's voice on the telephone had a soothing tone, the one he used on patients who would recover if they did just as he said.

His definition of *reasonable*. Victor was a brain surgeon, and he always tried that voice on her, too, before he brought out the big guns.

Bazookas of sarcasm, rocket launchers of scorn.

But not yet. "Jake, I was here at the hospital all along. The ward clerks must not have realized it, that's all."

"Uh-huh. And they didn't page you."

She knew they had. It was nine in the morning and she was sitting on a wrought-iron café chair, on the prettily landscaped terrace of their penthouse apartment overlooking Central Park.

The café chair was enameled absinthe green. The shrubs in the huge clay pots were Himalayan forsythia and dwarf Japanese maple.

On the wrought-iron bistro table, a grease-stained paper plate holding a slice of last night's pizza sat alongside a jelly glass stenciled with the image of Yosemite Sam.

There was a bite out of the slice. In the glass was some of the two-hundred-dollar bottle of wine she had opened once it became clear that not only was he not coming home for dinner as he'd promised, he wasn't coming home that night at all.

"If they did page me, I didn't hear it. Maybe I was catching a nap in the on-call room. I don't exactly always have the luxury of keeping a normal schedule, you know."

His tone shifted to the terse, coldly annoyed one he used on underlings, nurses or junior surgeons, who hadn't obeyed an order of his quickly enough. "Some of us have . . ."

Real jobs. Ones that matter. Life-or-death occupations whose demands trump everything else.

Including you, he didn't finish, but he might as well have. But she was immune to that now. Especially since she knew perfectly well that he hadn't been at the hospital last night, as he claimed.

She drank the red wine out of the Yosemite Sam glass in a couple of swallows, refilled it, then picked up the paper plate with the slice on it and sailed it out over the terrace's railing like a Frisbee, not watching to see where it went.

"I was there," she said. "At the hospital. You were signed out."

Brief silence from Victor. From down in the street came the blare of a car horn, possibly as a pizza-laden paper plate landed on a windshield.

"What?" Outrage now. "You mean you came over here to . . ."

"Check on you. Yes. At midnight when you hadn't shown up and you weren't answering your cell, I got worried. So I went out in my party dress and the diamond-and-platinum earrings you gave me when we got married."

She drank more wine. It was pretty good, actually. She'd have finished it the night before if she hadn't been distracted by the decanter of forty-year-old Scotch.

"To make sure that you were okay, that you hadn't had some kind of an accident on the way home, or gotten mugged. Because we had a date, remember?" she added gently, her voice breaking.

Which was silly, really. But the tears prickled in her eyes nonetheless, blurring the soft green tops of the trees in Central Park. It was spring, and the lovers down there were walking hand in hand along the paths beneath the flowering cherries.

No doubt. She swallowed hard. Probably her tears were only on account of the wine. Because she couldn't still care so much, could she?

"It was embarrassing," she said. "The ward nurses all looked at me with pity in their eyes." *Poor thing. Wouldn't you think she'd've had enough of it by now? Why doesn't she wise up?*

Why, indeed. "Yeah, I suppose it would be embarrassing," he retorted angrily. "How would you like it if I . . ."

I would like it, she thought. *If you cared enough to bother, I would like it very much.*

But he didn't. He didn't even care if she'd humiliated both of them; not really. It was only that this change of subject was convenient for him, focusing as it did on what *she'd* done instead of on what he'd been doing.

Which she also knew. Because while she'd lingered at the nursing station, waiting for them to page him even though he was signed out and then waiting some more while he didn't answer, she'd seen the nurses' schedule posted on a bulletin board.

The schedule listed who was on duty that night, and who was off. Most of the names were familiar; Victor had been a surgeon at the hospital for several years now.

But one name was new. It was also in the phone book, with an address. "I guess nurses must make pretty good money these days," she said.

"What?" he demanded in the kind of voice that meant someone was being difficult past all reason. "What are you . . . ?"

Talking about. "Monica," she said. "That Greenwich Village rowhouse she lives in? That your car was parked outside all last night? It's nice. The house, I mean."

Gotcha. Not that she took any pleasure in it. She was just tired of Victor thinking he'd put one over on her, was all.

Thinking that she was stupid. She drank the rest of the wine and resisted the urge to send the bottle over the railing, too.

"Good-bye, Victor," she said tiredly, and hung up. Probably he had an excuse for why he was at one of the nurses' homes last night instead of with her, celebrating their thirteenth wedding anniversary. But she didn't want to hear it.

Not, she reflected, tipping the empty wine bottle upside down sadly, that there was much to celebrate. The phone rang, the display showing Victor's hospital number.

Now he would try to shame her by telling her how paranoid she was, how her pathological suspicions were driving him to find solace in the arms of another woman.

Although she knew only too well that the arms weren't what interested him. Ditto the eyes, the ears, the face, or the brain.

Especially not that. The phone kept on ringing. She looked at it for a long moment, then picked up.

"Hello? Is that by any chance my lying, cheating, son-of-a-bitch husband calling me? Because if it is, listen to this."

She smashed the device hard against the terrace railing and smiled as its parts flew everywhere.

"And that goes double for your latest girlfriend, the poor little dope," she said into the phone's shattered shell.

Behind her, a blare of what at normal volume might've been music thundered through the penthouse apartment. But cranked up this way, it was more like a sound-wave-based demolition device.

She could practically feel the walls cracking. Any minute, the building superintendent would be up here. She hurried inside.

"Sam!" She hammered on his door. She'd have gone in, but he kept it locked.

He was twelve. "Yeah."

"Sam, turn it——"

The volume lowered abruptly.

"——down!" she shouted.

"Yeah."

She contemplated the door. "You okay in there?"

"Yeah."

She looked at herself in the hall mirror: showered, dressed, and with a little foundation and lipstick applied, in spite of everything. *Okay.* She'd run a comb through her short dark hair, too, and she had shoes on her feet.

Whoop-de-do, she thought bleakly, eyeing her reflection with skepticism. No beauty queen, but the navy slacks and jacket over a silk blouse were respectable enough, as were the black pumps. Luckily, she had the kind of lean, dark looks that didn't require much upkeep.

Yet. *Much more of this and I'll be laying on the makeup with a trowel just to look human.*

"Sam, I'm leaving for the office. I've got an appointment."

Brief silence. Then, "Okay."

Well, at least it wasn't *Yeah*. "You're going to school, right?"

He knew she'd call the school later to make certain he was there. The music volume went back up a little, but not as much as before.

She glanced at her wristwatch, the black Movado museum piece she'd bought for herself the first year she'd made any real money on her own.

Or what she'd thought of back then as real money. A few more minutes and she'd be late. "Sam?"

The music went up a notch. "Sam, this is your mother out here talking to you. Now you answer me this minute or I'll——"

What? she wondered despairingly. What would she do? Summon a locksmith? Or call 911 and have the door broken down?

There was no point talking to Victor about this. If she did, he'd have a fatherly chat with their son, and after Sam fooled him again with another tale about how she was just overreacting as usual, Victor would confront her.

And she didn't want to hear that, either. Didn't know what she would do, actually, if she had to——

Sam's door opened an inch. Through the crack, her son looked out flatly at her, and even as angry as she was at him, the sight was a relief.

She managed a smile. "Hi."

Sam had dark curly hair, long-lashed eyes, and a full mouth like his dad's. She wanted to ruffle his hair, but if she tried he would probably slam the door on her wrist.

"Sandra should be here in a minute." The housekeeper, she meant. "She'll drive you to school."

And make sure you go in. Sandra was fat, fair, and forty: not Victor's type. More important, she was onto Sam's tricks.

"I left you a casserole in the refrigerator, in case I'm late." Stouffer's, actually. But it didn't matter; he wouldn't eat it.

"Thanks." Patiently, waiting for her to leave him in peace.

"Are you going out with your friends later?"

Might as well at least pretend she still had any say in what her son did or didn't do. She thought lately he was hanging out with the Tooley boy from the fifth floor, but she wasn't sure.

The Tooley boy was sixteen and had already been in juvenile detention. Still, he was better than the crew Sam used to spend time with, shoplifting and riding the tops of subway cars at all hours of the day and night.

"Sam," she repeated, "are you . . . ?"

His door closed. The lock clicked. The music went up again, although not enough to bring the building super. It was as if Sam knew just exactly how far he could go.

What do you mean, "as if"? she asked herself bitterly as she left the apartment.

The lobby of her building on Central Park West had the kind of prewar glamour you couldn't find in new construction: art deco wall sconces, gleaming black marble floors, crystal chandeliers. Her heels clicked past the concierge's desk with the vase full of fresh florist's blooms on it, then the security guard's podium, and finally the low table spread with complimentary copies of the *Times* and *The Wall Street Journal*.

She picked up a *Journal* as she went by; she could read it as she cabbed to the office. "Mrs. Tiptree?"

Damn. She turned, trying to indicate by her expression and posture that she was late. Which she wasn't; not yet. But she did not want to talk to the building superintendent, Mr. Halloran.

Or rather, be talked to by him. "Mrs. Tiptree, I'm sorry to have to trouble you."

Have to. That was a bad sign. "But our other residents . . ."

She drew herself up. "There've been complaints?"

Her tone dared him. But of course there had been complaints. What with the threats and accusations flying between her and Victor, and Sam's music being played at volumes generally reserved for arena concerts, it was a wonder that the other tenants didn't assemble outside their apartment door with torches and pitchforks.

Inspiration hit her. "Talk to my husband about it."

"But——"

"The man of the house," she practically spat at the unlucky building superintendent. Really, he didn't deserve this.

But by now she *was* late, and anyway, there wasn't a thing in this world she could do about any of it, and especially not about the music; heaven knew she'd tried. So for now she thanked her lucky stars that Sam at least still lived at home, and not on the street half the time like the Tooley boy.

Outside, limos picking up other tenants sat idling along the curb while their drivers read the papers and drank coffee. On the sidewalks, elderly ladies in pastel Chanel suits tottered along behind tiny dogs on pastel leashes; nannies pushed Italian-made strollers and luxury baby carriages.

Changing her mind about the cab, she turned south, hoping a walk might clear her head. At this hour she could travel faster on foot than the traffic could move, anyway.

Thirty minutes later, at Madison and Thirty-fourth, the city was one part blaring cab horn, one part jackhammer, and three parts way too many people, all hustling like mad. In the deli on the corner, she got coffee and a bagel and carried them into her building, where they were nearly knocked from her hands by a man rushing past her out through the lobby.

Gray fedora, salt-and-pepper mustache, scarred face . . .

She knew him, and he must have recognized her, too, because he turned around and came back in. It was Jerry Baumann, known to his friends and associates as "Da Bomb."

She did not like thinking about why he was called this, or how she knew.

"Listen," Jerry growled, not pausing for niceties. "I went upstairs and told him the situation. It's not gonna change. He gets the money to us by tomorrow, or——" He drew a crooked finger across his throat.

"I beg your pardon?" Jake began, aware of the door-man listening with interest from his desk just inside the front door. "How did you even——"

The whole reason for having a doorman at all was that no one was supposed to be able to get upstairs without first being announced via intercom, and ap-proved.

But when she glanced over inquiringly, he was sud-denly extremely busy with some papers in one of the desk's drawers.

Come on, Jerry "Da Bomb" Baumann's face said clearly. *You think some freakin' rent-a-cop's gonna stop me?*

"You tell him," he repeated as he opened the door to the street. The sudden clamor of noise was so loud that it was almost comical.

"Don't let him get thinkin' anything else," Jerry Bau-mann said, and then the door swung shut.

"Some help you are," she said to the guard, who upon Jerry's departure found his paperwork less en-grossing.

"Yes, ma'am," the guard said evenly, unsmiling.

"Who's up there?" she demanded. Despite leaving home late, she'd made good time; her appointment wasn't for another ten minutes.

But just then the guard's desk phone rang, and the elevator doors opened. *The hell with it,* she thought as she stepped in, pulling the key to her office from her shoulder bag with one hand while balancing a paper bag with coffee and a bagel in it with the other; she'd find out who was there herself.

She didn't need the key, though, because the office door——no name, just the suite number——stood open. Inside, the anteroom smelled like Old Spice laced with bubblegum.

And something else. *Fear sweat,* she thought. "Hello?"

She didn't have a secretary or a receptionist. She wouldn't even have had an office, but some of her clients weren't the kind of people she wanted coming to her home.

Some of her clients, she didn't even want them knowing where she lived, although they probably did anyway. "Anyone here?"

The bubblegum smell was getting stronger. On the tan carpet, a few grains of something granular was sprinkled, like a trail of . . . She knelt and touched the stuff, and after a moment tasted it.

Sugar. What the . . . ?

"Hello."

She looked up. A little boy, maybe ten years old, stood in the doorway to her inner office, where she met clients.

The boy, scrubbed so clean he practically glowed and with an obviously fresh haircut under his kid-sized baseball cap, wore a blue blazer. Under it he wore a white dress shirt and a striped silk tie——a real one, not a clip-on. His slacks were belted, and from the way they broke just so over his oxblood shoes, they had obviously been tailored for him.

"Hello. Who are you?" She got up, brushing sugar granules from her fingertips while the kid went on eyeing her somberly.

"Steven. My mother calls me Junior." The boy blinked once, slowly. From the white bits around his mouth, she gathered that the ones on her carpet were from something that he'd been eating.

"Are you going to let the bad men kill my father?" he asked.

His voice held an odd, remarkably unchildish undercurrent of menace. Then it hit her, who he must be. *Oh, for Pete's sake.*

She should have known; under that new haircut of his, the kid's ears stuck out a mile.

Just like his dad's.

"Hi, Jake. Sorry we're a little early."

Steven Garner Sr. appeared in the doorway behind his son. "I slipped the guy downstairs a little something; he let us up," he confided.

Unlike the boy, he did not look freshly laundered. He wore rumpled slacks over white high-top sneakers that had seen better days, a polo shirt with dryer wrinkles still in it, and a blue cotton warm-up jacket with an egg splotch on the front.

"I saw Baumann in the lobby just now," she said, and watched Garner's face tighten with anxiety.

The kid was still staring at her. "You hungry?" she asked him, despite the evidence of a recent meal——a doughnut, probably——around his lips.

The boy nodded; what little kid wasn't always hungry? "But my mom doesn't let me . . ." he began as she brought out the bagel.

"Steven," his father told him gently, "go sit down

over there and eat the bagel, okay? Go on," he repeated as the boy looked doubtful. "I'll make it okay with your mom."

The boy rolled his eyes, giving Jake the idea that making things okay with his mom generally wasn't so easy. But he did as he was asked.

"And don't do anything else," his father told him, which Jake thought was a little strange. The look he gave the kid was odd, too: stern, but with a thread of fear in it. "Just sit."

"Come on," Jake said, waving Steven Sr. back into her inner office, which was even more spartan than the outer one.

The desk was a gray metal cube squatting in one corner, the chairs like ones in the Motor Vehicle Department's waiting area, square and serviceable. No pictures or diplomas hung on the walls or stood on the desk; venetian blinds covered the windows.

All business here, the room's bare, utilitarian chill said clearly. She sat at her desk, gestured at the seat in front of it, and watched Steven Garner sink onto it gratefully.

"So. How can I help you?"

Although she already knew. His hangdog expression, a mobbed-up minion down in the lobby . . . even the security guard had known enough to go deaf and blind with Baumann around.

Garner, by contrast, was just a low-level errand boy, the kind of guy who lived for the moment he would be invited along on a truck highjacking.

And who would die waiting, because guys who were always as much in need of cash as Garner was could never be trusted. So she would be his last hope, and his next words would be . . .

"I need money." He glanced up at her. At his day job he was a school photographer, she knew.

Not exactly a big earner. "A lot," he added, "of money." He leaned across the desk. "Because they're going to kill me if I don't get it to them."

"Yeah, so I just heard. But I'm not in the business of——"

Loan-sharking. Or whatever you wanted to call it. "I help people take care of their money, you know?" Jake said carefully. "Invest it, diversify it . . ."

Launder it, get it out of the country. She'd set this appointment up only as a favor to one of those other clients, and she was already regretting it.

"Yeah, I know," Garner conceded. "I just thought . . ."

"How much are we talking about?"

He looked up, his eyes alight with hope for a moment. But when he saw her expression, his own face fell again. "Fifty."

The amount he'd named shocked even her. "Thousand? You're into them for——"

"Yeah. Don't ask me how it happened, okay? It happened the way it always happens. You lose, you chase your losses, next thing you're on their shoot list."

Only Baumann didn't say *shoot.* "I've got a family. You saw the kid; he's a good boy."

Right, she'd seen the kid because she'd been intended to see him, maybe feel a little sorrier for Garner. She did, too.

Just not fifty grand's worth. She was about to say so when a small head peeped around the doorframe. "Dad?"

Garner frowned. "I told you, siddown out there, okay? Wait for me, I'll only be a——"

The boy didn't move. His big, not-quite-innocent eyes took in the room with its clinical lack of decoration, the metal cabinets and the shelves stuffed with file folders.

He didn't smile. He looked . . . sly. "Steven, maybe

you could just sit down in the chair out there until your father and I are finished here," she said gently.

His eyes didn't change, their expression calm and knowing. It gave her a chill, suddenly, realizing that the boy understood what his father was doing.

That he was begging for his life. But he'd come to the wrong place, because the only thing she knew for sure about Garner was that if she did lend him money, he would never return it.

Heck, he hadn't paid the mob back, and they were willing and able to kill him on account of it. So what chance would she have?

The boy went back to the outer office. She got up and closed the door. "What have you got?"

"What?" Garner looked confused. "I . . . What do you mean, what have I——"

"House? Car? Anything? A coin collection? Has your wife got any good jewelry?"

He was shaking his head. "There's the house, but it belongs to my wife. It was her parents' place, and anyway, what would you want with——"

She sat across from him again. "You're not getting it, what I'm saying to you. I don't want it. But they might."

Despair filled his face. "Just . . . you mean . . ."

He glanced at the door, beyond which his son waited. Right now the kid had a roof over his head, a place to go at night.

And tomorrow maybe he wouldn't. But his dad would be alive. "Steven, I'm suggesting you offer them something. It's harsh, I know. But it's the best I can do for you right now."

Or ever, she didn't add, but he understood. When he got up from the chair he moved like an old man.

She got up, too. "A house is a big thing, Steven. If you're lucky, maybe they'll take it."

"Yeah," he said bitterly. "If I'm lucky."

She didn't offer to put in a word for him. It wouldn't have done any good. He knew that, as well. He opened the door to the outer office, then turned.

"Listen, I was thinking I might take the kid out for lunch, maybe to a ball game. You know? But . . ."

He spread his hands helplessly.

He was tapped out, of course; his last twenty to the guard downstairs, probably. Without a word she opened her desk's top drawer and drew out five hundred-dollar bills.

She crossed the room and handed them to him. In the outer room, the little boy sat in a chair with his ankles crossed and his hands clasped in his lap, waiting. Watching.

"Thanks," Steven Garner said, stuffing the bills into the inside pocket of his cotton jacket. "C'mon, kid."

They turned to go. She followed them to the door, hoping Garner wouldn't decide to just take a flyer out the propped-open window at the end of the corridor.

He didn't. As they moved away down the hall, the little boy glanced back over his shoulder before they disappeared into the elevator. Those eyes . . .

Jake shivered, not liking the expression in them and glad when the elevator closed. And that was the last she ever expected to see of them:

Steven Garner Sr., his boy, and her five hundred bucks.

But she was only two-thirds right.